The Fo
by Pe

She tossed up
else was there to forgive?"

"Getting a woman pregnant and having to marry her."

Stunned, Stephanie stared, unable to believe that hearing him voice his transgression could have the same debilitating effect as it had when he'd confessed it to her so many years before.

Before she could cover her ears, he caught her hands and held them, forcing her to hear him out.

"I never loved Angela. That's not something I'm proud of, considering, but it's true. I loved *you*, Steph, with all my heart and soul. Your parents knew that and knew, too, how much it cost me to lose you." He tightened his grip on her hands. "Without them—" he dropped his chin to his chest and slowly shook his head "—I don't know how I would've survived it all."

Tempt Me
by Caroline Cross

ᗞ✷ᏇᏋ

"Let go of me!" Genevieve screamed. "Let go of me this instant or you'll—you'll be sorry!"

She was threatening him? Unbelievable. The woman clearly had more nerve than sense. Twisted together on the cold, snowy ground, Taggert locked his legs around hers and tightened the grip he had on her waist. "Pay attention, lady. I'm in charge now. You do what I tell you. Understand?"

A whimper escaped her throat. "Yes," she gasped.

"Now get up."

She stayed where she was.

He took a threatening step forward. "Now."

She flinched and threw up her hands. "Okay, okay!"

He reached down to help her up, and the moment he did, she threw her weight backwards, yanking him forwards. Off balance, he stumbled. It was all the advantage his adversary needed. She rolled away, sprang to her feet and bolted.

"Lady, you don't know who you're dealing with!" She had no idea at all.

The Forbidden Affair
PEGGY MORELAND

Tempt Me
CAROLINE CROSS

SILHOUETTE®
Desire™

First published in Great Britain 2007
Silhouette Books, Eton House, 18-24 Paradise Road,
Richmond, Surrey TW9 1SR

The publisher acknowledges the copyright holders of the
individual works as follows:

The Forbidden Affair © Peggy Bozeman Morse 2006
(Original title The Texan's Forbidden Affair)
Tempt Me © Jen M Heaton 2006

ISBN-13: 978 0 373 40223 6
ISBN-10: 0 373 40223 6

51-0107

Printed and bound in Spain
by Litografia Rosés S.A., Barcelona

THE FORBIDDEN AFFAIR

by
Peggy Moreland

PEGGY MORELAND

published her first romance with Silhouette Books in 1989 and continues to delight readers with stories set in her home state of Texas. Winner of the National Readers' Choice Award, a nominee for the *Romantic Times BOOKclub* Reviewer's Choice Award and a two-time finalist for the prestigious RITA® Award, Peggy's books frequently appear on the *USA TODAY* and Waldenbooks bestseller lists. When not writing, Peggy can usually be found outside, tending the cattle, goats and other animals on the ranch she shares with her husband.

You may write to Peggy at PO Box 1099, Florence, TX 76527-1099 USA, or e-mail her at peggy@peggymoreland.com.

Dedicated to the memory of
David Arthur Davidson
"Babysan"
Staff Sergeant
Special Forces
United States Army
March 8, 1947–October 6, 1971

Prologue

Older men declare war. But it is the youth that must fight and die.

—Herbert Hoover

June 14, 1971

It was a hell of a way for a man to spend his last night in the States. Given a choice, Larry Blair would have preferred to be curled up in bed with his wife rather than sitting in a smoke-filled bar watching his buddies get drunk.

But the Army wasn't into choices. Larry's orders were to report to San Francisco International Airport, 15 June at 0500. Five new soldiers assigned to his platoon—all Texas boys—had agreed to meet on Monday in Austin, Texas, to catch a late flight to San Francisco. There they would board yet another plane for the last leg of their journey.

Destination: Vietnam.

Larry looked around at the guys seated at the table. Fast Eddie. T.J. Preacher. Poncho. Romeo. Those weren't their real names, of course. Real names were all but forgotten two days after hitting boot camp and replaced with one better suited to the guy's personality. Since meeting up with the soldiers, Larry had lost one handle—Tex—and received another—Pops. He supposed the new one was a better fit, since he was the oldest member of the group.

He shook his head sadly. Twenty-one and the oldest. Proof enough of the youth and inexperience of the soldiers fighting this damn war.

He narrowed his eyes thoughtfully as he studied the soldiers sitting at the table, wondering if a one of them had a clue what he would be in for once he reached 'Nam.

He sure as hell did. Unlike the others, this was his second tour of duty in 'Nam. When he'd completed his first assignment, he'd re-upped for another six months. At the time it had seemed like the thing to do. In many ways Vietnam was a young man's wet dream. Whores, booze and drugs for the taking, plus the adrenaline high that came with engaging in combat and the thrill of cheating death one more day. With no family waiting for him back home, no job to return to, he'd thought, *Why not roll the dice and stay another six months?*

But during the thirty-day leave he'd received as a bonus for re-upping, he'd met and fallen in love with

Janine Porter and married her two weeks later. Now he'd give his right arm to be able to erase his name from that dotted line. He had a wife, and that was a damn good reason to stay alive.

But like they say, he thought, lifting his beer in acknowledgment of the old adage, *hindsight is twenty-twenty.*

Before he could take a sip, Romeo scraped back his chair and headed for the bar and a woman seated there. The soldiers remaining at the table immediately began laying bets as to whether or not he would score. Larry didn't bother to reach for his wallet. If what he'd heard about Romeo's reputation was true, the lady didn't stand a chance. According to the guys who'd gone through basic training with him, Romeo could charm the panties off a nun and receive them as a souvenir afterward.

A shadow fell across the table, and Larry glanced over his shoulder to find a man standing behind him.

"You soldiers headed for Vietnam?" the stranger asked.

Larry hesitated a moment, unsure of the man's purpose in approaching him. Americans' view of the Vietnam war varied, and he'd been called everything from a hero to a murderer. But he wasn't ashamed of the uniform he wore or the job he was doing for his country. And he sure as hell wasn't one to back down from a fight, if pushed.

Scraping back his chair, he stood, his head high, his shoulders square. "Yes, sir. We're catching a plane for San Francisco tonight, then shipping out for 'Nam tomorrow."

The man nodded, his expression turning grave. "Thought so. My son served in 'Nam."

Relieved that the man didn't appear to be looking for trouble, Larry asked, "What branch of the service was he in?"

"Army. Didn't wait for the draft to get him. Volunteered fresh out of high school."

"What's his name? Maybe I know him. This'll be my second tour."

"Walt Webber," the man replied, then shook his head sadly. "But I doubt you'd know him. He was killed in '68. Stepped on a mine four days before he was supposed to leave for home."

Larry nodded soberly, having heard similar stories. "I'm sorry for your loss, sir. A lot of good men didn't make it home."

The man nodded, then forced a smile and offered his hand. "I'm Walt Sr., though I reckon the *senior*'s no longer necessary."

Larry gripped the man's hand firmly in his own. "I'm pleased to meet you, sir. Larry Blair."

Walt shifted his gaze and nodded toward the others gathered around the table. "I'd consider it an honor if you'd let me buy you and your friends a drink."

Larry dragged up another chair. "Only if you'll join us."

The man's face lit with pleasure at the invitation. "Why, thank you, son. It's been a while since I've had the opportunity to spend time with any young folks."

After they were seated, Larry introduced Walt to the others, then gestured to the bar where Romeo was still sweet-talking the lady. "And that's Romeo," he explained. "He's with us, too."

"Romeo," Walt repeated, then chuckled. "Looks like the name fits."

Smiling, Larry nodded his agreement. "Yes, sir, it does."

Walt bought a round of drinks for everyone, then bought another round when Romeo returned, after losing his chance of scoring with his lady friend when her husband showed up. He received a good razzing from those who had lost money on the bet, then conversation at the table dwindled.

Walt studied the soldiers as they nursed their drinks. "You boys scared?" he asked bluntly.

Preacher, the meekest of the bunch and probably the most honest, was the first to respond. "Yes, sir," he admitted. "I've never shot a man before. Not sure I can."

"I 'magine you'll find it easy enough once those Vietcong start shooting at you," Walt assured him.

"Maybe," Preacher replied, though his expression remained doubtful.

Walt took a sip of his drink, then set it down and sighed. "Hell of a war. From what my son told me, it's like fighting ghosts. The Vietcong hit hard, then slip back over the border into the safe zone where the Americans can't touch them."

"True enough," Larry agreed. "To make matters worse, it's hard to tell who's the enemy. Old men. Women. Children. They all pose a threat, as they're just as likely to be carrying a gun or grenade as the Vietcong soldiers."

Walt nodded. "My son said the same thing. Claimed the number of casualties reported is nothing compared to the number of soldiers who've been maimed by booby traps or mines." He set his mouth in a grim line. "That's what got Walt Jr. After he stepped on that mine, there was nothing left of him but pieces to ship home."

Larry saw the shadow of sadness in the man's eyes and knew Walt was still grieving for his son. But there was nothing he could say to ease the man's sorrow. All he could do was listen.

"He was my only son," Walt went on. "Only child, for that matter. We lost his mother to cancer when he was in grade school, and with her all hope of having any more children. Walt Jr. was planning to work the ranch with me when he got out of the service. We were going to be partners." He dragged a sleeve across the moisture that filled his eyes. "Won't be doing that now."

Every soldier at the table ducked his head, obviously uncomfortable with witnessing a grown man's tears. But Larry couldn't look away. He understood Walt's grief. He may not have lost a son to the war, but he'd lost friends. Good friends. Friends whose memories he'd carry with him until the day he died.

He clasped a hand on the man's shoulder. "Your son was fortunate to have a father who cared so much for him."

Walt glanced at Larry and their eyes met, held a long moment. "Thank you, son," he said quietly, then swallowed hard. "My only hope is he knew how much I loved him. I never was one for expressing my feelings much."

Larry gave Walt's shoulder a reassuring squeeze before releasing it. "He knew," he assured him. "Words aren't always necessary."

Firming his mouth, Walt nodded as if comforted by the assurance, then forced a smile and looked around the table. "So. What do you boys plan to do when you get back home?"

Romeo shrugged. "Beats me. Haven't thought that far ahead."

"Same here," T.J. said, and the others nodded their agreement.

Walt glanced at Larry. "What about you?"

Larry frowned thoughtfully. "I'm not sure. I've never done anything but soldiering. Signed up right out of high school, intending to make a career of it." He smiled sheepishly. "But I got married a couple of weeks ago and that's changed things considerably. Army life is hard on a family. Once I finish up this tour, I'm hoping to find myself a new career, one that'll allow me to stay closer to home."

"Ever done any ranching?" Walt asked.

Larry choked a laugh. "Uh, no, sir, can't say that I have."

Walt glanced at the others. "How about y'all?"

Romeo smoothed a hand down his chest and preened. "I have. One summer, my old man cut a deal with a buddy of his for me to work on a ranch. Figured it would keep me out of trouble."

"Did it?" Walt asked.

Romeo shot him a sly look. "Depends on what you call trouble."

His reply drew a laugh from the soldiers at the table, as well as from Walt.

"Tell you what," Walt said. "Since my son can't be my partner on the ranch, why don't the six of you take his place? Everybody gets an equal share, and when I pass on, the ranch will be yours."

For a moment Larry could only stare. Was the man drunk? Crazy? Nobody just up and gave a ranch to total strangers. "Uh, that's awfully nice of you," he said hesitantly, "but we couldn't accept a gift like that."

"Why not?" Walt asked indignantly. "It's mine to give to whoever I want, and it just so happens I want you boys to have it."

Larry glanced at the others at the table, reluctant to voice his concerns out loud. "With all due respect, sir, there's no guarantee we'll make it home either."

Walt shot him a confident wink. "I'm bettin' you will." He slipped a hand into his shirt pocket and pulled out a folded sheet of paper and a pen. After spreading the paper open on the table, he began to write.

"This here is a bill of sale," he explained as he wrote. "I'm naming each one of you as part owner in the Cedar Ridge Ranch."

"But we don't know anything about ranching," Larry reminded him.

Walt waved away his concern. "Doesn't matter. I can teach you boys everything you need to know."

When he'd completed the document, he stood and shouted to the occupants of the bar, "Anybody here a notary public?"

A woman seated at a table on the far side of the room lifted her hand. "I am."

"Have you got your seal on you?" he asked.

She picked up her purse and gave it a pat. "Just like American Express. Never leave home without it."

He waved her over. "Come on, then. I need you to notarize something for me."

When she reached the table, Walt explained that he wanted her to witness the soldiers signing the document, then make it official by applying her seal. After she nodded her assent, he passed the piece of paper to T.J., who sat at his left. "Sign your name right here," he instructed, pointing.

T.J. hesitated a moment, then shrugged and scrawled his name. The piece of paper passed from man to man until it reached Larry.

Larry looked at Walt doubtfully. "Are you sure about this?"

"Never more sure of anything in my life," Walt replied. He shot Larry another wink. "I'll share a little secret with you. On the last tax appraisal the Cedar Ridge Ranch was valued at three million. Y'all knowing that you're part owners in a place like that is going to give you boys a reason to stay alive."

Three million dollars? Larry thought in amazement. He'd never seen that kind of money in his life! He puffed his cheeks and blew out a long breath, then thought, *What the hell,* and added his name to the bottom of the page.

After verifying that all appeared legal, Walt took the document and tore it into six pieces. He lined them up on the table. "Now it's your turn," he informed the notary public. "Sign your name on each and stamp 'em with your seal."

Though Larry could tell the woman was as stunned by Walt's generosity as he was, she dutifully signed her name on each slip of paper, then pulled her embosser from her purse and applied the official seal.

When she was done, Walt gathered up the pieces. "Keep this someplace safe," he instructed the soldiers as he handed each a section of the torn document. "When your tour of duty is up, you boys put the bill of sale back together and come to the Cedar Ridge and claim your ranch."

Larry stared at the scrap of paper a moment, unable to believe this was really happening. Giving his head a shake, he slipped the paper into his shirt pocket, then extended his hand to Walt. "Thank you, sir."

Smiling, Walt grasped his hand. "The pleasure's all mine." He stood and tucked the pen into his shirt pocket. "I reckon I better head for home. It's too late for an old man like me to be out." He leveled a finger that encompassed all the soldiers. "Now you boys be careful, you hear?" he warned, then grinned. "Y'all've got yourselves a ranch to run when you get home."

One

Stephanie Calloway had always prided herself on her ability to handle even the most complex situations with both efficiency and calm. As one of the most sought-after photo stylists in Dallas, Texas, those two traits were crucial to her success. On any given day she juggled six-figure budgets, kept track of prop inventories valued sometimes in the millions, and coordinated the schedules of the photographers, models and assistant stylists assigned to a particular shoot. If requested, she could transform an empty corner of a photographer's studio into a beach on the Caribbean, outfit a dozen models in swimwear to populate the space, then tear it all down and create an entirely different setting on the whim of a hard-to-please client.

So why, when faced with the task of disassembling and disposing of the houseful of items her parents had accumulated during their thirty years of marriage, did she feel so overwhelmed, so inadequate, so utterly *helpless?*

Because this is personal, she reminded herself as she looked around the den of her childhood home. Each item in the room represented a massive mountain of emotion she feared she'd never find the strength to climb.

"And standing here dreading it isn't accomplishing a thing," she told Runt, the dog at her side.

Taking a deep breath, she crossed to her father's recliner and laid a hand on its headrest. Oh, how he'd loved his recliner, she thought as she smoothed a hand over the impression his body had worn into the leather. When he wasn't out working on the ranch, he could usually be found reared back in the chair, with one of his dogs curled on his lap. He'd always had a dog tagging along with him, Runt being his most recent… and his last.

As if aware of her thoughts, Runt nudged his nose at her knee and whined low in his throat. Blinking back tears, she looked down at him and gave him a pat, knowing by his soulful expression that he was missing her father as much as she was. Runt—the name her father had given him because he was the runt of the litter—wasn't a runt any longer, she noted. The top of his head struck her leg at midthigh. Part Australian sheepdog and part Labrador retriever, he had inherited traits from both breeds, resulting in an intelligent long-haired dog with a sweet temper. But a long line of other canines had preceded him, and not all had been as endearing as Runt. Biting back a smile, she dipped her head in search of the section of frayed upholstery at the recliner's base, compliments of Mugsy—a Jack Russell terrier—and made during a chewing stage her mother had feared would never end.

The tears rose again at the thought of her mother, and she glanced over at the overstuffed chair positioned close to the recliner. Though her mother had preceded her father in death by two years, the floor lamp at its right remained angled to shed light on her hands and the endless knitting projects she worked on at night. An afghan for the church auction. A warm shawl for one of the ladies at the nursing home. A sweater for Stephanie.

Her chin trembled as she envisioned her mother and father sitting side by side, as was their habit each night, her mother's knitting needles clicking an accompaniment to the sound of whatever television program her father had tuned in at the moment.

How will I ever get through this alone? she asked herself, then sagged her shoulders, knowing she had no other choice. With no siblings to share the responsibility, the job was hers to do.

Releasing a shuddery breath, she said, "Come on, Runt," and forced herself to walk on.

They made it as far as the hallway before she was stopped again, this time by a gallery of pictures depicting her family's life. Her gaze settled on a photo of her and her father taken at a Girl Scout banquet when she was eleven. Few would guess by the proud swell of his chest that Bud Calloway was her stepfather and not her natural father. From the moment Bud had married her mother, he'd accepted Stephanie as his own and had assumed the full duties of a father. Never once in all the years that followed had he ever complained or made her feel as if she were a burden. She touched a finger to the glass, his image blurred by her tears. She was going to miss him. Oh, God, she was going to miss him so much.

Gulping back the grief, she tore her gaze away. She had taken no more than two steps when Runt stopped and growled. Linking her fingers through his collar to hold him in place, she glanced back over her shoulder. She strained, listening, and tensed when she heard the familiar squeak of hinges that signified the opening of the front door. Since she hadn't told anyone of her plans, she wasn't expecting any visitors—especially one who could get past a locked door. Mindful that burglars sometimes read the obituaries in search of vacant homes to rob, she whispered to Runt, "I hope your bite is as ferocious as your growl," and cautiously retraced her steps, keeping a firm hold on his collar.

As she approached the doorway that opened to the entry, she caught a glimpse of a man standing just inside the door. She might've screamed if she hadn't immediately recognized him. The thick sandy-brown hair that flipped up slightly at his ears, just brushing the brim of his cowboy hat. The tall, lanky frame and wide shoulders. The faded chambray shirt, jeans and scuffed cowboy boots.

No, she had no problem recognizing him. As she'd learned the hard way, Wade Parker was a hard man to forget.

Runt whined, struggling to break free. At the sound, Wade whipped his head around and his gaze slammed into Stephanie's. As she stared into the blue depths, she felt the old familiar tug of yearning and forced steel into her spine, pushing it back.

Runt wriggled free and leaped, bracing his front paws on Wade's chest.

Smiling, Wade scrubbed his ears. "Hey, Runt. How you doin', boy?"

She advanced a step, her body rigid with anger. "What are you doing here?"

The smile Wade had offered Runt slid into a frown. Urging the dog down to all fours, he gestured at the front window. "Drapes were open. Since they're usually closed—or have been since Bud's funeral—I figured I'd better check things out. Didn't see a car. If I had, I would've knocked."

"I parked in the garage," she informed him, then narrowed her eyes to slits. "How did you get in? The door was locked."

"I didn't break in, if that's what you're suggesting. Bud gave me a key after your mother passed away. Figured someone close by should have one in case anything happened to him and needed to get inside the house."

She thrust out her hand. "There's no need for you to have a key any longer. Bud's gone."

He whipped off his hat. "Dang it, Steph!" he said, slapping the hat against his thigh in frustration. "Do you intend to spend the rest of your life hating me?"

She jutted her chin. "If emotion ends with death, yes, at least that long."

Scowling, he tucked his hat beneath his arm and dug a ring of keys from his pocket. "I thought you went back to Dallas after the funeral," he grumbled.

"Only long enough to tie up a few loose ends."

He worked a key from the loop. "So how long are you planning on staying?"

"That's none of your business."

He slapped the key on her palm and burned her with a look. "Maybe not, but Bud's cattle *are.*"

She drew back to peer at him in confusion. "But I assumed Mr. Vickers was taking care of the cattle. He always helped Dad out in the past."

He snorted and stuffed the key ring back into his pocket. "Shows how much you know. Vickers moved to Houston over a year ago. When Bud got to where he couldn't do his chores himself, I offered to do them for him."

Her eyes shot wide. "*You* worked for my father?"

"No," he replied, then added, "Not for pay, at any rate. I offered, he accepted. That's what neighbors do."

She stared, stunned that her father would accept anything, even a favor, from Wade Parker. "I...I had no idea."

"You might've if you'd ever bothered to come home."

She jerked up her chin, refusing to allow him to make her feel guilty for not visiting her father more often. "Dad and I talked on the phone three or four times a week."

He snorted. "That was mighty nice of you to squeeze him into your busy schedule."

His sarcasm rankled, but before she could form a scathing comeback, he held up a hand.

"Look," he said, suddenly looking tired. "I didn't come here to fight with you. I only came to check on the cattle."

She wanted to tell him that she didn't need his help, that she would take care of the livestock herself. But it had been years since she'd done any ranch work, and she wasn't at all sure she could handle the job alone.

She tipped up her chin. "Hopefully I'll be able to free you of that obligation soon. When I finish clearing out the house, I'm putting the ranch on the market."

He dropped his gaze and nodded. "Bud said he didn't think you'd keep the place."

She choked a laugh. "And why would I? I have no use for a ranch."

He glanced up and met her gaze for a long moment. "No, I doubt you would." He reached for the door-knob, preparing to leave. "Have you talked to Bud's attorney?"

She trailed him to the door. "Briefly. We're supposed to meet after I finish clearing out the house." She frowned. "Why do you ask?"

He lifted a shoulder as he stepped out onto the porch. "No reason. If you need anything—"

"I won't."

Her curt refusal dragged him to a stop at the edge of the porch. Dropping his chin, he plucked at the brim of his hat as if he had something to say but was having a hard time finding the words. Seconds ticked by, made longer by the silence, before he finally spoke.

"Steph…I'm sorry."

Scowling, she gave Runt's collar a firm tug to haul him back inside and closed the door without replying.

As far as she was concerned, the apology came years too late.

Wade exited the barn and headed for the house, exhausted after the long hours he'd put in that day. No, he mentally corrected. His exhaustion wasn't due to the amount of time he'd worked or the effort expended. His weariness was a result of his run-in with Steph. The woman frustrated the hell out of him and had for years.

He knew it was his fault she felt the way she did about him, but what the hell had she expected him to do? He'd made a mistake—a big one—and had tried his best to rectify it by doing what was *right*. In doing so, he'd hurt Steph. But dammit, he'd suffered, too. He wondered sometimes if she realized how much.

As he neared the house, music blasted from the open windows, the bass so loud it reverberated through the soles of his boots and made his teeth ache. Stifling a groan, he made a quick detour to his toolshed. He wasn't in the mood for another argument and he knew if he went inside now he was bound to wind up in one. Meghan called that junk she listened to hip-hop. He considered it trash and had forbidden her to play it. Unfortunately she hadn't docilely bowed to his wishes. Instead she'd screamed and cried, accusing him of ruining her life—which was nothing new, since she accused him of that at least once a day.

He slammed the door of the toolhouse behind him and succeeded in muffling the sound of the irritating music only marginally. Sinking down on an old nail keg, he buried his face in his hands. How the hell was a father supposed to deal with a rebellious daughter? he asked himself miserably. If Meghan were a boy, he'd take her out behind the woodshed and give her a good spanking, the same as his father had when Wade had disobeyed the rules. A few swats on the behind had made a believer out of Wade, and he figured it would Meghan, too…if he could bring himself to spank her.

Groaning, he dropped his head back against the wall.

When had his life gotten so screwed up? he asked himself. There was a time when his daughter had idolized him, thought he all but walked on water. Not so any longer. In fact, she'd told him on more than one occasion that she hated his guts and wished she could go and live with her mother. There were days when he was tempted to pack her bags.

He shook his head, knowing full well he'd never allow Meghan to live with Angela. Hell, that was why he'd fought so hard for custody of his daughter in the first place! Angela wasn't fit to be a mother. Even the judge, who historically ruled in favor of mothers, had recognized Angela's deficiencies and awarded Wade custody of Meghan.

No, Wade wasn't going to allow Meghan to browbeat him into letting her go and live with her mother. He'd deal with her rebellion, the same as he'd dealt with every other stage of her development. But damn, he wished there was someone to share the responsibility with, someone he could at least talk to about his problems with his daughter! He'd give his right arm to be able to sit across the table from his mom and dad right now and seek the wisdom of their years and experience as parents.

But his parents were gone, he reminded himself, victims of a random murder, according to the police. Random or not, his parents were dead, and the carjacker who had killed them was currently sitting on death row.

He'd taken the loss of his parents hard—and inheriting the millions they'd left him had in no way softened the blow. If anything, it had only made things worse. He had been twenty-two at the time of their deaths and living on his own. After he'd buried his parents, he'd gone kind of crazy and done some things he wasn't too true proud of. He'd quickly discovered that when a man has money to burn, there's always somebody around offering to light the match. *Bottom-feeders,* his dad would've called them. Folks who thrived on another person's misery.

He still wasn't sure what it was that had made him realize he was traveling on a fast train to nowhere. But one morning he'd looked at himself in the mirror and was ashamed of what he'd seen. In a desperate attempt to put his life back together, he'd pulled up roots and bought the ranch in Georgetown, hoping to make a fresh start.

Less than two months after the move, he'd met Steph. He hadn't been looking for romance the day he'd delivered the bull to the Calloway ranch. In fact, romance had been the furthest thing from his mind. But it was on that fateful day that he'd met his neighbors' daughter, home for summer break between semesters. He remembered when Bud had introduced her to him how her smile had seemed to light up her entire face, how her green eyes had sparkled with a sense of humor and innocence that he'd envied. And he remembered, when he'd shaken her hand, how delicate yet confident her fingers had felt in his. By the time he'd left several hours later, he had been head over boot heels in infatuation and already thinking of ways to see her again.

From their first date on, they'd spent almost every waking minute together. With a ranch to run, Wade hadn't had a lot of time to spare for formal dates. But Steph hadn't seemed to mind. She'd ridden along with him when he'd needed to check his fences, sat with him in the barn through the night when his mare had foaled. She'd brought him lunch to the field when he was cutting hay and sat with him beneath the shade of an old oak tree, laughing and talking with him while he ate.

When summer had come to an end and it was time for her to go back to college, he had stood with her parents and watched her drive away, feeling as though a boulder were wedged in his throat. Before the first week was out he knew he couldn't live without her. That very weekend he'd taken his mother's wedding ring out of the safe where he'd kept it and headed for Dallas to propose.

In his mind's eye he could see Steph as she'd looked that day. He hadn't told her he was coming, and when she'd spotted him standing in the parking lot of her apartment complex, her eyes had widened in surprise, then she had broken into a run, her arms thrown wide. With a trust and openness that warmed his heart, she'd flung herself into his arms and he'd spun her around and around. He remembered the way she'd tasted when he'd kissed her, the weight of her in his arms. And he could still see the awe in her expression when he'd given her the ring, the love and tears that had gleamed in her eyes when she'd looked up at him and given him her answer. It was a memory he'd carry with him to his grave.

But dwelling on the past wasn't going to help him deal with his daughter, he told himself. Knowing that, he braced his hands against his thighs and pushed himself to his feet and headed for the house, already dreading the ugly scene that awaited him.

* * *

Stephanie didn't give another thought to her encounter with Wade Parker. As she'd learned to do with any unpleasantness, she blocked it from her mind and focused instead on something more productive—in this case, cleaning out her parents' home. It helped to know that the sooner she finished the job, the sooner she could leave Georgetown and close this chapter of her life once and for all.

She had started with the dining room, thinking that, as the only formal room in the house, it would hold fewer personal possessions, fewer memories. Wrong! After two days spent purging and packing, she'd already filled all the storage boxes she'd brought with her from Dallas…and emptied two boxes of tissues mopping her tears. It seemed everything held a memory, from her mother's silver tea service to the chipped ceramic Cookies for Santa plate that had graced their hearth every Christmas for as far back as Stephanie could remember.

Fully aware that this job was going to be tough, she had attempted to disassociate herself from the personal aspects attached to it by applying an organizational tool she'd picked up while watching HGTV. She had created three areas—Keeper, Trash and Donate—and set to work.

Sadly, after two days of what she'd considered cold-blooded sorting, the Keeper stack of boxes towered over the other two.

Promising herself that she would be more ruthless in her decision making, she tried to think where she could find more boxes. She was sure there were probably some in the attic, but the attic had always given her the willies.

Unfortunately the only other option was driving into town, and that prospect held even less appeal. Thirteen years later, and she still felt the sting of the pitying glances from people she'd once counted as friends.

With a sigh of resignation she turned for the hallway and the narrow staircase at its end, with Runt tagging along at her heels. It took some muscle to open the door at the top of the stairs, and once inside, her knees turned to rubber when she was confronted with the sheet-draped objects and cobwebs that filled the space.

She remembered well the last time she'd entered this room. She'd been ten years old and sent there by her mother to retrieve a box of canning jars. While searching for the requested box, one of the sheets had billowed as if someone was trying to fight free from beneath it. Convinced that she was about to be attacked by a band of killer ghosts, she'd run back down the stairs screaming bloody murder. Though her mother had assured her there were no such things as ghosts, from that day forward Stephanie had refused to step foot in the attic again.

Narrowing her eyes, she studied the sheet-draped objects, trying to remember which one had frightened her that day. *That one,* she decided, settling her gaze on a hump-shaped object in the corner. Determined to confront her fear and dispel it, she murmured a firm, "Stay" to Runt, then marched across the room and lifted the sheet.

Half expecting a ghost to come flying out, when nothing but dust motes rose in the air, she gave a sigh of relief and flung back the sheet to expose an old steamer trunk. Never having seen the trunk before, intrigued, she lifted the lid. Another sheet, this one free of dust, protected the truck's contents. Beneath it she found a variety of boxes, each tied with string. Her curiosity piqued, she selected the largest box and sat down on the floor, anxious to see what was inside. After removing the lid, she folded back the tissue paper.

She clapped a hand over her heart. "Oh, my God," she murmured as she stared at the Army uniform folded neatly inside. Sure that it was her father's, she gently lifted the jacket and held it up to examine it more closely. A name tag attached above the breast pocket read Sgt. Lawrence E. Blair.

"Oh, my God," she whispered, awed by the sight.

Unaware that her mother had saved anything that belonged to her biological father, she shoved the box aside and pulled out another. After quickly untying the string, she lifted the lid. Bundles of letters, each bound with pink ribbon faded to a dusty rose, filled the space. She thumbed through the envelopes, noting that each was addressed to Janine Blair. Though the months of the postmarks varied, all were mailed in the same year, 1971. Stunned by her discovery, she pulled out another box, then another, and found more letters in each.

She stared at the stacks of letters scattered around her, unable to believe that her mother had never told her of their existence. Was it because the memories were too painful? she asked herself. Or was it because her mother had chosen to bury the memories of her first husband along with his body?

She knew her parents' marriage had been impulsive, spawned by him leaving for the war. She remembered her mother telling her that he'd shipped out for Vietnam just two weeks after they were married. But Stephanie

really didn't know much else about her natural father—
other than his name, of course, and that he had been
killed in the war. She remembered asking her mother
once if she had any pictures of him, and she'd claimed
she hadn't.

Wondering if her mother had secreted away pictures
along with the letters, she pushed to her knees and dug
through the box until she found what looked to be a
photo album. Hopeful that she would find pictures of
her father inside, she sank back down and opened the
book over her lap.

The first photo all but stole her breath. The picture
was a professional shot of a soldier and probably taken
after he'd completed his basic training, judging by his
buzzed haircut. He was wearing a dress uniform and
had his hat angled low on his forehead. The name tag
above the breast pocket identified him as Lawrence E.
Blair.

He looks so young, was all she could think. And so
handsome. She smoothed her fingers over his image.
This is my father, she told herself and waited for the
swell of emotion.

But she felt nothing. The man was a stranger to her.
Her *father,* yet a complete stranger.

Emotion came then, an unexpected guilt that stabbed
deeply. She should feel something. If she didn't, who
would? His parents had preceded him in death. Her
mother—his wife—was gone now, too. There was no
one left to remember him, to mourn for a life lost so
young.

Along with the guilt came another emotion—resentment toward her mother. *Mom should have shown me this*

trunk, she thought angrily. She should have made sure
that I knew my father, that his memory lived on in my
heart. He had courageously served his country and
fathered a child he'd never seen. Surely he deserved more
than a trunk full of memories tucked away in an attic.

Firming her jaw, she pushed to her feet and began
gathering up the boxes. She would read the letters he
left behind, she told herself. She'd get to know him
through his correspondence and the album of pictures.
She wouldn't let his memory die. He was her father, for
God's sake, the man who had given her life!

Two

Later that night, as Stephanie passed through the kitchen dragging the last bag of trash she'd filled that day, the house phone rang. She didn't even slow down. It was her parents' phone, after all; anyone who wanted to speak to her would call her on her cell.

Ignoring the incessant ringing, she strong-armed the bag through the opening of the back door, then heaved it onto the growing pile at the foot of the steps. Winded, she dropped down on the top step to catch her breath.

Although the sun had set more than an hour before, a full moon lit the night sky and illuminated the landscape. From her vantage point on the porch she could see the roof of the barn and a portion of the corral that surrounded it. Beyond the barn stretched the pastures where the cattle grazed. Though she couldn't see the cattle, she heard their low bawling and knew they were near. Runt let out a sharp bark, and she winced, feeling guilty for having banished him to the barn. But it was for his own good, she told herself. She'd seen a mouse earlier that day and had set out traps. Runt, God love him, had already activated two—due to his curiosity or greed, she wasn't sure which—and had a bloody nose to prove it.

Knowing that spending one night in the barn wouldn't hurt him, in spite of the pitiful look he'd given her when she'd penned him there, she let the peacefulness of her surroundings slip over her again.

Though raised on the ranch, she'd spent her adult years surrounded by the big-city noises of Dallas and had forgotten the depth of the quiet in the country. Closing her eyes, she listened closely, separating the sounds of the night: the raspy song of katydids perched high in the trees, the closer and more melodious chirping of crickets. A quail added its plaintive call of "bob-white" to the chorus of music, and she smiled, remembering the first time she'd heard the call and asking Bud who Bob White was and was that his mommy calling him home.

Enjoying the quiet and the pleasant memories it drew, she lay back on the wooden planks of the porch and stared up at the sky, letting her mind drift as she watched the clouds float across the face of the moon.

Her earliest memories were rooted here on this ranch, she thought wistfully. Prior to her mother marrying Bud, she and her mother had lived with her mother's parents in town. Stephanie had vague recollections of that time, but she wasn't sure if they were truly hers or a result of images she'd drawn from stories her mother had shared with her of those early years. A natural storyteller, her mother had often entertained Stephanie with tales of when Stephanie was a little girl.

But she'd never told her any that had included Stephanie's father.

The resentment she'd discovered earlier returned to burn through her again. Why, Mom? she cried silently. Why didn't you tell me anything about him? Why did you refuse to talk about him when I asked questions? Was he funny? Serious? What kind of things did he enjoy? What were his fears?

Her cell phone vibrated, making her jump, and she quickly sat up, pulling it from the clip at the waist of her shorts. She flipped up the cover to check the number displayed on the screen and recognized it as Kiki's, her assistant.

Swiping at the tears, she placed the phone to her ear. "Kiki, what are you doing calling me?" she scolded good-naturedly. "You're supposed to be on vacation."

"Vacation?" Kiki repeated. "Ha! Being stuck at home with three-year-old twins isn't a vacation, it's a prison sentence!"

Laughing, Stephanie propped her elbow on her knee, grateful for the distraction Kiki offered from her whirling emotions. Five foot nothing, Kiki had flaming red hair that corkscrewed in every direction and the personality to match it. Talking to her was always a treat. "Don't you dare talk about my godchildren that way. Morgan and Mariah are angels."

"Humph. Easy for you to say. You haven't been locked up in a house with them all day."

"Wanna trade places?" Stephanie challenged. "I'd much rather be with the twins than doing what I'm doing."

Kiki made a sympathetic noise. "How's it going? Are you making any progress?"

Stephanie sighed wearily. "None that you'd notice. I had no idea my parents had so much stuff. I've spent three days in the dining room alone and I'm still not done."

"Found any hidden treasure?"

Stephanie thought of the trunk in the attic and the letters and photos she'd found hidden inside. "Maybe," she replied vaguely, unsure if she was ready to talk about that yet.

"Maybe?" Kiki repeated, her voice sharpening with interest. "Spill your guts, girl, I'm desperate for excitement."

Chuckling, Stephanie pushed the hair back from her face and held it against her head. "I doubt you'd find a bunch of old letters and a photo album that belonged to my father all that exciting."

"You never know," Kiki replied mysteriously. "Bud could've had a wild side we weren't aware of."

"They weren't Bud's. They belonged to my real father."

There was a moment of stunned silence. "Oh, wow," Kiki murmured. "I forget that Bud had adopted you."

"I do, too, most of the time, which is what I'm sure Mom intended."

Although Stephanie wasn't aware of the bitterness in her tone, Kiki—who never missed anything—picked up on it immediately.

"What gives? You sound majorly ticked."

"I'm not," Stephanie said defensively, then admitted grudgingly, "Well, maybe a little." She balled her hand into a fist against her thigh, struck again by her mother's deception. "I can't believe she never told me she saved any of his things. She kept it all hidden away in a trunk in the attic."

"Why?"

"How would I know? She just *did*."

"Bummer," Kiki said sympathetically, then forced a positive note to her voice. "But, hey, the good news is you found it! Have you read any of the letters yet?"

Stephanie had to set her jaw to fight back the tears that threatened. "No, but I'm going to read every darn one of them. Somebody's got to keep his memory alive."

"Are you okay?" Kiki asked in concern. "You sound all weepy—and you *never* cry."

Stephanie bit her lip, resisting the urge to tell Kiki everything, from the resentment she felt over her mother's deception to seeing Wade again. "I'm fine," she assured her friend. "I'm just tired."

"Cleaning out your parents' home is hard enough, and now you gotta deal with all this heavy stuff about your dad. Do you want me to come and help?"

Stephanie smiled at the offer, knowing Kiki would drop everything and drive to Georgetown if asked. She was that kind of friend. "No, I can handle it. But thanks."

"Well, I mean it," Kiki assured her. "You say the word and I'm there."

Stephanie chuckled, imagining how much work they'd get done with the twins underfoot. "Thanks, but I've everything under control. You just caught me at a weak moment. Listen," she said, anxious to end the call before she caved and begged Kiki to come. "It's getting late. I'd better go. Give the kids a kiss for me, okay?"

"I will. And take things slow," Kiki urged. "If it takes

you longer than two weeks to finalize things there, so what? The advertising industry won't collapse without us. Once you get back home, we can work doubly hard to make up for any time lost."

Stephanie pressed her fingertips to her lips, fighting back the tears, realizing how lucky she was to have a friend like Kiki.

"Thanks, Kiki," she said, then added a hasty good-night and disconnected the call before Kiki could say anything more.

Within fifteen minutes of ending the call with Kiki, Stephanie was in bed, propped up on pillows, the bundles of her father's letters piled around her. She'd already sobbed her way through two and was reaching for a third when the house phone rang. She angled her head to frown at the extension on the beside table. It was the second time the phone had rung since she'd talked to Kiki, and the sound was beginning to grate on her nerves.

Since her parents were a decade or more behind technology and didn't have caller ID installed on their phone line, she couldn't check to see who was calling. And she wasn't about to answer the phone just to satisfy her curiosity. At this hour, she doubted the caller would be a telemarketer, which meant that one of her parents' friends had probably heard that she was at the house and was calling to offer his or her condolences over the loss of Bud.

Considering her current emotional state, Stephanie was afraid that one kind word would send her into a crying jag she wouldn't be able to stop.

After the fifth ring, the ringing stopped. With a sigh

of relief Stephanie sank back against pillows and
opened the letter over her propped-up knees.

> *Dear Janine,*
> *It's been a crummy day. Rain, rain and more rain.*
> *Sometimes it seems like it's never going to stop.*
> *This is the third day we've been guarding this LZ*
> *(that's Landing Zone to you civilians), and every-*
> *thing I own is sopping wet—including my under-*
> *wear. Ha-ha.*
>   *I got your letter before I left camp. The one*
> *where you asked about getting a dog? Honey,*
> *that's fine with me. In fact, I'd feel better knowing*
> *you have something (not someone!) to keep you*
> *company while I'm gone. What kind do you want*
> *to get? Make sure it's something that'll make a*
> *good guard dog. Not one of those sissy poodles.*
> *They are about as useless as tits on a nun.*

"Tits on a nun?" she repeated, then choked a laugh.
Obviously her father *had* possessed a sense of humor.
Pleased to discover that small detail about his person-
ality, she settled in to read more.

> *Have I told you that I love you? Probably about*
> *a million times, but it's worth repeating. I miss*
> *you so much it hurts.*

Stephanie placed a hand over her heart, knowing
exactly how he must have felt. She'd experienced that
depth of feeling only once in her life, and though it was
more than a decade ago, she remembered it as if it were

yesterday. A love so powerful it was a physical pain in her chest. Even now, after years with no contact, thoughts of Wade would occasionally slip unbidden into her mind and she would experience that same deep ache. Thankfully all she had to do was remind herself of what a jerk he'd turned out to be and the feeling would disappear as rapidly as it had come.

She gave her head a shake to clear the distracting thoughts and focused again on the letter, picking up where she'd left off.

I know I probably shouldn't tell you that because it'll only make you sad, but it's the truth. I'd give anything to be holding you right now. Sometimes at night I close my eyes real tight and concentrate real hard on imagining you. A couple of times I swear I thought I even smelled you. Crazy, huh? But it's true. That perfume you wear really turns me on. Remind me to buy you a gallon of it when I get home!

I better sign off for now. It's getting so dark I can't see, and we can't turn on so much as a flash-light when we're out in the field because it might give our position away. Man, I'll be glad when this damn war is over!

Yours forever,
Larry

Stephanie stared at the letter a long time, trying to absorb the words he'd written and what he'd revealed about himself through them. It was obvious that he'd loved her mother very much and was concerned for her welfare. Had her mother's feelings for him equaled his for her? Unsure of the answer, pensive, she refolded the letter and selected another from the pile.

Dear Janine,
I'm going to be a daddy?

Stephanie sat bolt upright, her eyes riveted on the words, realizing that she was holding the letter her father had sent after learning that her mother was pregnant. She squeezed her eyes shut, afraid to read any more. What if he was disappointed that her mother had gotten pregnant so soon after their marriage? Even mad? He may not have wanted any children.

"Please, God, let him have wanted me," she prayed fervently, then opened her eyes and read on.

*Whoa. That's some pretty serious sh** to throw on a guy when he's halfway around the world. Don't think I'm not happy about it, because I am! I'm just disappointed that I'm stuck over here and not there with you. The good news is, if my cal-culations are right, I should be home by the time our baby is born.*

"Oh, God," Stephanie murmured and had to stop reading to wipe her eyes. He not only had wanted her, he'd been looking forward to being home in time for her birth. The irony of that was simply too cruel for words. Blinking hard to clear her eyes, she scanned to find her place and began to read again.

Are you feeling okay? I know women sometimes throw up a lot in the beginning. I sure hope you're not one of those who stays sick for nine months. Are you showing yet? That's probably a crazy question, since you can't be that far along. I'll bet you look really sexy pregnant!

Man, I can't believe this! Me, a daddy! It's going to take a while for this to really sink in. As soon as I get home, we're going to have to find a place of our own. I'm really glad that you're there with your parents so they can take care of you while I'm gone, but when I get home I want you all to myself! Does that sound selfish? Hell, I don't care if it does! I miss you like crazy and don't want to share you with anybody, not even your mom and dad!

We'll need a place with lots of room, because I want a whole houseful of kids. We never talked about that, but I hope you do, too. I don't want our baby growing up without any brothers or sisters the way I did. Believe me, it can get pretty lonesome at times.

You mentioned in your letter that, for my sake, you hope it's a boy. Honey, I don't care what we have. I'll love our baby no matter what.

Preacher just walked by and I told him our good news—I hope you don't mind. He said to tell you congratulations. Remember me telling you about Preacher? He's the one who didn't think he could shoot a man. So far he's squeaked by without having to. I'm worried that if it ever comes down to shoot or die, he won't be able to

*pull the trigger. I try my best to keep an eye on
him, but it's hard to do that when things get
really hot, with enemy fire coming at us from
every direction.*

*I better sign off for now. I've got to find
somebody who's got a pass to town and see if
he'll bring me back a box of Cuban cigars. I've
got some celebrating to do!*
Love forever,
Larry

Unable to keep the tears in check any longer, Stephanie dropped her forehead to her knees and wept. She
cried for a life lost so young, for the brave young man
who'd worried about his friend and was willing to put
his friend's safety above his own.

And she cried selfish tears at the injustice of never
having gotten to know her father, tears of anger at her
mother for not sharing her memories of him with her.

And she cried for the love her father had felt for her
mother, a love that he had carried to his grave with him,
a love snuffed out before it had had time to fully bloom.

And when she would've thought there were no tears
left, she cried for her own lost love and the dreams
she'd once built around Wade Parker and the life they
might have shared together. A love, like her father's, that
was snuffed out before it could fully bloom.

Muttering curses under his breath, Wade slammed
the door of his truck behind him and cranked the engine.
He wasn't in the mood to go chasing across the coun-
tryside playing the Good Samaritan. Not when his head

was still aching from going three rounds with his daughter over the proper attire for a girl her age.

Swearing again at the reminder of the argument, he stomped the accelerator and aimed the nose of his truck for the highway. Like he had a clue about women's fashion, he thought irritably. But he knew one thing for certain: no daughter of his was going out in public wearing a shirt cut six inches above her belly button and jeans that rode so low on her hips they barely covered her privates!

Where did kids come up with these crazy ideas anyway? he asked himself, then snorted, already knowing the answer. Television, that's where. And the worst were those asinine reality shows. Hell, there was nothing real about a one of 'em! And even if there was, what was the fun in *watching* reality when all a person had to do to experience it firsthand was get off his or her duff and take a stroll outside?

Feeling his blood beginning to boil again, he forced his fingers to relax from the death grip he had on the steering wheel and refocused his mind to the problem at hand. And Steph *was* a problem, whether she was aware of it or not. And thanks to a telephone call from a complete stranger, she was now *his* problem. He supposed he could've refused the lady's request that he check on Steph, but then he would've had to live with the guilt—and he was already carrying a full load. He didn't know how long he was going to be required to make atonement before he was able to clear his conscience of what he'd done to Steph. Judging by the fact that he was driving down the road in the middle of the night, when he should've been sacked out in bed, it appeared it wasn't going to be anytime soon.

He'd thought a phone call would be the easiest and least aggravating method of accomplishing the duty dumped on him. Forget that he'd already tried to call her once that evening, on his own volition, and hadn't received a response. Still, he'd tried again—twice, to be exact. Receiving no answer either time, there was nothing to do but make the drive to the Calloways' ranch and make sure she was all right. For all he knew, she could've fallen off a ladder and broken a leg and was unable to get to the phone.

As he pulled to a stop behind her SUV, he noticed that the windows on the house were dark. Good, he thought smugly and strode to the door. He hoped she was in bed and he awakened her, so that he could ruin her sleep, the same as she was ruining his. He knocked, then waited a full two minutes before knocking again. When he still didn't receive a response, he frowned, wondering if she really had injured herself. Though he figured she was going to be madder than a hornet with him for using it, he lifted a hand above the door and felt along the ledge for the key Bud kept hidden there. Finding it, he dealt with the lock and pushed open the door.

"Steph?" he called as he stepped into the entry. "Are you here?" He waited a moment, listening, and frowned when he didn't hear a reply.

"Steph," he called again and flipped on the overhead light.

God almighty, he thought in dismay as he looked around. The place looked as if a tornado had passed through it! Boxes were stacked on the floor and against the wall. In the dining room, the doors of the china cabinet stood open, its shelves stripped bare. Sheets of newspaper draped the back of the chairs and littered the floor, and more boxes lined the walls. The table itself was covered with stacks of dishes and whatnots a foot deep.

Shaking his head, he turned for the den. Not seeing any sign of Steph amongst the debris in that room, he continued down the hall. A muffled sound came from the rear of the house, and he followed it to the door of what he knew was her old childhood bedroom. Opening the door a crack, he peeked inside and found her sitting on the bed, her face buried in a pillow she held on her lap.

He hesitated, not wanting to disturb what he assumed was a private moment of grief. But the heart-wrenching sound of her sobs pulled him into the room.

"Steph?" he said quietly. "Are you okay?"

She snapped up her head, exposing a face streaked with tears. She stared, her face pale and her eyes wide, as if she were looking at a ghost.

Realizing too late that he'd probably scared her half to death, he held up his hands. "I didn't mean to scare you. I called a couple of times, and when you didn't answer, I was worried you might've hurt yourself and couldn't get to the phone."

She turned her face away, swiping at the tears. "I'm fine. I wasn't in the mood to talk to anyone."

She wasn't physically hurt, that much was obvious, but as to being fine, he had his doubts. If her swollen eyes were any indication, it appeared she'd been crying for hours and wasn't through yet.

He shifted from one foot to the other, anxious to get out of there but reluctant to leave her in her current emotional state. "I can hang around for a while, if you want," he offered hesitantly.

"That's not necessary."

Though she kept her face turned away, he heard the tears in her voice and knew she was still crying. Silently cursing her stubbornness, he crossed the room and sat down on the edge of the bed.

"I know you're missing Bud," he said gently. "I miss him, too."

She kept her face turned away but shook her head. "It—it's not Bud." She hitched a breath and lifted a hand in which she held what appeared to be a letter. "It's from my f-father."

He stared at the back of her head in confusion. Had she lost her mind? Bud *was* her father. "Bud left you a letter?" he asked, hoping to snap her back to her senses.

She shook her head in frustration. "N-not Bud. M-my *real* father."

He hesitated a moment, then reached for the phone. "Maybe I should call a doctor."

Before he could lift the receiver, she clamped her hand over his wrist.

"I don't need a doctor," she said through bared teeth. "Bud was my *step*father!" Releasing her grip on him, she fell back against the pillows and covered her face with her hands.

Wade stared, trying to make sense of what she'd said. "Bud adopted you?"

Though she kept her face covered, she bobbed her head, letting him know he'd assumed correctly.

He slowly unwound his fingers from the receiver. "But...who's your real father?"

"Larry Blair." Drawing in a deep breath, she dragged her hands from her face. "He—he was killed in Vietnam."

Wade rubbed a hand across the back of his neck. "I always assumed Bud was your father."

"Which is obviously what my mother wanted."

He drew back to peer at her, surprised by the venom in her voice. "And what's that supposed to mean?"

She pushed a foot against one of the bundles scattered over the bed. "These are all letters from my father. I found them, along with a photo album, in the attic."

"So? What does that have to do with your mother?"

"I never knew they existed! She never told me."

Stunned by her level of anger, he tried to think of a logical explanation to offer. "Maybe she did and you forgot."

"Oh, no," she said, shaking her head in denial. "I didn't forget. I distinctly remember asking her if she had a picture of him and her claiming she hadn't saved any of his things. She never wanted to talk about him. Ever." She banged a fist against her thigh, her eyes filling with tears again. "She lied to me. My own mother *lied* to me!"

He held up a hand. "Now, don't go assuming the worst. Could be she was only trying to protect you."

"From *what?*" she cried, her voice rising in hysteria. "My heritage? From the opportunity to know the man who fathered me?"

"No, from being hurt." He tipped his head toward the letter she clutched. "Obviously reading his letters has upset you. Your mother probably knew they would and wanted to save you the pain."

"She had no right. He was my father, for God's

sake! Can you imagine what it's like not knowing anything about your father? To know that he died without
ever seeing you? He was excited when Mom told him
she was pregnant with me." She thrust the letter in
front of his face and shook it. "It says so right here. He
wanted me!"

Reluctant to comment one way or the other for fear of
setting her off again, he said vaguely, "I'm sure he did."

She dropped her hands to her lap, her shoulders
sagging dejectedly. "Never mind. You wouldn't understand. I'm not even sure that I do."

She dragged in a long breath, then released it and forced
a polite smile. "I appreciate you coming to check on me,
but there's no need for you to stay any longer. I'm fine."

As badly as Wade would've liked to hightail it out
of there and leave her to wallow in her misery alone,
there was no way in hell he could do that. Not and be
able to live with his conscience later.

"No rush. I can stick around for a while."

She flattened her lips, all sign of politeness gone. "Then
let me make myself a little clearer. I don't want you here."

He lifted a shoulder. "I guess that makes us even,
'cause I don't particularly want to be here either."

She tossed up her hands. "Then make us both happy
and *leave!*"

He shook his head. "Can't. Leavin' might make me
happy, but I suspect it's not gonna help you any."

Her eyes narrowed to slits. "Wanna bet?"

He hid a smile, having forgotten how feisty Steph
could get when riled. Seeing her exhibit that particular
trait made him realize that he'd succeeded in getting her
mind off her sadness for a while. Pleased with himself,

he bumped his shoulder against hers, making room for himself to sit beside her on the bed.

"What do you think you're doing?" she asked incredulously as he stretched his legs out alongside hers.

He folded his hands behind his head. "Gettin' comfortable. Looks like you're needin' to unload some emotional baggage." He lifted a shoulder. "Since I'm willin' to listen, I figure I might as well make myself comfortable."

She rolled to her knees, her eyes dark with fury as she faced him. "If and when I think I need a shrink, I'll hire one."

Ignoring her, he picked up an envelope and pulled out the letter it held. "What branch of the service was your father in? Navy?"

"Army," she snapped. "And you're not staying."

He scanned a few lines and glanced over at her. "Have you read this one yet?"

She folded her arms across her chest and pressed her lips together.

He bit back a smile. "I'll take that as a no. Probably best if you didn't," he advised and slipped the pages back into the envelope. "There are some things about her parents' life that a daughter is better off not knowing."

She snatched the envelope from his hand and pulled out the letter. He watched her eyes widen as she skimmed the first page.

"I tried to warn you," he said, trying not to laugh.

Her cheeks flaming, she stuffed the pages back into the envelope. "You did that on purpose," she accused.

He opened his hands. "How was I supposed to know

that letter was gonna have graphic descriptions of your parents' sex life?"

She burned him with a look before burying the letter at the bottom of the stack. "You could've just set it aside and said nothing. Saying what you did was the same as daring me to read it."

"You'd have gotten around to reading it eventually," he reminded her. "I was just trying to save you the embarrassment." He cocked his head and frowned thoughtfully. "Do you think it's really possible to do it in a—"

She held up a hand. "Please. I don't need that particular visual in my head."

"Why were you crying?"

She blinked at the sudden change of subject, then let her hand drop. "I don't know," she said miserably. "It's just all so sad. There's no one left but me to remember him, yet I know nothing about him."

He picked up a bundle of letters and bounced them thoughtfully on his palm. "And this is how you plan to get to know him?"

"It's all I have."

He studied the bundle a moment. "I guess you know you're setting yourself up for a lot of pain." He shifted his gaze to hers and added, "And probably an equal share of embarrassment. What he wrote in these letters was meant for your mother's eye, and hers alone."

She nodded tearfully. "I realize that, but this is all I have that was his. Reading his letters is my only way of learning about him."

His expression grave, he set the bundle aside. "I want you to promise me something."

"What?"

"Promise that you'll call me whenever you feel the need to talk."

"No, I—"

He pressed a finger against her lips, silencing her. "You helped me through a hard time after I lost my parents. I think I deserve the chance to even the score."

He could tell that she wanted to refuse his request, but she finally dropped her chin to her chest and nodded. He figured she was only agreeing so she could get rid of him, but that was okay. He knew how to make sure she kept her end of the deal.

With that in mind, he swung his legs over the side of the bed and picked up an empty box from the floor. Using the length of his arm, he raked the bundles of letters inside.

Her mouth gaped open. "What are you doing?"

He hitched the box on his hip—and out of her reach. "Helping you keep your promise. Every afternoon, when I come over to feed the cattle, I'll drop off a bundle of letters for you to read. After I'm done feeding, I'll stop back by and check on you. That way I'll know if you're honoring your promise."

"What will seeing me prove?"

"One look at your face and I'll know whether or not you need to talk."

She opened her mouth, then clamped it shut, obviously realizing it was useless to argue with him.

His job done for the moment, he turned for the door.

"Wait!"

He stopped and glanced over his shoulder to find her eyeing him suspiciously.

"How did you get inside the house? I made you return the key Bud gave you."

"I used the one he kept hidden above the front door."

Her eyes shot wide. "You knew about that?"

He lifted a brow. "Oh, I think you'd be amazed at all I know."

Three

The next morning Stephanie stormed around the house, stripping pictures off the walls and stacking them against the wall in the dining room. It was the only packing she trusted herself to do while in a blind rage.

She couldn't believe she'd agreed to Wade's ridiculous arrangement. Having him dole out her father's letters to her was demeaning enough, but then to be subjected to his perusal so that he could judge her mental and emotional state was masochistic! She didn't want to share her thoughts and feelings with him. She'd die a happy woman if she never had to *see* him again!

Hearing his truck stop out front, she groaned, then set her jaw and marched to the door. Before he could even knock, she yanked open the door, snatched the bundle of letters from his hand and slammed the door in his face, turned the lock. Pleased with herself for outsmarting him, she hurried to the den and settled into her mother's chair.

She had just pulled the ribbon, releasing the bow that held the stack of letters together, when the hair on the back of her neck prickled. Sensing she was being watched, she glanced toward the doorway and nearly jumped out of her skin when she found Wade standing in the opening.

He dangled the house key between two fingers. "Nice try," he congratulated her. "Too bad it didn't work."

His smile smug, he slipped the key into his pocket, letting her know in his not-so-subtle way that attempting to lock him out in the future would be a waste of her time, then touched a finger to the brim of his hat in farewell.

"I'll be back as soon as I finish feeding the cattle," he called over his shoulder before closing the door behind him.

Mentally kicking herself for not thinking to remove the hidden key, Stephanie scooped up the scattered letters and rapped them into a neat stack on her lap. She should have known that a locked door wouldn't stop Wade Parker. The man could all but drip sugar when it suited him and rivaled Attila the Hun when he wanted his way.

Her smile turning as smug as the one he'd gifted her with while dangling the key in her face, she plucked a letter from the top of the stack. Well, two can play this game as well as one, she told herself as she smoothed open the creased pages. She knew how to compartmentalize her emotions, if and when the situation required it. When Wade returned to check on her, he'd find her dry-eyed and busy packing. She wouldn't give him any reason to think she needed to "unload," as he'd referred to her emotional state the previous night.

Confident that she could outsmart him, she began to read.

> *Janine,*
> *Have you ever had the feeling that everybody in the world is going crazy and you're the only sane person left? That's how I feel right now. I swear, a couple of guys in my unit have gone nuts. If they're not drunk, they're smoking grass—or worse.*
>
> *Out in the field, we work as a unit and depend on each other to stay alive. But these guys are so out of it most of the time, I can't trust them to cover my back. I tried talking to them, told them the booze and drugs were messing with their heads and that they were going to get us all killed if they didn't cut that crap out. They just laughed and called me an old man and worse. Hell, I don't care what they call me. I just don't want their stupidity getting them—or any of the rest of us—killed.*
>
> *Sorry. I didn't mean to go off like that and I sure as heck don't want to make you worry. Sometimes I just need to unload—*

Stephanie pursed her lips at the word *unload*, wishing her father had chosen a term other than the one Wade had used to describe her need to talk. Giving the pages a firm snap, she began to read again.

> *but there's nobody that I can talk to about this stuff. If I go to the lieutenant, I'll feel like a rat for squealing and probably get my buddies in trouble.*

Enough of this. Telling you about it isn't going to change things any. How are you feeling? Has the morning sickness passed yet? How much weight have you gained? And don't worry about those extra pounds. It just gives me more to love! Have you thought of any names yet? If it's a boy, we could name him William, after my father, and call him Will for short. And if it's a girl, I've always liked the name Stephanie. I knew a girl once—not a girlfriend, just a friend—named Stephanie, and she was really cool. Stephanie Blair. How does that sound?

Better go. The chopper is due soon to pick up the mail, and I want this letter to be on it when it takes off.
Love forever,
Larry

Stephanie carefully refolded the letter and slipped it back into the envelope. He had named her. Her father, not her mother, had chosen her name. She quickly sniffed back the emotion that realization drew.

See, she told herself proudly as she slid the letter beneath the last on the stack without shedding a tear. She could do this. She'd read a letter all the way through without falling apart, and one that had the potential to set her off on a crying jag. Confident that she had a handle on her emotions, she pulled the next letter from the stack.

Dearest Janine,
We lost one of the guys in our unit yesterday. North Vietcong were spotted in our area, and our

unit was sent out to verify the report and to find out how many there were and how much firepower they packed. We'd been out two days without seeing any sign of the enemy and were ready to head back, when all hell broke loose.

We were near an old bomb crater and we made a run for it so we could form a defense and radio for a chopper. We managed to hold them off until aircraft could get there to give us cover from above. Just as we spotted the chopper coming in, somebody realized that Deek, one of the new guys in our unit, was missing.

We only had seconds to get into that chopper and get the hell out of there. There were still two of us on the ground—me and T.J.—when all of a sudden there was this sound like an Indian war whoop, followed by machine-gun fire. I glanced to my left and there was Deek, standing on the edge of that crater like he thought he was John Wayne, blasting away with his machine gun. I yelled for him to get down, but it was too late. The Vietcong had already spotted him.

He took the first hit in the neck, and that was probably what killed him. He took about twenty more before his body slid behind the rim of the crater and out of their sights. T.J. and I dragged him to the chopper and brought him back to base. I imagine his parents have gotten word by now. I just hope they never know that he was stoned out of his mind when he died.

Sometimes there's no satisfaction in saying "I told you so." That's the case with Deek. If he'd listened to me and stayed clear of drugs, he might be alive today. Of course, he might've caught one anyway. That's the hell of it. You never know when your number is gonna come up.

In some ways, I owe Deek my thanks. Watching him die changed my life. I was awake most of the night, thinking back over mistakes I've made in the past, and I've come up with a plan. In the future, I'm not going to be so slow about telling people what I think or how I feel about them. I'm going to be more open to new ideas and less judgmental of those I don't agree with. And I'm going to be quicker to forgive. You never know when you're going to run out of time to make things right.

I love you, Janine.

Larry

Stephanie lowered the letter and stared blindly at the wall, numbed by the vivid scene her father had described. She couldn't imagine what horrors he must have witnessed in Vietnam. Deek's death was probably only one of many he had witnessed during the eighteen months he'd spent overseas.

How did a person deal with that? she asked herself. What kind of emotional scars did it leave him with? And how did he ever sleep at night without being haunted by the memories?

She laid a hand over the page, thinking of the effect her father had claimed that Deek's death had had on his life. If he'd lived, what kind of man would he have been? she wondered. Certainly a wiser one, judging from the things he'd seen and the lessons he'd learned. Sadly he'd never had the chance to put into action his plan to improve his life even more.

Her eyes sharpened. But she could, she realized. She could take the things he'd planned to do and incorporate them into her own life. It would be a way of honoring her father, a way of giving his life purpose. It would be a means of making him a part of *her* life.

Wade stood in the doorway quietly watching Stephanie. She wasn't sobbing her heart out, which he considered a good sign. But she wasn't dancing a jig either. Her forehead was pleated, as if she were absorbed in some deep thought. And there were creases at the corners of her eyes and mouth, as if whatever she was thinking about was either sad or depressing.

"Did you finish reading the letters?"

She jumped, then placed a hand over her heart and released a long breath. "I didn't hear you come in."

Dragging off his hat, he stepped into the room. "Sorry. Next time I'll give a holler." He dropped down on the arm of the recliner. "So? How'd it go?"

Averting her gaze, she lifted a shoulder and drew the ribbon back around the stack of letters. "Okay, I guess. I only read two."

"Two?" he repeated and glanced at his watch. "They must've been long ones—I was gone almost an hour."

"Not long. Heavy."

"Oh," he said in understanding but offered nothing more. If she wanted to talk, he'd listen, but he wasn't going to force her to say anything she wasn't ready or willing to share.

Her expression growing pensive, she framed the stack of letters between her hands. "He was only twenty-one when he died," she said as if thinking aloud. "Yet he'd probably seen and experienced more than men twice his age."

"Yeah, I imagine he had."

She glanced up and met his gaze. "In the last letter I read, he wrote about a guy in his unit who was killed." Wincing, she shook her head. "It was awful just reading about it. I can't imagine what it must have been like to be there and witness it firsthand."

"War's no picnic. Ask any veteran."

Lowering her gaze, she plucked guiltily at the ribbon that bound the letters. "I'm ashamed to admit it, but most of my knowledge of war is purely historical. Dates, battles, the political ramifications. The kind of thing you learn in a classroom. And since I've never been a fan of war movies or novels, I've never had a visual to associate with it before." She shuddered. "And to be honest, I think I preferred it that way." She glanced up, her expression sheepish. "I guess that makes me sound like an ostrich, huh? Wanting to keep my head buried in the ground?"

Wade thought of his daughter and the current problems he was having with her and shook his head. "No. Innocence is a hard thing to hold on to in today's world. What with all the graphic and gruesome TV shows and movies being shown, I consider it a miracle that you've managed to hold on to even a smidgen of your innocence."

"Innocent? Me?" She choked back a laugh and shook her head. "I think I lost my innocence about the age of six, when Tammy Jones told me there was no Santa Claus."

He clapped a hand over his heart. "Please," he begged, "tell me it isn't so."

Hiding a smile, she set the bundle aside and drew her legs beneath her. "I didn't say there *wasn't* a Santa Claus. I was only repeating what Tammy told me."

He dragged an arm across his forehead in an exaggerated show of relief. "Whew. You scared me there for a minute. I'm counting on Santa bringing me the new Kubota tractor I've been lusting after."

"A tractor?" she repeated, then rolled her eyes. "Men and their toys."

"A tractor's not a toy," he informed her. "It's a machine."

She flapped a dismissing hand. "Whatever."

"Okay, Miss Smarty-Pants. What is Santa gonna bring you?"

She blinked as if startled by the question, then tears filled her eyes.

Wade swallowed a groan, realizing that with Bud gone, this would be her first Christmas alone—an actuality he'd just brutally reminded her of. Dropping to a knee, he covered her hand with his. "I'm sorry, Steph. I wasn't thinking."

Keeping her face down, she shook her head. "It's not your fault. I just…hadn't thought that far ahead."

Hearing the sadness in her voice and knowing he'd put it there made him feel about as low as a snake. In hopes of making it up to her, he caught her hand and pulled her to her feet. "Tell you what," he said. "As punishment for sticking my foot in my mouth, I'll give you an hour of slave labor. Haul boxes, carry out the garbage. You name it, I'm your man."

He sensed her resistance, but then she surprised him by giving her head a decided nod.

"All right," she said. "But remember, this was your idea, not mine."

Stephanie didn't know what had possessed her to accept Wade's backhanded offer of help…or maybe she did.

I'm going to be quicker to forgive. You never know when you're going to run out of time to make things right.…

It was one of the ways her father had planned to change his life…and one of the changes Stephanie would have to make in her own if she was going to honor her father's memory by adopting his plan.

But could she forgive Wade? *Truly* forgive him?

She gave her head a shake as she placed the wrapped platter inside the box, unsure if that was possible.

"What pile does this go in?"

Pushing the hair back from her face, she looked up to see what Wade was holding. "Oh, wow," she murmured and reached to take the round of white plaster from him. "I haven't seen that in ages."

He hunkered down beside her. "What is it?"

"Don't you recognize fine art when you see it?" she asked, then smiled as she smoothed her hand across the shallow indentations in the plaster. "I made this in Bible school. Our teacher poured plaster in a pie pan, then had us press our hands into it to leave a print."

He placed his hand over the one impressed in the plaster. "Look how little that is," he said in amazement. "Mine is three or four times the size of yours."

She gave him a droll look. "I was five years old when I made that. I've grown some since then."

"Mine are still bigger." He held up his hand. "Put yours against mine," he challenged. "Let's see whose is bigger."

She hesitated slightly, reluctant to make the physical connection, then took a bracing breath and placed her palm against his. The warmth struck her first, followed by the strength she sensed beneath the flesh. She closed her eyes as awareness sizzled to life beneath her skin, from the top of her head to the tips of her toes.

"A good three inches longer," he boasted, pressing his fingers against hers. "Maybe more. And the breadth of my palm is at least two inches wider." He shifted his gaze to hers, then frowned and peered closer. "Steph? You okay? Your face is all red."

Of course it is, she wanted to tell him. Her body felt as if it were on fire and her mind was spinning, churning up memory after memory of what his hands could do to drive a woman out of her mind.

Dragging in a breath, she forced a smile. "Just a little dizzy. That's all." Flapping a dismissive hand, she laughed weakly. "I guess I've been pushing myself too hard to get all this done." She attempted to withdraw her hand, but he slid his fingers between hers, locking them together. Startled, she glanced up and met his gaze. In his eyes she saw the same awareness, the same need that burned behind her own. Unable to look away, she stared, slowly realizing that he was going to kiss her.

"Steph…"

At the last second she turned her face away and shook her head. "No. Don't. Please. I—"

"You what?"

Gulping back tears, she met his gaze. "I don't want you to kiss me. What happened before…I can't forget that."

She saw the anger that flashed in his eyes.

"Can't or won't?" he challenged.

Shaking her head, she dropped her gaze. "It doesn't matter. The result is the same."

He clamped his fingers down hard over her hand. "It may not matter to you, but it does to me. For God's sake, Steph! All that's in the past. Why can't you let it go?"

She snapped her gaze to his, furious that he would think it was that easy. "Because it hurts," she cried, fisting her free hand against her chest. "All these years later, and it still *hurts*."

He stared, the muscles in his face going slack. "You still care," he murmured, as if awed by the realization.

She shook her head wildly and tried to pull her hand free. "I don't. I *can't*."

He clamped his fingers tighter over hers, refusing to let her go. "You may not want to, but you can't deny what I see, what you feel."

A tear slipped past her lid and slid down her cheek.

"Aw, Steph," he said miserably. "I never meant to hurt you. That's the last thing I wanted to do. I asked then for your forgiveness and you refused." He dropped his gaze and shook his head. "Maybe that was asking too much of you. Could be it still is." He lifted his head to meet her gaze again, and she nearly wept at the regret that filled his eyes. "I know I destroyed whatever chance we ever had of being together, but couldn't we at least be friends?" He gave her hand a pleading squeeze. "Please, Steph? Is that too much to ask?"

She wanted desperately to tell him yes, it was too much to ask, to scream accusations and shoot arrows of blame until his heart was filled with as many holes as hers had been.

But she found she couldn't. And it was more than her desire to carry out her father's pledge of granting forgiveness that kept her from exacting her revenge. It was the pleading in his eyes and the sincerity in his voice that reached out and touched a place in her heart she'd thought could never be breached again.

But she wouldn't let him hurt her again. She couldn't. She would try her best to be his friend—but nothing more.

Drawing a steadying breath, she squared her shoulders. "I suppose we can try."

He stared a long moment, as if not trusting his ears, then dropped his chin to his chest and blew out a long breath. "Well, at least that's a start." Releasing her hand, he picked up the plaster disk of her handprint. "So what's it going to be? Trash, keep or donate?"

Grateful that he seemed willing to put the emotional scene behind them, she blinked to clear the tears from her eyes, then frowned as she studied the piece he held. Sagging her shoulders, she pointed to the pile marked Trash. "I'll probably hate myself later, but pitch it."

"If you want it, keep it."

Shaking her head, she picked up a china cup to wrap. "I'm already going to have to rent a storage facility as it is."

"But if it's special…" he argued.

"That's just it. Everything's special!" She placed the wrapped piece in the box, then waved a hand at the stuff piled around the room. "There isn't anything here that doesn't have a memory attached to it." She rocked to her knees and plucked a crystal bowl from the dining room table. "Take this, for instance. It belonged to my mother's mother. Mom told me that her mother always used it to serve her special fruit salad whenever they had company. Mom used it for the same thing. She even used the same fruit salad recipe her mother had always used." She opened a hand in a gesture of helplessness. "How do you throw away a piece of history like that?"

Wade picked up a piece of newspaper from the floor and handed it to her. "You don't. You either add on a room to your house or rent another storage building."

Stephanie frowned as he picked up another piece of paper and began to wrap it around the plaster handprint. "What are you doing? I told you to pitch that."

"A piece of art like this?" Shaking his head, he leaned to place it in the box with the china. "No way. That thing is priceless."

Tears filled her eyes as she watched him tuck the wrapped handprint into the box. It was such a simple thing, silly really, a kindness he was probably not even aware of. Yet his refusal to throw away a souvenir from her childhood put another crack in the armor she'd placed around her heart.

Fearing he'd do something else to widen the crack even more, she quickly wrapped paper around her grandmother's bowl. "What time is it?"

He glanced at his wristwatch. "One thirty-five."

She tucked the bowl into the box and stood, dusting off her hands. "Which means you've more than ful-filled your hour of slave labor."

"I can stay a little longer, if you want."

"Uh-uh." She turned him around and gave him a push toward the door. "Though I really appreciate all you did and hate losing the extra set of hands, I know darn good and well you've got work of your own to do."

"Yeah," he said, glancing at his wristwatch again. "I do."

At the door he stopped and looked back at her. "Steph, I'm glad we're going to be friends again."

She had to swallow back emotion before she could reply. "Yeah. Me, too."

Stephanie gave up and opened her eyes to stare at the dark ceiling. She'd tried everything to lull herself to sleep. She'd counted sheep, hummed the mantra from the yoga class she attended twice a week. She'd even gotten up and made herself a warm glass of milk to drink. Nothing had worked. Her mind still refused to shut down.

He would've kissed her. That one thought kept circling through her mind over and over again, keeping her awake. If she hadn't turned her face away, Wade would've kissed her. A part of her wanted to rail at the heavens that he would have the nerve to even try. Another part wished desperately that she had let him.

And that was what was keeping her awake. The fact that she still wanted his kiss. How pathetic. What woman in her right mind would knowingly and willingly subject herself to that kind of pain again?

Groaning, she dug her fingers through her hair as if she could tear thoughts of Wade from her mind. But that didn't help either. It just made her head ache even more.

Dropping her arms to her sides, she stared at the ceiling again, praying that sleep would come soon.

Runt growled, and she tensed, listening. Not hearing anything, she slowly dragged herself to a sitting position and leaned to peer at the rug beside the bed, where Runt slept.

"What is it, Runt?" she whispered. "Did you hear something?"

In answer, he rose and crossed to the door, the click of his nails on the wooden floor sounding like gunshots in the darkness.

Stephanie swung her legs over the side of the bed and hurried to stand beside the dog. "Is someone out there?" she whispered to Runt.

Whining low in his throat, he lifted a paw and scratched at the wood.

Though the dog couldn't see her face in the dark, she gave him a stern look. "If this is nothing more than you wanting to go outside to relieve yourself, I'm going to be really mad," she warned.

He barked once, sharply.

"Oh, Runt," she moaned, wringing her hands. "I really don't need this right now."

When he continued to whine and claw at the door, she gathered her courage and slowly opened the door a crack to peer out into the hall. Not seeing anything out of the ordinary, she opened the door wider. Runt pushed past her legs before she could stop him and shot down the hall, barking wildly. Stephanie's blood turned to ice as images of burglars and mass murderers filled her mind. Remembering the shotgun Bud kept behind the door in the laundry room, she crept down the dark hallway. As she passed through the kitchen, she whispered an impatient, "Give me a minute" to Runt, who was scratching at the back door and whining.

After locating the shotgun and checking to see that it was loaded and the safety was securely in place, she returned to the kitchen. She curled her fingers around the knob. "I'm right behind you," she murmured nervously to Runt, then opened the door.

The dog took off like a shot for the barn, his shrill bark sending shivers down her spine. She hesitated a second, trying to decide whether or not to grab a flashlight. Deciding that she couldn't shoot the gun and hold a flashlight, too, she ran after him.

A thick layer of storm clouds blanketed the sky, obliterating whatever illumination the moon might have offered. Stifling a shudder, Stephanie lifted the shotgun to her shoulder and moved stealthily toward the barn, keeping her finger poised on the trigger while keeping her ear cocked to the sound of Runt's barking.

A flash of lightning split the sky, making her jump, and was followed moments later by an earthshaking rumble of thunder. Silently vowing to murder Runt if this turned out to be a wild-goose chase, she quickened her step.

When she was about forty feet from the barn, Runt suddenly quit barking. Frowning, she strained, listening, but could hear nothing over the pounding of her heart. Tightening her grip on the shotgun, she flipped off the safety and tiptoed to the barn's dark opening.

Bracing a shoulder against the frame to steady her aim, she yelled, "Come out with your hands up!" in the deepest, meanest voice she could muster.

"Steph?"

She jolted at the sound of the male voice, then squinted her eyes against the darkness, trying to make out a shape. "Wade?" she asked incredulously. "Is that you?"

"Yeah, it's me."

The overhead lights flashed on and she squinted her eyes, momentarily blinded by the bright light. When her eyes adjusted, she saw Wade walking toward her. Runt trotted at his heels.

She didn't know whether to pull the trigger and shoot them both for scaring the daylights out of her or crumple into a heap of weak relief. Deciding murder was beyond her, she put the safety back on, lowered the shotgun and resorted to using her tongue as a weapon.

"What in blue blazes are you doing out here in the middle of the night?" she shouted at Wade. Before he could answer, she turned her fury on Runt. "And you," she accused angrily, "carrying on like burglars are crawling all over the place. You're supposed to protect me, not scare me to death. I have a good mind to take you to the *pound*."

Wade dropped a protective hand on the dog's head. "Don't blame Runt. It's my fault. I should've known he would hear me and kick up a fuss."

"Hear *what?*" she cried. "I was awake and I never heard a thing other than Runt barking." Realizing the oddity in that, she whipped her head around to look outside, then swung back around to face him. "Where's your truck?"

"At home. I walked."

"You *walked* all the way over here?"

He shoved his hands in his pockets and shrugged. "Couldn't sleep, so I figured I'd check on a heifer that's about to calf. She's young," he explained further, "and Bud was worried about her having trouble with the birth. I penned her when I was here earlier, so I could keep an eye on her."

"You walked," she repeated, unable to get beyond the incredibility in that one statement.

"It's not that far. Not if you cut through the woods."

She pressed the heel of her hand against her forehead and shook her head in disbelief. "I can't believe you did that. There's no telling what kind of varmints are hiding out in there."

He hid a smile. "I didn't run into a single grizzly or mountain lion."

She dropped her hand to frown. "Big surprise, since neither have been seen around here in fifty years or more. But there are coyotes and rattlesnakes," she reminded him, "and they can be just as dangerous."

When he merely looked at her, she rolled her eyes. "Men," she muttered under her breath. "If you cracked open the heads of the entire gender, you might come up with enough brains to form one good mind."

Lightning flashed behind her, followed by a deafening boom of thunder that made her jump.

Chuckling, he took the shotgun from her and caught her arm. "Come on," he said, tugging her along with him. "You better get back to the house before the bottom falls out of the sky."

She hurried to match her steps to his longer stride. "What about you? How will you get home?"

"The same way I came. I'll walk."

She dug in her heels, dragging him to a stop. "But you'll get soaked!"

He shrugged and nudged her into a walk again. "I've been wet before. I won't melt."

The words were no sooner out of his mouth, then the bottom of the sky did open up and rain poured down in torrents.

He grabbed her hand and shouted, "Run!"

Stephanie didn't need persuading. She took off, slipping and sliding on the wet grass, as Wade all but dragged her behind him. He reached the back door a step ahead of her and flung it open. Stephanie ducked inside and flipped on the light and was followed quickly by a drenched Runt. Wade brought up the rear, stripping off his hat and propping the gun against the wall before closing the door behind him.

"Man!" he exclaimed, dragging a sleeve across his face to swipe the rain from it. "That's some storm."

Stephanie grabbed a couple of dish towels from a drawer and tossed one to him before squatting down to rub a towel over Runt.

"Don't try to make up to me now," she scolded as Runt licked gratefully at her face. "If not for you and your stupid barking, we'd both be high and dry instead of dripping wet."

Wade hunkered down beside her and took the towel from her hand. "Here, let me. I'm the one to blame, not Runt."

Scowling, Stephanie stood and folded her arms across her breasts. "You won't get an argument out of me." A chill shook her, and she turned for the laundry room, where she'd left a basket of clean laundry. "I'm going to change clothes," she called over her shoulder.

She quickly stripped off her wet nightgown, dried off

as best she could with a towel she pulled from the basket, then tugged on a tank top and shorts. Grabbing one of her father's T-shirts from a stack on the dryer, she returned to the kitchen.

She offered the T-shirt to Wade. "It probably won't fit, but at least it's dry."

"Thanks." With a grateful smile he took the T-shirt and began to unbutton his shirt one-handed.

Stephanie didn't intend to watch but found she couldn't look away, as with each short drop of his hand to the next button, more and more of his chest was revealed. She knew from the summer they'd spent together, he often worked bare-chested. As a result, the skin he bared was as tanned as that on his face and hands, and the soft hair that curled around his nipples and rivered down to his navel had been bleached blonde.

By the time he reached the waist of his jeans and gave the shirt a tug, pulling his shirttail from beneath it, her mouth was dry as dust. Embarrassed by her reaction to such an innocent sight—and fearing he would notice his effect on her—she quickly turned away. As she did, the lights blinked out.

"Oh, great," she muttered. "Now the electricity is off."

"There's a candle on the shelf to the right of the sink."

Already on her way to fetch it, Stephanie shot him a frown over her shoulder. "I know where the candles are kept."

"Sorry."

As she struck a match and touched the flame to the wick, she frowned. The fire flickered a moment, then caught, tossing shadows to dance across the room.

Turning, she held the candle up and eyed Wade warily as he tugged Bud's T-shirt over his head. "How do you know so much about everything around here?"

He glanced up, then set his jaw and pulled the T-shirt down to his waist. "You may have shut me out of your life, but your parents didn't choose to do the same."

"You mean, you— They—"

"Yep, that's exactly what I mean." He stooped to pick up the towel he'd dried Runt with, then stood to face her. "Your mother was a little slower to forgive than Bud, but I think she finally realized I'd done the only thing an honorable man could've done in a situation like the one I was caught in."

Afraid she would drop it, Stephanie set the candle-holder on the table and pressed a hand to her stomach, suddenly feeling ill. "But they never said a word. Never so much as mentioned your name to me."

He tossed the wet towel into the sink. "That was out of respect for you, knowing it would upset you."

She dropped her face to her hands. "I can't believe this," she said. "How could they *do* that to me?"

"Oh, come on, Steph," he chided gently. "They didn't do anything to you." When she didn't respond, he crossed to pull her hands down, forcing her to look at him. "You know your parents loved you. They'd never do anything to hurt you."

"But they forgave you!" she cried. "Knowing what you had done to me, they still forgave you."

"One has nothing to do with the other," he argued.

When she opened her mouth to voice her disagreement, he silenced her with a look.

"They forgave me for what I'd done," he told her

firmly, "but not for the pain I caused you. I don't think they were ever able to forgive me for that."

She tossed up her hands. "What else was there to forgive?"

"Getting a woman pregnant and having to marry her."

Stunned, Stephanie stared, unable to believe that hearing him voice his transgression could have the same debilitating effect as it had when he'd confessed it to her so many years before.

Before she could cover her ears, refusing to hear any more, he caught her hands and held them, forcing her to hear him out.

"I never loved Angela. That's not something I'm proud of, considering, but it's true. I loved *you*, Steph, with all my heart and soul. Your parents knew that and knew, too, how much it cost me to lose you." He tightened his grip on her hands. "But don't hold their kindness to me against your mom and dad. Without them—" he dropped his chin to his chest and slowly shook his head "—I don't know how I would've survived it all."

Heaving a sigh, he gave her hands a last squeeze and turned away. "I guess I'd better go so you can get to bed." He stooped to give Runt's head a pat. "You might want to take a couple of candles with you to your bedroom," he said, the suggestion directed to Stephanie. "The electricity might not come back on until morning."

She watched him cross the kitchen, her throat squeezed so tight she could barely breathe.

I loved you, Steph, with all my heart and soul.

Out of everything he'd said, that one single statement filled her mind, obliterating all else.

He made it to the door before she found her voice.

"I loved you, too."

His hand on the knob, he glanced back.

The tears clotting her throat rose to fill her eyes. "And you broke my heart."

Four

Wade stood, paralyzed as much by the desolation that etched Stephanie's face as by what she had just said. This was the woman he'd loved—still loved, if he was honest with himself—and, by her own admission, he'd broken her heart. He'd known he had—or at least had assumed that was the case—but it cut him to the bone to hear her say the words and see, this many years later, how much she still suffered from his infidelity.

He hadn't been able to comfort her then. How could he, when she wouldn't let him past her front door?

But he could now.

In two long strides he was across the room and had her face gathered between his hands. "I'm so sorry, Steph." He swept his thumbs beneath her eyes, swiping away the tears. "I never wanted to hurt you. I swear, if there'd been any other way…"

Realizing how inadequate the apology sounded, even to his own ears, he tightened his hands on her face, desperate to make her believe him. "You didn't deserve what I did to you. The sin was mine. You had no part in it, yet you paid a price." He swallowed hard. "But I paid, too, Steph. If you want the truth, I'm still paying."

He saw the flash of surprise in her eyes, the hope that rose slowly to glimmer in the moisture.

Helpless to do anything less, he lowered his face and touched his lips to hers. It wasn't a passionate kiss. A mere meeting of lips. But to Wade it was like coming home after a long stay away. He withdrew far enough to draw a shuddery breath, then wrapped his arms around her and pressed his mouth more fully over hers. He felt the shiver that trembled through her, swallowed the low moan that slid past her lips. With a groan he clamped his arms around her and opened his mouth over hers.

Her taste rushed through him like a swollen river, flooding him with memory after memory that he'd struggled for years to forget. The feel of her lying naked in his arms, the almost greedy race of her hands over his flesh. Her catlike purr of pleasure vibrating against his chest, the moist warmth of her laughter teasing his chin.

Rock-hard and wanting more of her, he hooked a hand beneath her knee, lifted and drew her hard against his groin. But it wasn't enough. Not nearly enough. With his mouth locked to hers, he backed her up against the wall and leaned into her, pinning her there with his body. Filling his hands with her rain-dampened hair, he held her face to his and took the kiss deeper still, until his breath burned in his lungs and his veins pumped liquid fire, until every cell in his body throbbed with his need to take her, to make her his again.

Bracing his hand in a V at her throat, he dragged his lips from hers. "I want you, Steph," he whispered and rained kisses over her face, her eyelids, across the hollows of her cheeks. "I want to make love with you." He pushed a knee between her legs and buried his face in the curve of her neck to smother a groan as her heat burned through his thigh.

Though he knew her need equaled his, he sensed her hesitancy in the tremble of hands she braced against his chest and feared he was pushing her too fast, too hard.

Drawing in a long breath to steady himself, he dragged his hand from her throat to cover her breast. Beneath his palm he could feel the pounding of her heart.

"Remember how good we were together?" Closing his fingers around her fullness, he gently kneaded. "I always loved your breasts." He lifted the one he held and warmed it with his breath. Humming his pleasure when her nipple budded beneath the thin fabric, he flicked his tongue over the swollen peak.

She arched instinctively, thrusting her breast against his mouth. He nipped, suckled, nipped again, but quickly became frustrated by the fabric that kept him from fully touching her, tasting her. "I want you bare," he said, then looked up at her, seeking her permission.

She gulped, nodded, then dropped her head back against the wall on a low moan as he eased her tank top down far enough to expose her breast. The candle behind him tossed light to flicker over her flushed flesh— the knotted bud, the pebbled areola that surrounded it, the lighter skin stained with the blush of desire. Mesmerized by the sight, he opened his mouth over her nipple, drew her in.

As he suckled, teasing her nipple with his tongue and teeth, he sensed her growing need in the hands she gripped at his head, her impatience in the fingers she knotted in his hair. Anxious to satisfy both, he released her and swept her up into his arms.

Leaving the candle behind in the kitchen, he made his way through the dark house, his familiarity with her parents' home guiding his steps. Once inside her bedroom, he pushed the door shut with his foot, in case Runt decided to follow, and continued on to her bed. He laid her down, then stretched out alongside her.

In the darkness he couldn't see her face, didn't need to in order to know that somewhere along the short walk from the kitchen to her bedroom her hesitancy had returned. He could all but feel the years that lay between them, all the days and months, stacked one on top of the other, in which she had clung to her resentment toward him, shored up a wall around her heart that he had only just begun to believe he could tear down. He had the power to seduce her. He knew that. He'd proven it in the kitchen only moments before. But he couldn't allow his physical needs to destroy whatever chance he might still have with her.

Placing a hand on her cheek, he turned her face to his. "You'll never know how much I've missed you," he said softly. "How many nights I've dreamed of touching you and holding you like this." He drew in a deep breath, anxious to make her understand how he truly felt. "But it's so much more than the sex. I've missed *you*, Steph. Your laughter, your smile. The way you always seemed to know exactly what I needed, whether it was a swift quick in the seat of the pants or a tight hug of encouragement. The hours we spent talking. And the times we spent in silence, content just to be together."

He caught her hand and drew it to his lips. "I'd be lying if I said I didn't want you right now. But more than the sexual release and pleasure that would give me—hopefully both of us—I need *you*. Back in my life, back in my heart. When we make love again, Steph, I want you to want me as much as I want you. I don't want there to be any regrets."

He heard her breath hitch and he swept his thumb across her cheek to catch the tear that fell. "Don't cry, Steph." He slipped his arm beneath her and drew her to him, tucking her head beneath his chin. "Just let me hold you. That's all I'll do, I swear, is just hold you."

Steph awakened and stretched her legs out, while wisps of sensations and emotions floated through her mind. Her eyes still closed, she separated each, naming them. Warmth. Tenderness. Comfort. Security. Lust. She stiffened at the latter and tried to remember if she'd had a dream that would explain why she'd wake with that particular thought on her mind.

Wade, she realized slowly as the events of the previous night returned. He'd aroused her with his seductive words, his lips, his touch. Even as she remembered the way his mouth had felt on her breast, the tremble of desire he'd drawn, she had to squeeze her thighs tight against the ache that throbbed to life deep in her womb.

She remembered, too, the trepidation that had grown inside her with each step he'd taken that had brought them closer to her bedroom. *Distrust.* It was such an ugly and debilitating word, one that she had lived with for far too many years. But as hard as she'd tried to banish it from her mind, it was always there in her subconscious, keeping her from giving her heart to any man—even, it seemed, the one responsible for planting the seed inside her in the first place.

But he'd claimed that he had suffered as much as she. And, if he was to be believed, he was still suffering. Remembering how he'd pulled her into his arms, telling her that he wanted only to hold her, she closed her eyes and gave herself up to the warmth and sense of security she'd found there.

Stiffening, she flipped her eyes open, suddenly wide-awake. Was he still here with her? she wondered. In her bed? Holding her breath, she dropped a hand behind her and groped. When her fingers met only cool sheets, she slowly brought her hand back to curl beneath her cheek, swallowing back the disappointment at finding him gone.

And why would you be sad about that? she asked herself. You should be relieved that he left. You don't need this, she reminded herself. You've got enough drama going on in your life without adding Wade to the mix.

With a sigh she flipped back the covers, preparing to get up, but froze when a piece of paper fluttered up from the pillow next to hers and drifted slowly out of sight on the far side of the bed. Making a dive for it, she flattened her stomach against the mattress and caught it before it hit the floor. Her heart in her throat, she sat up, bracing her back against the headboard and read.

Good morning, Sunshine. Sorry to leave without waking you, but you were sleeping so soundly I hated to disturb you, figuring you needed the rest. I'll be back around noon to drop off another bundle of letters. If you want, after I check on the cattle, I can stay for a while and help you pack.
Wade

She shifted her gaze to read the first line again, and a warm glow slowly spread through her chest. *Sunshine.* It was a nickname he'd used often the summer they'd met. Surprised that he would remember the endearment, she sank back against her pillow and stared out the window, her thoughts growing pensive as she wondered where all this was going.

Judging by the passionate scene in the kitchen the previous night, she had to believe that he was hoping they could be more than friends.

But she wasn't sure she could offer him anything more than friendship. He'd destroyed her trust, hurt her more than words could ever describe. How did a person get over that kind of pain, humiliation? Was it even possible? Forgiving was one thing, forgetting another. And if she couldn't forget, what was the point in getting involved with him again? Even if she were willing to agree to a strictly physical relationship, the past would always be there between them.

She shivered, remembering the way his mouth had felt on her breast, the desperate need that had burned through her body, leaving her weak and wanting. He had been right in saying that they'd been good together. They *had* been good together—though she had to give all the credit to Wade. She'd yet to meet the man who could satisfy her the way he once had. He had always seemed to understand her needs better than she did herself, knowing what pleased her, the areas of her body that were most sensitive, when she craved speed and when she preferred a slow seduction…and when she needed him to stop altogether.

He'd recognized the latter the previous night. Without her having to say a word, he'd somehow known that at some point between the kitchen and bedroom the ugly doubts had arisen, making her question what they were doing and whether or not she should allow things to go any further. Before she had even reached a decision, he'd removed her need to do so by voicing her fears aloud and refusing to make love with her until she could do so without regret.

She drew in a shuddery breath and slowly released it. How in the heck was a woman supposed to deal with a man like that? she asked herself. One who knew her fears as well as she did, then offered her his under-standing and patience while she dealt with them?

Hearing Steph's faint call of, "The door's open," Wade stepped inside.

"I'm back here!"

Since her voice was coming from the rear of the house, he assumed by "here" she meant one of the bedrooms. Taking the shortcut through the dining room, he glanced around and was surprised to find the table was clear and all the boxes were stacked neatly against one wall.

He stuck his head into the guest room and found

her standing on a ladder inside the closet, her head hidden from view. She was wearing shorts, and the view of her long, tanned legs and bare feet put a knot of need in his groin. Puffing his cheeks, he blew out a long breath to steady himself, then tossed the bundle of letters onto the bed. "Looks like you've been busy."

"And then some," came her weary reply. She backed down the ladder, balancing a stack of shoe boxes on the palm of one hand. Reaching the floor, she steadied the stack with her opposite hand and stooped to set them on the floor. Straightening, she blew a breath at the wisps of hair that had escaped the ponytail she'd pulled her hair into, then smiled. "But I'm making progress. I finished the dining room and now I'm working in here."

He looked around at the piles that covered the floor, amazed by the amount of junk she'd unearthed. "Where did all this stuff come from?"

She hooked her thumb over her shoulder at the closet. "In there. Can you believe Mom was able to cram all that junk in that small a space?"

He picked up a doll that lay on the foot of the bed. A black hole gleamed from the space where an eye should have been, and blond hair frizzed from its scalp. He lifted a brow. "Yours?"

Smiling fondly, she took the doll from him. "This is Maddy. I wagged her around from the age of three to about seven or eight, I think."

"What happened to her eye?"

"One of Bud's dogs got a hold of her and popped it out."

"The dog get her hair, too?"

She shook her head and attempted to smooth the

wild tufts. "No, that was my doing. I thought she'd look better with a short hairstyle."

He sat down on the edge of the bed. "Remind me to never get near you when you've got a pair of scissors in your hand."

Chuckling, she laid the doll on the dresser. "Coward."

In her reflection in the dresser mirror he watched her smile slowly fade and knew by the creases that appeared between her brows that something was bothering her.

"About last night," she began uneasily.

Not wanting to have that particular discussion with her halfway across the room, he stretched to catch her hand and tugged her over to sit down beside him. "What about last night?"

She glanced at him, then away, her cheeks flaming a bright red. "I'm sure that you must think I'm giving off…"

When her voice trailed off, he bit back a smile. "Mixed signals?" he suggested.

She looked at him, then dropped her chin and nodded. "One minute I'm stiff-arming you and the next I'm, well, I'm—"

"Melting into a puddle of rapturous joy at my feet?"

She shot him a frown. "I wouldn't go so far as to say *that*."

Chuckling, he slung an arm around her shoulders and hugged her to his side. "No need to get your panties in a twist. I was just trying to make you laugh so you'd relax a little."

She shot to her feet to pace. "That's the problem. It's way too easy to relax around you. So much so that I'm letting my guard down."

"And that's a bad thing?"

She whirled to face him. "Yes, it's a bad thing! You hurt me, and I can't forget that."

"But you've forgiven me."

It was a statement, not a question, and she stared, realizing it was true. She didn't know exactly when or even why, but she *had* forgiven him.

But what was the use of forgiving if she couldn't forget? she found herself thinking again.

"Give yourself time," he suggested as if he'd read her thoughts. "And me, too," he added. He caught her hand and tugged her to stand between his legs. "I'm going to win back your trust," he told her in a tone that left little doubt that he would succeed. Holding her gaze, he brought her hand to his lips and pressed a kiss to her knuckles. "The burden is mine to prove, not yours."

She blinked back tears at the depth of his determination, the tenderness with which he'd made the promise to win back her trust. Yet she couldn't help questioning her sanity for her willingness to breathe so much as the same air as him after what he'd done to her.

Again as if reading her mind, he took her hands in his. "I'm not perfect, Steph. I've made my share of mistakes. But loving you was never one of 'em."

Her face crumpling, she sank to his knee and dropped her forehead against his. "Oh, Wade," she said miserably. "Why does everything have to be so complicated?"

He turned her face up to his. "It doesn't have to be. At least, not the part that deals with us. We were good together, good for each other. And we will be again."

She lifted her head to search his eyes and knew by the warmth she found there that he was offering her a new beginning, one that she was finding difficult to refuse. He made it sound so simple, so easy. But was it really?

"Wade—"

He touched his lips to hers to silence her. "You don't need to say anything. I'm not pushing for something you're not ready to give."

She closed her eyes, gulped. When she opened them and met his gaze, saw the warmth and understanding there, what little hesitancy that remained to hold her back slipped soundlessly away.

She lifted a hand to his cheek, her fingers trembling as she traced the lines that fanned from the corner of his eye. "You don't have to push. I'm more than ready."

He stared, as if not trusting his ears. "Are you sure?"

"Yes," she murmured and touched her lips to his.

Groaning, he wrapped his arms around her and pulled her to his chest. With an urgency that left her head spinning and her heart racing, he stripped off her blouse, her bra, then twisted her around on his lap and fitted her knees on either side of his thighs.

"Sweet heaven," he murmured as his gaze settled on her breasts. He filled his hands with their softness. "So beautiful." Sweeping his hands around to settle beneath them, he lifted and placed a kiss on each peak. He tipped up his head to meet her gaze and stroked his thumbs over her nipples. "Exactly as I remember them, perfect in every way."

Knowing it wasn't true, she shook her head. "You're a wonderful liar, but age and gravity have taken their toll."

"Perfect," he insisted, then teased her with a smile. "I think I'm the better judge."

She tipped her head, willing to concede the point,

then gasped as he closed his mouth over a nipple. Dropping her head back, she clung to his head. "Wade," she said, his name rushing out on thready sigh, then gasped again as he caught the nipple between his teeth and tugged gently. "Oh, Wade," she groaned and knotted her fingers in his hair.

Desperate to have her hands on him, she reached for his shirt and fumbled open buttons. Halfway down, she grew impatient and shoved the plackets apart and sank against him to press her lips against the middle of his chest. She inhaled once, released it with a contented sigh, then inhaled again and held the breath, absorbing his male scent.

Dizzy from it, she braced her hands against his chest and began a slow journey of exploration, smoothing her palms over the swell of muscled chest, down, her fingers bumping over each rib, then bringing her hands together at the waist of his jeans. Finding the snap, she released it and eased the zipper down.

With her lungs burning for air, her chest heaving with her attempts to fill them, she found his mouth with hers and freed his sex. It sprang from the restraining clothing and filled her hands. Marveling at the feel of silk-sheathed steel, she stroked her fingers down its length until the heel of her hand bumped the nest of coarse hair at its base. She released a shuddery breath against his lips and stroked upward, gathering her fingers at its tip and swirling her thumb over the pearl of moisture there.

With a groan he fell back, bringing her with him, and toed off his boots, his socks, then, one-handed, stripped off his jeans and underwear. Letting his clothing fall to the floor, he dragged her up his body and captured her mouth again. He kissed her with an urgency that fed her own need, yet with a tenderness that twisted her heart.

Noonday sun shone through the windows at either side of the bed, filling the room with bright sunlight. Though she would've preferred candlelight to mask the changes age had left on her body, Stephanie was grateful for the illumination, as it provided her the ability to see Wade's face, the muscled lines of his body her hands traced. With each glide of flesh over flesh, the years fell away, leaving in their place the familiarity she'd once known with this man, the ease they'd once shared.

Desperate to have him inside her again, to experience the thrill of oneness she'd once known, she wiggled out of her shorts and panties, then positioned her knees on either side of his hips. Using her hand to guide him, she dragged his sex along her folds to moisten it, then positioned the tip at her opening. With her gaze on his, she drew in a deep breath, bracing herself, then plunged her hips down and took him in.

The sensations that ripped through her stole her breath and sent brilliant shards of white to explode behind her closed lids. His name became a fervent prayer for release she whispered as she pumped her hips against his. Again and again and again, until sweat beaded her upper lip, slicked her hands, making it all but impossible to keep them braced against his chest. The pressure built inside her, fed by a rising wave of need that gathered itself into a knot in her womb.

As if sensing her readiness, her need for satisfaction, Wade clamped his hands at her hips. "Come with me," he said breathlessly, then set his jaw and squeezed his eyes shut. A low growl rose from deep inside him, then he exploded inside her, and the heat that pulsed from him sent her soaring high.

Her lungs heaving like bellows, her hands fisted against his chest, she hovered a moment, suspended on that needlelike peak of pain and pleasure, wanting more than anything to hold on in order to capture the feelings and emotions that filled her. Unable to stave off the sensations any longer, she toppled over the other side into satisfaction.

Weak, sated, she sank to his chest and buried her face in the curve of his neck, every nerve in her body quivering liked plucked strings. "Oh, Wade," she whispered, unable to find the words to express the experience.

"Was it good?"

Inhaling, she stretched her toes out and curled her feet around his sweat-dampened calves. "Oh, yeah," she said, releasing the breath on a contented sigh. "Better than good."

Before she had time to draw another breath, she was on her back and he was on top of her, his face only inches from her.

"Honey, that was nothing but foreplay. What comes next ranks right up there with fantastic."

Laughing, she laced her fingers behind his neck and brought his face down to hers. "Then show me what you've got, cowboy."

Five

The next day Wade was in his toolshed early, anxious to get his work done so that he could go and see Steph.

After selecting a wrench from those hanging on the wall above his worktable, he hunkered down in front of the baler to adjust the belt's tension. He had made only two full turns when the wrench slipped and he had to stop and swipe the perspiration from his hands—and it wasn't the heat that had made his hands slick with sweat, although his toolshed held heat like a smokehouse. It was the thoughts of Steph that kept playing through his mind.

Aware of the dangers involved in working on a piece of equipment and knowing how much they escalated if a man wasn't giving his full attention to the job, he pulled the wrench free and braced it against his thigh. He still couldn't believe they'd made love. He'd hoped they would, planned on it even, but he'd thought it would take him a lot longer to persuade her.

He didn't know what had changed her mind and really didn't care. The only thing that mattered was that she'd given herself to him willingly and without any pressure from him. Not that he would have felt any compunction on applying a little, if she'd dragged her feet too much longer. From the moment he'd seen her standing in her parents' house a week ago he'd known that his feelings for her hadn't changed. Just looking at her had had the same debilitating effect on him that it had thirteen years before. And kissing her…well, he wouldn't even go there, seeing as he couldn't even hold on to a wrench, as it was.

"Dad-dy! I'm talking to you!"

Wade glanced over to find his daughter standing in the doorway, her hands fisted on her hips. Setting the wrench aside, he dragged a rag from his pocket to wipe his hands. "Sorry, sweet cheeks. Guess I was daydreaming. Whatcha need?"

She pushed her hands into fists at her sides, with an impatient huff of breath. "I *asked* if I could spend the night with Brooke."

Eyeing his daughter warily, he stuffed the rag back into his pocket, wondering whether this overnight was on the up-and-up or a smoke screen she was spreading for her to do God only knew what. "Did Brooke's mother say it was all right with her?"

She gave him a pained look, one she'd perfected over the last year, then said through clenched teeth, "Yes. She said I could ride the bus home with Brooke after school if it's okay with you."

Knowing from experience that this could all be a clever lie Meghan was weaving in order to cover her tracks, he pulled his cell from the holster at his waist. "I'll just give Jan a call and double-check things with her."

"Daddy!" she cried. "I told you Mrs. Becker said it was okay!"

He punched in the number, then looked down his nose at her as he lifted the phone to his ear. "If it's all the same to you, I'd like to hear that from Jan."

She folded her arms across her chest and pushed her lips out in a pout. "You don't trust me."

He listened through the second ring. "The last time you asked permission to go somewhere with a girl-friend, you ended up at the pizza parlor with a guy two years older than you." When she opened her mouth to spew a comeback, he held up a hand, silencing her.

"Jan?" he said into the receiver. "This is Wade Parker, Meghan's dad."

He listened a moment, then smiled. "Doing just fine. How about yourself?"

"That's good," he replied to her response that all was well in the Becker household, then scratched his head. "Listen, Jan. Meghan was telling me about her plans to spend the night with Brooke tonight, and I wanted to make sure that was all right with you before I gave her my permission."

He listened again, then breathed a sigh of relief at her affirmative answer. "No, riding the bus home with Brooke is fine with me," he told her. "Will save you and me both from having to haul them around."

He smiled and nodded again. "Yeah, I hear you. These girls would keep us in the middle of the road if they could." Anxious to end the call before Jan got started in on the trials and tribulations of being a single parent, he said, "I'd better go. I need to write a permission note for Meghan to give the bus driver before she leaves for school." He nodded again. "You, too, Jan. And thanks."

He disconnected the call and returned his cell to its holster.

Meghan lifted a haughty brow. "Well? Are you satisfied *now?*"

Wade pulled a tablet from a slot above his worktable and scrawled a note granting his permission for Meghan to ride a different bus from school. "Better watch your mouth, young lady, or you'll find yourself spending the night at home with me."

She snatched the note from his hand and spun for the house. "And wouldn't that be fun?" she muttered under her breath.

Wade heard the sassy comeback but chose to ignore it. He'd learned the hard way to choose his battles with his daughter, and this one wasn't even worth the energy required for a skirmish.

Heaving a sigh, he braced a hand on the doorjamb and watched her stalk to the house, her long blond hair swinging from side to side with each angry stride. Twelve going on twenty-two, he thought sadly. Why couldn't kids just be satisfied with being kids? he asked himself. Why were they so hell-bent on becoming adults? Didn't they realize that being a grown-up wasn't all it was cracked up to be? Kids didn't have the responsibilities and worries that adults faced every day. Hell, this was the best time of Meghan's life! She should be enjoying herself, instead of plotting and scheming ways to do things she wasn't allowed to do. Things that she was too *young* to be doing.

He shook his head, remembering the day she'd come home sporting three holes in each ear and knowing it was too late for him to do a damn thing to stop her from doing it. And what was with this new infatuation of hers with boys two and three years older than herself?

Snorting, he dropped his hand from the door and turned back to the baler he'd been working on. He may not know what his daughter was thinking, but he knew what was on those boys' minds. And that was the problem. It wasn't so long ago that he'd been a teenage boy that he couldn't recognize a hormone-raging stud looking for a girl he could charm out of her panties when he saw one.

He shuddered at the thought of his daughter being sexually active, then set his jaw and picked up his wrench, settling it into place over a bolt. "Not on my watch," he muttered and gave the wrench a hard turn, tightening the bolt into place.

Stephanie opened the door and blinked in surprise when she saw Wade standing on the stoop, his hat in his hand. "What are you doing over here at this time of day?"

His smile sheepish, he scuffed the toe of his boot at the doormat. "I'm embarrassed to admit to being this slow, but it only just occurred to me that it's Friday night and I've got nothing to do. I thought, if you weren't busy, we might go to a movie or something."

Stephanie would've laughed if he hadn't looked so

cute standing there like a lost puppy in search of a new home. She glanced down at her bare feet and the cutoff jeans she was wearing, then at her wristwatch. Wrinkling her nose, she shifted her gaze back to his. "By the time I shower and change, whatever movie is showing would be half over."

He grimaced. "Yeah, you're probably right. I should've called first. I started to, but I figured you wouldn't answer the phone."

"I wouldn't have." Taking pity on him, she opened the door wide. "Tell you what. We can watch a movie here. If there's nothing on, I'm sure I can find a video or DVD in my parents' stash for us to watch."

"Are you sure?" he asked even as he stepped eagerly inside. "If you're busy or have other plans, I can head back home. I'm sure I can find something there to do to pass the time."

Laughing, she closed the door behind him. "I'm not busy. In fact, I was just about to put a frozen pizza in the oven. Have you had dinner yet?"

He placed a hand over his stomach, as if only now realizing he'd missed the meal and was hungry. "No, as a matter of fact, I haven't."

She glanced at him over her shoulder as she led the way to kitchen. "Is pepperoni okay?"

He tossed his hat onto the counter. "Beggars can't be choosers."

She stopped, balancing a pizza on the palm of one hand, the other curled around the handle of the oven door. "If you don't like pepperoni, I can probably scrape up the makings for a sandwich."

Chuckling, he shook his head. "Pepperoni's fine. In

fact, that's all I ever eat. It's Meghan's favorite and the only one we keep stocked in our freezer."

Stephanie's smile faded.

Wade noticed the sudden change in her expression before she turned to slide the pizza into the oven and cursed his blunder, knowing it was his mention of his daughter that had robbed her of her smile. He crossed to her and caught her hand in his. "Steph, she's my daughter. I can't pretend she doesn't exist."

She squared her shoulders and forced a smile. "I know that. And I don't expect you to pretend she doesn't exist. You just—well, you caught me off guard when you mentioned her. You having a child is not something that I care to think about."

"But…" He stopped, knowing that anything else he said would only drag up more of the past. And he didn't want to spoil the one evening he had with her rehashing his mistakes.

"How about some wine?" he asked, changing the subject. "Bud usually kept a bottle or two around, if you haven't thrown them out."

She stepped around him and gestured to the far cabinet as she headed for the sink. "Up there, and the opener is in—" She stopped, hauled in a breath, then continued on to the sink. "Well, I'm sure you probably know where to find the opener, the same as you do the wine, since you seem to know where everything else is kept."

In two long strides he was across the room and turning her around to face him. His anger melted when he saw the gleam of tears in her eyes. "Aw, Steph," he said miserably. "I thought we'd already cleared that hurdle. Yes, I was friends with your parents. And yes, I know my way around their house probably as well as I do my own. But don't let that come between us. We've got enough old baggage to sort through without having to dredge up that particular subject again."

When she kept her head down, refusing to look at him, he hooked a finger beneath her chin and tipped her face up to his. "Come on, Steph. I know you feel like we all conspired against you, but that wasn't the case at all. Your parents knew that mentioning my name in any form or fashion would only upset you, so they didn't."

She closed her hand over his and drew in a breath. "I know. And I'm sorry. Really. It's just going to take time for me to get used to…well, everything. So much went on that I wasn't aware of." She held up a hand when he started to interrupt. "Which is my fault," she said, saving him from having to tell her it was. Drawing his hand to hold between hers, she gave it a reassuring squeeze. "Now about that wine…"

He dropped a kiss on her mouth. "Frozen pizza and wine. Is there something wrong with this picture?"

"I'd say it's right on par with every date I ever had with you."

"Hey!" he cried, looking insulted. "We went on a couple of real dates."

She folded her arms across her chest. "Name one."

He shifted from one foot to the other, trying to think of one to offer, then gave her a sheepish look. "I guess I did kind of drop the ball in the date department."

Laughing, she patted his cheek. "No, you didn't. I always enjoyed the time we spent together, no matter what we were doing."

Relieved that it appeared they had weathered another

storm, he pulled out a drawer and drew out the wine opener. "Remember the time you sat up all night with me when my mare was foaling?"

"Yes. That was the first equine birth I'd ever witnessed. And hopefully my last," she added with a shudder. "That poor mare. It was hard to watch her suffer when there was nothing we could do to ease her pain."

"Breach births are seldom easy," he said as he pulled the cork from the bottle with a *pop*. "I've probably lost as many babies as I've saved. Sometimes lost the mamas, too."

While he filled two wineglasses, Stephanie set the timer on the oven. "That's the one thing I don't miss about living on a ranch," she said thoughtfully as she crossed to stand beside him. "Losing an animal always made me so sad."

"Yeah, it does me, too." He handed her a glass, then draped an arm along her shoulders. "Want to sit on the patio while we wait for the pizza to cook?"

"Good idea."

Once outside, she brushed a hand over the seats of the chairs, sweeping away the dried leaves that covered them, then sat and patted the chair next to hers. "Take a load off."

He nudged the chair closer to hers, then dropped down with a sigh.

"I love this view," she said, her smile wistful as she stared out at the pastures and the low hills beyond. "The way the sun looks at sunset, as if it's melting into the hills."

He laced his fingers through hers and settled their joined hands on the arms of their pushed-together chairs. "It is pretty. I have almost this exact same view from the balcony off my bedroom."

Her gaze still on the setting sun, she hid a smile. "I remember both the balcony and the view." She waited a beat, then added, "I also remember you spreading a blanket on the balcony one night and getting me drunk on tequila shots."

He pressed a hand against his chest. "Me?" He shook his head. "You must be mistaken. I'd never take advantage of a woman that way."

She bumped her shoulder against his. "Oh, please. And that wasn't the only time you got me drunk. I distinctly remember a case of beer and an afternoon spent skinny-dipping in the creek that runs through your hay field."

"It was hot," he said defensively. "And as I recall, you only had two of those beers."

She lifted a shoulder. "What can I say? I'm a cheap drunk."

Biting back a smile, he tapped his glass against hers. "Drink up, then. Maybe I'll get lucky again tonight."

She drew back to look at him in surprise. "How long are you planning to stay?"

"All night, if you'll let me."

She dropped her mouth open, then slowly closed it to stare. "You mean...you can stay the whole night?"

He took her glass and set it, along with his, on the patio. "Yep," he said and tugged her from her chair and onto his lap. "The *whole* night."

She continued to stare, realizing the significance in that. "Do you realize this will be the first time we will have ever slept together?"

He grasped her thigh and shifted her more comfortably on his lap. "I think you're forgetting about the night it stormed."

"No. That doesn't count because you were gone when I woke up."

He lifted a hand to her cheek and met her gaze squarely. "This one might not count either, because I'm not planning on either one of us getting any sleep."

The heat in his blue eyes burned through hers, turning her mouth to cotton and twisting her stomach into a pretzel.

The timer on the oven went off, its loud buzz signaling the pizza was done.

Unable to tear her gaze from his, she wet her lips. "Are you hungry?"

He hooked a hand behind her neck and brought her face to his. "Only for you," he said before closing his mouth over hers.

Her breath stolen, Stephanie wrapped her arms around him and clung. She felt as if she were drowning, slipping deeper and deeper into a sea of desire, its waters at first tinted a soft, muted blue, cocooning her as she drifted down. Then the water changed, became a fiery-red tempest that churned, battering her senses. The heat it produced gathered into a tight knot in her middle, then slowly spread out to every extremity, making her skin steam and her lungs burn for air.

"Wade," she gasped, remembering their dinner. "The pizza."

He slid a hand beneath her shirt, cupping a breast, and found her mouth again. "Let it burn."

Though tempted, she pushed a hand against his chest, forcing him back. "We can't. The house could burn, too."

Frowning, he pulled his hand from beneath her shirt.

"Okay, so we'll take the damn thing out." He stood, hitching her up high on his chest, and carried her back to the kitchen. "You do the honors."

With one hand locked around his neck to keep from falling, she plucked a mitt from the rack on the oven's front panel, then opened the door and pulled out the pizza. Wade angled her toward the range so that she could shove the pizza onto its flat surface.

He lifted a brow. "Satisfied?"

Locking her hands behind his neck, she gave him a coy look. "Not yet, but I'm counting on you taking care of that little problem for me."

He choked on a laugh, then turned for the door, his long ground-eating stride covering the distance between the kitchen and her bedroom in record time. Once in her room, he dumped her on her bed, then dived in after her. Hooking an arm over her waist, he rolled to his back and pulled her on top of him.

Smiling, he combed his fingers through her hair to hold it back from her face. "Now let's see what we can do about satisfying you."

"Don't you think we should get rid of some clothing first?"

He dragged his hands down her back and pushed them beneath the waistband of her shorts. "Eventually."

With the cheeks of her buttocks gripped firmly within his broad hands, he lifted his head and claimed her mouth. Stephanie surrendered with a delicious shiver, willing to follow wherever he led.

The path he chose for them was a wild one. At times treacherously steep, while at others lazy and meandering. At some point during their journey—she couldn't

remember when or how exactly—"eventually" occurred, and he peeled off their clothing, letting the
pieces fall where they may. While he explored her body,
she explored his, marveling at the muscles that swelled
and ebbed beneath her curious palms, the thunderous
beat of his heart against her lips, the soft pelt of light
blond hair that shot down his middle to the darker nest
between his legs.

Sure that no other man knew her as well as Wade,
nor could please her in so many fascinating and breath-
taking ways, she gave herself up to him, to them, to the
moment. She refused to think about the yesterdays in
their lives or the worries that tomorrow might bring. She
focused only on *now*.

And when he entered her, joining his body with hers,
she squeezed back the tears of joy that sprang to her
eyes at the sense of oneness that swept over her, the
sense of rightness in being here at this moment and in
this place with this man.

And when he'd given her the satisfaction he'd promised—and hopefully received an equal measure for himself—she curled naked against his side, laced her
fingers through his over his heart and slept.

Stephanie decided that sleeping with Wade was
almost as satisfying as making love with him. Cradled
like two spoons, her back to his front, her buttocks
nudged into the bowl shaped by his groin and thighs was
truly a heavenly experience. Adding to the pleasure was
having his knee wedged between hers and his arm
draped over her waist, keeping her snugged close. It
wasn't a position that either of them had choreographed

or maneuvered into after a lot of fidgeting and adjusting. It had just…happened. Naturally.

And that made her smile.

She knew couples who struggled for years to find the perfect sleeping arrangement. Others who were still struggling. Yet she and Wade had slid naturally into this position and had slept comfortably and soundly throughout the night.

And he was still sleeping.

Careful not to wake him, she turned beneath his arm, wanting to see him…and smothered a low moan of adoration when she saw his face. Handsome awake, he was absolutely adorable when sleeping, looking more like a tousle-headed toddler than a man in his late thirties. His sandy-brown hair shot from his scalp in wild clumps and flipped endearingly just above his ears. Relaxed in sleep, his lips were slightly parted, the lower one a little puffier than the upper and all but begging for a kiss. A day's worth of stubble shadowed his jaw, chin and upper lip. Lighter than most men's, the blond stubble held the faintest hint of red.

Unable to resist, she touched her lips to his.

He flinched, blinked open his eyes, then smiled and drew her hips to his. "Mornin'."

His voice was rough with sleep, and the huskiness in it sent a shiver sliding down her spine.

"Good morning to you, too. Did you sleep well?"

He nuzzled his cheek to hers. "Like a rock. You?"

Finding the graze of his stubble on her skin unexpectedly erotic, she sighed and snuggled closer. "Never better."

Lulled by the soft stroking of his hand over her buttocks, she closed her eyes, content in the silence that settled over them.

"You never married."

She flipped open her eyes, startled by the unexpected statement. "No, I didn't," she replied, hoping he'd let the topic drop.

"Why?"

Because I never met a man who could make me forget you. That was the answer that came immediately to mind. Probably because it was the truth. But she was hesitant to admit that to him. Why, she wasn't sure, but she suspected it had a lot to do with her pride, which had suffered a mortal blow when he had broken their engagement and married someone else.

She shrugged, hoping by her nonchalance he would assume that she hadn't given the subject much thought. "I guess I just never met anyone I wanted to spend the rest of my life with."

She waited, holding her breath and praying that he wouldn't probe deeper. When he remained silent, his hand still rhythmically stroking her hip, she quietly released the breath and let her eyes close again.

"Do you think you'd want to spend the rest of your life with me?"

Her breath caught in her throat, burned there. Gulping, she slowly lifted her head to look at him. "Was that a rhetorical question or a proposal?"

Gripping her hips more firmly, he shifted her over to lie on top of him. "Since I'm not sure what *rhetorical* means, I'd have to say it was a proposal."

She searched his face, sure that he was teasing her. But

she didn't find even the slightest hint of amusement in his eyes or in his expression. His face was smooth, his eyes a clear crystal blue. If anything, he looked…expectant.

She wasn't ready for this, she thought, feeling the slow burn of panic as it began to crawl through her system. Not yet. Maybe never. She'd agreed to be his friend. They'd become lovers…but husband and wife? *Married?* She gulped as thoughts of all that marrying him would entail flashed through her mind. Giving up her home and business in Dallas. Moving into the house he'd once shared with another woman. Becoming a stepmother.

Dear God, she thought, feeling the revulsion churn in her stomach, making her feel sick. His daughter. The child, whose conception had caused a ripple effect the size of a tidal wave, ripping Wade from her arms and shattering her emotions, her very life. How could she live with that reminder on a daily basis? How could she look that child in the face every day and not be reminded of all that her birth had caused? The anger. The heart-break. The years lost that she might've shared with Wade. The loneliness. The regret.

"Steph?"

She gulped and made herself focus on his face. Seeing the concern there, she gulped again and eased back to kneel beside him. "I don't know, Wade," she said, trying to keep the tremble from her voice. "This is so unexpected." She pressed a hand to her heart, and gulped again, knowing that *unexpected* didn't even come close to describing her reaction to his proposal. "Everything is still so…new between us. We've only just begun to get to know each other again."

He braced himself up on one elbow and caught her hand. "Nothing's new, Steph. If anything, the feelings I have for you are stronger than they were before. I love you. Always have. And you love me, too. Or at least I think you do."

She dropped her gaze, unable to deny that she did still love him. But *marry* him? Oh, God, she wanted to. More than anything else in the world. But in marrying him, she had to be willing to accept all that he brought to their relationship, including his daughter.

Deciding that she had to be honest with him, she drew in a steadying breath and lifted her head to meet his gaze. "Wade, I do love you," she said and had to stop to swallow back the tears that rose to her throat. "But there's so much more to consider than our feelings for each other."

He wrinkled his brow in confusion. "What could be more important than what we feel for each other?" He squeezed her hand. "I love you, Steph. Everything else is secondary to that."

"Even your daughter?"

He stared, his hand going lax in hers. "Steph, please," he begged. "Don't do this."

She gripped his hand hard, knowing she'd hurt him by mentioning his daughter but desperate to make him understand, to see her side. "It's not that I don't like your daughter, Wade. How could I, when I don't even know her? But she was what tore us apart. Surely you realize how difficult it would be for me to see her, live with her, and not think of that every time I looked at her."

Pulling his hands from hers, he dragged himself to

a sitting position and braced his arms over his knees. "She's just a kid. An innocent kid. You can't blame her for what happened."

"I don't…not intentionally. But she would be a constant reminder." She crawled to lay a hand over his arm, hoping that in touching him she could ease the pain her confession was causing him. "I don't want to hurt you, Wade. I would never do anything to purposely hurt you. But I can't lie to you either. Your daughter presents a problem for me, and I can't promise you that I can accept her or even feel comfortable living in the same house with her."

"But you don't even know her," he said in frustration. "If you met her, spent some time with her, you might find you like her a lot."

"That's just it. I don't want to meet her. Not yet," she added quickly. She took his hands and grasped them between her own. "We've only just begun to heal old wounds and make a new start. Maybe in time…"

He searched her face. "So that's not a definite no? I mean, about marrying me."

"It's a maybe. A really strong I-want-this-to-work-out-too kind of maybe."

He opened his knees and dragged her up his chest. "I can live with one of those kind of maybes." Smiling, he swept her hair back from her face. "You're gonna like her," he said confidently. "Once you two meet, I just know that you're going to get along great."

Six

Scowling, Wade shoved the plate of pancakes in front of Meghan. "I said no, and begging isn't going to make me change my mind."

"But, Daddy!" she cried and jumped up from the table to follow him to the sink. "It's going to be the coolest party ever. Richie's parents have hired a DJ and everything!"

He shoved his hands into the dishwater. "Richie is fifteen years old," he reminded her.

"So? I'm going to be thirteen my next birthday."

"Which is still six months away." Frustrated, he dropped the pan he was scrubbing and turned to face her. "You're too young to be running around with guys Richie's age and you're definitely too young to date. Now the answer is no, and don't ask me again."

She pushed her hands into fists at her sides. "I hate

you and I wish you weren't my daddy!" Whirling, she ran from the room, sobbing uncontrollably.

Wade braced his hands against the edge of the sink and drew in a long breath. She didn't mean it, he told himself as he slowly released the breath. She was just mad. Blowing off steam. Kids said things like that all the time to their parents when they didn't get their way.

Setting his jaw, he picked up the pan again and began to scrub. She'd get over it. It wasn't as if it was the end of the world. There'd be other parties for her to go to. Other boys for her to date.

He glanced over his shoulder to the hallway beyond the kitchen and the empty staircase that stretched to the second floor.

But damn if being a parent wasn't hell.

Stephanie tossed the tattered book on veterinary medicine into the box marked Trash.

"Hey!" Frowning, Wade shifted to dig it out. "You can't throw that away."

"Why not? I have no use for it, and the library won't accept books in that bad a condition."

He smoothed a hand over the worn cover. "But this was like Bud's bible. Passed down to him from his father. He referred to it whenever any of his livestock fell sick."

She waved an impatient hand. "Then you take it. You have more use for it than I ever will." Rising to her knees, she pulled another stack of books from the shelves, then sat down to sort them.

His forehead creased in a frown, Wade watched her, wondering how she could be so indifferent about something that had belonged to her father, a book that Bud had cherished as much as another man might have gold. Giving his head a shake, he turned away and placed the book near the door so that he wouldn't forget to take it with him when he left.

"Bud had the weirdest reading taste," he heard Steph say and glanced her way.

Propped up on her knees, her elbows on the floor and her chin on her fists, she read the titles imprinted on the spines of the books stacked in front of her. "*Moby Dick, How to Win Friends and Influence People, Mommie Dearest*. And a couple of dime-store Westerns." She shook her head. "Weird."

"Well-rounded," he argued.

"Weird," she repeated, then picked up the books and dumped them in the Donate box. Dusting off her hands, she turned for the closet. "I guess I've put off dealing with his clothes long enough."

She opened the door and scooped up an armload of clothing and lifted, making sure the hooks had cleared the rod before turning and heaving the stack onto the bed. She picked up a coat, gave it a cursory once-over, then tossed it in the trash.

Wade dug it right back out.

She huffed a breath. "Wade, I threw that away."

"And I took it out," he informed her.

"Why? It's covered with stains and the cuffs are all frayed."

"It was Bud's favorite."

"That doesn't make it any less a rag!"

He folded the coat neatly in half and laid it in the Donate box.

"Wade!" Stephanie cried. "What are you doing? Nobody's gonna want Bud's old coat."

"There's nothing wrong with that coat. Just because it's seen some miles doesn't mean it can't keep a body warm. Besides, I think Bud would be pleased to know that somebody got some use out of it."

"Whatever," she mumbled, then picked up a shirt and laughed. "Oh, my gosh. Do you remember this?" she asked and held it up for Wade to see. The shirt's front sported a bold red-and-white-stripe fabric, the back a blue with white stars embroidered in neat rows. "Bud wore it to every Fourth of July parade ever since I can remember."

Wade dropped the sack of trash he'd just picked up and fisted his hands on his hips. "And I suppose you're going to throw that away, too?"

She looked at him in puzzlement. "Why would I keep it?"

"Because it was *his?* Because it was something that Bud obviously liked?"

Seeing her stunned expression, he turned away, dragged a hand over his hair, then spun back, unable to suppress the frustration he'd carried since his battle with Meghan that morning. "Do you realize that you never say *my father* or *my dad* when you refer to Bud? You say *Bud.*"

She opened her hands. "So? That was his name."

"But you never used it before! You always called him Dad, never Bud."

"What difference does it make what I call him? You know who I'm talking about."

"It doesn't make any difference to me, but it would probably make a helluva lot to Bud! Can you imagine how hurt he would be if he could hear you right now? Calling him *Bud* and throwing away the things he cherished most. For God's sake, Steph! He was your father, not an acquaintance."

Seeing her hurt expression and knowing he'd gone too far, he stopped and hauled in a breath through his nose. "I'm sorry," he said, releasing it. "I didn't mean any of that."

"Obviously you did or you wouldn't have said it in the first place."

Frustrated, he dragged a hand over his hair again, then dropped it to his side. "It's just that you seem to have forgotten that Bud was your dad. He was the one who raised you, took care of you. But ever since you found those letters, all you can talk about is your *real* dad."

"I haven't forgotten Bud," she said defensively. "I loved him. I will *always* love him. But I owe a certain allegiance to my real father, too. And the only reason I refer to Dad as Bud is for clarification. I have *two* fathers," she reminded him. "My natural one and the one who adopted me. Just because I'm determined to get to know my natural father in no way detracts from my feelings for the one who raised me."

Realizing how much he'd upset her, Wade gathered her into his arms. "I'm sorry," he murmured with real regret. "I guess I'm just a little touchy about fathers in general because of what Meghan said to me this morning."

She drew back to frown up at him. "What did she say?"

He ducked his head, reluctant to repeat his daughter's angry words. "That she hated me."

"What?" Steph cried.

"She didn't mean it," he hurried to assure her. "She

was just mad because I wouldn't let her go to a party with a guy three years older than her."

"But, Wade—"

He silenced her with a kiss. "Forget it," he said and turned away. "They're just words. And you know the old saying about sticks and stones...."

Stephanie hummed along with the song playing on the radio as she sorted through the linens she'd pulled from the closet. Most she tossed into the Donate box, as there was very little sentiment to be attached to sheets and towels. But the tablecloths, especially those crocheted by her grandmother, she placed in a separate pile, planning to keep.

"A lost art," she murmured and paused to finger the decorative filet crochet border on a set of linen napkins, trying to remember who had made them. All of the women on her mother's side of the family had done some type of handiwork. Whether it was quilting, knitting, crocheting or embroidery, each had excelled at her chosen craft and had generously shared the fruits of her labors with other family members.

"Aunt Colleen," she decided and set the napkins in the Keeper stack.

A knock on the door had her lifting her head to peer toward the front of the house. Glancing at her wristwatch, she frowned as she hurried down the hall, wondering who it could be. It was too early for Wade's daily visit, plus he'd told her he'd probably be late because he was working his cattle this morning. Murmuring a fervent prayer that it wasn't Mrs. Snodgrass, the nosiest busybody at her mother's church, she opened the door.

She lifted a brow in surprise when she found Wade standing on the porch. She sputtered a laugh. "And since when have you ever knocked?" She opened the door wider. "You're lucky I even answered the door. I almost didn't because I was afraid it might be Mrs. Snodgrass."

When he made no move to enter, she looked at him curiously and noticed the tension in his face. "Is something wrong?" she asked in concern.

"You could say that," he replied tersely, then released a long breath. "I need a favor." He gestured behind him to where his truck was parked. "Meghan's in the truck, and I'd appreciate it if you would keep an eye on her for me."

"Meghan?" she repeated, her stomach knotting in dread. "But—shouldn't she be in school?"

He set his jaw. "*Should* being the operative word. She got expelled this morning." He gave her a pleading look. "I know it's asking a lot, considering, but it would only be for a couple of hours."

"Why can't she stay at home? Surely she's old enough to leave by herself."

"I don't trust her, okay?" he said, his frustration returning. "She's already threatened to run away. If I leave her at home, the minute I'm out of sight, I'm afraid she'll haul butt."

Stephanie glanced toward the truck and tried not to wring her hands. "I don't know, Wade," she said uneasily. "What if she pulls a stunt while she's here? I wouldn't know what to do."

"You can call me. I've got my cell." Before she could think of another excuse or alternative to offer, he turned for his truck.

"Wade!" she cried, reaching out a hand as if to stop him.

But it was too late. He already had the passenger door open and a young girl was climbing down. Petite and with long blond hair styled with the sides pulled up and gathered into a clip at the crown of her head, she didn't look like the kind of person who would get expelled from school. She looked more like one of the little girls that came to Stephanie's door selling Girl Scout cookies...or at least she did until Wade took her arm and started her toward the house, and Stephanie got a look at the belligerent expression on her face.

Stephanie gulped once, then gulped again. She'd thought she didn't want to meet Wade's daughter before. Now she was sure of it.

Stephanie led the way into the den. "Would you like something to drink?"

Meghan dropped down on the sofa in a slouch. "I'm not thirsty."

Racking her brain to think what to do with the child, Stephanie saw the remote for the TV and reached for it. "How about watching some television?"

"Whatever."

Irritated by the girl's surly attitude, Stephanie slapped the remote on the coffee table in front of her. "Well, here's the remote, if you decide to. I'll be in the back, packing. If you need anything, you can find me there."

Halfway down the hall, she heard the TV click on, followed by spurts of different sounds as Meghan surfed through the channels. "Delinquent," she muttered under her breath. No wonder the child had been expelled from school. With an attitude like hers, it was amazing she was allowed to attend at all.

As she passed her bedroom door, she heard the musical peal of her cell phone and ducked inside to retrieve it from the bedside table. Checking the display, she smiled when she recognized Kiki's number.

"Hey, Kiki," she said, bringing the phone to her ear. "How's motherhood?"

"Don't ask. When are you coming home? I don't know how much longer I can take all this togetherness before I start tearing out my hair."

Laughing, Stephanie sank down on the edge of her bed. "What have the twins done now?"

"What *haven't* they done," Kiki shot back, then heaved a weary sigh. "I don't want to talk about the twins. It's too depressing. Tell me what you're doing."

Stephanie cast an uneasy glance toward the door, then stood and tiptoed to her bathroom. "Babysitting a juvenile delinquent," she whispered as she closed the door behind her.

"What? Speak up. I can't hear you."

"Babysitting a juvenile delinquent," she whispered a little louder.

"Who?"

"Wade's daughter."

"What!"

Being as Kiki was one of only a handful of people in Dallas who knew about Stephanie's past relationship with Wade, Stephanie could understand her friend's shock. "I know. Crazy, isn't it?"

"Does this mean you and Wade are…?"

She sagged down onto the commode seat. "I don't know what we are," she said miserably. "We've established a truce of sorts, but—" She glanced at the door, then turned her head toward the tub, fearing Meghan might be able to hear her, and said in a low voice, "His daughter's a problem."

"Because she's a juvenile delinquent?"

She frowned, a visual of Meghan's belligerent expression popping into her mind. "That, too," she muttered, then sighed. "But can you imagine what it would be like to have to look at her every day and know, if not for her, Wade and I would be married right now?"

"Did you tell Wade that?"

"Yes."

"Please, God," Kiki begged, "tell me you didn't."

Stephanie frowned at the dread in Kiki's voice. "Of course I did. There was no point in lying."

"Oh, no," Kiki moaned, then cried, "Steph, what were you thinking? That's his daughter, for cripes' sake! You can't tell a parent something like that. It's the same as telling him his child is ugly!"

"It is not," Stephanie replied defensively. "Besides, Wade knows she's not perfect. Heck, she was expelled from school! That's why he brought her over here in the first place."

"It doesn't matter," Kiki argued. "A parent can think or say anything they want to about his kid, but let someone else make a derogatory comment, and that same parent will fight to the death to defend the kid."

Stephanie caught her lip between her teeth. She knew that she'd hurt Wade's feelings with her refusal to meet his daughter, but what other choice had she had? He'd asked her to marry him. There was no way she could have refused his proposal without telling him why.

"He understood," she said, trying to convince herself it was true.

"Uh-huh," Kiki said doubtfully. "I'll just bet he did."

"He did," she insisted, then pushed to her feet and crossed to the window to look out. "I told him that maybe in time I would feel differently. There's still so much that he and I have to work through. Everything is so new, so—" Her eyes flipped wide and she whipped the drape back for a better view. "Oh, my God!" she cried, then whirled for the door. "Kiki, I've got to go."

"Why? What's wrong?"

"Meghan's running away!"

Before Kiki could ask any more questions, Stephanie tossed the phone onto the bed and ran out of her room, down the hall.

Once outside, she broke into a full run. "Meghan!" she shouted, racing after the girl. "Where do you think you're going?"

Meghan glanced back over her shoulder, her eyes wide in alarm, then took off at a run. Stephanie raced after her. "Meghan, stop!" she yelled.

Meghan stumbled, fell, then scrambled to her feet and ran again. Her fall, coupled with the awkward backpack she was carrying, gave Stephanie the edge she needed to close the distance between them.

With her lungs burning, her arms pumping like pistons, she knew she had only one chance to stop the girl. She dived, tackling Meghan around the legs and bringing her down.

Meghan twisted beneath her, trying to fight free. "Let me go!"

Gasping, Stephanie rocked back on her heels but

kept a firm grip on Meghan's arm. "Uh-uh. You're staying right here with me."

"You can't tell me what to do," Meghan yelled angrily. "You're not my mother."

"Thank heaven for that," Stephanie muttered under her breath, then gave Meghan's arm a yank and all but dragged her back to the house.

By the time they reached the porch, Meghan was sobbing. Setting her jaw against the heartbreaking sound, Stephanie marched her into the house and to the den. She released Meghan's arm and pointed a stiff finger at the sofa. "Sit."

Sniffling, Meghan flopped down on the sofa.

Stephanie yanked tissues from the box on the coffee table and pushed them into the girl's hand. "I don't know where you thought you were going, but I'm telling you right now that you better not pull that stunt again. Understand?"

Her chin on her chest, Meghan sniffed, nodded, then lifted her head. "Are you going to tell my dad?" she asked hesitantly.

It was Stephanie's first real good look at the child. Though dirt and tears smeared her face, she could see that she was pretty. White-blond hair hung past her shoulders and framed an oval face. Her eyes, the color of roasted chestnuts, were large, and her tear-spiked lashes were thick and long. In spite of her desire not to, Stephanie found herself searching for a resemblance to Wade but found nothing in the child's features that even remotely reminded her of Wade.

"Are you?" Meghan prodded.

Stephanie firmed her lips, refusing to be suckered by

the girl's puppy-dog look. "Your father entrusted you to my care. Your running away makes me look irresponsible, incompetent, and I don't think that's fair, do you?"

Meghan hung her head. "No, ma'am," she murmured.

Stephanie didn't know if the child's contriteness was an act to draw pity or if she really did feel badly for what she'd done. Whatever her reasons, Stephanie wasn't about to take a chance on her running away again.

"As punishment for disobeying your father's instructions, you're going to help me."

"What do I have to do?"

"Pack." Stephanie motioned for Meghan to follow her. "I've been going through the linen closet," she said tersely as she led the way down the hall. "I've already—" Realizing that Meghan wasn't following, she turned to look behind her and saw that Meghan had stopped in front of her parents' bedroom. "Meghan?" she said in frustration. "What are you doing?"

The girl turned to look at her, and Stephanie was shocked to see that her eyes were filled with tears again.

"What's wrong?" she asked in concern.

Meghan dragged a hand beneath her eyes. "It's just that I haven't been here since Mr. Calloway died and I guess I forgot for a minute, 'cause I expected to see him lying in his bed."

Stephanie gulped, knowing that this was no act. No one could fake the depth of sadness she saw reflected in the child's eyes. "Yeah, I know," she said as she walked to stand with her. "Sometimes I catch myself listening for him, especially around dinnertime."

Sliding an arm around the girl, she urged her away from the door and down the hall. "Did you visit him very often?" she asked, hoping to distract the girl from the image that must surely be stuck in her mind of Bud lying sick in bed.

Meghan lifted a shoulder. "Not too much after he got sick." She pursed her lips. "Daddy was afraid I'd wear him out with my talking."

Chuckling, Stephanie removed a stack of linens from the floor, then sat down on the floor, her back to the wall, and patted the space next to her. "Have a seat," she invited.

Meghan sank down with a youthful ease that Stephanie couldn't help envying.

"So you're a talker, huh?" Stephanie said as she began to sort through the stack of pillowcases.

Meghan stretched her legs out in front of her and tapped the tip of her tennis shoes together. "Daddy seems to think so."

"I guess you knew my mother, too," Stephanie said, curious to discover how well Wade's daughter knew her parents.

"Yeah. When I was little, sometimes she would keep me when I was too sick to go to school and Daddy had something he needed to do." She plucked absently at a thread on her jeans. "When I had chicken pox, I was itching real bad, and she made me an oatmeal bath to soak in. She was always doing nice things like that."

Stephanie had to swallow back emotion before she could reply, ashamed of the resentment she'd felt toward her mother. "Yes, she had a kind heart." Forcing a smile, she picked up one of the stacks of pillowcases she had sorted and passed it to Meghan. "These go in that box over there," she said, pointing. "The one marked Donate."

Hopping up, Meghan moved to place the linens in the box, then returned to sit at Stephanie's side again.

Feeling the child's stare, Stephanie glanced over at her. "What?"

"I was just wondering how come I've never seen you before."

Stephanie quickly looked away. "Well," she said, stalling while she tried to think of a plausible explanation to offer. "I live in Dallas and own a business there. It keeps me pretty busy."

"What kind of business?"

"I'm a photo stylist."

Meghan wrinkled her brow. "What's that?"

Stephanie set the linens she held on her lap, wondering how best to describe her job to a young girl. "You know the advertisements you see in magazines? The ones that have photographs?"

"Yeah."

"I set the scenes for the pictures. I gather all the props, set everything up, then the photographer—and the models, if any are needed—come in and the photographer takes the pictures."

Meghan stared, her eyes wide in wonder. "How cool is that!"

Stephanie chuckled. "It is a cool job. But it can also be a royal pain in the patootee."

"Patootee?" Meghan repeated, then fell over on the floor, laughing. "That's the lamest word I've ever heard."

Stephanie lifted a brow. "Beats getting my mouth washed out with soap for using the more popular expression."

Her eyes rounding, Meghan pushed up to her elbows.

"You mean, Mrs. Calloway washed your mouth out with soap?"

"She certainly did," Stephanie said with a decisive nod. "But it only took twice before I learned not to say words that she didn't approve of."

"Wow."

Amused by the girl's shocked look, Stephanie shook her head and reached for another stack of linens. "So what's your punishment for saying bad words?"

Meghan blinked, then shrugged. "There's not one."

Stephanie gave her a sideways glance. "Oh, please. Surely your father doesn't allow you to say curse words."

"He doesn't exactly *allow* me to curse, but if I slip and say something I shouldn't in front of him, he just gives me a mean look and says, 'You better watch your mouth, young lady.'"

Her impersonation of Wade was so funny Stephanie couldn't help but laugh. "Maybe I should give him some pointers I picked up from my mother."

Meghan grimaced. "Yeah, like he could be any meaner. He rags on me all the time about the way I dress and the music I listen to. And I don't *dare* have the channel turned to MTV when he's at home. If I do, he goes ballistic."

Stephanie drew back to peer at her, unsure whether she should believe her or not. "That doesn't sound like the Wade I know."

"You know my daddy?"

Realizing her mistake, Stephanie looked away and busied herself straightening linens. "He moved to the ranch next door while I was in college," she replied vaguely.

"Do you know my mom, too?"

It was all Stephanie could do to remain upright. "No, I've never met your mother. I was living in Dallas when your parents married."

"Oh," Meghan said, sounding disappointed.

Anxious to change the subject, Stephanie asked, "Are you thirsty?" She heaved herself up from the floor. "I know I am. Let's get a soda."

"Okay."

Stephanie led the way to the kitchen, with Meghan following close on her heels. Just as she stepped inside, the back door opened and Wade walked in.

"Well, hi," she said in surprise. "Meghan and I were about to have a soda. Would you like one?"

"Maybe next time." He tipped his head, indicating his daughter. "Did she give you any trouble?"

Stephanie glanced down and met Meghan's gaze. Seeing the girl's fear, she gave her a reassuring smile. "Nothing I couldn't handle."

Wade shifted his gaze between the two, his expression doubtful, then heaved a sigh and motioned for Meghan to join him. "Come on," he said, already turning for the door. "We need to go."

"Couldn't I stay here with Stephanie?" Meghan asked. "I was helping her pack."

"No, we've got—" He hesitated a moment, then said, "Company waiting."

Meghan's eyes lit with hope. "Mom's here?"

Wade pushed through the door and stepped outside without answering.

Meghan let out an excited squeal and ran after him. At the door she stopped and glanced back. "Thanks for not ratting me out."

Stephanie leveled a finger at her in warning. "Just don't make me regret it."

Meghan grinned. "I won't," she said, then charged out the door, shouting, "Hey, Dad! Wait for me!"

Stephanie tried not to think about Wade's ex being at his house.

But it was hopeless. Every time she pushed the thought from her mind, it dug a new hole and came crawling back in. Deciding that a nice hot bath was what she needed to get Wade's ex off her mind, she headed for her bathroom and turned on the tap. She was stripping off her clothes when her cell phone rang. Grabbing a towel to drape around her, she hurried into the bedroom to answer it.

"Hello," she said breathlessly.

"Were you just going to leave me hanging?"

She winced at the annoyance in Kiki's voice. "Sorry. I've been sort of busy."

"So did the runaway make good her escape?"

Remembering she'd left the water running in the bathroom, Stephanie retraced her steps. "No. I caught her. But I had to tackle her from behind and drag her to the ground to stop her."

"You've got to be kidding!" Kiki cried, then hooted a laugh. "Oh, to have been a fly on the wall and seen that."

Rather proud of her accomplishment, Stephanie buffed her nails against her chest. "It was a clever save, even if I do say so myself."

"Congratulations. Now tell me the good stuff. Why did Wade bring her to you, of all people? Does she know about you and Wade? Did she say anything about her mother? I want the dirt, so start shoveling."

Shaking her head at her friend's outrageousness, Stephanie squirted bath oil beneath the tap. "Has anyone ever told you that you're nosy?"

"Daily. Now spill."

Stephanie tested the water, then dropped the towel and climbed in. "I don't know why Wade brought her here, but I'd guess it was because he had nowhere else to take her. He was in the middle of vaccinating his cattle and couldn't keep an eye on her himself."

"Why didn't he just leave her at home? Good grief. Surely the kid's old enough to stay by herself."

"She is," Stephanie agreed. "But he doesn't trust her. He said she'd threatened to run away."

"Wow. I thought you were exaggerating when you said you were babysitting a juvenile delinquent. Obviously you were being serious."

Growing thoughtful, Stephanie lifted a toe to pop a bubble. "I may be wrong—God knows I don't have any experience with children—but I don't think she's really a bad kid. She certainly doesn't look the part. She has really long white-blond hair and the biggest eyes. She looks…well, almost angelic."

Remembering the belligerent expression on her face when Wade had first dropped her off, she added, "But she has the potential to turn bad. I got a peek of a darker side when Wade first dropped her off. Angry. Hostile. Rebellious. If he doesn't get her in hand fairly soon, I would think she could easily turn into a huge problem for him."

"Bet you five he's suffering from the Guilty Parent Syndrome."

Stephanie choked out a laugh. "The *what?*"

"Guilty Parent Syndrome. You see it all the time in divorce cases. Wade's the one who asked for the divorce, right?"

"That was the talk around town."

"Right. So he's taking heat from the daughter because she blames him for making her mother leave. He feels sorry for the kid, so he goes easy on her, trying to make it up to her. If the kid's smart—and it sounds like she is—she picks up on his guilt and plays him like a piano, and the cycle continues until—bingo!—the kid is a holy terror and totally out of control."

Shaking her head, Stephanie slid farther down into the bubbles. "You need to quit working for me and hang out a shingle. You'd make an excellent psychologist."

"Comes from all the years I spent in therapy."

Stephanie frowned. "Your mother should have been the one in therapy, not you."

"Try telling her that."

Stephanie shuddered at the thought of having any conversation with Kiki's neurotic mother. "Thanks, but I think I'll pass."

"What about the kid's mother? Wade's ex? Did the kid say anything about her?"

"Nothing specific, though she did ask if I knew her."

Kiki whistled softly. "Man, this just gets crazier and crazier. Like a soap opera."

"Tell me about it," Stephanie muttered drily. "The ex is at his house right now."

"Why? Is it her weekend to have the kid or something?"

"How would I know?" Stephanie snapped. "I just know she's there."

"Do I detect a hint of jealousy?"

"Why would I be jealous? They're divorced."

"Which doesn't mean squat. He might be through with her, but that doesn't mean she's through with him."

Since that was the exact thought that Stephanie had hoped to escape by taking a bubble bath, she remained silent, refusing to discuss it.

"Steph?"

"Yes?" she said tersely.

"Just wanted to make sure you were still there."

"I am."

"And obviously don't want to talk about his ex," Kiki deducted, then sighed her disappointment. "Okay, so tell me what you think about the kid after spending the morning with her."

"She's your average twelve-year-old," Stephanie replied, then amended, "except for the ugly rebellious streak."

"So you liked her?"

Stephanie considered the question for a moment and was surprised to find that she did like Meghan. "She's okay," she replied vaguely. "And obviously crazy about her mother."

"Which would make you the ugly stepmother if you and Wade should work things out."

Stephanie scowled, not having to stretch very far to imagine the kind of problems that could create for her and Wade. "Thanks, Kiki. I really appreciate you bringing that to my attention."

"Sorry," Kiki mumbled, then brightened. "But look

at it this way. The kid won't be around forever. She's twelve, so she should be leaving the nest in another five or six years. Then you and Wade would be alone."

If their relationship lasted that long, Stephanie thought sadly. Sharing a house with another woman's child and a bed with that child's father had the potential to destroy even the strongest of relationships.

Giving herself a shake, she said to Kiki, "There's no sense in worrying about that. Wade and I aren't married. We're just…friends."

"Steph?"

Stephanie jumped at the sound of Wade's voice, almost dropping the phone in the water. "In here," she called, then brought the phone back to her ear and whispered frantically to Kiki, "I've got to go. Wade's here."

"Friends, huh?" Kiki snorted a laugh. "I'd say you're more than friends, since you just invited him into the bathroom while you're in the tub."

"Goodbye, Kiki," Stephanie said firmly, then disconnected the phone.

Just as Stephanie leaned to lay the phone on the commode seat, Wade stepped into the bathroom. He stood there a moment, staring, then started toward the tub, unbuttoning his shirt.

Stephanie sputtered a nervous laugh. "What are you doing?"

His gaze on hers, he flipped back his belt buckle and pulled down the zipper on his jeans. "What does it look like I'm doing?"

She watched as he hooked the toe of one boot behind the heel of the other and pried it off, then lifted her gaze to his. "Stripping?" she asked meekly.

He pushed his jeans down his hips, kicked them aside. "No." He gave her a nudge and slipped into the tub behind her. "I'm bathing."

"But where's Meghan?"

He slid his arms around her waist and pressed his lips to the curve of her neck. "At home."

Since he'd claimed he didn't trust Meghan to stay alone, she had to assume her mother was there with her. Although she didn't find that thought at all comforting, Wade was with her, which had to say something about his preferences. She angled her head, giving him better access to her neck. "How long can you stay?"

He dragged his lips down to her shoulder. Nipped. "As long as it takes."

She closed her eyes, stifling a groan. "As long as what takes?" she asked breathlessly.

He turned her around to face him and sent water splashing over the edge. His blue eyes, dark with passion, burned through hers as he drew her legs around his waist. "To satisfy this hunger I have for you."

Water lapped against her body, adding to the sensations created by his erection nudging her belly. Looping her arms around his neck, she smiled as she lowered her face to his. "That might take a while."

"Yeah." He released a sigh against her lips. "That's what I'm hoping."

Later, snuggled against Wade in her bed, Stephanie found herself thinking about something Meghan had said to her that morning. "Wade?" she said hesitantly.

More asleep than awake, he hummed a lazy response.

"Meghan said something this morning that concerns me."

He groaned and buried his face between her breasts. "Please tell me she wasn't rude."

Biting back a smile at the dread she heard in his voice, she ran her fingers through his hair to reassure him. "No, though I have to admit, when you first dropped her off, she was sporting a pretty tough attitude."

Sighing, he drew his head back and placed it on the pillow opposite hers. "She's *always* sporting an attitude. That's nothing new."

"This has nothing to do with her attitude. It's something she said."

"What?"

"We were talking about cursing, and I told her that when I said a curse word, my mother would wash my mouth out with soap."

He smiled softly, as if at a fond memory. "My mom did that, too."

"Meghan said that when she says a bad word, you don't punish her."

"I damn sure do," he said defensively, then waved away Stephanie's concern. "She was pulling your leg, blowing hot air."

"I don't think so." Stephanie knew she was taking a chance on alienating Wade by discussing his daughter with him, but Meghan's comment concerned her enough that she felt she should speak her mind. "She said you only give her a mean look and tell her to watch her mouth."

His brows drew together. "So? That's the same as telling her I don't approve of that kind of talk."

Stephanie laid a hand against his chest, hoping to take the sting out of what she was about to say. "Maybe you need to be a little more firm. Let her know that in the future there will be specific consequences for bad behavior."

"And you think washing her mouth out with soap is going to keep her from cussing?" He snorted a breath. "Sure as hell didn't break me."

She pursed her lips. "Obviously not. The point is, Meghan doesn't seem to think there are any consequences for her actions. A mean look from you isn't enough of a deterrent. You need to be firmer with her. Establish rules and set specific punishments to be implemented when she breaks them."

He lifted a brow. "Oh? And how many children have you raised?"

For a moment Stephanie could only stare, his careless remark cutting deeply. "I haven't," she said and rolled away, swinging her legs over the side of the bed. "I was only offering an opinion after spending some time with your daughter."

He caught her arm, stopping her before she could stand. "Hey," he said softly. "I didn't mean that the way it sounded."

When she kept her face averted, refusing to look at him, he tugged her down to lie beside him again. "I'm sorry, Steph." He laid a hand on her cheek. "You're probably right. Maybe I am too easy on Meghan. But sometimes I just flat don't know what to do with her. You have no idea what kind of crap kids are getting into these days. Body piercings and tattoos, not to mention sex and drugs. She's twelve going on twenty-two. I try to keep a tight rein on her, hoping to keep her out of trouble. But she kicks and screams about how strict I am and threatens to run away and live with her mother. I'm afraid if I come down on her too hard, she will."

"Maybe she should live with her mother."

By the look on Wade's face, Stephanie knew she'd said the wrong thing.

"Wade," she said and reached for him, wanting to explain.

He shoved her hand aside and rolled from the bed and to his feet to face her. "You think her mother would do a better job of raising her?" he asked angrily. Without waiting for an answer, he strode to the bathroom, scooped up his clothes and returned, jerking on his jeans. "Well, let me tell you something Dr. Know-It-All," he said, pointing a stiff finger at her face. "On my worst day I'm a better parent than Angela will ever be. I fought for custody of Meghan for that very reason and won. Angela's nothing but a—" He clamped his lips together and spun for the door, pulling on his shirt.

Stephanie bolted from the bed and grabbed a robe, shrugging it on as she ran after him.

"Wade, wait!"

He didn't even slow down.

She caught up with him at the front door and grabbed his arm. When he tried to jerk free, she tightened her grip. "No," she said, her anger rising to match his. "You're not leaving until I have a chance to explain. I wasn't suggesting that you are a bad parent. Meghan's a *girl*, Wade, and a young girl needs her mother. If she were a boy, maybe it would be different. But she's not a boy. She's a *girl* and she's at an age where she needs to talk about things that she may not feel comfortable talking about with you. That's why I said what I did. I was simply suggesting that maybe she needs a mother right now more than she does a father. I wasn't suggesting that her mother is a better parent than you. How could I? I don't even know the woman."

He grabbed her arms, making her blink in surprise. "No, you don't know her. If you did, you'd understand why I've fought so hard to keep Meghan away from her. Why I insist that a court-appointed guardian be present at all times when she visits Meghan. Angela is a drug addict, a whore who'll sell herself to any man who'll give her another fix."

He dropped his hands from her arms and took a step back, suddenly looking tired, beaten. "Do you know how I know that, Steph?" he asked quietly. "I know because I was once one of those men."

Seven

Stephanie walked around in a daze the next morning, still numbed by Wade's confession. She couldn't believe he'd ever been the kind of man he'd described. Sure, when they'd first started dating, he'd told her a little about his life prior to his move to the ranch next to her parents. How he'd gone a little crazy after his parents' deaths and done some things he wasn't proud of. But Wade involved in drugs? Associating with a woman like the one he described Angela to be? She couldn't believe it. He was so straight, so *good*.

Frustrated by her inability to come to grips with the man he'd described to her, she moved to the front window and looked out. What difference does it make if he had done those things? she asked herself. He wasn't the same person he was back then. That was all in the past. He'd changed, made a fresh start. He was a good person, kind. Hadn't he looked out for Bud after her mother had died? Hadn't he comforted Stephanie when he'd found her crying over her father's letters? Hadn't he fought for custody of his daughter, wanting to protect her from the environment in which her mother lived? A man who did those things wasn't a bad person. He was good and kind.

She should've told him that, she realized with a suddenness that clutched at her chest. She shouldn't have let him walk out of her house without telling him that his past didn't matter. That he was a wonderful man, kind and generous, and that she loved him with all her heart.

She glanced at her watch and was surprised to see that it was past noon, the time that Wade usually dropped off a bundle of letters for her to read. Praying that nothing had happened at home that would have prevented him from leaving, she hurried to the front door, wanting to make sure he hadn't gone on to the barn and pastures without stopping first.

Two steps onto the porch her left foot connected with something hard, making her stumble. Catching herself from falling, she glanced down to see what she'd tripped over and found a box sitting on the porch. Her heart seemed to stop for a moment when she recognized it as the one Wade had used the night he'd carried away the bundles of her father's letters.

She stooped to pick it up, wondering why he'd left it for her to find rather than bringing it inside. And why would he drop off the entire box instead of the usual single bundle?

She gulped, afraid she already knew the answer. She'd let him leave the night before without telling him that his past didn't matter to her, without assuring him of her love. She'd even suggested he allow his daughter to live with his ex, told him that she couldn't consider marrying him because she couldn't bear the thought of living with the child who would serve as a daily reminder of the choice Wade had made and all the hurt she'd suffered at his hand.

She'd let him down. When he'd needed her most, she had denied him her love, her understanding, and instead chose to batter him with the resentment she had hoarded through the years, the bitterness she had clung to.

Her heart heavy, her eyes filled with tears of regret, she gathered the box close and went back inside.

Janine,

I don't know how I survived the year I spent in Vietnam before I met you. Your letters are what keep me going, what help me deal with the tragedy and death I see every day.

I've just about worn out the pictures of you I brought with me. I can't tell you the number of times a day I pull them out just to look at them, to remind myself that there is a world beyond the hell I'm living in right now, one where there is normalcy, laughter and love.

Sometimes it's hard to remember what it's like back home. To sleep without being afraid someone is going to slip up on you in the night and slit your throat. To walk without fear of stepping on a mine or a booby trap. To be able to eat food other than C-rations. To wear clothes that aren't all but rotting off my body.

I don't understand this war. Why people would want to kill each other. Surely there's a better way to resolve differences, to make peace between nations and keep it. The loss of lives—on both sides—is unimaginable, and that's without considering the lives of the people that are destroyed or changed forever by the loss of their loved ones.

A couple of guys I knew back home went to Canada to avoid the draft. At the time I remember thinking they were cowards for choosing to leave their country rather than fight for it. Now I'm not so sure. I still don't believe I ever would've run, even knowing what I know now. But I don't feel the same about the guys who did choose to run. I don't consider them cowards anymore. Doing what they did took courage. Granted, it was a different kind of courage than the one required to stand and fight. But it took guts to do what they did. Leaving your home and family behind and knowing that you may never see them again... well, that takes a certain kind of courage, too. In some ways, it's the same sacrifice or chance a soldier makes when he puts on a uniform and goes to war.

Unable to read any more, Stephanie let the letter drop to her lap and stared out the window at the darkness beyond the house. Her father had only been twenty-one when he'd written the letter, yet there was a wisdom in his words, a wealth of experience which exceeded that of most men his age. Women, too, she thought. At twenty-one she'd been in her third year of college and living in an apartment in Dallas, near the campus of Southern Methodist University, and without a care in the world. Her education was paid for by her parents, who covered her living expenses, as well, which allowed her to focus on her studies without worrying about supporting herself. The only fear she had faced was making good grades in the courses she was enrolled in, and the only tragedy she'd suffered was when Wade had broken their engagement.

The latter had been devastating and it had taken weeks, months even, for her to drag herself from the depression that losing him had plunged her into. But she hadn't resurfaced fully healed or unscathed from the occurrence. From the darkness she'd brought with her her resentment toward Wade, and used it like a talisman to keep herself from ever being hurt again.

The broken engagement had changed her life in so many ways…most not very flattering. She'd remained in Dallas but had withdrawn from her classes, which had put her a semester behind in graduating. For months she'd refused to come home, unable to bear the thought of possibly bumping into Wade and his new wife. She'd let that fear control her actions for years, making only brief visits home to see her parents and, while there, refusing to step so much as a foot outside their house.

And she'd allowed the breakup to affect more than just her family life. For more than a year she had refused to go out on any of the dates her friends set up for her. And when she had finally begun dating again, she'd kept a firm grip on her emotions, her feelings, determined to never let a man hurt her again.

But the most regrettable fallout from their breakup

was holding on to her anger with Wade and never forgiving him for hurting her. In the days immediately following their breakup she'd refused to see him or talk to him. It was easy enough to do. She'd simply monitored her phone calls and deleted the messages he'd left on her answering machine without listening to them, tore up the letters he'd sent without ever opening them.

She dropped her chin in shame as she realized the domino effect her stubbornness and bitterness had had on the people she loved most—as well as many whose lives she'd touched only briefly. By stubbornly refusing to visit her parents more often, she had foolishly robbed herself of precious time she could have spent with them. And by not granting Wade her forgiveness, she'd thought she could punish him, and all but reveled in the guilt she knew he carried.

She didn't deserve his love, she told herself miserably. He'd tried so many times to tell her he was sorry, begged her repeatedly for her forgiveness. Yet in spite of her spitefulness, when he'd found her crying over her father's letters, he'd comforted her. Offered her his ear, as well as his shoulder to cry on, when he'd insisted upon being with her when she read the letters that remained.

And what had she given him in return? she asked herself. Had she given him her forgiveness when he'd admitted making a mistake? Offered him her understanding when he'd shared with her his past? Her acceptance when he'd asked her to share his life with him and his daughter?

No, she thought, shaking her head sadly. She'd used his mistake like a battering ram to beat him with. Remained silent, horrified even, as he'd confessed to a past that still shamed him. And she'd refused his proposal to share his life with him, insisting that she needed time to come to grips with her resentment toward his daughter.

She'd promised she'd be his friend, told him that she loved him. But how could a woman who professed those things turn her back on a man when he most needed her understanding and her love?

She rose, the letter she'd been reading falling to the floor, forgotten. She had to talk to him, she told herself and hurried for the door. See him. Tell him that his past didn't matter. Grant him the full forgiveness that she'd selfishly withheld. And she would deal with her conflicting feelings for his daughter, she told herself as she climbed into her car. Perhaps even help him see that Meghan needed his discipline as much as she needed his love.

It didn't occur to Stephanie that Wade's ex-wife might still be at his house until she pulled to a stop and saw the strange car parked on the drive. For a moment she was tempted to turn around and return home. She didn't want to meet his ex, doubted she could look the woman in the face without wanting to claw her eyes out.

But she couldn't let another moment pass without sharing her heart with Wade. Stiffening her resolve, she climbed out.

In spite of the lateness of the hour, a light burned in the kitchen window. Hoping not to disturb the entire household, she walked around back. At the door she hesitated a moment, then squared her shoulders and knocked.

She jumped, startled, when the door was immediately snatched open and a woman appeared in the space.

Backlit by the overhead light in the kitchen, the woman's face was shadowed, but Stephanie had a feeling she was confronting Wade's ex-wife for the first time.

Gulping, she asked uneasily, "Is Wade here?"

"Who wants to know?"

Stephanie set her jaw at the woman's hostile tone. "Stephanie Calloway. I'm a neighbor."

The woman gave her a slow look up and down, then stepped back and shouted, "Wade! That snotty little bitch from next door is here to see you."

Stephanie stared, while shock and anger fought for dominance of her emotions. Managing to push both back, she jutted her chin and strode inside.

Wade's ex had moved to the sink and was standing with her hips braced against its edge, her lips pursed in a smirk. Bone-thin, she wore a shockingly short denim skirt and a low-cut tank top. Her breasts—obviously silicone-enhanced—were as large as grapefruits and looked totally out of proportion to her emaciated frame.

"Didn't your mother teach you any manners?" the woman snapped, making Stephanie jump. "It's rude to stare."

Her cheeks flaming, Stephanie tore her gaze away. "I'm sorry. I didn't mean to—"

"Steph?"

She spun to find Wade standing in the doorway that opened from the kitchen to the den. She sagged her shoulders, almost weak with relief at seeing him. "I'm sorry to barge in like this. I had no idea you had—"

The woman quickly shifted in front of Stephanie, blocking her view of Wade.

"Well, well, well," she said as she folded her arms

across her chest and gave Stephanie another slow look up and down. "Looks like I've screwed up your plans." She lifted a brow plucked pencil-thin and added pointedly, *"Again."*

"That's enough, Angela," Wade warned.

She kept her gaze on Stephanie and smiled. "Oh, I don't think so. In fact, I haven't even gotten started good yet. I've wanted to give this lady a piece of mind for years."

"Angela," he warned again and took a step toward her.

"What's wrong, sugar?" Though her eyes were fixed on Stephanie, her question was directed at Wade. "Afraid I'll say something you don't want Miss Goody Two-shoes to hear?"

Wade lunged and caught Angela's elbow, whirled her around. "I said enough, Angela," he said, then released her and pointed a stiff finger at the hall and the stairs beyond. "Now go upstairs before you make me do something we'll both regret."

She shoved her face within inches of his. "You can't tell me what to do. Not anymore. I followed your orders for six long years, while you tried to shape me into what you considered the perfect wife. Well, guess what, Wade?" She opened her arms wide. "I'm not perfect and I never was. Not even while I was pretending to be the Stepford wife you wanted me to be. While you were off working, I'd drop Meghan off at day care and drive to Austin and have me a good ol' time. Those college boys really know how to party. All the booze and drugs I wanted, and all they expected from me in return was a piece of my ass."

He grabbed for her again, but she ducked to the side,

managing to dodge him. "I like drugs and the way they make me feel," she said, then smiled and dragged a fingernail down between her breasts. "And I like sleeping with a different man every night, especially one who isn't grieving over some old flame."

"I'm warning you, Angela," Wade said, his face red with rage, "either you shut up or I'll fix it so you'll never see our daughter again."

"*Our* daughter?" she repeated, then dropped her head back and laughed, the sound so evil it sent a shiver chasing down Stephanie's spine.

"Meghan isn't *your* daughter," she said. "I just told you that so you'd have to marry me. You thought you could just up and leave me in Houston, taking all your money with you." She snorted a laugh. "Well, I showed you, didn't I? You and Miss Goody Two-shoes here had your future all planned out, but I messed things up for you good, didn't I, when I showed up in town pregnant out to here."

Wade grabbed her again, and this time Angela was too slow to dodge him. He all but dragged her from the room and to the stairs, with her kicking and cursing him every step of the way.

Stephanie stood as if her feet had rooted to the floor, sickened by the ugly scene she'd just witnessed, the infidelities Angela had confessed to. She remained there, a hand pressed to her stomach, forcing herself to take slow, deep breaths until the nausea slowly faded and only one statement remained to circle in her mind.

Meghan isn't your daughter.

She closed her eyes, hearing again the vindictiveness in Angela's voice, envisioning the hate it had carved into her features as she'd hurled the confession like a knife to pierce Wade's heart.

Wade, she thought, and her gaze went instinctively to the stairs, wondering if it was true that he wasn't Meghan's father. Angela might only have said that to hurt him. To punish him for the injustices she felt she'd suffered at his hand.

As she continued to stare at the spot where she'd last seen him, Wade appeared on the stairway, his steps slow, his shoulders stooped as if he was burdened beneath the weight of the world. She started toward him, then stopped and wrung her hands at her waist, unsure what to say to him, what to do.

"Wade?" she said hesitantly.

He glanced her way, held her gaze a moment, then continued down the stairs.

She watched, her breath burning a hole in her chest as he reached the end and turned toward her.

"I'm sorry you had to listen to all that. You didn't deserve to hear any of what she said."

She shook her head, unable to push a word past the emotion that clotted her throat. Catching his hands, desperate for that contact, she gave them a reassuring squeeze. "It's not your fault. I should've called first. It never even occurred to me that she might still be here. I was so anxious to see you, talk to you, I didn't think about anything else. When you didn't come by at noon, I went outside and found the box of letters on the porch. When I saw it, I knew it meant you didn't want to see me, that you probably wouldn't be coming by anymore."

Tears filled her eyes, and she stubbornly blinked them back.

"But it wasn't until earlier this evening, after I'd read one of my dad's letters, that I realized it was all my fault. I let you leave last night without telling you how I feel. I should have told you then that your past doesn't matter to me, that I love you with all my heart and that I want to marry you."

Throughout her speech, he had listened quietly, his gaze steady on hers. And now that she was done, had said everything that was in her heart, and he still said nothing, she felt a moment's unease.

"Wade?" she asked hesitantly. "Is something wrong?"

"You didn't mention Meghan. When I asked you to marry me, you said you needed time, that you didn't think you could live in my house with her there as a constant reminder of the past."

"Yes, I did say that, but that's not a problem anymore."

"Why? Because Angela said that Meghan isn't mine?"

Numbed by the chill in his voice, the steely gleam in his eye, she shook her head. "Well, no. Of course not. I—"

Pulling his hands from hers, he took a step back. "What Angela said was true…to a point. Until the day Meghan was born, I did think she was mine. But when the nurse told me that Meghan weighed only four pounds and was considered a preemie, I knew that Angela had lied and was trying to stick me with another man's child.

"But here's a news flash for you, Steph," he continued. "It didn't matter. Not to me. Not then, and it sure as hell doesn't now. From the moment that doctor put Meghan in my arms she was mine. There was no way I was going to walk away from that baby and leave her with Angela to raise. I knew what kind of person Angela was, how she lived. And I knew that was the kind of life Meghan would have if I walked out on her. That's why when I divorced Angela I fought so hard for custody of Meghan."

Shaking his head, he took another step back, putting even more distance between him and Stephanie. "But it was more than Angela's lifestyle that made me want to keep Meghan with me. I love that girl as if she were my own. And because I love her, I would never marry a woman who didn't love her as much I do, who wasn't willing to put Meghan's happiness above her own. That's what parents do, Steph. They love their children unconditionally. Even when that child is not their own flesh and blood."

He turned and walked away.

Stephanie made the short drive home, her eyes fixed on the road ahead, her hands gripped tightly around the steering wheel. The tears were there in her throat, behind her eyes, yet she couldn't cry. She needed to. Oh, God, how she needed to.

She'd lost him. She'd allowed her resentment and bitterness to cost her a second chance to be with the one man she'd ever loved.

She didn't deserve to cry, she told herself. Didn't deserve the release it offered, the emptying of all emotion. She'd let him down. The man who had freely and generously offered to share everything he cherished most in the world—his heart, his daughter, his home— she'd let him down when he'd needed her most.

She understood now why he'd become so angry with

her for referring to Bud by his given name rather than her usual "Dad," and for what he considered her careless disregard of Bud's favorite possessions. He was bound to have seen himself in Bud, as they'd both raised daughters that weren't their own, and he'd probably feared that someday Meghan might find her real father and transfer her affection and allegiance to him, as Wade had thought Stephanie had transferred hers to her biological father.

Wade was wrong, though. Stephanie's determination to get to know her real father in no way changed how she felt about Bud. He was the only father she had ever known. He'd raised her, cared for her, loved her, and she would always love him. He was her father in every way but blood, and nothing would ever change that.

But she'd never have the chance to tell Wade that. She'd let him down, and now he was gone from her life forever.

For two days Stephanie packed like a wild woman, managing to accomplish more in that short space of time than she had in the entire previous week. Twice she saw Wade drive by the house on his way to check on the cattle, and though she watched from the window, praying with all her heart that he would stop, he passed by without so much as glancing toward the house. Each time, her heart would sink a little lower in her chest, and she would resume her packing, more determined than ever to finish the job and return to Dallas, putting as much distance as possible between her and the memories that haunted her.

On the third day, with most of the packing complete,

she placed a call to Bud's attorney and scheduled an appointment for that afternoon, then phoned a moving company and made arrangements to have the items she planned to save picked up on Friday and hauled to a storage facility in Dallas.

As she walked through the house on her way to her bedroom to shower and dress for her appointment with the attorney, an indescribable sadness slipped over her. The walls she passed were blank, save for the occasional rectangle of brighter paint where a picture had once hung. Boxes and furniture lined the walls and segmented the rooms, creating walkways that led from one room to the other. By Friday afternoon the house would be completely empty, listed for sale, and within a few short months, according to the Realtor she'd spoken to, a new owner would be moving in.

At the doorway to her bedroom she stopped and looked back down the hall, her heart breaking a little at the thought of another family living in the house she'd considered home for most of her life. Closing her eyes, she could almost hear the sounds that had once filled the house. The slam of the back door and Bud's voice as he called his standard greeting of, "When's dinner? I'm starving." The bark of the dog that always followed him in. Her mother fussing, "Wipe your feet, Bud Calloway! I just mopped that floor." The whir of the box fan that Bud kept aimed at his recliner in the summer months to keep him cool. The steady ticktock, ticktock of the clock that had sat on the fireplace mantel for more years than Stephanie could remember. Bud's soft call of, "'Night, Stephie," as he passed by her door on the way to his room.

Dragging an arm across the moisture that filled her eyes, she turned into her bedroom.

Stephanie settled in the chair opposite the lawyer's desk and offered Mr. Banks, Bud's attorney, a smile. "I appreciate you making time for me on such short notice."

He waved away her thanks. "No problem. I know you're anxious to get back to your own home and your work."

Stephanie released a long breath. "Yes, I am."

Getting down to business, Banks shuffled through the papers on his desk, then passed Stephanie a sheaf of papers he pulled from the stack. "A copy of Bud's will," he explained, then settled back in his chair, holding his own copy before him. "Most of this is standard language and the bequeaths what you'd expect, so I'll only bring to your attention the things I think might overly concern you or that you might question the validity of."

Stephanie looked at him curiously. "Why would I question anything? I'm familiar with Bud's wishes. He gave me a copy of his will shortly after Mom passed away."

Mr. Banks averted his gaze. "Well, uh—" He cleared his throat. "Well, you see, uh, Bud made a few changes."

A chill of premonition chased down Stephanie's spine. "What kind of changes?"

He flapped a hand, indicating the papers she held. "If you'll turn to page six, paragraph three." While she flipped pages, looking for the spot mentioned, he went on to explain, "As Bud's only child, you inherit everything. All stocks, bonds, insurance policies, the house and all its contents." He paused to clear his throat, then added, "But Bud left the land to Wade Parker."

Stunned, Stephanie could only stare. "He left the ranch to Wade?"

His expression grim, Banks nodded. "I know you must be shocked to learn this and I regret that it's my duty to deliver the news. I tried to get Bud to talk to you about it before he made the change, but he refused. Said he couldn't."

Stephanie choked out a laugh as the irony of the bequest set in. "No, Bud would never have mentioned Wade's name to me."

Banks leaned forward, his face creased with sympathy. "I'm sorry to be the one to tell you all this," he said with real regret. "I can only imagine how upsetting it must be for you. But I assure you, Bud was in sound mind when he made the change. I would never have done what he asked if I hadn't been absolutely sure he was sane."

Stephanie offered Banks a soft smile, hoping to ease his concern. "You needn't worry. I have no intention of contesting Bud's will. He knew that I wasn't interested in the land or in returning to Georgetown. Giving the land to Wade was his way of seeing that his ranch remained intact and wasn't cut up into a subdivision."

"He did mention that he feared that was what would happen to the place if it were ever put up for sale."

Rising, Stephanie extended her hand. "Thank you, Mr. Banks. I appreciate your concern for me. I truly do. But you can rest assured that I will honor Bud's wishes and will do nothing to stand in the way of Wade obtaining the deed to my father's ranch."

* * *

Late that night, unable to sleep, Stephanie sat on the front porch swing, slowly swaying back and forth, thinking over what Bud had done. Mr. Banks had been right when he'd assumed that Stephanie would be shocked by the discovery. She was more than shocked. She was stunned.

But that had lasted only a moment or two. She knew better than anyone how much Bud had loved his ranch, and it made perfect sense to her that he would want someone to have it who would love it as much as he had. Not that Stephanie didn't have strong feelings about the home where she was raised. She did. But she'd never made a secret of the fact that she had no desire to ever live there again. The truth was, she'd avoided coming home most of her adult life. Even though that must have hurt Bud, he had never held it against her. He'd loved her unconditionally throughout his life and, after his death, had generously left her with everything that was his, with the exception of his land.

Wade was the natural choice to receive the ranch. He would honor the gift and care for the land as much—if not more than—Bud had, and certainly more than Stephanie ever would. He'd already proved his dependability by taking care of things for Bud when Bud's health had declined, making it difficult, if not impossible, for him to do his chores himself. The gift to Wade was a large one, the value of the land alone worth probably close to a million dollars. But Wade would never sell the land to get the money it would bring. He had plenty of his own.

Closing her eyes, Stephanie examined her heart,

searching for any signs of resentment or bitterness toward Wade for receiving something that by all rights should have been hers. Oddly she felt nothing but a swell of pride that Bud had thought enough of Wade to give him something that had meant so much to him.

Sighing, she laid her head back and pushed a bare toe against the floor of the porch, setting the swing into motion again. Tomorrow the movers would come, she reminded herself, and she would be returning to Dallas and her own home.

She remembered when she'd first arrived to clean out her parents' house, she'd been anxious to close this chapter of her life once and for all and return to Dallas and her home there.

Now the mere thought of leaving made her want to cry.

Eight

Runt's sharp bark all but snatched Stephanie from a deep sleep and into a sitting position on the bed. Her heart thumping, she looked around.

"What is it, Runt?" she whispered.

He barked again, then trotted to the bedroom door.

Stephanie swung her legs over the side of the bed and grabbed her robe, pulling it on. Just as she reached the door, she heard a loud pounding.

"Steph? Open up! It's me. Wade."

Fully awake now, she flung open her bedroom door and ran down the hall, dodging boxes as she passed through the den. When she reached the front door, she fumbled the lock open, then flipped on the porch light as she swung the door wide, sure that he had come to reconcile with her.

Seeing the worry that etched his face, she wrapped

her robe more tightly around her and stepped outside. "What's wrong? Has something happened?"

"It's Meghan. She's gone. She was in bed asleep not more than four hours ago and now she's gone."

"Are you sure?"

"Of course I'm sure," he shouted impatiently. "I've searched the house, the barn, and there's no sign of her anywhere. I thought maybe she had come over here."

"Here?" she repeated, stunned that he would think Meghan would run away to her house.

Dragging a hand over his hair, he paced in front of her. "She likes you. Was mad when I wouldn't let her come back over and help you pack."

Stephanie gulped, unaware that Meghan had felt anything toward her, much less affection. Gathering the collar of her robe to her neck, she shook her head. "I haven't seen her. Have you called any of her friends."

"No. I hated to wake people up in the middle of the night until I was sure she was missing. I was so sure I'd find her here." He stopped and dropped his head back. "Oh, God," he moaned, his face contorted with what looked like pain. "She's gone to Angela's. I know she has."

Stephanie shuddered at the very suggestion, understanding Wade's concern, then set her jaw, knowing one of them had to remain calm. "You don't know that she has. Have you called Angela? Maybe she's talked to Meghan, knows where she is."

"I tried. She didn't answer, which doesn't surprise me." He scowled. "She was mad at me when she left the other day."

"How she feels about you isn't important right now,"

Stephanie reminded him firmly. "Meghan's safety is what you need to focus on. Now think. Where would she go? Who would she call?"

Wade tossed up his hands. "Hell, I don't know! When she's threatened to run away in the past, it's always been to her mother's. There isn't any other place I can think of where she'd go."

"Houston is almost three hours from here," Stephanie said, trying to think things out. "She couldn't very well walk there." Her eyes sharpened. "The bus station," she said and grabbed Wade's arm, shoving him toward his truck. "She'd probably catch a bus. Check there. Show her picture around. See if anyone remembers seeing her."

Wade dug in his heels. "But she'd have to get to town first."

Stephanie yanked open the door of his truck. "She could've walked. Hitchhiked. How she got there isn't important, and the more time you waste, the colder her trail is going to grow." She gave him a push. "Go! Find her and bring her home."

His expression grim, Wade started the ignition. "If she shows up here or contacts you—"

"I'll call you on your cell," she said, cutting him off. "And you call me if you find her."

Nodding, he slammed the door and gunned the engine and drove off with a squeal of tires.

Hugging her arms around her waist, Stephanie moved to stand in the middle of the drive and watched until his taillights disappeared from sight.

Drawing a deep breath, she turned for the house, knowing she wouldn't get a wink of sleep until she knew Meghan was safe and praying that Meghan was with one of her girlfriends and not on her way to Houston and Angela's house.

Her eyes burning from lack of sleep and her nerves tingling with worry, Stephanie walked through the house, directing the movers as they loaded the furniture and the boxes she'd marked as keepers.

Wade had called around four o'clock that morning to let her know that Meghan had bought a bus ticket for Houston and he was on his way there, hoping to intercept her before she reached Angela's. Since then, the phone had remained frustratingly silent.

She wanted desperately to call him, but each time she reached for the phone, she pulled her hand back, telling herself that he would contact her if there was any news.

Her nerves shot, she watched the movers load the last piece of furniture into the van. "I gave you the address of the storage facility, right?" she asked.

The driver patted his pocket. "Yes, ma'am. Got it right here."

She forced a smile. "Okay, then. I guess you're all set."

He lifted a hand in acknowledgment, then climbed behind the wheel while his partner hopped up onto the passenger seat on the opposite side.

With nothing left for her to do, Stephanie returned to the house and closed the front door behind her. The sound echoed hollowly in the empty house. She looked around, unsure what to do. One of the local charities had sent a truck by earlier in the day to pick up the items she had opted to donate. All that remained to signify the passing of her parents' lives was the huge pile of trash bags out back, and that, too, would be gone by morning, as she'd made arrangements with a garbage company to have it hauled off.

She'd originally planned to leave right after the moving van pulled out. Her bag was already packed and propped by the back door. But she couldn't leave now. Not with Meghan still missing. Worried that the phone company had misunderstood her instructions and shut off the phone today, rather than next week as she'd requested, she hurried to the kitchen and picked up the phone to make sure it was still working. Hearing the buzz of the dial tone, she replaced the receiver quickly, fearing she'd miss Wade's call.

"No news is good news," she reminded herself. Finding no consolation in the old adage, she began to pace—and nearly jumped out of her skin when the phone rang.

Leaping for it, she snatched the receiver to her ear. "Hello?"

"She's not at Angela's. Nobody is."

She pressed her fingers to her lips, her heart breaking at the defeat she heard in Wade's voice. "What are you going to do now?"

"I'm staying here. I know a couple of Angela's old hangouts, people she used to run around with. I'm going to make the rounds, find out if anybody has seen her."

"But what if Meghan comes back home? If you're gone, she might leave again."

"I was hoping you would go over there. Keep her there until I could get back."

"Of course I will."

"There's a key under the mat at the back door."

"I'll find it."

She started to hang up, but Wade's voice stopped her. "Steph?"

She pressed the phone back to her ear. "Yes?"

"Thanks."

Tears filled her eyes, but before she could respond, the dial tone buzzed in her ear, letting her know that he'd broken the connection.

Stephanie felt odd being in Wade's house. She was familiar with his home's layout, as she'd spent a lot of time there the summer they'd dated, but she chose to remain in the kitchen and near the phone hanging on the wall.

She made a pot of coffee to keep herself awake and drained cup after cup while sitting at the table. The clock on the oven recorded a digital time of 10:00 p.m., reminding Stephanie that she'd been at his house for over four hours.

The phone rang, startling her, and she lunged for it, catching it on the second ring.

"Hello?" she said breathlessly.

"Wade Parker, please."

Disappointed that it wasn't Wade calling, she brushed the hair back from her face. "I'm sorry, but he isn't in right now. Can I take a message?"

"No, I need to speak with him directly."

She frowned, wondering at the insistency in the man's voice. "I have his cell number. Would you like to try that?"

"I've already tried his cell. The call went straight to his voice mail. Hang on a second."

Her frown deepening, she listened, trying to make out what was being said, but whoever was on the other end of the line had covered the mouthpiece with his hand.

"Who am I talking to?"

Surprised by the question, she said, "Stephanie Calloway. I'm a neighbor."

"Just a sec."

Again the man covered the mouthpiece. Stephanie tightened her hand on the receiver, wondering if the call had something to do with Meghan.

"There's a young girl here who wants to speak to you," the man said.

The next voice Stephanie heard was Meghan's.

"Stephanie?" she said and sniffed. "Do you know where my daddy is?"

Fearing Meghan would hang up before Stephanie found out where she was, she said, "Where are you, Meghan? Your father is worried sick."

Meghan sniffed again, then said tearfully, "At the police station. In Austin."

Stephanie's eyes shot wide. A thousand questions crowded her tongue, but she couldn't ask them. Now was not the time. "Sweetheart, your daddy is in Houston looking for you."

Meghan burst into tears, and Stephanie had to swallow hard to keep from crying, too. "Meghan, listen to me," she said firmly. "Is the man with you a police officer?"

"Y-yes, ma'am."

"Let me speak to him."

"Okay. Stephanie?"

"Yes, sweetheart?"

"Will you come and get me?"

"Oh, honey," Stephanie moaned, her heart breaking at the pleading in the girl's voice. "I don't know if they'll release you to me. I'm not family."

"Please," Meghan begged and began to cry again. "I'm so scared."

"I'm on my way," Stephanie said quickly, having to raise her voice to be heard over Meghan's sobbing. "Give the phone back to the police officer so he can give me directions."

It was Stephanie's first visit to a police station...and she prayed it was her last. She supposed it could be the lateness of the hour that made the place appear so spooky, but she wouldn't bet on it. People—hoodlums, judging by their appearance—lounged outside the building and stood in loose groups in the hallway inside. Hugging her purse to her side for fear one of the thugs eyeing her would snatch it, she approached the desk.

"I'm here to see Meghan Parker," she told the officer on duty.

He looked at her, his expression bored. "You family?"

"No. A friend."

He shook his head. "We can only release her to a family member."

She bit down on her temper. "I'm aware of that, but she's just a child and she's frightened. I only want to stay with her until her father can get here."

He lifted a brow. "He's on his way? Last I heard, he couldn't be reached."

Anxious to see Meghan, she balled her hands to keep herself from throttling the man. "That's true, but I've left him a message on his cell phone and I'm sure as soon as he receives it he'll get here as quickly as he can. Now may I please see Meghan?"

With a shrug he stood and motioned her to follow him. He led her down a long hall and stopped before a door marked Interview and gave her a warning look. "Don't try sneaking her out. You'll only get yourself thrown in jail. She's a minor and can only be released to a family member."

She burned him with a look. "You needn't worry. I have an aversion to jails and have no intention of staying here a second longer than is necessary." Pushing past him, she opened the door.

Meghan was stretched out on a grouping of chairs, her face buried in the crook of her arm. She looked so small lying there. So incredibly young.

"Meghan?" Stephanie called softly.

Meghan sat up, blinked. Her eyes rounded when she saw Stephanie, then she shot off the chairs and into Stephanie's arms.

"Oh, Stephanie," she sobbed. "I was so scared you wouldn't come."

"Shh," Stephanie soothed. "There's no need to cry. I'm here and I'm going to stay with you until your dad arrives. Now why don't you tell me what happened? Why did you run away?"

Meghan's sobs grew louder. "Mom said Daddy didn't want me anymore. That I wasn't his. She told me to go to the bus station and buy a ticket to Houston. I did, but then she came to the station and got me. Said the ticket was just to fool dad. She took me to Austin and to a friend of her's house. It was awful," she cried and clung tighter to Stephanie. "People were snorting coke and doing all kinds of bad things.

"I begged her to leave. Take me somewhere else. But she wouldn't. She told me to shut up and have some fun for a change. I was so scared. These men kept looking at me all weirdlike. So I went into the bathroom and locked the door."

Stephanie stroked a hand down Meghan's hair, horrified to think of what might have happened to Meghan, the danger her mother had placed her in. "That was a very smart thing for you to do."

"I thought so, too. But then the police came and started beating on the door. Only I didn't know it was the police. I was crying and screaming for them to go away, and they beat the door down. I tried to tell the cop that I didn't want to be there, that my mother had brought me and made me stay. But he wouldn't listen. Said I had to go with him, that he couldn't leave me there alone. He made me get into the back of a police car with a couple of other people and brought me here."

Stephanie tried to block the awful images that rose in her mind. The kind of people that Meghan would've been sequestered with. The things she'd seen at that house. What might've happened to her if the police hadn't arrived when they had. Squeezing her eyes shut, she made herself focus on what Meghan was saying.

"When we got here, this woman cop brought me to this room. I gave them Daddy's name and number. She called him, but he wasn't home. So I gave them his cell number, but he didn't answer it either."

"I tried to call him, too, sweetheart," Stephanie told her. "His battery must be dead or he's out of range."

Gathering Meghan beneath her arm, she moved her toward the chairs. "But he'll come as soon as he gets the message."

Meghan sat, her eyes round with fear and fixed on Stephanie. "What if he doesn't?" Tears welled in her eyes. "Maybe he doesn't want me anymore. Mom said he didn't."

Stephanie pulled her into her arms. "That's not true. Your father loves you very much."

"But that's just it," Meghan sobbed. "He's not my father. Mom lied to him. She said she told him she was pregnant and the baby was his so he'd have to marry her."

Stephanie set her jaw hard enough to crack a tooth and hugged Meghan tighter against her chest. "I don't care what your mother told you. Wade loves you. Don't you ever doubt that for a minute."

Swearing, Wade yanked his battery charger from the adapter on his dash and hurled it out the window. Of all times for the stupid thing to break, this had to be the worst. He dragged a hand down his face and focused on the road, trying to think what to do. Seeing a gas station up ahead, he wheeled his truck into the parking lot and braked to a stop in front of a pay phone hanging on the side of the building.

Jumping out, he fished a quarter from his pocket, fed it into the slot, then punched in his cell phone number, silently praying Stephanie had called and left him a message telling him Meghan was home. When the recorded message started, asking him to leave a message, he quickly punched in the numerical code to take him directly to his voice mail. Pressing the phone to his ear, he listened. "Oh, no," he moaned and braced a hand against the wall to hold himself upright while he listened to a man, who identified himself as an Austin police officer, inform him that his daughter, Meghan Parker, was currently being held at the Austin Police Department on Seventh Street.

Wiping a shaky hand over his brow, he waited for the next message to begin.

"Wade, it's Stephanie. I talked to Meghan and she's at the Austin Police Department on Seventh Street, right off I-35. She's fine," she added quickly, "though understandably scared. I'm leaving now to go and stay with her. They won't release her to me, so you need to get to Austin as soon as possible."

Swearing, he dropped the receiver and jumped back into his truck. He was going to kill Angela, he told himself. If he ever got his hands on her, he was going to wring her lying neck. He knew she was behind this. How she'd pulled it off, he didn't know. But if Meghan was at a police station, Angela was the one responsible for her being there.

The door of the interview room flew open and Wade rushed in. He took one look at Meghan curled against Stephanie's side, then whipped his gaze to Stephanie's, the blood draining from his face.

Realizing that he thought Meghan was hurt, she shook her head. "She's fine," she whispered. "Just exhausted."

Meghan lifted her head and blinked. "Daddy?" she murmured sleepily. Tears filled her eyes when she saw Wade, and her face crumpled. "Oh, Daddy. I'm so sorry."

Wade crossed the room in two strides and gathered

her up in his arms, fitting her legs around his waist. "It's okay, baby," he soothed, then had to bury his face in her hair and gulp back his own tears. "Thank God you're all right. That's all that matters. You're safe."

Meghan clung tighter to him. "I just want to go home, Daddy. Please take me home."

"Don't worry, sweet cheeks," he assured her and headed for the door. "I've already cleared things with the police. We're good to go." He stopped at the doorway, as if only then remembering Stephanie was there, and glanced back, a brow lifted in question. "Do you need a ride?"

Stephanie rose, realizing that now that Wade and his daughter were reunited, her services were no longer needed. Though she should have been relieved that all had seemingly turned out well, she felt an inexplicable sadness.

She forced a smile. "No, I have my car."

Stephanie debated her options as she drove north on I-35 toward Georgetown, relieved to be leaving Austin behind. She was too tired to drive all the way to her home in Dallas, yet there was no place for her to sleep at her parents' house. All of the furniture had either been hauled away by the charitable group she'd donated it to or was currently sitting in a storage facility in Dallas.

Seeing a sign for a motel at the next exit, she slowed, considering stopping and getting a room. She sped up and passed the exit by, deciding that after the night she'd just spent, she needed the comfort and familiarity of her parents' home, even if it did mean she'd have to sleep on the floor.

Upon arriving, she parked beneath the shade of a tree near the back door rather than hassle with raising the garage door, Climbing out, she moaned softly as she stretched out the kinks sitting so long had left in her body. Hoping to find something she could use as bedding, she opened the rear doors of her SUV and dug through the items she kept stored there. She found a paper-thin blanket in the bag of emergency gear, tucked it under her arm, then dug around some more until she unearthed the inflatable neck pillow she used when traveling on airplanes. As an afterthought, she picked up the box containing her father's letters and headed for the house.

Once inside, she walked from room to room, feeling like Goldilocks as she searched for the most comfortable place to sleep. Deciding that the carpet in her bedroom was the cushiest, she set the box on the floor, then sank down beside it and blew up the neck pillow. Satisfied that she'd done all she could to make herself comfortable, she stretched out on her side, tucked the neck pillow beneath her cheek and drew the thin blanket up over her shoulder.

She released a long, exhausted breath, drew in another…and slept.

"Daddy?"

"Yeah?"

"Mom said that you and Stephanie used to be engaged."

Wade tensed, then forced his fingers to relax on the wand he held and twisted, closing the blinds and blocking out as much sunlight as possible from Meghan's room so that she could get some rest. "Yeah, we were."

"Mom said she broke y'all up so that you'd have to marry her."

Adding yet another item to the long list of reasons Meghan had already given him during the drive home to despise his ex, Wade crossed to sit down on the side of his daughter's bed. "In a way, I guess she did," he replied, not wanting to burden her with the details.

Tears welled in her eyes. "It was my fault, wasn't it? Because Mom was pregnant with me, you had to break your engagement to Stephanie."

He leaned to brush her hair back from her face. "No, sweet cheeks," he assured her. "The fault was mine. You had no part in it."

"You still like her, don't you? Stephanie, I mean."

He smiled sadly and drew his hand to cup her cheek. "Yeah. I guess I always will."

"You could still get married, couldn't you? I mean, it's not like you're married to Mom anymore."

He dropped his gaze, not sure how to answer. "It's more complicated than that."

She pulled herself up to sit, dropping her arms between her spread knees. "How?"

He hesitated, searching for a way to explain why he couldn't marry Stephanie that wouldn't make his daughter feel as if she were to blame. "Marriage is a big commitment," he began.

She rolled her eyes. "Duh. Like I don't already know that."

Chuckling, he scrubbed a hand over her hair. "If you're so smart, then you tell me why I *should* marry her."

"Because she's a hottie."

He choked out a laugh. "Hottie?" He shook his head. "Only a shallow man marries a woman for her looks."

"That's not the only reason," she said drily, then lifted a hand and began to tick off items. "She's smart, hip and really, really nice." She dropped her hands, her eyes filling with tears. "She came all the way to Austin to stay with me because I was scared. And she held me real tight when I cried, just like a real mom would. She made me feel safe, loved. Even knowing how bad I'd been, she didn't yell at me or anything. She was just…nice."

Wade stared, wondering if Stephanie's kindness to Meghan was a sign that she no longer resented his daughter. "Meghan?" he said hesitantly. "If Stephanie and I were to get married, she would become your stepmother. How would you feel about that?"

Meghan frowned, as if she hadn't considered that aspect, then smiled. "I think that would be really cool."

"Are you sure? Now think about this before you answer," he warned. "She'd be living in our house with us, and I'm sure she'd have her own set of rules she'd expect us to follow. Consequences, too," he added, remembering his conversation with Stephanie about cursing.

She drew back, eyeing him warily. "Gosh, Dad. You make her sound like some kind of witch."

He shrugged. "I just want to make sure that you understand that if Stephanie and I were to marry, I would expect you to give her the respect any mother deserves."

She lifted a brow and looked down her nose at him. "*Any* mother?"

He rolled his eyes, knowing she was referring to Angela. "You know what I mean."

"I will. I promise." She gave him a push. "Go and ask her. I'll bet she says yes."

He gaped. "Now?"

She flopped to her back and pulled the covers to her chin. "Why not? It's not like you have anything better to do."

He rose slowly, fighting a sudden attack of nerves. "No, I guess I don't."

Wade wasn't sure if he'd find Stephanie at her parents' house, but he figured that was as good a place as any to start his search.

He prayed it was a good sign when he found her SUV parked beneath the shade tree near the back. Unsure how she'd respond to another proposal, he crossed to the front door and knocked. He waited, shifting nervously from foot to foot. When he didn't receive a response, he lifted a hand above the door and felt along the edge for the key. Finding it, he unlocked the door and let himself in.

He glanced around and was shocked to see that the house was empty, not a stick of furniture or a box in sight. Realizing that Steph had completed the job she'd come to do and would be leaving soon made his stomach twist with dread.

Runt trotted out from the kitchen and bumped his nose against Wade's hand.

"Hey, Runt," he said and gave the dog a distracted pat as he looked around. "Where's Steph?"

In answer, the dog started down the hall. Wade followed, his hands slick with sweat, his throat dry as a bone.

At the door of her bedroom Runt dropped down on his haunches and looked up expectantly at Wade.

"Good boy," Wade murmured and gave the dog a pat as he leaned to peek inside.

Guilt stabbed at him when he saw Steph asleep on the floor with only a blanket for cover. Silently kicking himself for not thinking to ask her to come to his house when they'd left the police station, he tiptoed into the room and sank down to his knees at her side.

"Steph?" he whispered and gave her arm a nudge.

She moaned softly and pulled the blanket over her head. "Not now, Runt," she complained. "I'm sleeping."

Biting back a smile, Wade stretched out on his side to face her. Careful not to startle her, he lifted the edge of the blanket. "It's not Runt, Steph," he whispered. "It's me. Wade."

She blinked open her eyes. Blinked again, then tensed. "Is Meghan okay? Has something happened to her?"

He laid a hand against her cheek, touched by the alarm and concern in her voice. "She's fine. When I left, she was sleeping."

Obviously relieved, she closed her hand over his and let her lids drift down. "Good. Poor baby was tired."

Poor baby. Hearing her use that one endearment told Wade all he needed to know. He eased his body closer to hers. "Steph? I need for you to wake up."

"Tired," she moaned. "So tired."

"I know you are, sunshine, but there's something I need to ask you."

"Can't it wait?" she complained.

Chuckling, he placed a finger on her eyelid and forced it up. "No, it can't," he told her firmly.

Heaving a sigh, she rolled to her back and scrubbed her hands over her face. "What?" she asked wearily.

He sat up in order to better see her. "I wanted to thank you for going to Austin and staying with Meghan until I could get there. That meant a lot to me."

Yawning, she rolled back to her side and pulled the blanket over her shoulder. "You're welcome."

"Meghan sends her thanks, too."

"Poor baby," she murmured sympathetically. "I can't imagine how frightened she must have been."

Because he knew only too well the kind of horrors his ex had subjected his daughter to, Wade scowled. "Yeah, she was scared all right." Heaving a sigh, he focused on Steph's face again. "Meghan said that you were really nice to her. Held her tight, like a real mom would."

Though her eyes remained closed, a tender smile curved Steph's lips. "That's really sweet. She's a good kid."

"You think so?"

Something in his voice must have caught her attention, because Steph opened her eyes and looked up at him. "Yes, I do."

"You said before that you didn't think you could live in the same house with her. Do you still feel that way?"

Her gaze on his, she slowly pushed herself up to an elbow. "Wade, what are you saying?"

He dipped his chin, shrugged. "Meghan and I had a little talk before I came here. She seems to think we should get married."

Her eyes shot wide. "Meghan said that?"

"Yeah. Angela told her that we were engaged before,

and Meghan was worried that it was her fault that our engagement was broken."

She shifted to sit and dropped her face onto her hands. "Oh, no," she moaned. "That is so unfair, so wrong. Angela should never have said that to her. Meghan wasn't to blame."

"Don't worry. I straightened Meghan out. I told her it was my fault, that she had nothing to do with it."

She opened her hands enough to peek at him. "And she believed you?"

He lifted a brow. "What choice did she have? It's kind of hard to argue with the truth. It *was* my fault."

She dropped her hands to frown. "No, it wasn't. It was Angela's."

He lifted a shoulder. "No matter who was to blame, I don't regret the decision I made. I only have to look at Meghan and know I did the right thing."

"Oh, Wade," she said, her face crumpling. "After all that woman put you through, you never once turned your back on Meghan."

"And I never will," he said firmly. He caught her hand and squeezed. "And I hope you won't either."

Her tears welled higher. "I won't. I couldn't."

He gulped and gripped her hands more tightly. "There's something you need to know. Something that might make you angry. I probably should've mentioned it before, but I didn't think it was my place."

A soft smile curved her lips. "If it's about Bud leaving you his land, you needn't worry. I already know."

His eyes widened in surprise. "You knew?"

"I met with Bud's lawyer. He told me."

"And you're not mad?"

She shook her head. "No. Surprised, yes, but not mad. Bud willed you his land because he knew you would love it as much as he did." She sputtered a laugh. "And I wouldn't be surprised if he didn't do it in hopes it would bring us together."

Smiling, he nodded. "That sounds like something Bud would do." Growing solemn, he shifted to kneel before her and brought her hands to his lips. "Stephanie Calloway, would you do me the honor of marrying me and becoming my wife?"

She stared at him as if afraid this was a dream she would wake from.

"Will you?" he prodded.

Laughing, she flung her arms around his neck. "Yes, yes, a thousand times yes!"

He squeezed his arms tightly around her and buried his face in her hair. "I've waited so long to hear you say that," he murmured, then drew back to look deeply into her eyes. "We're going to be a family. You, me and Meghan."

A sharp bark had him glancing toward the doorway, where Runt sat, looking at him expectantly.

Smiling, he added, "And Runt." He turned to look at Steph again and the smile melted from his face. "I love you, Stephanie Calloway."

"No more than I love you, Wade Parker."

He framed her face between his hands. "We're going to make it this time. Nothing is ever going to separate us again."

"Nothing," she promised and lifted her face to his.

Epilogue

Stephanie turned her hand slowly, watching as light from the bedside lamp caught the emerald-cut diamond of her ring and made it shimmer. It was the same ring Wade had slipped on her finger almost thirteen years ago. His mother's ring. Two weeks after he'd placed it on her finger, she'd ripped the ring off and thrown it at him. Closing her eyes against the unwanted memory, she curled her fingers to her palm as if to protect the ring and silently vowed never to take it off again. Ever.

Sighing, she opened her eyes to look at the ring again, then dropped her hand and reached for the last stack of letters sitting on the bedside table. She'd read them, just as she'd promised herself she would, and only one remained before she could say she'd read them all. Slipping the last envelope from the stack, she pushed back the flap and pulled out the folded pages.

As she opened them, a torn piece of paper fell to her lap.

"What's this?" she murmured and picked it up to examine it. Finding a jumble of handwritten words on one side, she turned it over to look at the back. Impressed into the paper was a notary's seal and a woman's signature. *Helen Thompson.* Frowning at the unfamiliar name, she flipped the paper back over and tried again to make sense of the words. She quickly gave up. Whatever message was originally written on the piece had lost its meaning when the document was torn.

Hoping to find an explanation in her father's letter, she set the piece of paper aside and smoothed open the pages of the letter over her propped up knees.

Dearest Janine,

I'm enclosing part of a document that I want you to have. I have no idea if it'll ever be worth anything, but keep it somewhere safe, just in case. I never mentioned it to you before, but I honestly thought the guy who gave this to me was either crazy or drunk. Maybe I'd better explain.

The night before I left for 'Nam I was in a bar in Austin with the guys I was traveling with and this man came up to our table and offered to buy us all a drink. We invited him to join us and he told us that he'd had a son who was killed in Vietnam. It happened several years before, but I could tell the man was still grieving. Anyway, he said, now that his son was dead, he didn't have anybody to leave his ranch to and said he wanted to leave it to us. He wrote out this bill of sale, had each one of us sign it, then tore it into six pieces and gave each one of us a piece. He told us, when we got back from Vietnam, we were to put the pieces together and come claim our ranch.

Like I said, I don't know if anything will ever come of this, but I want you to have it, just in case I don't make it home. Kind of like insurance, I guess.

I've never really thought about dying, but lately it's been on my mind a lot. Maybe it's because I'm going to be a daddy. I don't know. I've been worrying how you and the baby would make it if something were to happen to me. You'd get money from the Army. I know that for sure. But what I don't know is if it would be enough to support you and the baby without you having to work. And I don't want you to have to worry about working or money or anything like that.

I want you to be able to devote yourself to being a mommy.

I hope I haven't depressed you by telling you all this. My only purpose in writing it all down is so that you can take advantage of this opportunity, if it should ever present itself. If something should happen to me, the other guys will know what to do and they'll contact you. You can trust them. They'll see that you get your fair share.

I'd better go. We're heading out early in the morning and moving to an area where there's been some trouble. The guys and I have already

*decided that we're going to kick butt and get this
war over with so we can come home.
Love forever and ever,
Larry*

Blinking back tears, Stephanie carefully refolded the
letter, then picked up the torn piece of paper. Insurance,
she thought sadly, turning the yellowed and ragged
piece of paper between her fingers. Since Stephanie
was unaware of her mother ever having received a
windfall, she had to believe that her father's assumption
was right. The man who had given him the piece of
paper had either been drunk or crazy.

"You still awake?"

Stephanie glanced up to find Wade in the doorway.
Though she'd agreed to stay in his house, she had
refused to sleep in his bedroom with him until they
were properly married. With his daughter in the house,
she'd thought it only proper.

Smiling, she patted the spot on the bed beside her.
"I was just reading the last of my father's letters."

He hopped up onto the bed and settled beside her,
stretching his legs out next to hers. "So? How was it?
Any new revelations?"

She frowned thoughtfully. "I don't know." She
passed the torn piece of paper to him. "Take a look at
this. It was inside the letter."

He studied first one side, then the other, then
shrugged and passed it back. "What is it? Some kind of
secret code?"

She laughed softly. "It looks like it, doesn't it?" Her smile faded and she shook her head. "He sent it to Mom and told her to keep it someplace safe. Said it was insurance, in case he didn't make it home."

He took the piece of paper back from her to look at it again, then snorted. "Sure doesn't look like an insurance policy to me."

"It's not. A man gave it to him the night before he left for Vietnam. Him and five other soldiers. It's like a deed, I guess. Supposedly his son died in Vietnam, and since he didn't have anyone to leave his ranch to, he wanted my father and his friends to have it."

He snorted a laugh. "What man in his right mad would give his ranch to six complete strangers?"

"My father thought the same thing. He said in the letter that he thought the guy had to be drunk or crazy to do something like that." Growing thoughtful, she rubbed the torn edge of the paper across her lips. "I wonder what happened to the other five men?" She glanced at Wade. "There's a chance that some of them, if not all, made it back home."

He lifted a shoulder. "You'd think so."

"Wade," she said as an idea begin to form in her mind. "Do you think it would be possible to locate those soldiers? Find out what happened to them? Maybe where they live?"

"I don't know," he said doubtfully. "That was—what?—thirty-five years ago?"

"Give or take a few months." Catching her lower lip between her teeth, she tried to think how to go about locating the men. "I could write a letter to the Army," she said, thinking aloud. "Find out the names of the men that were in Dad's unit at the time he was killed."

"Yeah," he agreed. "That would be a start."

"Wonder how many men there were?"

"In his unit, you mean?" At her nod, he shrugged. "I have no idea. A lot, I'd imagine."

She firmed her mouth in determination. "It doesn't matter. I don't care if I have to write a thousand letters, I'm going to track down the five men who have the other pieces of paper."

"You don't really think it has any value, do you? Even if the guy who gave it to them was serious, that was thirty-five years ago. A lot could have happened in that amount of time."

Smiling, she dropped a kiss on his cheek. "Doesn't matter. Not to me. The only thing I'm interested in is finding my father's friends."

"Would you mind waiting until after we're married to start your search?"

She looked at him curiously. "Why?"

He curled up close to her and nuzzled her neck. "Because I don't want anything distracting you from planning this wedding and causing a delay. Having you in my house and not in my bed is driving me crazy."

She slid down until her face was even with his. "Doesn't Meghan ever have sleepovers with her friends?"

A slow smile spread across his face as he realized what she was suggesting. "Yeah, she does. Remind me to call Jan tomorrow and set one up."

She drew back to peer at him in surprise. "Isn't that rather bold to ask if your daughter can spend the night at someone's house? Shouldn't the invitation come from Jan?"

He looped an arm around her waist and drew her to him. "Jan'll understand." His lips spread across hers in a smile. "She's a single parent, too."

* * * * *

Don't miss the next book in
Peggy Moreland's latest series.
Watch for
The Convenient Marriage,
available in April 2007 from Silhouette Desire.

TEMPT ME
by
Caroline Cross

PLAY THE
Lucky Key Game

and you can get

Do You Have the LUCKY KEY?

FREE BOOKS
and a FREE GIFT!

Scratch the gold areas with a coin. Then check below to see the books and gift you can get!

YES!
I have scratched off the gold areas. Please send me the 2 FREE BOOKS and GIFT for which I qualify. I understand I am under no obligation to purchase any books, as explained on the back of this card. I am over 18 years of age.

▼ DETACH AND POST CARD TODAY! ▼

Mrs/Miss/Ms/Mr	Initials	D7AI

BLOCK CAPITALS PLEASE

Surname

Address

Postcode

 2 free books plus a free gift   1 free book

2 free books   Try Again!

Visit us online at
www.millsandboon.co.uk

The Reader Service™ — Here's how it works:

NO STAMP NEEDED!

THE READER SERVICE™
FREE BOOK OFFER
FREEPOST CN81
CROYDON
CR9 3WZ

If offer card is missing write to: The Reader Service, PO Box 676, Richmond, TW9 1WU

NO STAMP
NECESSARY
IF POSTED IN
THE U.K. OR N.I.

CAROLINE CROSS

always loved to read, but it wasn't until she discovered romance that she felt compelled to write, fascinated by the chance to explore the positive power of love in people's lives. She grew up in Yakima, Washington, the "Apple Capital of the World", attended the University of Puget Sound and now lives outside Seattle, where she (tries to) work at home despite the chaos created by two telephone-addicted teenage daughters and a husband with a fondness for home-improvement projects. Pleased to have recently been No.1 on a national bestseller list, she was thrilled to win the 1999 Romance Writers of America RITA® Award for Best Short Contemporary Novel and to have been called "one of the best" writers of romance today by *Romantic Times BOOKclub*. Caroline believes in writing from the heart—and having a good brainstorming partner. She loves hearing from readers and can be reached at PO Box 47375, Seattle, Washington 98146, USA. Please include an SAE (with return postage) for a reply.

One

John Taggart Steele stood motionless in the shifting shadows that edged the towering stand of evergreens.

Snowflakes swirled in the icy air around him, swept from the treetops high overhead by a capricious wind. Narrowing his eyes against the October sun, he raised his binoculars to zero in on the tidy A-frame cabin in the clearing five hundred yards away, only to jerk the glasses away as his cell phone vibrated. Ripping it from the clip on his belt, he glanced at the screen and saw the call was from Steele Security's Denver office. He hit the receive button and slapped the instrument to his ear. "What?"

"Looks like it's her, all right." As calm as a summer day, his brother Gabe's voice held neither reproach at the brusque greeting nor satisfaction as he delivered the long-awaited confirmation.

Taggart said nothing, merely waited.

"The truck was recently registered to a woman calling herself Susan Moore. The previous owner is a Laramie grad student who says he sold the vehicle three weeks ago to a cocktail waitress at the bar he frequents. He described Bowen to a T, said she was 'a real sweet little thing.' She paid cash for the vehicle and confided she was headed south to see her ailing grandpa."

"Laramie, huh?"

Gabe seemed to know exactly what Taggart was thinking. "Yeah. When she left Flagstaff, she bolted *toward* Denver, not away. Totally unexpected, completely illogical." There was a pause, then he added thoughtfully, "It was a damn good strategy."

Good strategy wasn't quite how Taggart would describe it—not when he'd been chasing the elusive Ms. Genevieve Bowen for close to three months. Still, he shoved away the rude comment that sprang to mind, along with his uncharacteristic impatience. Emotion didn't have a place in the job he did as a partner in Steele Security, the business he and his brothers ran out of their home base in Denver, Colorado. The kind of work they did—hostage and fugitive recovery, personal protection, threat management, industrial security—required clear but creative thinking, situational analysis, high-stakes decision making.

Taggart regarded being cool and impartial an absolute necessity. It ought to be chiseled in stone, if you asked him—his brother Dominic's recent marriage to a wealthy debutante he'd rescued from the clutches of a ruthless Caribbean dictator notwithstanding.

He shifted his gaze from the cabin to the ancient

Ford pickup parked at the far end of it. Just because the vehicle's recent history fit with his quarry's MO—blend in, deal in cash, vanish after dropping false hints about your destination—that didn't automatically mean it was Bowen. There was still a chance she'd again eluded him—and gained the gratitude and ensuing silence of yet another needy young woman matching her general description—by giving away the truck the way she had three previous vehicles.

Only Taggart didn't think so. And not merely because his instincts were clamoring that his luck had finally turned. Because *this* time, damned if he hadn't seen her himself, bold as brass, driving out of the Morton's Grocery parking lot on the outskirts of Kalispell.

The cabin door swung open. "I've got movement," he told Gabe. "I'll catch you later." Not waiting for a reply, he disconnected and shifted the binoculars into place as a woman stepped out onto the porch that skirted the cabin.

With icy calm, he let his gaze climb her length, starting at her fleece-topped boots and moving up her slim, blue-jeaned legs, past a serviceable green parka until he arrived, at long last, at her face.

He let out a breath he hadn't known he was holding. It was her, all right. After the dozen weeks he'd spent on her trail, interviewing her friends and showing her picture around, her features were as familiar to him as his own. There was the full mouth, the straight little nose, the big dark eyes and the slightly squared chin. Her glossy brown hair, which she'd once worn in a thick braid that reached to her waist, was now cropped short and, after a number of cut-and-color transformations, back to its original color.

He frowned as something nagged at him, and then his face smoothed out as he realized he was simply surprised by how small she was. Even though his information on her included the fact that she was only five foot three, for some reason he'd expected her to appear taller.

Nevertheless, it *was* her—Ms. Genevieve Bowen, Silver, Colorado, bookstore owner and literacy booster, teen mentor, animal lover, occasional emergency foster mother. A woman so well-known for her random acts of kindness that her friends fondly referred to her as their own little Pollyanna.

Polly-pain-in-the-butt was more like it, Taggart thought, recalling the absolute futility of the past three months. Given Ms. Bowen's glorified Girl Scout reputation, and the fact that your average model citizen didn't know jack about being on the lam, he'd assumed he'd be able to track her down without breaking a sweat.

Wrong. First to his surprise and then to his exasperation—and his brothers' not-so-subtle amusement—little Genevieve had made none of the usual beginner's mistakes. Hell, she hadn't made any mistakes. Instead, she'd simply vanished, turning a job that should have been a week-long romp into a test of Taggart's cunning and perseverance.

It was just too damn bad for her that he was very, very good at his job.

That, being a methodical son of a bitch, he'd decided after losing her trail yet again to revisit all the places he'd initially pegged as being potential bolt holes for her, including her late great-uncle's northern Montana cabin where she and her brother—who was currently being held without bail on charges of capital murder—had spent several long-ago summers.

And that, in an unpredictable turn of luck, he'd just happened to pull into that grocery store lot at the same time she'd been pulling out. Otherwise, he not only would have missed her, he'd have once again struck the cabin off his list for now and most likely spent another few weeks fruitlessly trying to locate her.

Instead, he'd called in the pickup's plates to Gabe and followed her back here, managing to remain undetected only because he'd been pretty damn sure where they were going. Once again, what had been good for him had been bad for her.

But then, Genevieve hadn't exactly had a banner year, what with her brother's arrest for killing James Dunn, his client's only son; her own unwanted role as the prosecution's key witness and her dumb-ass decision to flee rather than testify.

Because now she was *his*. With a distinct surge of possessiveness, he watched as she reached the truck, keeping the binoculars trained on her vivid face as she retrieved a bag of groceries and trekked back the way she'd come.

Suddenly, just as she reached the stairs that led up to the cabin's railed porch, she stopped. Swiveling her head, she looked straight at him.

Taggart knew damn well she couldn't see him. Still, he felt her gaze like a lover's touch. Rooted in place, he forgot to breathe, stunned as his skin prickled and he felt the oddest tug of recognition….

It seemed like an eternity before she looked away, gave the rest of the clearing a careful once-over, then squared her shoulders and went quickly up the trio of steps. Pausing under the wide overhang that sheltered the door, she abruptly glanced one last time directly at the spot where he stood before she disappeared inside.

Annoyed, he blew out his pent-up breath, asking himself what the hell had just happened. Just who did she think she was? Some sort of psychic? His long-lost soul mate?

Yeah, right. It'd be a cold day in hell when he started believing in that kind of delusional mumbo jumbo.

Jaw clenched, he stowed the binoculars and surged into motion. Carefully hugging the shadow of the trees, he began to work his way toward the back of the cabin, his powerful body making short shrift of the thigh-high snowdrifts.

Enough cat and mouse. It was time to take her down.

Genevieve set the bag of groceries on the kitchen counter. Chilled despite the warmth of her parka, she rubbed her arms and did her best to dispel her lingering sense of unease.

Try as she might to downplay it, she'd had the most uncomfortable sensation of being watched while she was outside. It had been sharp, overwhelming, eerie— as palpable as an actual touch. Alarm had flickered along her spine; gooseflesh had erupted on her arms and prickled the nape of her neck.

She'd felt a powerful urge to run.

That's what you get for staying up late last night reading Stephen King. Keep it up, and the next thing you know, you'll start to think the trees are alive. Or that a mutant squirrel is coming to get you....

A wry little smile tugged briefly at the corners of her mouth. Okay. So maybe she was a wee bit jumpy. It wasn't really surprising, not when her stop in town to get supplies had filled her with such conflicting feelings.

Typical of her current existence, she'd been scared to death that someone might recognize her while also wishing fervently that she might see a familiar face. Which was not only illogical and contradictory, but also highly improbable since the last time she'd been in the area for more than a night she'd been barely fifteen, nearly half the age she was now.

Still, she knew she was taking a chance by coming here. *How to Vanish without a Trace,* the book that had been her bible these past months, warned against seeking out known and familiar places.

And yet... Not only was she running dangerously low on money, but she'd changed her identity so many times they were starting to run together. She needed a break—just a week or maybe two—to rest and regroup. And surely, after all this time, anyone still looking for her would have written this place off.

Lord, she hoped so, she thought, turning to glance fondly at the cabin's simple interior. The structure was a standard, open-concept A-frame. Toward the back, an L-shaped kitchen occupied one side, while the bathroom and a sleeping area with a massive built-in bed occupied the other, the two areas separated by a narrow stairway that led up to a small loft.

A bank of windows stretched across the cabin's front, divided by a floor-to-ceiling native-stone fireplace equipped with a glass-fronted heat insert. Although the oversized navy couch, the trio of maple occasional tables and the pair of padded rocking chairs were new, chosen by the property management company she'd hired when the place had passed to her and her brother, they had clean, uncluttered lines, like the old furniture she remembered, and were placed to make the most of the sweeping view of the surrounding peaks.

If she closed her eyes, she could almost believe it was fourteen years ago and that any second her great-uncle Ben would come clattering through the door, an adoring twelve-year-old Seth dogging his heels. The two would snatch away whatever book she happened to be reading—her little brother complained that Genevieve was *always* reading—and tug her out on the deck to see the sunset or watch an eagle soaring overhead.

Except that Uncle Ben had been gone more than a decade, the last to pass of the quintet of elderly relatives who'd done the best they could to provide their great-niece and great-nephew with some occasional normalcy. While Seth...

Her heart clenched at the memory of the last time she'd seen her brother. Dressed in an orange jumpsuit, his hands weighed down with shackles, Seth's normally easygoing expression had been closed and implacable as he faced her through the mesh divide of the visitors' room of the Silver County Jail. "No. No way, Gen," he'd said flatly. "You go into court and refuse to testify, they're going to throw you in jail, too."

"But—"

"*No.* It's bad enough that you're probably going to

lose your house—and for what? To pay an attorney who thinks I'm guilty? But I swear to God I'll confess before I'll let you sacrifice your freedom."

"Seth, don't be foolish—"

"I'm not kidding. It's a slam dunk I'm going to be convicted." His voice had been even, almost uninflected, but his eyes had been so defeated it had taken all her strength not to lay her head down on the scarred counter between them and weep. "The best thing you can do is accept that I'm a lost cause and just…move on."

As if, Genevieve thought fiercely now. The mere thought of giving up on her little brother was inconceivable. They'd never known their father, and it had been just the two of them ever since their mother had abandoned them for good when Genevieve was ten and Seth was seven. She certainly wasn't about to sit back now and do nothing while he was punished for something he hadn't done. Any more than she would play a part, however unwilling, in making him appear guilty.

So, after considerable agonizing, she'd decided to run. It was far from a perfect solution—she accepted that eventually she'd have to pay for defying the court—but so far, at least, she'd done what she'd set out to. The trial had been delayed, buying Seth some time. And there was always a chance that one of the dozens of people she'd written to over the past three months— policemen, attorneys, private investigators, her congressman—might actually decide to do what she'd begged and look into the case.

In the meantime, she was doing okay. Sure, she was lonely—just as *How to Vanish* warned, the hardest part of disappearing wasn't constructing a new identity or not leaving a paper trail or even not staying too long in any one place.

The hardest part was having no one to talk to. She couldn't count the number of times during the course of a day that she longed to hear a familiar voice or see a familiar face. As much as she missed home, what she missed even more was someone to confide in, someone she could trust.

Still, as long as she had her books, her freedom and her sincere belief that if she just continued to insist on Seth's innocence somebody somewhere would eventually listen, she could survive anything.

Uh-huh. Except for that killer squirrel that's lurking outside, just waiting to get you.

Well, really. What was she going to do? Let herself be controlled by a nonexistent bogeyman, animal or otherwise? Crawl under the bed, cover her eyes and hide?

She drew herself up. Heck, no. She had enough legitimate worries without letting her imagination into the act.

Before she could lose her nerve, she zipped up her parka, strode to the door and flung it open. Marching outside, she caught her breath as a blast of frigid air swept over her, but she didn't falter. Planting herself at the top of the stairs, she scanned the clearing one more time, determined to put an end to her foolish fears. She scoured the snow for telltale footprints and searched the shadows at the base of the pines for anything out of place.

Nothing. Yet she still had the strangest feeling....

Determined to be thorough and be done with this once and for all, she turned and marched out onto the large, prow-shaped section of the deck that jutted from the cabin's front. Again she looked and listened, but there wasn't a thing to suggest another human presence. There was just a glint of sun on snow, the intermittent call of a hawk and the whisper of the wind sighing through the surrounding trees.

See? There's nobody here but you.

Blowing out a breath, she forced her stiff shoulders to relax. Everything was fine. She and her memories were the only ones here. And once she had the rest of her things out of the truck and got started on the soup she planned to make for dinner, she'd feel even better. She turned and took a step toward the stairs.

Like a ghost come to life, a man materialized out of the shadows of the overhang.

Her heart slammed to a stop along with her feet as she stared at him, the blood suddenly roaring in her ears.

Like her, he was dressed for the weather in a parka, boots and jeans. But that was where all similarity ended. He was huge, six foot four at least, with powerful legs and shoulders like a linebacker's. His hair was coal-black, cropped close to his head, and his hooded eyes were a pale, icy green.

His face was all angles, with a slash of high cheekbones, a straight blade of a nose, a stubborn chin and firm lips set in a straight, uncompromising line.

He looked dangerous as hell, and Genevieve hadn't stayed free for three months without learning to trust her instincts.

Whirling, she ran for her life.

Two

Well, hell.

Feeling a distinct stab of annoyance, Taggart launched himself after little Ms. Bowen, who appeared to be operating under the delusion that now that he'd found her, he might actually let her get away.

He swallowed a snort. There was about as much chance of that as of him dancing in the Denver Ballet.

She might be fast, but he was faster. Not to mention bigger, stronger and trained—by the US Army Rangers—to take down considerably tougher, rougher members of society than Genevieve would ever be.

Although he had to admit, closing this case was going to make his week. Hell, who was he kidding? It was going to make his *year.*

Catching up to her with ease, he tackled her, hauling her close as they reached the edge of the deck, crashed into the railing, flipped over the top and plunged toward the snowbank below.

Instinctively—he wanted to take her into custody, not put her in the hospital, damn it—he twisted, taking the brunt of the impact as they slammed to the ground. He winced as his hip struck a rock and he heard a distinct crunch of plastic as his cell phone bit the dust. Then he winced again as the back of Bowen's head slammed into his collarbone.

Baring his teeth at the pain, he loosened his grip a fraction, only to bite out a curse as his captive drove her heavily booted heels into his shins at the same time as she punched him hard in the stomach with one sharp little elbow.

That did it. Setting his jaw, he locked his legs around hers and tightened the grip he had on her midriff. "Knock it *off.*"

"Let go of me!" she countered. "Let go of me this instant or—" her voice wavered as he increased the pressure on her solar plexus, making it impossible for her to get a deep breath "—I swear...you'll—you'll be—sorry—"

She was threatening *him?* Unbelievable. The woman clearly had more nerve than sense. He tightened his hold even more. "Pay attention, lady. I'm in charge now. You do what I tell you. Understand?"

He waited a beat for her to answer.

When she didn't, he increased the pressure until she couldn't breathe at all, knowing from experience that the more he could dominate and demoralize her now, the less likely she'd be to give him trouble on their return trip to Colorado. *"Understand?"*

A whimper escaped her throat. "Yes," she finally gasped. "Yes!"

"Good." Satisfied, he loosened his hold, dumped her unceremoniously onto her side and climbed to his feet.

Knocking the snow from his pants, he considered her as she lay sprawled in the snow. With her shiny mop of hair, her eyes squeezed shut so that her inky lashes shadowed her smooth cheeks, her mouth trembling each time she took a greedy gulp of air, she looked small and defenseless, almost childlike.

Except that thanks to their recent tussle, the lush curve of her ass and the soft swell of her breasts were imprinted on his brain, leaving him in no doubt she was a thoroughly grown-up female.

And a treacherous one at that, he reminded himself, his shins throbbing annoyingly from where she'd kicked him.

"Get up," he ordered.

She drew in one last shuddering breath, then opened her eyes. He watched her struggle to control her fear, and felt a grudging admiration as she willed herself to present a semblance of calm.

She pushed herself upright, watching him warily. "What do you want with me?" she demanded.

"I work for Steele Security. James Dunn's parents hired us to find you."

"Find *me?*" She widened her dark eyes in an excellent imitation of surprise. "But why would—"

"Forget it. I know who you are, *Genevieve*—so whatever you're trying to sell, I'm not buying. Now, get up."

She stayed where she was. Probing the back of her head, she winced and dropped her gaze. "I will. It's just—I'm a little dizzy."

He took a threatening step forward. "Now."

She flinched and threw up her hands. "Okay, okay!" Brushing the hair out of her eyes, she gave a defeated sigh and reached up for assistance getting to her feet.

Normally he'd have taken a step back and left her to deal on her own. But not only were her lips trembling again, but her outstretched hand was suddenly shaking, too.

With a faint, exasperated sigh of his own, he reached down. Her delicate palm slid across his calloused, much larger one. Yet the instant he tightened his grip, damned if her other hand didn't swing up and clamp around his wrist. With surprising strength for such a little bit of a thing, she threw her weight backward, yanking him forward at the same time she drew up her legs and lashed out.

She was quick, he'd give her that. Luckily, however, he was quicker. He threw himself sideways, and instead of her boot heels catching him in the groin as she'd obviously intended, they thudded heavily into his right thigh.

The blow caught him squarely in the femoris muscle and hurt like hell. Off balance, he stumbled, his leg twanging as if comprised of overstretched guitar strings.

It was all the advantage his adversary needed. Giving him one final kick, this time in the knee, she rolled away, sprang to her feet and bolted toward the trees.

"Son of a bitch." He couldn't remember the last time

he'd lost his temper, having learned early on to regard intense emotion of any kind as the enemy.

Yet suddenly he was on the verge of being genuinely pissed.

He tore after her. Catching up with her handily, he snagged the neck of her parka in his fist, then set his feet and yanked, jerking her off her feet.

"Let go of me! I'm warning you—" Twisting, she struck out at him, and damned if one of her flailing hands didn't connect with a glancing blow to his mouth.

If he'd been Gabe, he probably could've soothed her with a few reasonable words. If he'd been Dominic or Cooper, he most likely could've charmed her into submission. But he had neither a gift for reassurance nor a way with women and he was sick and tired of being used as a punching bag.

"That's *it!*" Ducking his head, he caught her by the thighs and tossed her over his shoulder.

This can't be happening, Genevieve thought, kicking and squirming as her captor strode effortlessly through the snow. It wasn't right. This big, scary-looking stranger with his hard body and shuttered eyes couldn't just appear in her life, overpower her and drag her back to Silver.

Somebody obviously forgot to tell him that, though, because that seems to be exactly what he's doing. And you can pummel and threaten him all you want, but he's still going to be able to overpower you.

It was clearly time to change tactics. She was no match for him physically, which meant if she was going to have a chance at escape, she was going to have to outwit him—easier said than done when she was hanging upside down, the blood rushing to her head, her stomach jouncing painfully against his hard shoulder with every step.

She thought hard for a moment, then blew out a breath, forced herself to quit struggling and went limp.

Nothing happened for what felt like an eternity. Finally, however, she felt the faintest hesitation in her adversary's long, effortless stride. "You all right, Bowen?" he asked.

"No." Sounding weak and pathetic didn't require any effort. "If you don't put me down, I'm going to lose my breakfast."

Darned if he didn't shrug, lifting and lowering her with a hitch of his shoulder as if she weighed nothing. "Tough."

"But—"

"No." He paused for a beat. "And if you get sick on me, you're gonna regret it."

His low voice held just enough menace that she believed him totally. Even so, he couldn't really expect her to control something like that—could he?

Deciding she'd prefer not to find out, she swallowed. Hard. "What—what's your name?"

He was silent so long she didn't think he was going to answer. Finally, he said, "Taggart."

"Is that your first name or your last?"

"Just Taggart's all you need to know."

Nobody was ever going to accuse him of being a chatterbox. She gulped as he hefted her a little higher. "Okay, Just—" She started to call him Just Taggart, then thought better of it. Antagonizing him more than she already had couldn't be wise. "Listen, please? I'm not rich, but whatever you're getting paid, I'll double it if you'll let me go."

"No."

"Then how about if you just put off taking me back for say…a week?" Surely she could find a way to escape in that space of time. "We can stay here. You'll still be doing your job, but I'll pay you, too, and I've got lots of supplies and—"

"No."

"Then what about a day? Just one day. Surely twenty-four hours can't matter—"

"Not gonna happen, Genevieve." Without warning, he dumped her on her feet next to the truck. Towering over her, he gave her a quick once over, his ice-green eyes impossible to read. Then he caught her by the shoulder and spun her around. "Now shut up, keep your hands where I can see them and spread your legs." Planting a palm between her shoulder blades, he gave her a nudge.

She had barely enough time to throw up her hands and brace herself against the fender before his big, hard hands were on her. They skimmed impersonally down her arms and skated over her back, breasts and sides, then slipped downward to explore her legs and thighs.

Humiliation painted her cheeks with fire as he patted her hips, then gave a huff of satisfaction as he encountered the car keys she'd zipped into her coat pocket. Before she could voice a protest, he took possession of them, then resumed his exploration. By the time he finished, she was shaking all over from the indignity of his touch.

"Okay," he murmured, reaching around her to open the truck door. "Get in."

"But my things—"

"Are in back where you left them."

"But I can't just leave!" She twisted around to face him. "What about the cabin? The fire's going and I've got groceries sitting out and—"

"I'll arrange for somebody to come and close things up."

"Okay, but—but we really shouldn't take the truck. The heater's shot and the brakes aren't reliable and the lights don't always work and it'll be dark soon—"

"No sweat. My rig is parked on the next track south."

"But—"

"Enough." The look he sent her was frigid enough to flash-freeze boiling water. "You can babble until hell freezes over, but I still plan to be back in Colorado— with you in custody—this time tomorrow. Got it?"

She thought about Seth, about his threat to confess rather than allow her to forfeit her own freedom and felt a spurt of desperation. Surely there had to be some way to reach this man, some way to change his mind. "I know you have a job to do, but you have to understand. I can't go back. Not yet."

"Oh, yeah. You can. You are."

"Please! Just listen. My brother's innocent. But if you take me back, he'll feel obligated to try and protect me and—"

"Get in the truck, Bowen." He took a step closer, the toe of one big boot bumping her smaller one.

It took every ounce of her courage, but she stood her ground. "Damn it, Taggart, if you'll just listen—"

"No." With a speed that was surprising for a man his size, he caught her under the arms and boosted her onto the seat. Then he gripped her right arm with one hand, reached under his coat with the other and the next thing she knew, he was slapping a handcuff around her wrist.

"Don't!" She tried to twist away but it was too late as he snapped the other bracelet around the door handle. "Surely that's not—"

"I don't like surprises when I'm driving."

Frightened, furious, she watched helplessly as he slammed the door and headed around to the driver's side of the truck.

Think, she ordered herself as he slid the seat back as far as it would go to accommodate his mile-long legs and climbed inside.

Taking a firm grip on her emotions, Genevieve turned to face him. "I don't have much money, most of it went to pay for Seth's attorney, but you can have my house. I'll sign it over. My business, too. I'll—I'll give you anything you want. Just name it."

For a moment it was as if he hadn't heard her. Then he abruptly twisted on the seat and leaned over so that only inches separated them. His cool compelling gaze slid from her hair to her eyes to her mouth, then flicked back up. "Anything?" His eyes gleamed dangerously.

He was so close she could see each individual inky whisker shadowing his cheeks, as well as a faint, razor-thin scar that cut through one corner of his hard, unsmiling mouth.

Her stomach dropped and what was left of the moisture in her mouth dried up. She told herself not to be a fool, to say, "Yes, of course, whatever it takes," but

when she parted her lips, the words wouldn't come out.
"I—I—"

His head dipped even closer. Swallowing hard, she
squeezed her eyes shut, her heart slamming into her
throat as his hair—cool and unexpectedly soft—tickled against her cheek.

Then he abruptly straightened and she felt the pressure as he dragged her seat belt across her waist. Her
eyes flew open as he jammed the end into the clasp with
a distinctive click.

He sent her a mirthless smile as their gazes meshed.
"Yeah. I didn't think so. Which is just as well, since the
only thing I want from you—" he fastened his own seat
belt and slapped the truck into Reverse "—is your word
that you won't give me any more trouble."

Embarrassed, insulted, affronted, disgusted—Genevieve couldn't decide what she felt most. "Go to hell."

He gave a faint sigh. "Too late. Already been there,
done that," he murmured. Depressing the clutch, he
backed the vehicle out of its slot. He shifted, straightened the wheel and began to guide the truck down the
narrow, tree-lined track that led to the road.

The deer came out of nowhere. One second there
was nothing in front of them but an unobscured ribbon
of white. In the next, a rangy young stag bounded
squarely into their path, its dun-colored hide seeming
to fill the entire windshield.

"Watch out!" Genevieve cried as Taggart wrenched the
wheel to the left. He hit the brakes and the old Ford
bucked wildly, fishtailed across the snowy ground and
slammed driver's side first into an enormous ever-
green tree.

Taggart's head hit the door frame with a sickening crunch.

Genevieve watched with a mixture of awe and horror as he slumped, his big body suddenly as limp as a rag doll's. *Dear God, what if he's dead?*

Fast on the heels of that thought came another. *Dear God. What if he's not?*

Three

Taggart surfaced slowly.

As he did, several things seemed noteworthy. One was that his head felt as if a stake were being driven through it.

The other was that somebody—a woman, judging from her soft voice and even softer hands—was touching him. "Come on now," she murmured, her husky voice tickling along his spine while her fingers sifted featherlight through the hair at his temple. "It's time to quit fooling around. Wake up now. I know you can do it."

She knew he could do it. Her faith gave him pause. The first and last female to unswervingly believe in him had been his mother. Yet he knew damn well that the woman murmuring to him wasn't Mary Moriarity Steele.

She smelled entirely different, for one thing, like sunshine and soap instead of lavender and baby powder. Plus her hands were smaller and her voice was lower. Besides, his mother had been gone…

How long? Drawing a blank, he struggled to punch through the fog hazing his brain. For a frustrating moment his mind remained shrouded and sluggish. Then the knowledge abruptly bubbled up.

Twenty years. She'd died twenty years ago last month, the anniversary of her passing falling on the day after his thirty-third birthday.

What's more, with another burst of returning memory he knew that it was Genevieve Bowen who was showing him such gentle concern. He recognized her voice at the same instant the recollection of tossing her over his shoulder and heading for her truck came rushing back at him. Yet after that… Nothing.

He didn't have a single, solitary doubt who was to blame.

Marshaling his strength, he opened his eyes. He felt a perverse flicker of satisfaction as his quarry—hell, no, his *prisoner*—sucked in a startled breath and jerked back, snatching her hand away from his face.

"Genevieve." Even to his own ears, his voice sounded raspy.

"You're back."

"Yeah." He blinked, tried to make sense of the timbered ceiling above his head and failed. With a prickle of uneasiness, he realized he was lying on a bed in a room he'd never seen before.

"How do you feel?"

He told himself to focus. Okay, so his brain seemed

to be a few cards short of a full deck and he had a son of a bitch of a headache—so what? He'd survived worse. He concentrated on what he did remember and tossed out an educated guess. "The truck. There was an accident."

"Yes." She nodded. "There was a deer. In the road. You swerved to avoid it and hit a tree."

"I knew that," he lied. "What I meant was—how long have I been out?"

"You don't remember?"

"No."

A spark of something—it looked a lot like compassion except he knew damn well that couldn't be right—flared in her eyes. "You've been in and out, but mostly out, the past hour. And in case you're wondering, you're in the cabin. My great-uncle's cabin."

Of course. He glanced around, taking note of the comfortable-looking furniture, the fire dancing cheerfully behind the glass doors of a big stone fireplace, the stretch of windows looking out on the jagged Montana peaks stabbing into the sky. Bringing his gaze back to her, he wondered how she'd managed to get him inside, given that he was twice her size, then decided there was a different question he was far more curious about. "And you're still here...why?"

She was silent a moment, then gave a dismissive little shrug. "You took a pretty nasty knock to the head. I couldn't just go off and leave you. Not until I was sure you were okay."

Yeah, right. Pollyanna reputation or not, she wasn't stupid and *nobody* was that good-hearted. More likely she was tired of being hunted and, having finally come

face-to-face with what she was up against—that would
be *him*—had realized the futility of continuing to run.

Then again, she'd saved him a boatload of aggrava-
tion by hanging around. If she wanted to pretend she
was Doris Do-right, what the hell did he care? He inclined his chin a fraction, ignoring the ensuing howl of
protest from his aching head. "Thanks."

"You're welcome." Even as she took a step back,
putting a little more distance between them, an uncer-
tain smile kissed the corners of her full mouth.

He scowled as part of him that was unapologetically
male whispered *pretty*. Reminding himself sharply that
she was his assignment, not his date, for God's sake—
and he never mixed his personal and professional
lives—he stared expressionlessly at her. "Don't get the
wrong idea," he said flatly as he carefully pushed himself upright. "You're still my prisoner and I'm—*what
the hell?*"

Something heavy was dragging at his arm. He
sensed Bowen moving even farther away as he glanced
down, confounded to see that a handcuff was locked
around his left wrist. What's more, the adjoining stainless-steel bracelet had been threaded through the end
links of a heavy chain that had been passed around the
end support of the massive built-in bed frame.

He was trapped like a wolf in a snare.

Ignoring the pounding in his head, he didn't think but
acted, launching himself at his one chance at freedom.

He was within inches of grabbing her when it
dawned on him that instead of bolting the way she
ought to be, his nemesis was holding her ground, and
a warning shrieked through his brain.

Too late. Unable to check himself, he reached the end of his tether and was damn near jerked off his feet.

The handcuff cut into his wrist. His arm felt as if it was being ripped from his shoulder. Then his momentum snapped him around and his head exploded in agony.

Gritting his teeth against the howl crowding his throat, he staggered back the way he'd come, braced himself against the bed frame and sank down onto the quilt-covered mattress.

So much for his luck having changed, he thought savagely. With a snap of her fingers, Lady Fortune had snatched away success and turned him from victor to casualty, from hunter to captive.

It was a road he'd traveled before, he reminded himself. Under far worse circumstances, with far graver consequences.

But he wasn't going to think about that. It was over. In the past. Beyond his reach to change. He needed to focus on the here and now. On Genevieve.

Locking firmly onto that single thought, he squeezed his eyes shut and forced himself to hold perfectly still as he waited for the worst of the pain to pass.

Enduring, after all, was what he did best.

"Here." Genevieve set the pill bottle and the glass of water on the nightstand, all the while keeping a wary eye on the big man hunched on the bed. "This should help."

Mindful of the terrifying show of speed and strength he'd put on just minutes earlier, she quickly stepped back out of reach. And waited.

Nothing. He continued to sit perfectly still, head slumped, eyes shut, broad shoulders rigid.

"It's ibuprofen. My first aid book says that's okay for someone in your condition."

Still no reaction. With an inner shrug, she decided that if he wanted to imitate a boulder there was nothing she could do about it. She'd give it one more try; then she was done.

"If you think a cold compress would help, let me know. The fridge hasn't been on long enough to make ice, but there's plenty of snow outside." Silence. "Hokay then, J.T." With a shrug, she started to turn away. "I'll just give you some space—"

"Don't call me that."

Turning back, she found his gaze fixed on her, his eyes hooded and impossible to read. "What?" Her response was automatic even though she knew perfectly well what he was referring to.

"J.T.," he gritted out. "Don't call me that. I don't like it."

For a second she was speechless. Of all the things she might've expected him to object to, her flippant abbreviation of Just Taggart wasn't even on the list. Still, given that she had the upper hand, she supposed she could afford to be gracious. "All right. Plain old Taggart it is then." She felt a fleeting flash of amusement as she considered what he'd say if she called him by *that* acronym.

Moving carefully, and looking as if *he* hadn't smiled about anything in years, he reached for the pill bottle and thumbed off the cap. To her dismay, he proceeded to toss back considerably more than the recommended dosage. Setting down the water glass, he eased back farther on the bed, then sliced her a sharp look. "What?"

"I—nothing." She wiped the concerned look off her face, telling herself not to be foolish. He was a grown-up, and bigger than average, and if he wanted to suck down the entire bottle of pain reliever, it was none of her business. While she obviously hadn't been ruthless enough after the accident to shove him out of the truck and abandon him to his fate, she was neither stupid nor naive enough to think anything had changed.

He was her enemy.

A crucial little fact she couldn't afford to forget, she reminded herself, turning away. Sure, she was lonely. Sure she was dying to talk openly to somebody. And yes, the sight of anyone injured or hurting tended to trigger what Seth had always claimed was her overdeveloped nurturing streak.

But she'd be grade-A certifiable, lock-me-in-the-asylum-and-throw-away-the-key crazy to let down her guard even an inch where the man on the bed was concerned.

And it wasn't only the risk he posed to her freedom, his obvious mental toughness, killer physique or ability to handle himself that she found so threatening, she mused as she walked over to the kitchen and began methodically putting away the groceries.

No, there was something else, some intangible quality he possessed that made her feel off balance and not quite herself. Something that tugged at her senses and alarmed her recently awakened sense of self-preservation all at the same time.

Uh-huh. That's called the thrill of danger, the call of

the wild, Genevieve. Women have been drawn to dangerous men like moths to the flame since the beginning of time.

Add to that the fact that he wasn't exactly ugly and it was perfectly reasonable that he inspired such conflicting feelings in her. Not that he was pretty-boy handsome. Far from it. Along with that dark hair and those pale eyes, he had the strongly sculpted, slightly ascetic face of a medieval warrior.

But she wasn't attracted to him, for heaven's sake. She absolutely was not. Even if she'd met him under different circumstances—say, when he wasn't doing his damnedest to hijack her life—he was so far from her type it wasn't even funny. He was too big, too tightly wound, too…male.

Plus he had an air of watchfulness, of being apart, that troubled her. Most people had a need to be liked, to connect with others, to smooth their path through life with at least a pretense of mutual experience or interest.

Not him. He seemed walled off, although she had a feeling she didn't question that beneath that carefully controlled surface there were strong emotions at play. Perhaps that was why, even chained and hurting, he filled the cabin with his blatantly masculine presence, making her aware of him without ever saying a word.

Why even now, as she dragged a large cast-iron pot out of the cupboard, set it on the stove and busied herself with sautéing meat and chopping vegetables for the soup, she could *feel* him watching her. Just as she'd sensed him observing her earlier.

She gave a rueful little sigh. God. What she wouldn't

give for her earlier foreboding to have been caused by a good old killer squirrel, mutant or not.

Instead, she was stuck with a much more terrifying human male.

Of course, she supposed things could have turned out worse—far worse. She'd gotten incredibly lucky with that deer. And Taggart, for all his aura of imminent threat, hadn't hurt her despite having had plenty of opportunity, not even in retaliation when she'd struck him first. In all fairness, she supposed she had to give him points for that—and consider the possibility that he was more civilized than she imagined.

"You don't really think you're going to get away with this, do you, Bowen?"

Then again, maybe not. Despite her prisoner's uninflected tone, she recognized a threat when she heard one. Which, she reflected, as she added a can of tomatoes, broth and seasonings to the meat, really did take an incredible amount of nerve given their respective situations.

"Do yourself a favor. Undo these cuffs. I swear I'll go easy on you."

Oh, right. Like she believed that. And even if it was true, what exactly did it mean—that he'd use velvet ribbon to truss her up when he delivered her back to Silver?

Rolling her eyes, she transferred the raw carrots and potatoes she'd sliced into the pot. She put the lid in place, turned down the heat on the burner and moved to the sink to wash her hands.

"Okay, I get it now. This—tying guys to your bed— is how you get your kicks."

She turned off the water and dried her hands. Surely she hadn't heard that right?

"Normally, I don't go for the Suzy Homemaker type. But I suppose I could make an exception. Of course, first I'd want to see you nak—"

She swiveled around. "Are you out of your mind? Are you *trying* to tick me off?"

Propped up against the headboard, his legs stretched out, he hitched his shoulders a scant half inch. "Got your attention, didn't I?"

"Oh, yes, you did do that." She gave a theatrical sigh. "And to think three hours ago I was actually pining for the sound of another human voice." She leveled her gaze at him. "So what is it you want to say that I just have to hear?"

"How long do you plan to keep me chained like this?"

"That depends."

"On what?"

She gave a little shrug. "A variety of things. Your health. My mood. Whether you persist in making any more objectionable personal comments."

One level black eyebrow rose. "Is that a threat?"

"More like a promise," she said sweetly.

"What am I supposed to do when I need to use the facilities?"

"Bathroom's right there." She indicated the door some four feet down the wall from the bed. "The chain will reach."

"What are you going to do?"

"There's a half bath up in the loft. Not perfect, but it'll do."

He started to scowl, then appeared to reconsider. "Look, my offer still stands. End this now, let me take you back and I'll make sure the judge knows you co-operated."

"How generous of you. But I think I'll pass. You may not understand, but as I tried to explain earlier, I don't care what the judge thinks—not about me. It's my brother who matters."

"Damn it, Bowen—"

"You know, if I were you, I really wouldn't swear at me. What's more, I'd at least *try* to be nice. Otherwise, I may forget to tell someone where you are once I'm gone."

His face hardened. "Sorry, sweetheart, but I'm not buying. If you meant to take off and leave me to rot, you'd have done it earlier. You're going to have to come up with a better threat than that."

"I don't think so." She came to a sudden decision. So he thought he could predict her behavior, did he? Well, maybe he could as concerned this particular issue—damn him—but that didn't mean she had to make it easy. It would do his character good to worry a little for a change.

Grabbing her parka off the hook near the door, she slid it on, checking her pocket to make sure the keys to his rig were still in it. "I guess I'll see you later. Or then again—maybe not."

"What the hell's that supposed to mean?" he demanded.

She smiled without humor and scooped up her purse. "You think you know everything. Figure it out." Her hand on the doorknob, she glanced back at him over her shoulder. "Oh, and just so we're clear? I wouldn't sleep with you if you came dipped in chocolate."

Without looking back, she flicked him a wave and sailed out the door.

Four

Gripping the bathroom doorjamb, Taggart glanced narrowly at the silvery twilight rapidly fading beyond the cabin windows.

Terrific. Just frigging terrific. It was getting dark and there was still no sign of Bowen.

He walked unsteadily to the bed and sank gingerly down on the edge. Careful not to jar his head, he unlaced his hiking boots and slid them off, then lay back and stretched out, letting himself stew as he scowled up at the plank ceiling overhead.

Not that he was worried. At least, not much. While he still didn't buy the concept that anyone could be as pure of heart as she was reputed to be, he was confident little Ms. Genevieve was coming back—and for reasons that had nothing to do with her supposed concern for his health.

She had, for example, gone to considerable effort putting together whatever was simmering deliciously on the stove. Why do that if she didn't plan to return to eat some of it? It sure as hell wasn't as if *he* could reach it, he thought, trying to ignore the pathetic way his mouth was watering in reaction to the rich, savory aroma.

What's more, there was no way she would've taken off without the duffel bag and the box of books that were currently parked by the door, which she must've hauled in from the truck while he was in la-la land. It would also be reckless and stupid of her to have left so late in the day without a plan—and from everything he'd seen so far she was plenty smart.

By now, she was bound to have figured out it would be a day or two before anyone would expect them to show up in Silver. It wouldn't take much additional brain power for her to realize that even when they were a no-show, an alarm most likely wouldn't be immediately raised since he was so obviously not the kind of guy to tolerate a short leash.

Which was why the prudent thing for her to do would be to remain at the cabin and take some time considering her next move.

The alternative—that she'd taken off for good—was unacceptable.

Because, damn it, he'd already searched every inch of space he could reach and hadn't found a thing he could use to pick the lock on the handcuffs. Just as he'd tested each chain link as well as the bed frame for weakness and scored a big fat zero.

So if Bowen didn't come back, short of gnawing his hand off he'd have no choice but to wait to be rescued.

The mere thought of *that* set a nerve ticking in his jaw. And not just because of the obvious humiliation factor. Or that his brothers were guaranteed to give him serious grief the second they learned he'd let an amateur—and a woman at that, for God's sake—get the drop on him. Or even because he'd be forced to start the hunt for a certain annoying little brunette all over again.

No, what was really going to rankle was that he'd have no one to blame for her decision to run but himself.

So what if he had a monster headache? So what if the past three months had been beyond frustrating? Who gave a rip that being at someone else's mercy seriously teed him off? Or that it was a well-known fact, at least in his portion of the universe, that he sucked at charming chitchat.

Only a freaking idiot would antagonize his jailer without a specific goal or a damn good reason.

Yeah, but that's precisely what you did, Ace. And you might as well admit that what really pushed you over the edge was Bowen herself. Face it. There's just something about her that rubs you the wrong way.

The ache in his head ratcheted up a notch and with a stab of impatience he realized every muscle in his body was as tightly strung as a trip wire. More than a little exasperated—control, after all, was his middle name—he blew out a pent-up breath and ordered himself to get a grip.

Okay, so being around her made him feel…itchy. As

if his skin was too small for his body. And for some in-explicable reason, probably because the blow to his head had temporarily disconnected a wire, he kept getting unwanted flashes of the way she'd felt against him, all small and soft and perfectly curved, when they'd wrestled in the snow earlier.

It didn't excuse the fact that he'd screwed up. That he'd flat-out failed the first rule of Hostage 101, which was to make your captor see you as a fellow human being. Worse, he'd let his mouth get ahead of his brain and gone out of his way to antagonize her.

And now all he could do was wait—and reflect on his numerous and varied mistakes.

So that when Bowen did return—and she *would,* by God—he'd be ready to make nice, to channel some of his brothers' winning ways with women and try to forge a bond between them, however slight.

But then, slight was all he needed. His goal, after all, wasn't to become her best friend or her lover. It was simply to get her to stick around long enough for him to regain control of the situation. To regain control of her.

He didn't have a doubt in the world he could do it. God knew, he'd faced far tougher situations doing recon missions in Afghanistan. And while the make-friends, play-nice-with-others thing wasn't going to be easy, nothing that mattered ever was.

Besides, it wasn't as if he had to share his life story with her. Or talk about anything he cared about. Like being banished as a kid to Blackhurst. Or the disaster at Zari Pass, which had put an end to his military career—and been the last time he'd allowed anyone to call him J.T.

No, his personal private business could, and would, remain just that. Personal and private.

All he had to do was be nominally civil. To offer Bowen—no, *Genevieve,* he admonished himself—the proverbial olive branch until either she lowered her guard enough for him to get the drop on her or he figured out how to free himself. As for payback…he'd see to that later.

For now, all he needed, all he wanted, he thought, finally giving in to the hammering in his head and letting his eyes drift shut against the fading light, was for this frigging headache to take a one-way hike.

And for Genevieve to be predictable for once and walk back through the door.

Nighttime fell like a heavy ebony cape.

Caught midway along the track that led to the cabin, Genevieve slowed the pickup to allow her eyes time to adjust to the swift slide from hazy dusk to inky darkness.

Despite the choppy rumble of the engine, she could hear the wind as it surged restlessly through the towering evergreens around her, making the snow-shrouded trees sway like uneasy ghosts. Overhead, a pack of marauding clouds took ever bigger bites out of the sky, obliterating the moon and swallowing stars a constellation at a time.

A shiver skated down her spine. She tried telling herself she was just chilled—she hadn't been kidding earlier when she'd told Taggart the truck's heater didn't work, and in the past ten minutes her fingers, nose and toes had started to go numb—but she knew that wasn't all it was. There was simply something spooky, a sort of bone-deep dread, that came with being alone in the dark, surrounded by an untamed wilderness, with the threat of a storm lurking in the wind.

Add to the cold and the declining weather the fact that she was tired, as much from the stressful events of the day as the three-mile hike through the snow she'd made to complete her errand, and it was no wonder she was ready to get back to the cabin.

Even if that meant having to share space with one John Taggart Steele. Whose complete name she now knew courtesy of the registration in his rig, which she'd confirmed by finally taking a look at the ID in his wallet, which she'd liberated when he'd been unconscious.

Not, she told herself hastily, that she cared what he called himself. Except for a mild curiosity about his aversion to being referred to as J.T, which, as it turned out, really were his initials, it was no skin off her nose if he went by Bozo the Clown.

What did matter was her discovery that he and the firm he worked for carried the same name. It might not be a hundred percent proof-positive, but when factored in with his relentless, self-assured personality, it made her strongly suspect that he was a principal in the enterprise rather than simply an employee.

If that was true, it was good news for her since it meant he had not just power but autonomy, and that made it a lot less likely anyone would be checking up on him anytime soon or expecting him to report in regularly.

It wouldn't be smart to count on it, however, she reflected as the truck shuddered over the last rise and the cabin came into sight. Grateful that she'd had the fore-sight to switch on the stove and porch lights before she left, she drove down the shallow hill and parked, mus-cled open the badly dented driver's-side door and headed inside, his lightweight pack slung over her shoulder.

No, she was a firm believer in hoping for the best but doing whatever was within her power to make things go her way. Which was why, she thought, as she climbed the cabin steps, retrieved the distributor cap from her pocket and dropped it with a satisfying thunk behind the wood pile, Taggart was going to have to make a trip to the auto parts store in the near future if he wanted his big black SUV to run. Of course, first he'd have to find it in the abandoned barn where she'd hidden it.

Stomping the snow off her boots, she said a sincere thank-you to the book gods for *Alan's Guide to Auto Engine Basics*. Then she pushed open the door and stepped inside, mentally straightening her spine as she braced to go another round with her less-than-charming captive.

To her surprise, no sarcastic remark greeted her re-turn. Instead, except for the faint hiss and pop of the fire, the dimly lit room was eerily quiet.

Her heart stuttered. In the space of time it took her to toss away his pack and pivot toward the bed, her imagination conjured the worst possible scenario: Tag-gart had somehow gotten loose. Any second now he was going to explode out of the shadows, wrap his iron-banded arms around her and yank her against his big, hard-as-steel frame—

But no. *No.* Relief sucked the starch right out of her as she made out the solid, long-legged shape sprawled on the bed. Locking her shaking knees, she fought to regain her composure, only to abandon the effort as fear for her safety reluctantly gave way to concern for his well-being.

She felt a stir of alarm at his continuing silence. Driven to make sure he was still breathing, she crossed the room and crept as close to the bed as she dared. To her gratification, from her new vantage point she could see his chest in his gray flannel shirt rising and falling as steadily as a metronome.

The breath she hadn't known she was holding sighed out while her legs once again went as weak as spent flower stems. In need of a moment to regroup, she marshaled her strength and prepared to step away and leave him to sleep.

Before she could do more than think of retreat, up snapped Taggart's eyelashes—thick, black as the night outside and the only part of his angular face that could possibly be described as soft looking—and then she was trapped in the pale-green tractor beam of his eyes.

"Hey." For all the intensity of his gaze, his voice was as rough as a weathered board and more than a little groggy. "You're back."

"Yes."

He glanced beyond her toward the darkened windows and frowned. "What time is it?"

"A little past seven."

"Huh." He raised his unfettered hand and she prepared to lunge for safety, but he only scrubbed it across his face. "Feels later."

"It's been a long day."

"Yeah. I noticed." His hand fell away and something she couldn't define flickered in his eyes. "You had me worried."

She wondered what he expected her to say. *I'm sorry?* Not a chance. *Good, it serves you right?* Well, that might be closer to the truth, but it wasn't in her nature to gloat. Even if he so richly deserved it. She gestured toward the pack she'd deep-sixed near the door. "I brought your things."

His gaze flicked over, took note, came back again. Speculation flashed across his face, but he didn't say anything.

She cleared her throat. "How do you feel?"

"You really want to know?"

"I wouldn't have asked otherwise."

He hiked himself higher on the pillows and gave a slight shrug. "Except for my vision being blurred, my stomach churning and my head feeling like the Green Bay Packers used it for a practice ball, I'm terrific."

Well, great, she thought with a sinking feeling. He'd just described all the things her first aid book listed as indicative of a concussion. Although, the upset stomach *could* be the result of the megadose of pain reliever he'd recklessly gulped earlier....

"How about you?"

She gave a start of surprise. "How about me what?"

"You okay? No worsening aches or bruises, that sort of thing?"

"I'm fine."

"Okay. I just…" He glanced away, clearly unwilling to meet her gaze and gave another dismissive little shrug. "Somebody I once knew said the same thing after a car accident. And then… It turned out later she had some internal bleeding."

He sounded so cool and detached he might have been commenting on the weather. So why was she suddenly certain that the outcome for the "she" in question hadn't been good? And that beneath his tough-as-nails, don't-give-a-damn exterior the incident still haunted him, at least a little?

Because you're a bleeding-heart romantic with a vivid imagination, Gen. A sucker, as already noted, for anyone even the slightest bit wounded.

Uh-huh. More likely she was just a sucker, period. Because the chances were excellent that he was simply making the whole thing up, creating a fictitious person and a fictitious event in an attempt to get to her. Just as he was feigning concern for her well-being in hopes that she'd make a misstep he could use to his advantage.

And if he wasn't?

Well, that didn't matter either, she told herself firmly. Whatever the truth, she strongly doubted he'd welcome her sympathy, and she certainly didn't want *his*.

"I'm fine," she said again, turning her back on him and walking away. Tugging off her gloves, she shed her parka and hung it up, then sat down on the ottoman next to the sofa to divest herself of her boots. "Look, I realize you may not feel like it—" she pushed to her stocking feet and padded into the kitchen "—but would you be willing to try to eat something? I mean, I'll understand if you're not up for it, but it might help settle your stomach." Lifting dishes down from the cupboard, she glanced at him over her shoulder.

"I can give it a try." Shutting his eyes, he rubbed gingerly at his temple.

Well, great. Here she was, trying to ply him with food to prove that he was well enough that she could take off in the morning with a clear conscience, and he had to choose now not only to be a good sport but actually to show a hint of weakness. Annoyed, she concentrated on ladling soup, steadfastly ignoring the clink of chain behind her that was followed by the slap of the bathroom door.

Seconds later, as she was rummaging around for a tray, she heard the toilet flush, followed by the sound of the faucet coming on. Pushing the hair off her forehead, she glanced around just as Taggart reappeared, his shirtsleeves rolled up, water dotting his rugged face. Standing there, he seemed to dominate the room in a way that had nothing to do with his size.

And that was why—the only reason why—her throat suddenly felt dry.

She swallowed. "You all right?" She waited as he sat back down on the bed, stuffed a pillow behind his back and leaned against the headboard before she started toward him with his food.

"Yeah."

She stopped while she was still well out of reach. "Look, I'm just going to set this on the end of the mattress, okay? I strained the meat and vegetables out of your soup, so it's just broth, but it's still hot. One false move and you'll be wearing it, understand?"

"Relax," he rumbled. "I'm not up for a wrestling match." His gaze flicked from her to the tray she slid his way with its helping of broth, soda crackers and

7-Up, and back again, and a sort of resigned exasperation that she didn't understand flashed across his face.
"For now, anyway."

Shaking her head—he really was the most perplex-
ing man—she got her own food and carried it over to
the couch.

To her surprise, she was suddenly ravenous. Grateful for once that Taggart wasn't much for small talk, she
applied herself to the hearty soup and thick slice of but-
tered French bread she'd fixed for herself.

Yet as much as she tried to pretend she was alone in
the room, she couldn't completely shake her awareness
of him. Which was why she knew to the second when
he was done, even before he picked up the tray and
stood.

She looked up warily as he approached.

Coming as close to her as the chain would allow, he
set the tray on the floor and gave it a shove in her direction with his foot. "Thanks," he said gruffly. "That
was good."

"You're welcome," she murmured, feeling a twinge
of surprise at his display of manners. Glancing up into
his hooded green eyes, she once again found herself
wondering about him.

Where did he live when he wasn't terrorizing fugitive booksellers? Was he single, divorced or—she felt
an inexplicable little pang—married? Did he have kids
or other family? Did he *ever* smile?

Finishing the last spoonful of her soup, she watched
him retreat, then retrieved the tray, added her dishes to
it and hauled everything over to the counter.

She frowned as she saw that he'd eaten every scrap

she'd served him. Suddenly wondering if maybe he felt well enough for more but pride wouldn't let him ask, she swiveled around, only to find him perched on the edge of the bed, unbuttoning his gray flannel shirt. She watched, mesmerized, as the shirt parted down the middle, then gave herself a sharp mental shake. "What are you doing?"

"Getting ready for bed." He shrugged out of the garment, exposing the sleeveless black tank beneath. The dark color was the perfect contrast to the gold-tinted olive skin stretched over an acre of to-die-for muscle that bunched and flexed with his every breath.

She swallowed. "Already? It's only eight." She wasn't sure why she was protesting; she was tired, too.

"Yeah, well, if you have to know, my head hurts." He scowled at the flannel as it dangled from the chain by the right sleeve, then shook his head and slid it away.

"Oh." In contrast to his flat stomach and ridiculously narrow hips, both faithfully delineated by the clinging black knit, his shoulders looked immense. "Of course."

"Don't worry." Oblivious to her sudden paralysis, he carefully stood and stripped off his jeans, exposing an impressive length of hairy leg between his gray wool socks and black BVDs. "I promise not to slip into a coma and die in my sleep."

Oh, God. She hadn't even thought of that, she realized, as she tried—and failed—not to stare at the impressive bulge straining the front of his clingy cotton briefs. "No. Certainly not."

To her profound thankfulness, she managed to drag her gaze away a heartbeat before he glanced her way and gave her a critical once-over of his own. His eyes, the color of new leaves in the room's soft light, narrowed. "You look beat. I'd suggest you get some rest yourself."

Their gazes meshed and for an instant she saw her surprise at his concern mirrored in his face. Then his expression closed like a slamming door and he looked away.

"Or not. Doesn't matter to me one way or the other."

His abrupt change of attitude was like a bucket of ice water, snapping her out of her distraction with his physique. A sharp retort rose to her lips, but before she could get out so much as a single word, he flipped back the covers, climbed into bed and turned his back.

Shaking her head, she walked over to the closet, yanked down the sleeping bag and extra pillow and carried them over to the sofa. Killer bod or not, she thought, as she dug her nightshirt out of her bag, Taggart was, without doubt, the most impossible, arrogant, exasperating man she'd ever met.

If she were a different kind of woman, she'd be out of here so fast tomorrow morning the draft would probably blow him against the wall.

Whether he was better or not, she mused as she washed her face and brushed her teeth in the kitchen sink.

It was therefore beyond annoying that when she climbed into her makeshift bed, she couldn't make herself forget her first aid book's warning that the first twenty-four hours after a head injury were crucial. Although she could probably safely cut that time in half for Taggart, who was harder headed than anyone she'd ever known. In the meantime, however...

She threw off the covers and climbed back out of bed to set the oven timer for two hours. In the meantime, she supposed she had no choice but to keep an eye on him.

Slipping back into the sleeping bag a moment later, she switched off the light and tried to settle into sleep. Only to have Taggart's image—bare legged, broad chested, unmistakably, blatantly male—promptly muscle its way into her mind. She fought to cast it out, but like the man himself, it obstinately refused to leave.

She huffed out a heartfelt sigh.

It was going to be a long night.

Five

Taggart jolted awake.

Muscles flexed, he braced for attack, his heart pounding painfully in the half second before reality rushed in and he remembered where he was.

The mountains. Montana. In a cabin. With Genevieve.

He sagged back against the mattress. Squeezing his eyes shut, he willed away the images crowding him of another ink-black night, of another set of mountains in a country half a world away, where he'd found himself in a nightmare from which there'd been no escape.

Don't go there, he ordered himself. Think about something, anything else. The trip to Africa you've always meant to make. How pissed Dom is going to be when he finds out there's a Steele Security pool on how long it'll take him to make us all uncles. Or—what the hell—think about…Genevieve. Even she has to be a better choice than anything that pertains to Dominic's sex life.

Genevieve. Who, judging by the kitchen clock that showed it was coming up on 2:00 a.m., would soon be joining him for what would be the third of their bedside encounters tonight.

"Taggart?" she'd whisper, after she tumbled out of bed and flipped on the light above the stove so she could see to switch off the trusty oven timer. "You awake?"

"Oh, yeah," he'd answer, having learned the hard way that ignoring her would earn him a jab with the broom.

"Do you know who you are? Where you are?"

"Yeah, Genevieve, I do." Suppressing a sigh, he'd rattle off the desired information since he'd also discovered she wouldn't leave him alone until he did. It was galling to admit, but it really did seem she was hell-bent on doing what was best for him. And since somewhere in one of her damn books she'd read that periodic checks were necessary to ensure he didn't slip into a coma, interrogating him every few hours appeared to be her mission for the night.

Even though it was obvious she was exhausted. That she was finding it harder as the hours passed to shake off the steadily increasing cold. Although he supposed, in light of her persistent death grip on the broom, that at least part of the reason for her shivering might be that on some level she sensed the growing danger of poking at him as if he were a caged bear.

Oh, not for the reason she no doubt supposed—that as adversaries, for one of them to win the other had to lose. Although that was true.

But because the longer he lay in the dark and the more tired he became, the greater the likelihood that sometime in the next few hours she was going to startle him out of a sound sleep.

And God help them both, he couldn't predict how he might react or what he might do, whether in a moment of sleep-fogged confusion he might surge up off the bed and go for her throat…. That uncertainty was why he always slept alone, and always kept more than one light on. It was the same reason he'd forced himself to accept that he'd never marry. Much less find the sort of blazing happiness Dom and Lilah had—

The timer sounded, shattering the silence. Even though he'd expected it, he couldn't stop the way his pulse spiked and his muscles jumped. It was a testament to the deteriorating state of his nerves, he realized. His gut twisting with self-disgust, he shifted onto his side and latched onto the only distraction available.

With a rustle of fabric and a harsh whine of her sleeping bag's metal teeth, Genevieve emerged from her cocoon on the couch. Backlit by the glow from the fireplace, her hair gleamed, as shiny as a child's. There was nothing childlike about the body momentarily revealed in silhouette as she stood, however. The upward tilt to her breasts, the lissome curve where her waist nipped in, the delicate dip at the small of her back that flared into a tight little rear end that would fit perfectly in his hands….

"Taggart?" Yawning, she pushed the thick, silky tendrils of her hair off her face and glanced in his direction.

Unsure why he did it, except that the sight of her and the undeniable response of his body made it even harder to decide what to do about the situation, he closed his eyes and feigned sleep.

He sensed more than heard her sigh. Then came the muted thump of her feet as she crossed the floor, the click of the oven light and the merciful return to relative silence as she switched off the buzzer.

Except for his slow, measured breathing, he lay perfectly still.

"Hey, come on." He heard the faint swish as she picked up the broom, felt the air around him stir at her approach. "Say something."

He forced himself not to react to the gentle poke in the shoulder.

"I know you're awake." She was quiet for a moment, then prodded him again moving closer. "Damn it, Taggart, this isn't funny." The first faint note of panic sounded in her voice. "It's cold out here and—"

Without warning, he snatched at the broom handle and yanked.

He wasn't sure who was more surprised. Him, since he didn't know what he was planning to do until he did it. Or Genevieve, who was so stunned she forgot to let go until it was too late.

With a startled shriek, she toppled forward into his waiting arms. There was a second's stunned silence as they lay face-to-face, bodies intimately nestled together, gazes locked.

A second after that, she started to struggle, kicking

and thrashing and letting him know in impressively graphic terms exactly what she thought of him.

Face set, Taggart took it as long as he could. Then, not knowing what else to do, he took a grip on the chain, rolled her beneath him and silenced her the only way he could.

Catching her flailing hands, he pressed them into the bed, lowered his head and covered her mouth with his own.

Genevieve gave a choked cry as Taggart molded his hard lips to her softer ones. His big, muscular body was hot and heavy as he pinned her to the bed, and there was no doubt, as he hitched himself higher and increased the heated pressure against her mouth, that he was all man.

Whatever she'd expected, it wasn't…this. Never in her wildest dreams would she have imagined someone so closely guarded could kiss with such reckless abandon.

But oh, he could. And though his embrace was raw and unyielding, it was also the most exciting thing she'd ever experienced.

Are you out of your mind? she asked herself hazily. You barely know him. And what you do know, you don't like. And even if you were the sort of woman to jump into bed with a big, brooding, disagreeable stranger, this one should be your very last choice.

Chained and injured, he was a threat. Up close and on the mend he was guaranteed trouble.

Yet as she'd already acknowledged, her fear of him wasn't physical. And really, what could he do? The key to the handcuffs was across the room in her pants pocket.

She told herself she ought to resist anyway. She should press her lips together, hold herself rigid, avert her head, do whatever she could to make it clear she didn't want this or him.

Except…it would be a lie—and she knew it. Which she proved when he slid his hands from her wrists to entangle their fingers, and instead of trying to escape, she held onto him with all her strength.

She could tell herself anything she chose, but the fact was her body was on fire. Hard as it was to admit, she'd never wanted anyone the way she wanted John Taggart Steele.

The realization was staggering. Stupefying. Sex had never impressed her much. Her first time had been quick, awkward and had left her feeling exposed, empty and dissatisfied. A handful of subsequent encounters hadn't been much better. When her last experience had ended with a very nice man regretfully informing her she lacked whatever it took to achieve satisfaction, she'd swallowed her hurt and humiliation and decided he was probably right.

She'd certainly never believed herself capable of the kind of breathless need that was blowing through her now like a hurricane.

But oh, wonder of wonders, she burned to wrap herself around Taggart and soak him up. She ached to stroke and taste, to burrow even closer. She wanted—oh, how she wanted—to explore every hot, powerful inch of him.

Never had she been so aware of a man. With his weight bearing down on her, she could feel the ridges of his washboard abs, the slabs of his pectoral muscles, the sinew roping his heavy thighs, the thick, solid proof of his arousal.

She probably ought to be alarmed by all that hot flesh and blatant masculinity pressed against her.

Instead, she felt a fierce gratification. And a desperate desire to experience more. Much more.

The realization stole what was left of her breath along with the last of her caution. When the tip of his tongue seared the seam of her mouth—probing, promising, demanding—she parted her lips and drank him in.

He groaned and thrust his tongue deeper. He tasted darkly exotic, his sheer, overpowering maleness as foreign to her as uncharted territory. Her head went light, as if she'd just chugged a bottle of champagne. For the first time in her life she understood the term *drunk with desire,* as deep down at her core, a liquid flame sparked and caught fire.

Desperate to touch him, she tugged, trying to liberate her hands.

She heard his breathing hitch, felt a tremor rack the big hard body molded to her own. Then, without warning, he released her and rocked up on his forearms, the abrupt movement sliding his cotton-covered arousal along the slick, aching cleft of her sex. "Shit." He jerked away.

Her eyes flew open. Staring up at his shadowed face, she saw his jaw clench and his lips compress and realized in an instant of absolute clarity that he'd misinterpreted her attempt to free herself. For a moment she couldn't think what to do. And then from somewhere came an answer: Take a chance. Show some courage. Tell him what you want.

Latching on to the advice, she reached up, buried her fingers in the cropped thickness of his hair and tugged. "Don't stop," she whispered, skimming her fingertips over the hard planes of his face. "I want this. I want *you*." She stroked the pad of her thumb across the unyielding line of his lips. "Please."

"You don't know what you're asking for," he said flatly.

"You're wrong." It was her first, her only, lie. "I know exactly."

"No. You don't. Trust me."

"That's just it—I do. I trust you to give me what I want. What I need." Guided by desperation, her fingers found their way under the hem of his shirt. She looked directly at him as she drew her hands up the firm, hot flesh of his back.

She explored the sleek muscle that bracketed his spine, then pressed her fingers into the glorious breadth of those velvet-over-steel shoulders. Slowly, languidly, she worked her way down, kneading gently when she reached the small of his back.

He gazed impassively down at her. Her stomach clenched as she realized she didn't have a clue what was going on behind the guarded green of his eyes. Dampening her kiss-tender lips, she tried once more to get through to him. "I want you. Don't make me beg. Please, John."

He flinched at her use of his name. He stared at her for a long, endless second, then a nerve jumped in the hollow of his cheek. "Damn you, Genevieve," he rasped as his control shattered like a dropped pane of glass.

With a savage curse that would have frightened her

under any other circumstance, he rolled away and off the bed. Towering over her in the darkness, his body outlined by the glimmering firelight, he tore off his T-shirt, swore briefly as it got hung up on the chain, then abandoned it to shuck off his underwear.

She barely had time to feel her stomach jump with nervous anticipation before he was on her. Dragging her up, he yanked her nightshirt over her head and tossed it away. Then he laid her down, pinning her in place with his free hand splayed lightly across her throat.

"Is this what you want?" He lowered his head and his mouth whispered like molten fire along the vulnerable underside of her jaw. "*Is it?*"

"Yes." She swallowed, stunned anew by how incredibly exciting it was to be touched by him. "Oh, yes."

"Yeah, well… We'll see about that." Despite his sardonic tone, he was exquisitely gentle as he brushed his lips down her throat and nuzzled the notch of her collarbone, then plunged lower.

She gasped as the cool silk of his hair tickled the undersides of her breasts. She gasped again as he slipped his hands under her, gripped the mounds of her bottom and lifted, the chain making a clinking noise with the movement.

Squeezing her eyes shut, she shivered as his lips grazed the hollow of her hip. "Your skin's so damn soft." He nuzzled her, unhurriedly exploring her with his mouth as he made his way toward her navel, then zeroed in on the shallow indentation and pressed a single suggestive kiss to it.

When he finally lifted his head to stare up at her with hot-eyed intensity, her whole body was throbbing and she was shivering violently—and this time not from the cold.

She felt...dazed—by the way he seemed to regard her as a feast to be savored, by his continuing display of bone-melting patience. By her body's riotous response.

He slid higher, dragging his metal tether in his wake and cupped her breast. His long fingers felt deliciously hot against her cooler flesh, and delight flared along her nerve endings. She felt poised on the edge of something big even as she tensed, expecting him to squeeze her already throbbing nipples.

A jolt of surprise rippled through her as he lowered his head and gently rubbed his beard-roughened cheek against her instead. Surprise quickly transformed into excitement as he licked a path along the tender crease where her breast met the top of her midriff.

Enthralled, mesmerized and just a touch alarmed by the power of the wave of need crashing through her, she wondered what unexpected thing he'd do next.

She didn't have to wait to find out. Shifting, he unhurriedly moved higher to trace a circle around her aching nipple with his tongue.

A rough sound of pleasure rumbled in his chest. With infuriating slowness he dampened the pebbled crest, then blew a soft stream of air over the supersensitive area. He paused as she inhaled sharply, leaned in, gently raked her with his teeth.

Then he clamped his mouth around her straining flesh and sucked. Hard.

Her world exploded. Back bowing, she dug her nails into the solid anchor of his hard shoulders and held on for dear life as pleasure pierced her like a thunderbolt. "Oh, oh, *oh!*"

Taggart couldn't believe it. He felt Genevieve coming apart, heard the shocked surprise in her voice as the climax took her, and his own body quivered like an overstrung bowstring with the need for release.

She was just so damn responsive. All her little moans and whimpers and shakes and shivers were making him wild—and that was before the stunning discovery that he could make her come just by feasting on her pert, pretty breasts.

He knew he wasn't going to be able to wait much longer to be inside her. But he also knew that if he didn't rein himself in, didn't take some time to get a firmer grip on the need pounding through him, he could hurt her, and he was damned if he'd take that chance.

He blew out a breath as her body finally quieted and she slumped back onto the mattress like a rag doll. Releasing the velvet plumpness of her nipple, he ignored the greedy urge to knee her thighs apart and plunge himself deep into her slippery tightness.

Fighting for control, he shifted onto his side, thrust the chain out of his way, propped himself on one elbow above her and prepared to drive himself crazy just a little longer, telling himself he couldn't go wrong with kissing her.

He started to lower his head, only to check his movement as her eyes opened.

"Oh." She stared up at him, her gaze luminous. "That was…" She exhaled shakily. "That was wonderful, John."

The last time he'd been called by his first name he'd

been thirteen; he'd stubbornly seen to it that it was buried along with his mother. Oddly enough, however, now that he was past the first shock, it sounded right coming from Genevieve's lips.

Yet he couldn't bring himself to say so. Couldn't imagine admitting that for reasons he didn't understand she'd been able to blow past the defenses he'd spent two decades perfecting.

It seemed better just to concentrate on the physical. Safer. Smarter. "We're not done." His voice sounded rough, even to him.

"No." She ran her hand up his arm, rubbed her palm against his biceps.

"So tell me what you want. What else turns you on." Her hand stilled. She wet her lips. "You."

"Me what?"

"You. You turn me on. I never…I didn't expect—" As light as a whisper, she trailed the tip of her index finger down his cheek. "More than anything—" Her hand shook almost imperceptibly as she sketched the shape of his upper lip "—I want you inside me."

Five words. Five mind-blowing little words and his hands—hands that could defuse a bomb without a quiver, hold a rifle rock-steady and take out a target hundreds of yards away while he was taking enemy fire—shook.

His vaunted control vanished like smoke on the wind.

He took her mouth, and she opened for him, meeting him eagerly as his free hand swept down her silky, delicately curved body into the narrow triangle of curls between her legs.

She was as soft there as she was everywhere else. Cupping that warm, feminine mound, he thrust his tongue into the honeyed sweetness of her mouth at the same time that he parted her satiny folds. Settling the broad tip of his finger on the wet nub at the seat of her desire, he stroked.

She made a keening sound and he echoed it with a low guttural one of his own. Yet somehow he managed to keep his touch light as he stroked again and she bucked, straining against him.

The blood was racing through his veins like a river at flood tide. Sliding his arm beneath her, careful to keep the handcuff away from her satiny skin, he snugged her torso against his own, relishing the feeling of her tightly budded nipples pressed against him. The position gave him greater freedom to move and he put it to good use, rubbing her now with a tight little circular motion. When she moaned, then moaned again, he slid his middle finger deep into her clutching, quivering heat.

She tore her mouth free of his. "Oh! No. No! I can't. I—oh!" She gulped a desperate draught of air as her head fell back and her body exploded, her tight inner muscles clamping around him.

All that slick, snug heat milking his finger demolished his restraint.

Breathing as though he'd just run ten miles uphill flat-out, he centered her beneath him and settled his hips between her thighs. Then he rocked up on one arm, guided himself into place against her and pushed.

Genevieve couldn't contain a slight cry at the squeezing fullness of that first broad inch. She was

small; he absolutely wasn't. Still she felt far more pleasure than discomfort, far more excitement than appre-
hension at his possession.

She hadn't lied. She wanted him. She just hadn't
known, hadn't ever envisioned, that sex could be like
this. That she could want, no, need, to have a man—to
have John—buried deep inside her and find that she
wanted even more.

She felt him hesitate and wrapped her legs around
him, locking him in place. "Don't stop. Don't. Stop."
Though it took all of her strength with his weight resting against her, she rocked her pelvis, propelling him
forward.

That slight movement shoved him over the edge.

With a rumble of sound that seemed to be torn from
somewhere deep inside him, he gave up the fight and
drove deep until he was socketed to the hilt inside her
tight, quivering depths.

Genevieve forgot to breathe as he withdrew, then
pushed into her again, and her body stretched to accommodate his rigid length. Despite the enormous pressure,
the promise of pleasure shimmered on the horizon in a
golden haze that danced just beyond reach as he settled
into a steadily escalating rhythm.

She arched against him, cradling him with her arms
and legs, and felt the tension ridging his big body. She
felt the sweat sheening his shoulders and the flex and
bunch of muscle in his broad back as he abruptly shifted
forward, balancing his weight on the arm sporting the
handcuff. He slipped his other forearm under her hips,
lifting her up and deepening the angle of penetration
even more.

She cried his name as his pubic bone bumped against her, stunned to find she had a frantic craving to be touched just there, like that, with exactly that grinding pressure. Gripping his hair with shaking hands, she kissed him, long, hard, wanting everything he was, everything he had to give.

They strained together, hips pumping, hearts pounding, bodies slick. Her heels drummed the back of his thighs as he rocked her higher and higher, hammering into her. She heard a distant, muffled sound and vaguely realized it was him. That he was saying her name, over and over.

The orgasm slammed into her, an eruption of pleasure that started small, deep where they were joined, and radiated outward, robbing her of breath, blanking her mind, sending out wave after wave of melting sensation, making her body quake.

She felt John thrust harder, faster, felt him above her, around her, buried deep inside her, and then he was driving toward his own satisfaction, his hips pistoning like a pile driver. She heard him cry out, felt him shudder and jerk and instinctively she bore down, stunned as she was slammed with another rush of pleasure.

He collapsed against her, crushing her into the bed. Clinging to him, she sobbed for breath, trusting him as she'd never trusted anyone else in her life to be her anchor and keep her safe.

Six

"I'm sorry." Scrubbing at the tears streaking her face, Genevieve swallowed audibly as she slowly opened her eyes. "I don't know what's wrong with me."

Lips compressed, Taggart stared down at her, careful to keep his expression blank. Outside, the weather had deteriorated. Wind buffeted the cabin, making the timbers sigh and creak, while sleet clicked against the window panes like a legion of skeletal fingertips.

It had nothing on the turbulence swirling inside him.

The waterworks had started just minutes after their mutual, mind-blowing climax. Oh, Genevieve had done her best to hide it, not making a sound except for an occasional shuddery breath.

But twined together the way they were like two strands of the same rope, there'd been no way to miss the way her shoulders shook. No way to overlook the warm slide of her tears on his skin as she clung to him, her face buried in the crook of his neck.

It cut. Unexpectedly deep. Clearly, he'd hurt her. Which shouldn't be such a big surprise given that she was half his weight and stood no taller than his shoulder. Yet that hadn't stopped him there at the end from totally losing control.

No, not *losing* it, damn it. That somehow implied his actions had been unintentional. There'd been nothing the least accidental about the way he'd kicked his control to the curb and stomped it to paste because he'd been in a fever to bury himself deep inside of her.

And Genevieve—who'd nearly stopped his heart with the inexplicable gift of herself—had paid the price. She'd been so small and tender and tight and he'd been too big, too impatient, too rough.

Oh, yeah, he thought grimly. His fault. Proof once again that he wasn't a man to trust.

Although, when he stopped to consider, part of him was of the opinion that, given the reason they were there together in the first place, she damn well should have figured that out for herself.

Yeah, well—if she didn't get it before, she does now.

Yet guilt still pricked at him. Frustrated—with himself, with the entire situation—he peeled her hands from his neck, shifted the damn chain out of his way and eased onto his back, putting some much needed distance between them. "I'm the one who should apologize," he said stiffly. "I never should've touched you."

"What?" Her response was punctuated by a watery little hiccup.

"I hurt you." He stared sightlessly into the dark. "I'm sorry."

"No. *No.*" He froze, caught completely off guard as she swiped one more time at her eyes, then twisted onto her side, propped herself on her elbow and scooted right back up against him. "You didn't hurt me. Absolutely not."

"Yeah, right."

"No, really—"

"Uh-huh. You always cry after sex," he said caustically, doing his best to ignore his body's brazen response to the warm curves plastered against him. "There's just something about coming that makes you feel all weepy and sentimental—"

"I never had an orgasm before."

The quiet statement shocked him into silence. Forgetting himself, he turned his head to stare at her and felt something deep inside him flinch as he saw the tears still clinging to the sweep of her eyelashes.

He was damned if he knew what to say.

Another blast of wind shook the cabin. In the time it took before it darted away, twin apples of color had stained her cheeks. Averting her eyes, she gave a weary little sigh, then surprised him all over again by settling trustingly against him, resting her cheek on his shoulder. "I thought…I couldn't. That there was something wrong with me. And then tonight, with you, everything changed. I guess it just got to me."

Totally at a loss, he cradled his arm around her, not knowing what else to do.

"I'm sorry," she went on. "I didn't mean to worry you."

She didn't mean to worry him. God. How was he supposed to respond to *that?*

Well, that was easy. *Don't say anything, dumbass. Do the woman a favor and blow her off. Tell her you were glad to be of service, but now that the fun and games are over it's time to get back to reality.*

And the reality was, he wasn't her friend and God knew he'd rather have burning splinters shoved under his fingernails than be her confidant. So the best, the only thing to do, was tell her to get the hell away from him while he was still in such a benevolent mood.

"Trust me, there's absolutely nothing wrong with you, sweetheart. Except that the guys in your past were incompetent morons." *Sweetheart?* Holy mother of mercy. Where had that come from? And why should the idea of somebody else touching her all of a sudden make his jaw tight?

"Maybe," she said uncertainly.

"No maybe about it."

"Unless—"

"What?"

"Maybe it's just…you." She was silent a moment, as if considering her own words. Then she raised her head and pressed her lips to the underside of his jaw. "Thanks," she said softly.

Alarm rumbled through him. It seemed no matter what he did or said, he just kept making things worse. If he didn't shut up *now,* she might actually get some twisted idea that he was worth caring about or something.

And if she knew the first thing about him, she'd realize that nothing could be further from the truth. "Forget it," he said brusquely. "Just…try to get some sleep, okay?"

She pushed up on her elbow and stared down at him. "But—"

"Look, this isn't open for discussion. You're sleeping right here, with me, tonight. The sound of your teeth chattering earlier annoyed the crap out of me, and I'm not about to give you another chance to poke me with that damn broom. So just shut up, close your eyes and let's call it a night." Tightening his arm around her, strictly to underscore his words, he pulled her back down to his side, ignoring the aches and pains in his bruised muscles that were once again making themselves known. "There's not much time left before daylight gets here anyway."

Wisely, she kept her mouth shut and resettled her head on his shoulder. They lapsed into a silence which, if not exactly companionable, was still a hell of an improvement over the sound of him babbling things he was sure to regret in the morning.

Taking a firm grip on the excess of emotion roiling around inside him, he did his best to relax. He doubted he'd sleep, but he could at least try to rest.

"John?"

"What?"

"Do you think we could pull the covers up? I'm starting to get a little chilled."

She wasn't just starting, he realized, as he felt her shiver and realized her skin had grown cool to the touch. Feeling grim all over again, he shifted her away from him, rolled onto his side, then pulled her back into the cradle of his body and yanked the covers up to her chin.

"Better?" he said gruffly.

She spooned her round little butt into his lap and rested her silky back against his chest. "Yes."

That made one of them happy, he thought, inhaling the faintly flowery scent of her hair. Swallowing a sigh, he snugged an arm around her waist to anchor her in place and propped his cheek on his tethered arm.

"John?"

"*What?*"

"Just…thanks."

Oh, yeah, no doubt about it. When his time came, he was going straight to hell. "Get some sleep, Genevieve."

God knew, he wasn't going to.

Wrapped in the delicious heat of Taggart's arms, Genevieve drifted in a dream world between waning sleep and dawning consciousness.

Then the source of all that scrumptious warmth shifted, bumping the part of himself that was exclusively male against her thigh and she was catapulted into full awareness.

Her stomach jumped. No way had she dreamt *that* up.

Cautiously, she opened her eyes, greeted by a flood of gray-white morning light. To her bemusement, she realized the satiny cushion under her cheek really was the bulge of muscle padding the underside of Taggart's arm. And that the muscle-ridged expanse of bronze rising and falling inches from her face was his chest and not that of a Michelangelo statue come to life.

Warily shifting her gaze downward, she saw that their legs were indeed tangled together.

Unable to help herself, she studied him *there,* taking a good long look at the masculine anatomy framed by a cloud of jet-black hair. Its shape was exotically different from her own. Even in sleep it looked substantial, and, as she now had good reason to know, Taggart certainly knew just what to do with—

Heat slapped her cheeks. She squeezed her eyes shut, but there was no retreat as the ribald thought tripped a floodgate in her mind, spilling memories into it of the previous night.

She saw herself clinging to Taggart like a vine to a trellis. She recalled her explosive response to the greedy pull of his mouth on her nipples. She remembered explicitly what it felt like to have those big, hard hands on her and those long, clever fingers inside her. And even if she lived to be ninety, she'd never forget the incredible sense of being irrevocably claimed that had come as he'd pushed himself into her, making them one.

A tangle of need, desire and longing reignited inside her, making her heart thump in the back of her throat. It was hard to believe that a mere twenty-four hours ago she hadn't known such feelings existed, much less made the acquaintance of the man who'd inspired them. It was equally difficult to accept how quickly she'd come to crave both Taggart and the pleasures he'd taught her.

Yet most illogical by far was her realization that, for the first time since she'd walked into her home and found Seth with a gun in his hand, standing over his best friend's lifeless body, she actually felt safe.

That wasn't merely foolish; it was dangerous. She might have been forever changed by last night's events, but her situation remained the same. She didn't think for a minute that Taggart was going to wake up this morning, announce he was quitting his job and demand she run away with him to Tahiti.

No, whatever destination she settled on in the next few hours, she'd be making the trip alone.

Still, one way or another, she *was* leaving. Just as soon as she could put together some food for him and collect her things.

She staunchly ignored the unexpected squeeze of her heart, assuring herself its only cause was the thought of all the stunning sexual fulfillment she'd never experience now.

It had nothing to do with the idea of cutting herself off from the man who'd provided it. After all, there was always a chance she'd eventually find someone else with whom she would share such electric, stomach-hollowing chemistry.

Even if based on her past history she highly doubted it.

Even if before this her sexual experiences had never even come close to what they'd shared last night.

Even if she felt repelled by the mere thought of being with anyone but John.

She shook off her misgivings, reminding herself that the only thing that was one-hundred-percent certain was she couldn't stay here. Because if it was hard to leave him after just one night, what would it be like after two, three or four? If she felt this sort of connection to him in the wake of a few hours spent sharing the sheets, how would it feel to get acquainted to the point where they actually made love?

It didn't bear thinking about it.

So she wouldn't. *That* at least—refusing to dwell on what was beyond her reach and getting on with her life because she had no other choice—was something with which she had experience.

She forced open her eyes, then blinked as she saw with more than a little fascination that the part of Taggart that had initially inspired her soul-searching was now more impressive than it had been before.

Her pulse quickened. Easing her head back, she shifted her focus to his face—and found herself staring straight into his limpid, jade-colored eyes. To her surprised relief, they were still clouded with sleep.

She took the opportunity to study their owner. Without his usual guarded expression, he looked younger, she decided. Younger, more approachable—but not a jot less masculine. From his rumpled hair to the beard shadowing his cheeks to the hard play of muscle that flexed with his every breath, he was the embodiment of all things male. Just looking at him made her feel quivery inside. "Hey," she said softly.

His heavy-lidded gaze flicked from her eyes to her mouth, lingered for the space of a heartbeat, then came back up. "Hey yourself."

His voice was morning-husky and tickled deliciously along her nerve endings. With a little jolt, she realized she no longer felt any fear when she looked at him. Oh, he was still a formidable opponent, and the knowledge that he was the one who'd be after her in the near future was scary without a doubt.

But when it came to the man himself… He'd more than watched out for her in the past hours, displaying a gruff gentleness, a near-tenderness, that was a direct contradiction to his tough outer shell.

Even though she knew she shouldn't, she surrendered to temptation. She leaned forward and pressed her mouth to his hot skin, slowly stringing kisses from his collarbone to feast on the pulse of his smooth, strong throat.

His skin smelled faintly musky and made her senses swim. By the time she finally lifted her head, she realized with a mixture of amusement and despair that her hands were shaking.

Good job, Genevieve. Why don't you make this even harder by torturing yourself with fresh reminders of what you're about to walk away from?

She blew out a breath, trying to resurrect her composure, then blew it out again in a little gasp as Taggart cupped the back of her head. "John—"

In one fluid movement he slid lower and silenced her by closing his mouth over hers.

She told herself it was just a kiss. Men and women all over the world kissed every day. Lips met and clung. Teeth nipped plump flesh, mouths parted, tongues tangled lazily, then thrust and retreated, kindling inner fires and evoking images of another type of invasion....

Her body flushed as want became need, making her ache for his possession. She tore her mouth away from his. "*No.* Don't. We can't."

He jerked back. "What's the matter?"

Her heart stuttered and her courage faltered as she saw the very real concern on his face. In that moment she wanted nothing more than to turn back the clock, resume their embrace, follow it to its natural conclusion. "I... That is—" She swallowed. "How's your head?" What on earth was she doing? Could she possibly make a worse hash of this?

He now appeared not simply wide awake, but unmistakably wary, as well. "It's okay."

"Good. That's good."

"It is, huh?" His eyes narrowed and every vestige of warmth slowly drained from his face. "Maybe you better tell me what's going on."

Clutching the sheet to her breasts like a shield, she shifted away from him and sat up, hating that she was about to end their fragile truce and make him angry.

She forced herself to meet his gaze squarely anyway. "Under the circumstances, it wouldn't be right for me— for us— I just can't take advantage of you this way. It wouldn't be fair."

His eyebrows winged up and something—disbelief, dismay?—flashed across his face, then was gone behind that controlled facade. He sat up, dragging the chain with him, and for a second his attention fixed on something beyond her before once more settling over her like an enfolding cloak.

He propped himself against the headboard and considered her, seemingly unaffected by both the cold and his own nudity. "Define circumstances," he said finally, after what felt like an eternity.

"Well...you're my prisoner." She made no attempt to evade him as he reached out with his free hand and skimmed his fingers down her arm. "You need to know, you have the right to know—" surely her next words would set him off "—that since you're so clearly okay, I plan to leave. Today." *While I still can.*

"Huh." Measuring his words, he slowly stroked his thumb over the pulse now pounding in her wrist. "And that's why we're sitting here talking instead of—"

"*Yes.*" Perplexed and more than a little unnerved by his reaction—or lack of one—she fought to keep her voice steady. "I'm leaving, John. And nothing you say or do is going to stop me." She flicked her gaze to the warm weight of his hand, then back to his face and lifted her chin. "I mean, obviously you can delay me for a while but you can't keep me by your side indefinitely. Sooner or later you're going to get hungry or sleepy or have to answer the call of nature and that'll be the end of it."

"You think so?"

"I know so. I wish—" She started to say she wished she could stay, then caught herself. Not only wasn't it strictly true, but it wouldn't change anything and he probably wouldn't believe her anyway. "Well, never mind that. No matter what I wish, I have to do what's best for Seth."

"And you actually believe defying the court, taking the law into your own hands, is it?"

"Yes. No." She raked a hand through her hair. "I don't know. But until something changes or I come up with a better solution, it's all I have."

Again, for a moment that stretched interminably, he simply stared at her. Finally, he gave a slight shrug. "Yeah, well, then I don't imagine you're going to like what I'm about to say. Because you're not going anywhere, Genevieve. Not today. Probably not tomorrow. Maybe not even the day after that."

Her stomach hollowed. Not certain if it was because

he was finally being unreasonable after she'd done her best to be honest—or the deplorable flutter of excitement she felt at the idea of being trapped in bed with him a little while longer—she did her best to ignore it. "Who's going to stop me, John? You?"

Again he glanced toward the far side the room, then deliberately released his hold on her and folded his arms behind his neck, ignoring the heavy chain as if it weighed nothing. "Nope." He inclined his head. "That."

Exasperated, she twisted around—and felt her stomach plummet.

Because beyond the windows, the world had been transformed into a sea of white. Snow fell in swirling, relentless sheets that choked the air, reducing visibility to zero as it blanketed everything in sight.

And try as she might, Genevieve couldn't see a single sign that it might let up anytime soon.

Seven

"So how come this place doesn't have a woodstove?"

Seated at the kitchen table, Genevieve gave a start of surprise. Except for a few unavoidable utterances of "yes," "no" and "thanks," it was the first time Taggart had spoken to her since she'd climbed out of bed, dragged on her sleep shirt and trudged to the windows to stare forlornly out at the snow more than nine hours ago.

In the interim, they'd both washed and dressed, shared a trio of meals and not much else.

Deliberately rattling the chain that still tethered him, he'd made the bed, brooded, exercised, stared at the ceiling, paced, brooded some more.

She'd reorganized the kitchen, hauled firewood, read an entire mystery cover to cover, hauled more wood and wondered how long it would be before the power, which had begun to flicker at midmorning, went out for good.

She'd gotten the answer an hour after dusk, she thought, glancing at the oil lamp providing her with light, one of three currently staving off the darkness. At least they had plenty of kerosene, a generous supply of food and enough heat from the fireplace to keep them alive, if not exactly toasty.

"There used to be a stove," she told him. "When my uncle was alive." Frowning in concentration at the piece of paper before her, she tucked one side of the blanket covering her legs a little tighter.

"So what happened?"

She felt the weight of his gaze like a touch. Reluctantly, she stilled her pen and glanced over at him.

And wished instantly she hadn't.

Half an hour earlier he'd embarked on his second exercise routine of the day, doing several hundred each of sit-ups, push-ups, ab crunches and the like at a bruising pace. One that would have put her in the hospital for sure, but had left him barely winded.

Now he sat sprawled on the floor, stripped down to his jeans, back propped against the bed, one long leg cocked. The ends of his cropped, inky hair were damp from exertion, the perfect frame for his compelling face with its straight nose, strong cheekbones and hard mouth. Sweat sheened his shoulders as well, gleamed on the hard planes of his chest and the sinewy ripples of his abdomen, while the lamplight tinted his skin to toasted gold.

Need punched low and deep, making her breath

catch and squeeze in her lungs. Appalled, annoyed, she
sat up a little straighter in the chair. What was it about
him that stripped away her usual defenses? What dark
magic did he possess that made her burn to scrub her
palms against the muscle bulging in his arms, to rub her
cheek against his chest, to sample the salt on his skin
with her tongue?

She didn't have a clue, so she jerked her gaze away,
returning it to the papers spread out on the tabletop.

"After my uncle died—" *come on, come on, get a
grip* "—this place became a summer vacation rental.
Apparently fireplaces are sexy and woodstoves aren't,
and the agency that manages things didn't feel there
was room for both. Luckily they allowed for a heat insert along with the glass doors; otherwise we'd be freezing our fannies off for sure."

"Huh."

She held her breath. When he didn't say anything
more, she relaxed just a fraction and picked up her pen,
hoping he couldn't see the tremor shaking her fingers,
praying he'd leave her in peace.

"What are you writing, anyway?"

Darn it. For a man who hadn't shown an inclination
toward conversation for most of time that she'd known
him, he was certainly chatty all of a sudden. Maybe if
she pretended to be too absorbed to hear him—

"A book? Your memoirs? *Genevieve's Life on the
Run?*"

Her mouth tightened. "A letter."

"To your brother?"

"No. A detective agency. In Denver."

"Why?"

"Because eventually somebody is actually going to listen to me and take a hard look at Seth's case."

He was silent just long enough for her to start to hope he'd taken the hint. And then—

"So you're…what? Contacting private investigators, asking them to take up your case?" His voice held a hint of incredulity he made no attempt to camouflage.

It was like a sharp jab at a raw wound. Her head came up. "I'm writing everybody. I have been for months. Police. Politicians. Attorneys. I'd write Oprah herself if I thought she could help."

"Is that what you meant this morning about waiting for something to change before you'll consider turning yourself in?"

She nodded. Although she didn't recall saying the words, she'd said a number of things earlier that day she hadn't exactly planned. "Yes. I suppose it is."

He pursed his lips. "And if someone does take that hard look?"

"Then they'll have to at least consider what I already know. That Seth's telling the truth. He isn't the one who killed Jimmy."

He started to shake his head. "Damn it, Genevieve—"

"Don't," she said sharply, coming to her feet. She was tired, cold and off balance from what they'd shared. Not to mention overwhelmed by her own unfamiliar emotions, and in no mood to be lectured, particularly by him. "You don't know anything about it."

He surged upright as well. "I know enough to be damn skeptical about your brother's version of events. He had means, motive and opportunity, and there's nothing in the police report to support his claim that he saw a stranger fleeing the scene. Which, just so we're clear, is a really lame defense, as anybody who's ever seen *The Fugitive* knows."

Ignoring the gibe, she stared at him in surprise. "You read the police report?"

"I do my homework. When it comes to finding people, Steele Security has a firm policy about not taking on ambiguous cases. We do the best we can to make sure we're not tracking down innocents and returning them to the bad guys."

"If you read the police report," she persisted, kicking the blanket out of her way as she came around the table to meet him face-to-face, "you know the gun was Jimmy's, not Seth's."

"So? Your brother knew where it was kept, had easy access and out of the three people at the scene—you, him and the victim—he was the only one with powder residue on his hands."

"That's because he took a shot at the real killer—"

"Yeah, right. Come on, Genevieve, you're smarter than that. Forget the one-armed man and focus on the gun. For your brother's version of events to work, James Dunn would've had to bring it with him to your house and conveniently surprise an intruder who felt compelled to confront him, wrest away the gun and shoot to kill. It makes no sense. There's no gain, no motive and absolutely no evidence—not a hair, not a single fingerprint—to support it.

"Seth, on the other hand, had a damn good reason for what he did. The money from Dunn's life insurance was just enough to save his precious ski shop. But he had to move fast since Dunn had come back from vacation with the news he'd met someone and they were getting married. Soon. At which time he no doubt intended to change his will and everything else, making his new wife his beneficiary."

"Are you finished?"

"Yeah, pretty much."

Words crowded her mouth, clamoring to be given a voice. She had at least a dozen things she wanted to say, a dozen facts she wanted to share, a dozen arguments she could make as to why he was wrong.

Yet staring at him, taking in the stubborn set of his jaw, she realized she didn't think she could stand it if he refused to listen. The only thing that would be worse was if he did agree to hear her out and then, like everyone else, flatly rejected the possibility that Seth might be innocent.

It would be a major blow. More, she thought, than she could handle.

She tried to tell herself she was being dramatic. That it was her exhaustion speaking, that she was having some sort of unprecedented overreaction to the events of the past forty-eight hours.

Yet she still couldn't risk it. At this moment in time, defying logic, defeating common sense, he mattered to her, and that was all there was to it.

"Well that makes two of us." Coming to a sudden decision, she turned on her heel, marched into the kitchen and blew out the lantern glowing on the counter. Swiveling, she backtracked to the table, jammed her nearly finished letter into the correspondence folder and snatched up the blanket.

"What the hell are you doing?"

"Going to bed."

"Now? We're not done—"

"I am. It's been a long day and I'm tired. I don't want to deal with this—" *with you* "—now." Her movements stiff with suppressed emotion, she leaned forward to snuff out the second lamp.

"Just leave it, all right?" Taggart said sharply.

Surprised at the vehemence in his voice, she jerked away. "Sure. Whatever." Unable to help herself, she turned to look at him, but his expression was closed, his gaze shuttered.

And just like that, the memory of how safe she'd felt in his arms the previous night came rushing back. Before she could get a grip, her lips trembled.

His mouth tightened. "Damn it, Genevieve—"

"Let it go, John. Please." Walking to the couch, she quickly peeled off her jeans and one of the two sweaters she had on over a thermal shirt. Then she extinguished the lantern on the end table, climbed into her sleeping bag and dragged it and the blanket up to her ears. "Just…let it go."

Closing her eyes, she curled up and prayed for the oblivion of sleep.

Taggart stared at the shadows cast by the glow of the lamplight as they danced gently on the ceiling above his head.

Outside, the wind still surged and gusted, but it had settled down from a constant howl to a whispered growl. Inside there was only silence, except for the occasional crackle of the fire and the soft ebb and flow of Genevieve's breathing.

Taggart's mind, however, was anything but quiet.

Thoughts clashed and emotions rumbled, twisting, tangling and battling for recognition as he tried to sort out what it was he was feeling. Yet when he boiled everything down to the basic facts, he found himself pretty much where he'd been for most of the day.

Genevieve found him sexually appealing. That he at least understood, since he felt the same for her.

It was the rest of it that kept hanging him up.

She believed he had "rights" that obliged her to be honest. She worried about being fair to him. She'd even insisted on forgoing pleasure because—he blew out a pent-up breath—she didn't want to take advantage of him.

And what had he given her in return? Great sex. Zero companionship. One minute of conversation and a brutal recap of all the reasons why she should doubt herself and abandon her brother.

Man, was he a prince or what?

He scrubbed his hands over his face and tried to wrestle things back into perspective. It wasn't as if he'd deliberately set out to be the world's biggest bastard, he reminded himself. Last night, at least when he'd first yanked her into bed, it had been with a vague but genuine desire to save her from potential harm.

He sure as hell hadn't planned what had happened next. But then, there'd been no way he could have foreseen such a simple contact sparking a blaze that would consume them both. And in his own defense, in what had probably been the only time in his life he'd actually deserved a medal, when it had seemed that she wanted him to stop, he had.

She'd been the one who'd thrown gasoline on the fire and caution to the wind.

She'd also made the first move this morning. It had been her mouth branding a trail up his chest, her lips nuzzling his throat, her soft little body lighting him up as she snuggled close. And yeah, presented with such an unmistakable invitation, he'd kissed her back and been fully prepared to do even more, but really—who could blame him?

He was a man, not some pious saint, and he'd spent half the night with her all over him like jam slathered on toast. Yet for the second time in less than a dozen hours, when she'd called a halt, he'd stopped.

If he had it to do over again, knowing what he did now, he'd be damn tempted to just kiss her senseless, bury himself as deep as he could get in her sweet, squeezing heat, and skip the whole incredible, mystifying, logic-defying conversation that had followed.

Because, sweet holy mother of God, just how the hell *was* he supposed to respond to a woman who, instead of taking a strip off him for taking advantage of her and then doing everything she could to keep him at arm's length, seemed dead set on looking out for him?

Well, here's an idea: Ignore her most of a day, then get right in her face and demand she admit her brother's a stone-cold murderer.

Okay, so maybe that hadn't been the best way to go. Although, according to every shred of evidence he'd seen, it was a slam dunk that Seth Bowen had killed his friend Jimmy Dunn.

Only Genevieve didn't think so. But then, that was hardly a surprise. If she'd give him, someone she'd known for a mere handful of days, the benefit of the doubt, then it was to be expected that she'd fight with her last breath for her brother. God knew, he'd do the same for any of his.

And yet... Would he give up his home, his livelihood, his reputation, his freedom, based on nothing more than blind devotion?

He didn't think so.

And from what he knew of Genevieve—smart, resourceful, overly responsible Genevieve, who had a moral code strong enough to dictate she stay and care for a wounded enemy rather than exploit another's misfortune and make tracks while she could—neither would she.

And that meant...what, exactly? He blew out a breath. Damned if he knew. Which, he supposed, went a long way toward explaining why he felt all tied up inside.

The swishing sound of nylon rubbing against itself whispered through the darkness. Gratefully, he pounced on the distraction, drawing back deeper into the shadows as one of the couch springs gave a groan and Genevieve unexpectedly sat up.

Smothering a yawn, she stood. After a quick glance in his direction, she crossed to the hearth, added a piece of wood to the fire, shut the glass doors and straightened.

Turning, she looked briefly toward the ladder leading to the loft, then glanced his way again. Appearing to reach a decision, she scrubbed her hands up her arms as she tiptoed across the room, past the bed and disappeared into the bathroom.

Well, hell. Now what?

Even as asked the question, he knew. Just as he knew that for once in his life he wasn't going to think it to death, weigh every last pro and con, try to calculate everything that could go wrong.

She had, after all, left a light on for him.

He was on his feet and waiting for her, his decision made, his resolve firmly in place, when she opened the door.

"Oh!" With a stutter of surprise, she took a half step back and clapped a hand to her heart. "God, John, you scared me. What are you doing up?" She sidled to her left, clearly intending to brush past him.

He mirrored her movement, blocking her path. "Get in the bed, Genevieve."

She jerked to a stop, her gaze flying to his face. "What?"

"You can be as mad at me as you want, but that's no reason to be stupid. It's cold and we've got a limited amount of firewood. It makes sense to share our body heat."

"Sense?" She took another sideways step. "I don't think—"

"Good." Again, he planted himself in her path. "Go with that."

Her head tipped back and her eyes narrowed. "Get out of my way."

"No."

She conferred a long, searching look on him, her gaze for once impossible to read.

He gave a faint sigh. "I'm not going to jump you, if that's what's worrying you."

At that, she lowered her head, ensuring he had no chance of getting so much as a glimpse of her expression. "I never gave it a thought," she said coolly.

His kitten had claws. Not sure whether to be annoyed or amused, he reached out, cupped her shoulder, nudged her toward the bed. "Go on then. Get in."

Her chin came up stubbornly, but the effect was ruined as she shivered, this time more violently than before. "Oh, all right. If you insist."

Shrugging away his hand, she stepped over the trailing chain, walked the few paces to the bed, ignoring him as he backed out of her way, continuing to bar her escape. She tossed back the covers, slid between the sheets and turned away, her face to the wall.

His mission accomplished, he peeled off his jeans and crawled in beside her. For half a second, he considered honoring the not-so-subtle request implicit in her ironing-board posture that he leave her the hell alone.

But nobody had ever accused him of being a sensitive, New Age kind of guy. With a ruthless directness that felt good after too many hours spent foundering in the quicksand of his emotions, he slung his arm around her and crowded close.

Her bare legs and the exposed curves of her butt were icy cold. Rather than recoil, he threw his leg over hers, sharing what warmth he could.

He did hesitate, however, if only for an instant, before he smoothed the thick, soft ends of her hair away from her nape, bent his head and settled his mouth there.

After all, the issue of where he'd be spending eternity was a done deal. And the part of him pressing against the curve of her firm little bottom was already as hard as an iron rod. But what decided the issue was the taste of her on his tongue, like sunlight and sweetness and the promise of summer to a man who'd lived with his soul's winter bleakness far too long.

Still, he had every intention of going slowly, of testing the waters, of backing off at the first sign of resistance.

But even before he began the slow slide of his parted lips toward her ear, she was twisting around, anchoring her fingers in his hair, deciding their fate with the soft cry of his name.

"John. Oh, yes." She pressed even closer at the same time as she arched her neck to provide him even greater access. "Yes."

Not gasoline on the fire this time, he thought, as desire scorched him. Rocket fuel.

Her back bowed as she strained toward him. It seemed the most natural thing in the world to slip his fingers beneath the layers of shirts she had on, slide his hand up the satin tautness of her stomach, over the sturdy bump of her ribs and under the band of her bra.

Both of them groaned as he rubbed his palm over the exquisite softness of her stiff little nipple.

Then they groaned again as she reached for him, skimming her hand under his waistband to close around his turgid length.

"Easy," he choked out. "We've got the whole night—"

"No." She measured him with a stroke of her palm that had him clenching his teeth. "*Now.* Now, now, *now.*"

Not rocket fuel, either. Nitroglycerine, explosive and volatile.

Breathing hard, arms and hands colliding, they hurried to strip away each other's clothing. He was easy; his briefs took a single slide and jerk. Genevieve's panties and various tops took longer, and he swore under his breath as he rapped himself in the elbow with the chain as he grappled with the clasp of her bra. Finally winning the battle, he tossed the flimsy undergarment away.

Before the strip of nylon and lace could hit the floor, she was straddling him, her silky thighs gripping his hips, her fingers digging into his straining biceps, her teeth grazing his throat. "Hurry, John. Hurry up."

Her urgency filled some deep, profound hunger he hadn't known he possessed. He wanted her, only her, in a way he'd never wanted anything or anyone else.

He felt her hands tremble as she cupped his face and then her lips were on his. The kick from that simple contact reverberated in every nerve and fiber of his being as her sweetness filled him, washed him clean, sustained him.

He slicked his hands the length of her back, down the satiny skin that covered the delicate curves of rib and spine, the bend of her waist, the swell of her hips.

She quivered beneath his touch. She rocked her pelvis with more instinct than finesse, rubbing herself against him, and the suggestion of what was to come made his vision dim. Bringing his hand around, he gently slicked the pad of his thumb along the valley of her sex.

She was wet, ready for him, and he—who'd always prided himself on his restraint—had none.

He needed this joining, needed her display of trust, needed *her*.

Needed. And took.

With a flex of his hips he positioned himself and thrust, sliding deep inside her.

He felt her clench around him, and wasn't sure which of them was more shocked as the first wave of pleasure ripped through her. Unprepared for her hair-trigger response, he still managed to catch her startled cry with his mouth.

Cupping the warm swell of her breasts in his palms, he squeezed her distended nipples with slowly increasing pressure and fought the urge to ravish her. Instead, although the effort had sweat beading across his nose, he forced himself to keep still, to let her ride the crest, ride him. Hearing her call his name, feeling her drive herself over the edge, holding her as she took the long, shattering fall to completion, he couldn't imagine how she'd ever thought herself passionless.

It seemed an eternity before she finally lay spent, her shuddering breath fanning his throat, her fingers slack on his shoulders.

"Genevieve." His voice was thick.

"Hmm?"

He pressed a kiss to her temple, smoothed a shaking hand over her hair. "Can you sit up?"

She didn't reply for a second, then slowly raised her head. "What?"

"I want to see you." Catching her by the shoulders, he pushed her upright, swallowing hard as he got his first good look at her face.

Her lips were passion-swollen, her cheeks flushed,

her hair tousled. But it was her eyes, heavy-lidded, opaque with pleasure and dark with wonder as she gazed down at him, that set the muscle ticking in his jaw.

He wasn't some callow kid. And though he didn't claim to understand it, there was a certain kind of woman who'd always seemed to find his very indifference a challenge, so he'd never lacked for sexual partners.

As he'd admitted to himself earlier, lust he understood. But this... He'd never looked at a woman and felt this kind of gut-twisting tenderness, much less this confounding compulsion to brand her as his own.

He felt his heart pounding, even before she reached down and touched her fingers to his mouth. "It's all right, John. It's all right."

He told himself there was no way she could know what he was feeling. Told himself, but didn't believe it. There was a connection between them, a bond, and for this moment in time, he was done fighting it. "Take me. Take all of me."

"Yes. Oh, yes."

Gripping her waist, he lifted her up until they teetered on the edge of separation, then brought her sliding down, his breath hissing out at the squeezing tightness.

Yet as good as it was, it wasn't enough. He needed more. He needed everything.

In a single, powerful movement he caught her to him and reversed their positions, keeping himself buried deep inside her even as he shoved the excess chain out of their way. Bringing his mouth down on hers, he kissed her with barely contained violence as he began to move.

He couldn't get close enough. Deep enough. Muscles straining, he drove forward and felt something inside him give way as she didn't simply welcome him, but rose up, met him stroke for stroke, and begged for more.

He lost it then, going wild, slamming against her, again and again, feeling as if the top of his head was going to blow off when the velvet glove of her body tightened and quivered once more, and she mindlessly cried his name.

The sound shivered through him, triggering a colossal landslide of his senses. His body exploded in a climax that blew him apart, turned him inside out.

Yet even as his strength deserted him and he collapsed into her cradling arms, some part of him recognized that what had just passed between them wasn't merely sex, but a mating.

Because somehow she seemed to have freed a portion of the heart that he'd walled off long ago.

Eight

Genevieve lay cradled in the curve of Taggart's arm, her head pillowed on his shoulder.

Despite the intensity of their lovemaking, she could feel the tension still thrumming through him. She wondered at its cause, but at the same time she understood him well enough to realize he was accustomed to relying on himself, on working through matters in his own time and way, and that it wouldn't be wise to push.

Besides, if he was feeling even half as unsettled as she was, his restlessness was understandable. Because something was happening between them, she thought, as she slowly stroked her fingers over the warm taut skin above his hip. Something beyond the powerful physical attraction that had them firmly in its hot-fingered grip.

And it was happening fast—too fast for comfort or easy answers. In the space of mere days they'd gone from being total strangers to sharing a connection that was as strong and elemental as the storm that had stranded them together. It was daunting and more than a little frightening, yet Genevieve could no more deny it than she could reverse the weather.

She could do something about the oppressive silence that lay over them like a smothering weight, however. "John?"

"Hmm?"

"How come you didn't tell me your last name was Steele the day we met?"

He tensed a fraction, but then to her gratification the muscle beneath her cheek noticeably relaxed. "No reason to mention it."

"Oh. So what are you saying? That you only share your name on a need-to-know basis?"

"Yeah. I guess I am."

"Good grief." She raised her head to stare at him. "What exactly is Steele Security? Some sort of secret society?"

Her faintly alarmed question pried a brief, rusty laugh out of him. "Not even close."

She waited for him to go on. When he didn't, she had to fight the urge to roll her eyes. He could give a clam lessons in being closemouthed. "Explain."

His shoulders hitched. "Not much to it. It's a family business now, a partnership with my brothers, that started when Gabe—he's the oldest—left the service. He took what he'd learned in SOCom—"

"SOCom?" She settled back against him.

"Special Operations Command. It's the part of the military that has to do with the special forces units, like Delta, SEALs, Green Berets. Gabe decided he'd take a shot at offering some specialized services to the private sector that regular law enforcement can't."

When he fell silent again, she gave his hard stomach a gentle poke. "Why not?"

"A variety of reasons. A lack of time, money, manpower. Jurisdictional restrictions. Turns out he hit a real nerve, and the work just poured in."

"But what do you do?"

"Risk assessment, security evaluations, providing short-term protection for personnel and structures, that sort of thing. Mostly it's pretty tame."

"And when it isn't?"

"It depends, but the riskier stuff tends to be case-specific—hostage recovery, protecting a high-value target, going after someone who's determined not to be found."

"Like me."

"I wouldn't exactly classify you as high risk, Genevieve." He couldn't quite keep a trace of amusement from creeping into his voice. "Frustrating, yeah, and definitely annoying. But not dangerous."

"Gee, thanks." Despite her tart reply, she wasn't able to contain a slight smile of her own as they lapsed into silence, listening to the wind as it darted in to rattle the windows before streaking away. She liked his rare flashes of understated humor, even when they were directed at her. "Just how long *have* you been chasing me?"

"A while."

This time she did roll her eyes, even though he couldn't see it. "Define a while."

He answered with obvious reluctance. "A few months."

"A few *months?*" It wasn't admirable, but she felt a certain satisfaction that she'd managed to elude him for so long without even knowing he was on her trail, and it showed in her voice.

"Yeah." He made an unmistakable sound of disgust. "You care to explain where you learned how to disappear like that?"

"Oh, come on, that's a no-brainer."

"Indulge me. Lately my brain seems to be lodged somewhere other than my head. At least the one above my shoulders."

"I own a bookstore. Hence, I learned from a book. You can learn anything if you know where to look."

"Jesus. I take it back. You *are* dangerous."

Delighted, she laughed. "Thanks."

With just the whisper of a touch, he rubbed the ball of her shoulder with his thumb. "So, you gonna complete my humiliation and finally tell me how the hell you got me inside after the accident?"

"Gosh, I don't know. I'm not sure it would be wise to give away all of my secrets—"

Without warning, he twisted effortlessly so that he was above her, her body caged by his arms. His gaze drilled into her. "Talk."

She bit her lip to prevent a smile, and then unable to help herself, reached up and cupped the side of his face, enjoying the prickle of his beard against her palm. "Isn't it obvious? I carried you."

"Uh-huh. You and what army?"

"Oh, all right. If you must know—" she did her best to sound put-out, which wasn't easy when he caught the pad of her thumb between his lips and sucked, making the breath jam in her throat "—you brought yourself in. You were only unconscious for a few minutes—"

"Long enough for you to find the key to the handcuffs and get loose," he murmured, eyes suddenly gleaming dangerously.

"—before you came around enough that I could get you to slide across the seat so I could back the truck up to the cabin. You were pretty out of it, so it took some work to keep you upright and pointed in the right direction, but the end result is that you walked in under your own power."

"And let you put my own handcuffs on me, like a lamb to the slaughter."

"Yes."

He was silent a moment. "Where'd you get the chain?"

"It was in the bed of the truck."

"Lucky for you."

"No, lucky for you," she countered matter-of-factly. "Without it you'd be on a much shorter leash."

Only inches apart, they stared at each other, the seconds slowly ticking past until, to her shock, the corners of his mouth quirked an entire eighth of an inch while the skin around his eyes crinkled a similar fraction. "Pretty damn pleased with yourself, aren't you?"

Not by the wildest reach of imagination could he be said to be smiling. Still, there was something in his look that made the heat rush into her cheeks—as well as a few other places—and set her stomach to tap-dancing. She swallowed, fighting the urge to throw her dignity to the wind and just grab him. "Yes. I suppose I am."

"Yeah, well…" He lowered his head and trailed his lips from her temple to her cheek to the edge of her mouth, watching her all the while "…maybe you deserve to be."

Pleasure made her heart thump in her chest. Then he slowly flexed his hips and sank his flesh into her welcoming wetness and her already tenuous restraint vanished like dust in the wind.

Wrapping him in her arms, she claimed his mouth and eagerly gave herself up to the melting pleasure she'd only ever known with him.

Sweet holy hell, Taggart thought, as he and Genevieve lay tangled together a full two hours later, flesh damp and lungs winded, muscles quivering and bodies spent.

He didn't know what was worse. The fact that without any apparent effort she seemed able to separate his mouth from his brain and turn him into a frigging babbling brook.

Or that he couldn't keep his hands off her.

Always before he'd viewed sex like food: just another essential one needed to get by. A man got hungry, a man ate and then he pushed back from the table and walked away. Maybe every once in a while he got an unexpected taste of dessert, but it wasn't anything he couldn't live without.

But with Genevieve… Nothing was the same. *He* wasn't the same. His desire for her felt more like the inescapable need he had to breathe than a lesser, more controllable urge.

The thought sent a shiver of uneasiness shooting down his spine. Or would have, he thought caustically, if he had a nerve left to carry it.

"John?" The cause of his alarm skimmed a fingertip over the nape of his neck.

"Hmm?"

"How many brothers do you have?"

He raised his head from where it rested against the crook of her neck. "What?"

"You said you and your brothers are partners. How many of them are there?"

He hesitated, but he couldn't see the harm in answering. As topics went, in fact, it was a hell of a lot safer than the one his mind had been zeroing in on. "There are nine of us all together."

"Nine?"

"Yeah."

"Good Lord."

"What?"

"Nothing. I just…I'm trying to imagine eight more of you and it's making me a little dizzy."

Damned if her slightly horrified admission didn't handily dislodge the last of his disquiet and leave a kind of fuzzy-edged tenderness for her that was completely unlike him in its place. "I guess we do all sort of look alike: tall, dark hair."

Telling himself the feeling would pass, that it was the consequence of great sex, nothing else, he rolled more completely onto his side. He flexed his tired muscles, before settling back down so their eyes were on a level.

Genevieve stared at him expectantly.

"What?"

"Gosh, I don't know. Maybe you could tell me a little more?"

His brows knit. "Like what?"

Something flickered across her face that was either despair or amusement or a mixture of both. "Let's see. You said Gabe's the oldest. What are you? The youngest?"

"No. That'd be Jake."

"While you are…?"

"Ten months younger than Gabe. Then comes Dominic, Cooper and Deke."

"Okay." She worried her full bottom lip. "That's six. What about the other three?"

He supposed he might as well just lay it out and be done with it. "Look, we're a military family. I told you about Gabe. I was an Army Ranger, Dom, Deke and Coop were all SEALs—get the picture? Right now there are five of us in the business, while Josh, Eli and Jordan are all currently on active duty overseas. Then there's Jake. He's in his last year of college."

She blinked, trying to take it in. "Wow. Your parents must be proud. Exhausted, but proud."

He gave a little shrug. "The old man's in Florida, retired from the army, doing his own thing the way he always has. My mom passed away a long time back, when we were all still kids."

"Oh, John, I'm sorry. How terrible. That must've been hard."

There was no doubting the genuine sympathy in her voice. Still, he was shocked to hear himself agree. "Yeah. It sucked."

She reached out, stroked his upper arm as if to try and soothe away that long-ago hurt. "I'm so sorry," she said again.

Maybe because she didn't press, he found himself wanting to tell her about it. "She was in a car accident, just a minor fender bender in a parking lot, except she wasn't wearing a seat belt and she hit the steering wheel. It was the day before my birthday, and she had things to do, so she just blew the accident off. And then…something inside her was torn and…that was it. She was standing in the kitchen, icing the cake and then she was just gone."

Genevieve remained quiet, simply touching him in an age-old gesture of comfort, but her eyes were indelibly sad for him.

"I didn't handle it very well. Gabe took care of things, the way he always does, but I got angry. Skipped school. Got into fights. Broke windows and busted up fences and didn't come home at night. Eventually I got caught boosting a car. Not even Gabe could fix that, so I got shipped off to Blackhurst, a military school. It saved me." *For all the good it did—*

"I slugged a social worker once."

"What?" Genevieve's quiet statement jerked him back from the abyss. He gave a faint snort. "Yeah, right."

"I did. It was after my grandpa died. This woman told me that Seth and I might not be able to stay together in the same foster home and I punched her."

"Jesus, Gen, what are you talking about?" Except for the information that she had no known living family except her brother, and the notation that she sometimes acted as an emergency foster mother, there hadn't been a hint, either in the file he'd been given on her or among her friends, of anything like this. "How old were you?"

"Eleven."

"Where were your folks?"

"We never knew our father—or fathers. And our mom had dumped us on Gramps a year or so earlier and disappeared for good. Responsibility—" her voice took on an unfamiliar, caustic note "—was never her thing."

"And you wound up in foster care?"

"That, and group homes. It wasn't too bad, once they realized I wouldn't tolerate our being separated. We got to spend some of our vacations with Gramps's brothers and sisters, until they were gone, too. I got emancipated at seventeen, got a job, my own place and custody of Seth and that was the end of it. When my uncle Ben died, he left me this cabin and enough money to make a down payment on the bookstore."

He didn't know what to say. But Genevieve being Genevieve, he didn't have to worry about filling the silence for too long.

"I've always thought it would be sort of nice to be part of a big family," she ventured unexpectedly. "To have other people around who know your history, who know *you*. People who care what happens to you."

The hint of wistfulness in her voice, which he doubted she even realized was there, made him want to go out, track down her long-lost loser parents and give them exactly what they deserved. Yet as he knew all too well, there was no going back, no fixing the past.

There was only the here and now. "Big families do

have some benefits," he told her. "But trust me, there are drawbacks, too."

"Like what?"

"Well…" Inexplicably determined to banish the last trace of melancholy from her eyes, he considered. "I don't think I ever slept in a room alone or made a phone call without somebody listening in until I scraped together enough money to rent a hotel room when I was eighteen.

"Nothing else is sacred, either. Food, shoes, your toothbrush—you name it and it's open season. And you can forget the whole idea of "your" clothes. In a big family, if they're clean, they're fair game. Blackhurst was the first place I didn't have to hide my damn underwear against marauders."

She chuckled. "Listen to us. If we wrote a book, we'd have to call it *Poor Pitiful Childhoods*." The chuckle got swallowed by a yawn, but when it was over, the soft smile he was starting to crave was back on her face. "God, we're a pair."

For an instant Taggart found himself thinking she was right. Then he gave himself a sharp jerk back.

No. No way would they ever be a pair, a couple, a twosome.

Because she still didn't know the truth about him. And it would be a cold day in hell before he'd allow that to change.

Nine

Genevieve jiggled from foot to foot as she rummaged through her duffel bag, searching for the bottom half of her long johns.

She was dressed in nothing but socks, panties and bra, shivering in the room that had yet to warm from the fire she'd built up first thing after climbing out of bed. The cold, as brisk as it was, wasn't the main cause of her inability to stand still, however.

That had just strolled out of the bathroom and was standing a dozen feet away, one broad shoulder propped against the doorjamb, one jeans-clad hip cocked, both muscular arms crossed over his naked chest.

She could feel Taggart's gaze like a velvet touch, making every nerve ending in her body jump.

Rationally, she knew her reaction was beyond foolish. They'd made love a dozen different ways the previous night; there wasn't any part of her body that those big hands hadn't touched, that hard mouth hadn't tasted, those always hard-to-read green eyes hadn't seen.

She was nevertheless very much aware that their intimacies had all taken place in the soft, shadowy cocoon of darkness lit by only the gentle glow of a single lantern's light.

Now she was standing, exposed, in dawn's unforgiving glare.

Yet it wasn't mere modesty alone that was making her jittery, she conceded. No, it was that Taggart's opinion of the view he was currently taking in mattered to her. Far more than she could have imagined just days ago. Definitely more than was prudent or wise.

Swallowing, she pawed through her belongings, triumphantly closing her fingers around the object of her search just as she heard Taggart make an odd sound, one that was neither sigh nor curse but a mixture of both.

Snatching the long johns to her chest, she swiveled to face him straight on. "What?"

"Nothing," he said instantly, his voice the slightest bit hoarse. His gaze skated over her. "I just—it never occurred to me Pollyanna would have a taste for killer underwear."

She glanced down at her cherry-red bra and panties, frilly lingerie being one of her few indulgences, then back at him. She frowned. "Pollyanna?"

It took a second for her question to penetrate his fascination with the embroidered roses twined strategically across various bits of sheer, transparent fabric.

When it did, his gaze shot to her face. "Forget it," he said hastily. "You look...good."

Pleasure washed through her—until she remembered what had sent her scurrying for her clothes in the first place. She watched, her pulse tripping irregularly, as he pushed away from the wall and strode a few feet closer, the chain gripped in his hand to prevent the trailing links from rapping him in the ankles.

Conflicting desires froze her in place. Her heart urged her to cross the space that separated them, step into his arms, run her hands across the taut skin of his chest and abdomen and watch the glint in his eyes turn to fire.

Her head preached caution, warning her that for both their sakes, the best thing she could do was stay out of his reach, at least until she figured out for sure if—

"What's wrong?"

"Nothing. I—" Darned if she didn't start to take a step toward him, only to be brought up short when the warmth suddenly vanished from his face as he looked past her.

His eyes watchful, he gestured toward the fleece shirt and thermal vest she'd laid out in addition to her usual jeans, winter silks and pair of sweaters. "Looks like you're getting geared up to go someplace."

She wondered what it would take to win his trust. Or if it were even possible, given the reason they were together in the first place.

The one thing she didn't question was that it mattered—that *he* mattered—since the question of how much was precisely what was fueling her urgent need for some space. Even if it came at the cost of a potential case of frostbite.

"It occurred to me that I may have paid a few years back to replace Uncle Ben's old generator," she said. "I thought I'd make a trip to the shed to see if I'm right, and if I am, to see if I can get the thing running."

He glanced out the window, contemplating the sullen gray sky and the snow that could now be measured in feet rather than inches. Thanks to the ever-present wind, huge drifts of white, some of them taller than she was, dominated the frigid landscape.

"Forget it," he said flatly, that pale, enigmatic gaze coming back to her. "We can live without power a while longer."

Thinking that she knew what was worrying him, she dredged up a reassuring smile. "Don't worry. I'm coming back. Even I know I wouldn't get far in the truck with this much snow on the ground."

His mouth tightened, but he was silent as she pulled on her silk bottoms, long johns and then her one pair of flannel-lined jeans. "That's not the problem."

"Oh? Then what is?"

"Get real, Genevieve. It's probably ten below out there if you factor in the wind chill." He stooped down and slid his own shirts up the chain, then impatiently began the process of putting them on, dragging the black cotton knit over his head, then untwisting the arms of his big flannel shirt and shrugging into it. "If anything goes wrong, if a branch comes down or you stumble into a drift that's over your head… Hell, it's not worth taking the chance for a generator that may not exist. God knows—" his voice darkened as he gave the chain a disgusted rattle "—I won't be any help."

So he did care. At least a little. Her heart swelled,

much the way it had when she'd been perched on the edge of the bed a little while ago, mooning over him as he stood at the bathroom sink scraping the beard off his cheeks and she'd found herself thinking—

No. Don't go there. Not here in front of him.

"I'll be fine." Her own multiple layers of clothing in place, she zipped up her vest, stepped into her boots, then bent down to tie them, glad for the excuse to hide her face. "I really want to check it out. I mean, I can live without heat or lights but not hot water," she said, injecting a false cheerfulness into her voice. "And I'd rather not have to cook outside on the barbecue if I don't have to—"

"Okay, fine." His voice was brutally clipped. "If it means so damn much to you, then undo this frigging handcuff and let me take care of it. If there is a generator out there, I'll at least be able to get it to run."

Straightening, she hesitated, unexpectedly tempted to do what he asked. To go ahead, roll the dice, turn him loose and see what happened next.

And what about Seth?

The thought of her brother had her taking a step back. If it was just her, she'd take the chance. But to take such a huge risk with Seth's future as collateral...

"All right. I'll give you the key." She braced for his reaction. "Just as soon as you promise me that when the weather improves you'll let me walk out of here, free and clear."

"Goddamn it, Genevieve, that's not fair—"

"None of this is," she cut him off sharply, zipping up her coat and slinging her scarf around her throat. Not waiting for his reply, since the last thing she wanted was for him to see the foolish tears suddenly stinging her eyes, she turned and walked toward the door. "Like I said, I'll be back."

She pulled open the door and stepped outside, welcoming the cold that immediately slashed into her like a razor-edged knife. Flipping up her collar, she struggled to get her breath as the sub-zero air burned her lungs.

Yet even as she trudged through the snow piled high on the porch and down the stairs, her thoughts were on the man inside. And what he would say if she told him the true reason for her sudden flight: That she was very much afraid she was falling hopelessly, irrevocably in love with him.

Jaw clenched, hands fisted, Taggart stalked a path parallel to the bed.

Damn, damn, *damn.* He'd just made what had to be his umpteenth search of every inch of cabin within his reach and he still couldn't find one stinking thing—not a bobby pin, paper clip or even a twist tie—that could possibly be used to pick the lock on the handcuffs.

Emotions churned through him. He was sick and tired of being a prisoner. Fed up with being chained like somebody's pet tiger. Up to his eyeballs with having to depend on St. Genevieve of the soft heart and luscious little body for every damn thing.

Sorry, pal. But even you've gotta admit, it's hard to steal a key or anything else off a woman who only gets near you when she's either naked or close to it.

One who, despite her soft-voiced concern and supposedly forthright manner, hadn't made one lousy mistake he could capitalize on.

And who was outside now, in the killing cold, taking unnecessary chances because he hadn't had the balls to lie and tell her what she wanted to hear. "Sure, baby. Give me the key and I'll not only let you go, I'll do anything else you want. You just name it—it's yours."

It would have been the expedient way to go, the smart thing to say. But when it came to Genevieve, words like *smart* and *expedient* didn't apply to him.

You've got that right. Whipped *and* enthralled *seem to be more your thing.*

The caustic thought shoved him over the edge. In a sudden fit of frustration, he snatched up the tray holding his empty breakfast dishes from the bed and hurled it across the room.

Shame had him by the throat even before the crockery struck the wall and shattered in a grinding explosion of sound.

What the hell was his problem?

What the hell *wasn't?*

Raking a hand through his hair, he stood stock still as he faced the demon driving him and reluctantly admitted it was him. That as a man whose self-restraint in every aspect of his life had always been paramount, he felt precariously out of control. And—the irony had his mouth twisting in a humorless smile—it was making him crazy.

Since meeting Genevieve, none of his behavior had been typical. From their first encounter out on the deck, when her unexpected bid to escape had resulted in the flying tackle that could have injured them both, to her recent insistence on venturing outside that he could have quashed with a few well-chosen words, he'd been one step behind and a few bricks shy of a full load.

He could remember, as a kid, his old man grumbling that no good deed ever went unpunished. Well, score one for Master Sergeant Richard Steele's life's-a-bitch-and-then-you-die take on life. And not because in the past few days his second son had been outwitted, imprisoned, beguiled and disarmed by a slip of a woman.

But because Taggart had broken the paramount rule of his life. He'd started to care about her.

Hell, who was he kidding? He hadn't *started* anything. He was solidly there. At some point when he wasn't looking—most likely because his brain had been in a sexual fog so complete he'd been rendered temporarily blind—Genevieve had crept right past his defenses and wedged a little sliver of herself deep into his heart that he was powerless to excise.

Not that it changed anything, he was quick to remind himself. He had an obligation to his brothers, to the Dunn family and to his own rapidly shrinking integrity to see this job through.

And if that wasn't enough of a reason to do what he was supposed to, there was Genevieve's long-term welfare to consider.

As much as it galled him, he had to admit she was pretty damn good at being a fugitive. But she could be the reincarnation of Mata Hari and it wouldn't matter. If she kept it up, it was just a matter of time before she got hurt.

Either she'd encounter a predator who'd use her isolation against her, or somebody with far fewer scruples than him would come after her in hopes of claiming some if not all of Steele Security's fee.

There was also the fact that the longer she was AWOL, the deeper the hole she was digging for herself with the judge whose order she'd defied in the first place.

He could no longer avoid the truth. The sooner he wrapped this up, the better for everyone, Genevieve included.

Cocking his head, he heard the faint crunch of boots on snow that signified her return. He took a forceful hold on his unruly emotions, shoving them back into the sealed inner compartment where they belonged, and tried to decide, as he tracked her progress up the steps, just what he was going to say to her. He frowned a little as there was a pause and he heard her say, "Oh, for heaven's sake—"

And then her voice abruptly cut off, replaced with the sound of crashing and rolling wood followed by an alarmed cry, a muffled thump and then absolute, paralyzing silence.

"Genevieve!"

Genevieve had never heard another human being actually roar, although the word was used in fictional conversations all the time.

But it was exactly the way she'd describe the manner in which John was yelling her name.

Then again, she thought hazily, as she lay flat on her back, desperately trying to suck in a breath to replace the air that had been knocked out of her, *bellow* might be an even better description. Although, come to think of it, she didn't think she'd ever heard anybody do that, either. Until now.

"Genevieve! Goddamn it, answer me!"

Gee. Talk about having your panties in a twist. Here she was suffocating, her vision starting to go dim, and he was having a major hissy fit, carrying on as if he'd slammed a drawer on his—

The thought was mercifully lost as the terrifying sensation of having a giant squatting on her chest abruptly vanished and she was finally able to drag a desperately needed breath into her starving lungs.

Except that it was colder out here than a Siberian meat locker, and the influx of icy air made her feel as if she'd inhaled a pissed-off porcupine.

Coughing and wheezing, she flopped onto her stomach and from there onto her elbows and knees, bringing her hands up to do what she could to warm the breath finally flowing in.

After what felt like an eternity, but was more likely a mere score of seconds, she decided she was going to live after all. And while she was likely to have a few bumps and bruises, she seemed for the most part to have survived unscathed.

She wasn't sure the same could be said of the cabin, she realized, as a loud crash came from inside. "*Genevi—*"

"I'm here," she called, doing her best to sound reassuring as she climbed gingerly to her feet. Encouraged by another quick inventory that found all her parts in working order, she picked up the hat she'd lost in the fall and did her best to dust the snow off it and whatever other areas of her clothing she could reach. "I'll be inside in a second. Don't worry."

Not worrying—about her discovery that she loved

him—was what *she'd* decided to do. Of course, first she'd had a minor meltdown courtesy of the bright and shiny new generator she hadn't been able to start. Then, when she'd realized her tears were freezing like sleet on her face, which wasn't a sensation she cared ever to repeat, she'd gotten a grip, taking a hard look at everything that had transpired between Taggart and herself.

It hadn't taken her long to realize that, while denying what she felt for him might make her feel better in the short run, it wasn't going to change anything in the larger scheme of things.

Yes, she hadn't known him very long. Yes, there was a host of things she didn't know about him. And yes, if she'd met him under different circumstances, she'd have deemed him too big, too tough and too intimidating to warrant a second look.

But none of that mattered now. She wasn't a person who gave her heart lightly or easily—that was obvious given that this was the first time she'd ever fallen in love. Sexually, she shared a bond with him she'd never felt with anyone else, while the chance to learn more about him made her feel like a kid at Christmas who'd been gifted with an abundance of presents.

As for his dangerous demeanor and aura of leashed power, she no longer found them threatening. She'd discovered he had too many honorable characteristics to offset them, including being committed to doing what he considered the right thing. They might be on opposite sides of the issue regarding Seth, he might break her heart by not returning her feelings, but she knew unequivocally that he'd never deliberately hurt her if there was any way he could avoid it.

The furnishings inside, on the other hand, sounded as if they were under a major assault. Wondering what on earth was going on, she blew out a breath, stomped as much of the snow off her boots as she could and walked through the door.

"My God." Her mouth formed a soundless O as she looked around. Not quite believing what she was seeing, she took in the easy chair that she'd placed next to the bed lying drunkenly on its side in the kitchen, the bright blue shards of broken dishes littering the hearth and, incredibly, the deep scars in the leg of the bed frame that anchored the far end of the chain.

Straining toward her at the opposite end of the chain was John, a bracelet of blood welling from the handcuff biting into his wrist. Her stomach dropped. "Oh, dear. What happened?" Scooting into the kitchen, she grabbed a clean towel and hurried toward him. "What did you do to yourself?"

"Me?" His expression savage, he caught her hand in a careful but inescapable grip as she reached to blot the blood from his wrist. "You just took a frickin' decade off my life."

"But you're bleeding."

He said something so profane it would have gotten his mouth washed out with soap in every foster home she'd ever lived in. "So are you."

"I am?" Confused, she followed his gaze to her hand, surprised as she saw the blood smearing her fingers and palm. "I don't think—"

"Be quiet." Taking the towel from her, he gently pressed it against her lips and chin, scowling as he

lifted the red-stained cloth away and he surveyed her
face. He blew out a breath. "It doesn't seem to be anything major. Looks like you bit your lip."

She blinked. Now that he mentioned it, her mouth did
feel a little tender. Still, that didn't do a thing to explain—

She gave a startled squeak as without warning he
peeled off her coat, unzipped her vest and began checking her out for further damage. "Really, I'm all right,"
she protested. "Which is more than I can say for this
place—"

He made a sound as if he were grinding his teeth.
"What the hell happened?" he demanded fiercely as he
gently examined her arms and legs.

"Oh." She tried to ignore the little kernel of heat
blooming shamelessly in response to his businesslike
touch. "I fell. I caught the end of my scarf on one of
the logs in the woodpile, tried to yank it free, then lost
my footing getting out of the way when some pieces
fell. I guess I went down kind of hard, because it
knocked the wind out of me." She laughed unsteadily.
"I think I actually saw a few stars."

His hands moved instantly toward her head, and it
was then that it sank in how much she'd frightened him.
Tenderness flooded her, and she reached up to intercept
him.

"John." Linking her fingers in his, she waited for his
gaze to meet hers. "I'm fine," she said softly. "Really."

For an instant his fierce expression didn't alter. Then,
with the speed that always surprised her given his size,
he pulled her into his embrace, cradling her against
him as he rested his cheek on the top of her head.

With a sigh of contentment, she burrowed closer, basking in his strength and the glorious heat he radiated.

Then, just as quickly as he'd reeled her in, he was pushing her away. "Genevieve. Look at me."

He sounded so serious her heart gave a little thump of alarm as she tipped up her chin. "What? What is it?"

"I've decided to agree to your terms. Get this damn handcuff off me and when the time comes, I'll let you walk out of here with a forty-eight-hour head start."

"You will?"

That familiar muscle jumped once in his jaw and then was still. "Yeah." Cupping his hand around the back of her neck, he anchored his long fingers in her hair and tipped her head back for the gentle assault of his mouth. "Absolutely."

Ten

"This is nice." With a contented sigh, Genevieve shifted a little closer to Taggart as they sat on the couch by the fireplace.

Apparently there was a technique for constructing a blaze that actually gave off adequate heat, she mused, enjoying the warmth on her face as she gazed into the softly dancing flames. It was a discovery she'd made not long after freeing the owner of the broad shoulder she was currently nestled against.

In just a matter of hours, after first stripping her out of her damp outerwear, wrapping her in several blankets and depositing her in an easy chair with a book, John had put the cabin to rights, got the generator running, cleared the snow from the steps to the door, split a dozen logs into kindling and done his magic with the fire.

That hadn't been all. He'd put dinner together and done the dishes as well, and while Genevieve had found it all very impressive and endearing, his nonstop action had also driven home just how difficult being confined must have been for someone powered by such immense energy.

Happily, however, he now seemed as satisfied as she was to sit quietly and enjoy the night. For the first time in days, the wind had died to just an occasional gust, while the sky had cleared enough that a scattering of stars was visible. Beyond the frost-edged windows, the merest sliver of a silver moon peeked above the jagged silhouette of the mountain peaks looming on the horizon.

"Yeah, you're right. It is nice." Taggart traced the curve of her jaw with the pad of his thumb. "God knows, it beats the hell out of being shackled to the bed."

"Oh, I don't know. I'm sort of fond of that particular item of furniture. At least, when you're in it."

He turned his head to give her a quelling look.

She stared blandly back at him before returning her gaze to the fire. "Hey, I can't help it if I think there's something sexy about a guy in chains. At least when he's you, with that hard body and outlaw face—"

"Genevieve," he said warningly.

Virtuously, she quit talking. Then, unable to help herself, she glanced sideways at him, delighted when she saw the slight edge of embarrassment he was manfully trying to hide.

She swiveled her head toward him and widened her eyes. "Still, you do know it's true, right? I mean, women must come on to you all the time—"

"Genevieve."

She sighed and with a little pout turned back to the fire. "You know, I happen to be as fond of my name as the next person, but between you repeating it now, and all that earlier roaring and bellowing, I think you've about worn it out—"

She glanced sideways to see how she was doing and found herself squarely in the crosshairs of his visual sights. Only now there was a glint in his slightly narrowed eyes that warned he was on to her.

Deciding she'd pushed her luck as far as it would go, she raised an eyebrow. "Too much?"

"Oh, yeah."

"What gave me away?"

He raised an eyebrow of his own. "Outlaw face? Give me a break."

She gave an unapologetic shrug. "Hey, it sounded good when I read it in a book. And you have to admit, it did take you a while to catch on." She gave in to the impish grin she could no longer contain.

For the longest moment his reproachful expression didn't change. Then without warning, he caved. With a faint shake of his head, he finally let his mouth curve in a crookedly charming smile.

It was the best gift he could have given her. With a soft sigh of satisfaction, she shifted around and kissed him, treasuring the unfamiliar upturned tilt of his lips.

Once again she felt passion flare between them, a banked fire that seemed to grow stronger with every hour they spent together. Yet rather than give in to it, this time when they finally stopped to take in air, she gathered her crumbling willpower and, after pressing a lingering kiss to the corner of his mouth, forced herself to sit upright and move a few inches away.

"You okay?" he asked quietly, a flicker of disquiet in the green eyes meeting hers.

She reached out and brushed a tendril of his thick, straight hair off his forehead. "Of course. But there's something I'd like to talk to you about."

He looked the slightest bit wary for an instant, then his expression smoothed out. "All right."

She considered how best to start, and then realized that like most things, just being forthright was the way to go. "I want to tell you why I think Seth is innocent. And I want you to listen."

"Genevieve—"

"I know." She raised her hand in a plea for patience. "All the evidence points to him. And you think I'm acting out of blind devotion."

"You're right. I do. Hell, having brothers of my own, I even admire your loyalty. But at some point you've got to face reality—"

"Please, John. Just hear me out."

His lips thinned momentarily, but then he relented. "Okay."

She breathed a sigh of relief. "I do love Seth. I also think I know him better than anyone else since I helped raise him. I know—I *know*—he's not capable of what he's accused of. He might be able to kill in self-defense, or to protect me or someone else he loved, but for money? Never.

"However—" she sent him a quelling look when it looked as if he were going to interrupt "—that's not the only reason I know he's innocent. There's also the fact that, despite what everyone thinks, he didn't have a motive."

She stopped to take a breath, and to his credit, Taggart simply waited for her to continue.

She gathered her thoughts. "Four days before he died, Jimmy told Seth he was going to change his will and his life insurance, making Laura, his fiancée, his beneficiary. He planned to do it the next day. Not only that—" she spoke a little faster since she could sense Taggart's sudden exasperation with what he clearly considered her naiveté at accepting at face value her brother's version of anything "—but Seth also had no reason to hurt Jimmy because *I'd* already agreed to lend him the money to bail out the ski shop."

"What?"

She nodded. "I told this all to the police, but they didn't believe me. I suppose I can't blame them too much, since all they've got is my word on it. I had part of the money in savings—" which had since gone to Seth's attorney "—and I intended to borrow the rest. But Silver's a small town and, because I deposit the bookstore's receipts several times a week, I knew the bank's loan officer was out on a family emergency. I was just waiting for his return to make the arrangements.

"Obviously, there's no way I can prove that," she said earnestly. "Except *I* know that I'm telling the truth, and that means Seth didn't have a motive."

Shifting, Taggart stretched out his legs and mulled it over for a minute. "So we're back to the mysterious stranger theory?"

"No. I don't think so. I've had a lot of time to think

about it, and I think Seth's wrong. I don't believe Jimmy just happened to be carrying the gun and had the misfortune to walk in on something. That explanation relies on too many coincidences. I think somebody took the gun from his house, and either waited for him at my place or followed him there. I think he was killed on purpose."

To her relief, he didn't instantly shoot her down. "Okay, but why? From what I understand, he was a nice kid."

"He was." She felt the familiar ache, but saw no reason to go into how much she'd cared about Jimmy, how much he'd been like a second little brother. When this was finally all over, when Seth was safe, *then* she'd allow herself to mourn.

Taggart, however, seemed to sense her sadness, and settled her back into the curve of his arm. "But?" he prompted.

"But I read a lot, including mysteries and true crime stories, newspapers and magazines, and most of the time when someone's murdered, the crucial question is who gains from the victim's death."

"Which in this case happens to be Seth," he said quietly.

"Yes. But as I just explained, Seth believed just the opposite. And even if he didn't, even if he thought he was still Jimmy's beneficiary, he didn't need that money—which he probably wouldn't have received in time to save his business anyway—because he knew I was going to help him out."

He sifted the ends of her hair through his fingers and slowly blew out a breath. "Okay. But going with your theory, who other than Seth stood to profit from Dunn's death? The fiancée?"

She shook her head. "No. She's not my favorite person, but in her defense, I didn't know her long before all this happened, and despite what Jimmy told Seth, nothing was left to her. Besides, she has a pretty good alibi—she and her brother were with Jimmy's parents, waiting for him to show up so they could have dinner."

"Then who?"

"I don't know," she admitted.

He must have heard the dejection in her voice, because he gathered her closer as they both lapsed into silence. To her surprise, he was the first to breach it.

"I'm not sure what I think at this point," he said slowly, choosing his words with care. "I'm no cop, but I do know you're not going to solve anything being on the run. The longer you defy the court, the worse you're making things for yourself—and I'm pretty damn certain that's tough as hell on your brother.

"Still, the bottom line is that sometime in the future you *will* be going back, whether you want to or not. It wouldn't hurt for you to consider that it might be easier if you had somebody you could trust at your side."

Like him. Even though he didn't say it, his meaning was clear. Not certain what she felt—disappointed that he hadn't endorsed her theory about the murder, frustrated that despite his earlier promise he still clearly intended to come after her when her forty-eight hours were up, or moved by his offer to stand by her—she sighed. "I guess we both have some things to think about," she said softly.

"Yeah." Linking the fingers of one hand with hers,

he drew her onto his lap and brushed his lips over her temple. "I guess we do."

He remained still for a moment, and then his mouth began a lazy slide lower, pausing to bestow kisses on the corner of her eye, the top of her cheek, the edge of her mouth.

"Although," she said as she shifted to provide him easier access, unable to stifle an "oh" of appreciation when she felt him growing hard in reaction, "I suppose we don't have to do it right this minute."

"No." In a single deft move, he wrapped an arm around her and twisted, neatly positioning her underneath him. "I don't suppose we do."

The nightmare came near dawn, creeping into Taggart's sleep like deadly tendrils of smoke slithering under a doorway.

For one endless second, he felt the horror slyly twine itself around him. Then he was dragged away from Genevieve's comforting warmth and sucked deep into the bottomless abyss of the past, only to be spat out high in the Hindu Kush, the brutally beautiful mountain system that rose like a crown atop northern Afghanistan.

He'd been here before and knew what was coming. Knew, dreaded and despaired, yet was powerless to save himself from reliving the event that had nearly destroyed him.

It was a beautiful early-summer night. Stars spangled the vast bowl of the sky, while desolate spears of rock rose like a jagged picket line on either side of the steep, twisting defile that was the Zari Pass. A new moon hovered overhead, painting the landscape with eerie light.

As in every other nightmare before this, Taggart was both observer and participant.

Even as he hovered nearby and watched himself, he also felt the familiar weight of the pack on his back, the comforting shape of the M-16 in his hands, the slight burn in his lungs from the thin mountain air. He felt the rocky ground under his feet and heard the occasional murmured comment from another member of the unit through his headset.

"So what do you think, J.T.?" His lieutenant's quiet voice floated back to him on the breeze as the other man unexpectedly bypassed his mike.

"I don't know, Laz," he answered quietly and also off-mike.

Usually he walked point, since he preferred being out in front of the team, his senses strung tight, knowing that whatever happened the enemy would have to get by him first.

Tonight, however, he'd taken the tail, so he could help the CO keep an eye on Caskey, the new kid who was sandwiched between them.

A fatal mistake, the watching part of himself knew. If he had the lead, the coming tragedy wouldn't happen. He wouldn't allow it.

Still, to his credit, the him at the back of the pack sensed...something. Yet a glance up the track where Bear, Willis, Alvarez and the rest of the guys were strung out ahead of them like floats on a fishing line revealed nothing out of place.

He went with his gut anyway. "I can't put my finger on it, but it just doesn't feel right."

"Yeah. I'm getting that, too." With the decisiveness

that typified him, the other man thumbed on his mike so everyone could hear him. "Team, this is Alpha. Listen up, guys. We're packing it in for the night. We'll set up camp at that bend in the trail a quarter mile back."

"Sweet," Willis remarked, making the word into two syllables with his lazy Alabama drawl. "'Cuz I aim to tell you, sir, this place is creepin' me out. Plus I gotta take a leak."

"Again?" Alvarez's snort of good-natured disgust was pure east L.A. "Man, what is your problem? You must have a bladder the size of a friggin' thimble."

"Yeah? Well that still makes it way bigger than your—"

Whatever part of his teammate's anatomy Willis intended to insult was lost forever as he lowered his gun, reached for his fly and took a handful of steps toward the edge of the trail.

Without warning, a ferocious blast went off, flinging him up into the air.

For what seemed like an eternity, the young communications expert seemed to hang in the air, his body silhouetted by the glare from the land mine's explosion. His agonized wail shrieked through his mike until he abruptly crashed to the ground and went mercifully silent.

In the next instant the night disintegrated into a thousand disparate pieces, blown apart as the team was hit by a barrage of enemy fire that seemed to come out of nowhere.

Taggart registered the whistle of incoming rocket-propelled grenades; the staccato cough of automatic weapons fire; the deeper pop of older, Turkish-made bolt-action rifles. The smell of gunpowder and cordite filled his nostrils, along with the coppery scent of fresh blood.

Laced through that devil's brew were the shouts as men scrambled for cover, followed by screams as their paths intersected with the rest of the landmines slyly hidden along the trail's outer perimeters. Like human dominos set into motion by the hand of hell, his second set of brothers toppled one after the other.

Hunkering down to return fire, he heard himself shout, "Damn it, Caskey, *no!*" but it was too late as the younger man bravely raced forward toward the source of the incoming fire, only to be slammed back a dozen feet by a hail of gunfire.

In a series of freeze-frames burned forever on his mind, he saw Laz go down, too, then felt a scalding rush of relief as he heard his friend curse through the headset and realized he was only wounded.

"Hold on!" he shouted, ignoring the bullets he sensed whizzing past as he scrambled forward.

"J.T.?" Laz's amplified breathing was labored. "Get the hell out of here, *now!* That's an order."

"No way." Reaching the other man, he hefted Laz in a fireman's hold, swiveled back around and began to run. "Hang on. You just hang on, damn it," he ground out, too hyped on fury, fear and the resultant overload of adrenaline even to register that he was carrying two-hundred-plus pounds as he sprinted full out. "We're gonna be fine."

All he had to do was make it to that hairpin twist in the trail that Laz had mentioned, and he knew he could hold off whatever the enemy threw at him. And praise God, it wasn't that far away now, he was only a stone's throw away—

The flash of the RPG hitting the totem of rock to his right was blinding. He felt the concussion roll over him a second before the sound reached his ears, and then he was flying, tumbling through an endless darkness, falling down, down, down, knowing he was dead since he couldn't even hear his own desperate screams—

"John? *John.* Listen to me. It's okay. You're okay."

The woman's faraway voice whispered through the dark, a glimmer of light breaking through the blackness of his despair.

"Wake up. You're having a dream."

An angel? No. Angels didn't exist in hell. What's more, that voice, and the comfort and peace it promised, felt familiar somehow. As if she'd held off the dark and given him refuge before...

"Come on, wake up now, John. It's just a dream. A bad dream. You're safe."

Genevieve. He snapped his eyes open and was abruptly assaulted by the sound of his own harsh breathing, the taste of blood from having bitten his tongue, the sour stench of fear rising off his sweat-slick skin.

Shivering violently, he stared up at her propped above him, her eyes dark with worry. Saw her hand come down to soothe him, and instinctively reached out to block it. *"Don't."*

"But—"

"Just give me a minute." He waited for her hand to withdraw, then squeezed his eyes shut and, ignoring the fact that his guts felt as if he'd just bungee jumped off the Empire State Building, concentrated on the simple act of breathing.

Time spun away. He wasn't sure how long it took

him to clamp down on his emotions, to banish the ghosts of Laz and Willis and the others, to will away the shakes, although it probably wasn't even a minute.

However long it was, when he finally opened his eyes, he had himself firmly under control. "Sorry," he said, reaching down deep to dredge up a rueful smile.

"Are you all right?"

"I'm fine. Just a bad dream, like you said. Had me going pretty good there, but I'm okay now."

Despite his assurance, the concern didn't leave her face. "Are you sure?"

"Yeah."

"Do you want to talk about it?"

"No." Somehow he managed not to flinch as she laid her hand on his cheek. "You know how it is. Even if it wasn't already fading, I probably couldn't explain it."

For a moment longer she continued to search his face, as if she knew damn well he was lying. He braced, fully expecting her to call him on it, but to his profound relief, she seemed to accept what he'd said at face value.

"Okay. If you're sure," she said softly, settling back down and laying her head on his shoulder.

"I am." He gave her arm a reassuring squeeze. "It'll be light soon. Try to get back to sleep."

"You, too."

"Sure." Even as he said it, he knew it wasn't going to happen.

So it wasn't any great surprise to be lying awake, watching the darkness in the room gradually lighten, long after her breathing had deepened into the sound sleep of the good and the righteous.

It was the kind of sleep he hadn't experienced since that night in the Hindu Kush when every member of his unit had died.

Everyone but him.

Eleven

Genevieve watched through the kitchen window as Taggart chopped wood like an automaton. Feet spread, shoulders bunching beneath the clean denim shirt and dark-green down vest he'd retrieved from his bag that morning, he appeared impervious to the spectacular beauty of the day.

Instead of taking time to appreciate the brilliant sunshine that made the snow sparkle like diamond dust, or looking up long enough to notice the lone eagle riding the thermals like a teenager out for a joyride, he wielded the ax with an unrelenting rhythm that was exhausting to watch.

At the rate he was going, they'd soon have more kindling than logs. Not that she cared. Wood was wood, and whatever its size it would burn.

She had far more pressing matters on her mind. Like whether John was out there for the exercise the way he claimed. Or if, as she suspected, his real goal was to keep her at arm's length.

Despite his reassurance of the previous night that he was fine, which he'd doggedly repeated again this morning, she knew he wasn't. Before he'd escaped outside, she'd had ample time to see the strain around his mouth, hear the detachment in his voice he couldn't entirely hide, practically *touch* the barrier he'd thrown up around himself.

If that wasn't enough to clue her in, being on the receiving end of his too-frequent smiles—which never quite reached his eyes—was.

She wondered if he had any idea he talked in his sleep.

With a slight shudder, she recalled the heartbreaking sound of his despair that had jolted her from sleep. His mumbled narrative may have been too disjointed for her to glean exact details, the when or where or how or why, but she'd heard enough to know he'd been in some sort of firefight that hadn't gone well. Men had died. Men he'd cared about.

It was also clear he'd sooner have his tongue extracted through his nose than share what had happened. Although she'd taken pains to keep her voice mild and her expression composed, simply asking if he wanted to talk had triggered a response similar to a heavily fortified gate slamming shut.

One moment he'd been there with her, haunted and hurting; in the next, the essence that made him the man she loved had been securely locked away behind an unbreachable wall.

Genevieve tapped a distracted finger against the kitchen counter.

She might not be able to get him to open up, but surely there was something she could do to stop his brooding and put an end to his self-inflicted isolation.

She stood there a moment longer, considering the golden gift of the sunshine, the heavenly blue of the sky, the pristine expanse of the snow, and realized the eagle had it right.

It was a day made for play. And while she might not be able to get through John's defenses, she thought she might know a way to get him to lower them all by himself.

Wasting no time, she gathered her snow gear, pulled it on, then slipped outside. Unconcerned with detection, since John was so absorbed in pulverizing another log he probably wouldn't notice if a flying saucer touched down beside him, she picked her spot and made her preparations.

When she was ready, she dusted off her palms, hefted one of her arsenal of snowballs in her hand and waited until her target was positioning the next log for its execution. The instant he straightened, she took a steadying breath, wound up for the throw and let loose.

Bull's-eye! She allowed herself a second of satisfaction as her missile struck Taggart squarely between the shoulder blades and sent a spray of snow shooting up to lodge at the back of his neck.

Ducking back around the cover of the stairs, she watched as he dropped the ax handle and spun around. "What the—"

She popped out and hurled snowball number two before he could complete the sentence. Unfortunately, her aim was off this time so she missed him entirely, the icy orb whistling harmlessly past his ear.

He scowled, clearly not amused. "Knock it off, Genevieve. I'm not in the—"

"Oh, jeez." She winced as her third try went high, hitting him in the chin instead of the chest. Yet the look of disbelief on his face as snow showered him, coating him from eyebrows to lips, was priceless. She didn't even try to hold back the laugh that rolled out of her.

He reached up, wiped himself off with his gloved hand. "You think that's funny?" he demanded, his narrowed eyes as green as his vest.

"As a matter of fact—" Wham! To her delight, this time she got him smack in the open neck of his shirt "—I do."

He swore, apparently not enjoying the sensation of ice-cold snow mixing with the sweat he'd worked up with the ax.

"You wanna know what else?"

"What?" While he sounded mightily aggravated, he couldn't entirely suppress the slight twitch at one corner of his mouth.

She took it as a hopeful sign. "The way you're getting all pissy? I think that makes you what my friend Arnold calls a girlie man."

Her gleeful insult did it.

He was moving before she had time to blink, easily dodging the snowball she tossed hastily his way as she gave a shriek and bolted away. Forced to stick to the path he'd carved on his trips to the shed, she was an easy target as he scooped snow up by the handfuls as he ran.

Wadding it together, he peppered her with a series of hits that came one after the other in the short time it took him to catch up with her.

Then his arms came around her and he lifted her off her feet. She laughed breathlessly as they tumbled to the ground, her relief as she saw a smile finally flit across his face mixed with tenderness as he took care to absorb the brunt of their fall.

The second they quit skidding across the icy ground he flipped her onto her back, caged her in with his elbows, and made a show of glowering down at her. "Laugh all you want, angelface," he growled. "You're in serious trouble now."

Angelface. The endearment made her feel warm all over. She did her best not to let on, however. "Ohhh," she hooted, "aren't you the big bad."

Much as he had the previous night, he gave it his best shot but couldn't quite sustain his dark and dangerous look. "Big bad?" A tiny V of disbelief formed between his eyebrows. "Where the hell do you come up with this stuff?"

Willing to forgo her dignity and act silly if it would keep his demons at bay for even a little while, she shook her head. "Forget it. No way am I telling you all my secrets."

"You're not, huh?"

"Not a chance."

"Yeah, well, we'll see about that." Pinning her in place with one big hand, he scooped up a handful of snow with the other. His gaze raked her front, zeroed in on her waist where she'd run up the double zipper to allow herself greater freedom of motion, then came back to her face. The smile he finally unleashed on her wasn't nice.

"Don't you dare."

"Yeah, like I'm going to feel threatened by you."

"John—"

"Too late." Releasing her long enough to shove up the hems of her shirts, he clapped the icy mass in his hand against her bare stomach.

"Ohmi—" Gasping, protesting and laughing, she bucked and twisted, doing her best to shake him off.

She might as well have been trying to shift a bulldozer.

Changing tactics, she wrapped her arms around his neck and her thighs around his hips, figuring if she was going to suffer he might as well share the pain.

Surprise, surprise. He really *was* the big bad. Or at least the big, she amended, as she registered the solid length of his arousal pressed eagerly against her.

Her gaze flashed to his face to find his eyes riveted on her with such desire in their mossy depths it stole her breath. "Oh, John," she said softly, her amusement ebbing as everything she felt for him filled her up and took its place.

"Yeah," he murmured in the instant before his arms came around her and his mouth settled hungrily over hers.

His lips were cold and tasted of snow. His kiss was hot and greedy. Genevieve sank into it, welcoming the avid thrust of his tongue, glorying in this further proof that he wanted her. She could feel his heart pounding, despite their layers of clothing, and the knowledge that she had such an effect on him thrilled and enthralled and humbled her.

When he shifted onto his knees, scooped her into his arms, climbed to his feet and headed for the cabin, she didn't protest.

She wanted him and anything—everything—he was willing to give.

"I've never made love during the day before," Genevieve said softly, watching Taggart undress as she knelt naked on the bed.

Being here with him, like this, at this time of day, felt different, she mused. Daring and a little risqué and incredibly intimate. There were no shadows to hide in, no escape from the shafts of glittering sunshine striping the room and painting everything they touched a pale, shimmering gold.

"I have," he volunteered unexpectedly, peeling off his shirt to reveal the wide, smooth shoulders and sculpted chest that never failed to put a hitch in her breath. "Once."

Amazed that he'd willingly share such information, she told herself to concentrate, even as her pulse tripped. She'd never seen him completely naked in broad daylight, she realized. "How was it?"

He unsnapped his jeans and slid the zipper down. With an economy of motion that was laudable, he stripped off his jeans and briefs together. "Fast." The look he tossed her way was unexpectedly rueful. "I was sixteen."

"Ah." The thought of him as a teenager made her wistful. She wondered what he'd been like, if he'd been open and hopeful for the future. But no, she realized an instant later. By then he'd already lost his mother and been shipped away from home to military school.

It made her want to gather him close, protect him, keep him from ever feeling more pain, even though she knew not only that it was impossible, but that he'd never allow it. He had too much pride to let her or anybody else shelter him.

"What?" he said, searching her face as he stretched out beside her.

"Nothing. I just…" Chiding herself for putting concern in his voice, she smiled. "This was one of your better ideas, that's all." Coming up on her knees, she saw his surprise as she braced her hands on either side of him, then lowered her head and pressed an open-mouthed kiss to the shallow oval of his navel.

This—the gift of pleasure—was something he would accept, and was well within her power to bestow.

Deliberately leaving the best for last, she ignored the velvety thrust of his straining arousal and slowly skimmed her lips over the washboard ripple of his abdomen. He had the most magnificent body she'd ever seen, and truth be told, having it stretched out like this for her delectation made her feel all fizzy inside.

Taking her time, she explored with her hands and her mouth. She trailed her fingers over every inch of those glorious abs first, then the curves of his pectorals from his sides to his middle. She flicked her tongue over the hardened bead of his nipple, delighted to hear a soft sound rumble from his throat. Intrigued, she did it again, and felt his hand slide into her hair a moment before he tugged her head up.

"Genevieve," he said, his voice smoky, his eyes dark with a look she'd never seen in them before.

"What?" With a pinch of concern, she reached up, touched her hand to his face. "What is it?"

"I want—" He stopped, and she saw his struggle to get out the words. "I need to see your face when I'm inside you."

The words alone were enough to trigger a liquid flutter inside her. It got stronger as he slid his hand around and traced her lips with his thumb. "Now," he said hoarsely.

"Yes." Scooting up, she claimed his mouth, giving herself over to him completely as he held her close and reversed their positions.

In a blink of an eye, the kiss went from soft and tender to greedy and heated. In the next instant, he was tearing his mouth away, holding himself still for the heartbeat it took her to open her eyes. Then he plunged inside her.

She was wet, slick and yielding, more than ready, and she could feel herself stretching to accommodate his considerable size as he began to pump. His hips slowly pistoned as they continued to watch each other, their gazes locked.

He was so beautiful, she thought, as the first ribbon of pleasure made an immediate arrival and curled through her. From that strong, austere face to his wide palms and long fingers, from the warm, corrugated surface of his stomach to the powerful, lightly haired thighs wedged now between her smooth, softer ones, he was utterly, quintessentially male.

Never in her life had she been so aware of being female, of the fundamental drive to claim and be claimed by a man.

Not any man, she amended as she felt herself slide a little closer toward completion, that single ribbon of toe-curling sensation having given birth to a silken web that had her firmly in its grip.

Just John. Only John. Always John.

She watched, enthralled, as his eyes began to blank and his breathing quicken as his control started to evaporate. Teeth clenched, perspiration misting his skin, he shifted, sharpening the angle of penetration and began to drive. "Damn it," he gasped. "I can't— I can't hold back."

"It's all right," she whispered, her head going light as pleasure began to squeeze her.

Nothing in her life had prepared her for this, she thought hazily. The delicious heat of his big body. The raw, drugging sensuality of the act they were sharing. Her own wildly eager response.

Emotion overran her as if she were the top wine flute in a champagne fountain. It was too much to contain. Too precious to hoard.

Reaching up, she dug her hands into his hair, rising up to meet him at the same time that she tugged his head down to hers. "I love you, John," she said clearly, her gaze never leaving his. Clamping around him with sleek, inner muscles, she felt herself reaching, reaching… "Come with me," she implored.

He quivered as if she'd struck him. Then his eyes squeezed closed and his mouth crushed down on hers, a welcome marauder.

Every muscle in his big body shuddering, he held on to her as if she were his only anchor as the storm broke and pleasure swept them away.

Twelve

"You shouldn't do that," Taggart said quietly, his shoulders still heaving as he sat up and swung his feet to the floor.

"Do what?" Genevieve said blankly to his back.

He heard the sheets rustle and knew she'd sat up. "Say things you don't mean."

"Like I love you?" There was a telling pause, and then she said evenly, "Pardon me, but I think I know my own mind."

Frustrated, he twisted around to face her. The last thing he wanted was to hurt her; why couldn't she just acknowledge she'd spoken in the heat of the moment and let it go? "You're wrong. You're confusing great sex with…something else."

"Trust me. I know the difference between the two."

Her expression was serene as she met his gaze. "And I didn't tell you because I was hoping you'd say it back or because I'm looking for a commitment, if that's what's bothering you. I just wanted you to know. Love, freely given, is a gift, John. Not a burden. Or at least it shouldn't be."

How the hell was he supposed to respond to that? Feeling all tied up inside and hating it, he stood, scooped up his jeans and yanked them on, then paced to the window and stood looking blindly out. "There are things you don't know about me."

"You're right. It's also true that if you only count the time in hours, we haven't known each other very long. But none of that matters. I feel closer to you than I've ever felt to anyone except Seth. And I trust my judgment. I know you, John. Maybe not every little detail, but the things that are important. I know you care— about your brothers, your job, about doing the right thing. I know you light me up inside. I know you're a good man."

"Oh, yeah?" He wheeled around, surprised to find she'd flown under his radar once again and was standing just a few feet away, wrapped in his shirt. "What if I told you nine guys are dead because of me?"

"I wouldn't believe you."

He turned back to the window, the sunshine unable to touch the endless winter that lived inside him. "Then you'd be deluding yourself."

"No," she said firmly.

"*Yes,* damn it." He told himself just to shut up and let it go, but now that he'd gone this far, he couldn't seem to stop the words from flowing out of his mouth.

"You know I was a Ranger. My last deployment was to northern Afghanistan. My unit had been there nine months when word came down from CentCom that they had reliable intel an old trade route was being used as a pipeline by terrorists coming in from Pakistan. We were ordered to check it out.

"The trip out took a week, but there was zilch to indicate that anybody but us had been over that pass in years." He took a shallow breath and an iron grip on the bitter emotions burning his throat. "Until we started back. It was night, we were maybe two days from our base camp, pushing it a little because heavy rains earlier in the day had slowed us down. One minute everything was fine."

Willis's amused drawl whispered through his mind but he shook it off.

"The next, we were taking heavy fire, with nowhere to hide because the trail had been mined since we'd come through. The whole thing lasted five, maybe ten minutes. When it was over—" he shrugged "—I was the only one left."

"Dear God." Her face, always so expressive, was a telling mixture of shock and horror.

Taggart told himself he ought to be glad; after all, wasn't this what he'd wanted? For her to see him as the bastard he really was?

Damned right it was.

So why did he feel as if he'd just lost a vital piece of himself? Something he wasn't sure he could go on without?

"How—" Genevieve swallowed. "However did you survive?"

He smiled humorlessly. "I was carrying my CO, who'd been hit, when a grenade went off beside us. He took the brunt of the blast; I got blown over a cliff. I got lucky—" the word felt like acid on his tongue "—and hit a ledge about a hundred feet down."

Genevieve tried to picture it in her mind; the noise and the confusion and the urgency and the fear, and then what must have seemed like an unending fall. That was the memory, she now realized, that must have prompted his agonized cries at the end of his nightmare. The ones that had sent shivers down her spine and pushed her even harder to wake him up.

She drew in a deep breath, blew it out, fought for composure as her heart broke just a little more for him. "How badly were you hurt?"

He shrugged dismissively. "I was a little banged up from the fall."

"Define *banged up*."

His mouth set stubbornly, and she knew before he answered that he was going to lie. Clearly, the last thing he wanted was sympathy, of any kind. "Nothing major. I told you. I was lucky, remember?"

She heard the self-loathing in his voice, and suddenly it all made sense. The air of isolation; the tightly controlled emotions; the stubborn, misplaced conviction that he didn't deserve to be loved. "What did you do?"

"I climbed up the cliff, checked to see if anyone else was alive." His voice was suddenly uninflected, his expression cool, as if what he was saying was of no significance whatsoever. Genevieve didn't buy it for a minute. "All our comm units were shot to hell, so I had to wait to radio for help until I got back to camp."

He'd said they were two days out. She pictured him—injured, since no one could fall that far and escape damage to their body—with no one to talk to about the carnage he'd witnessed or the friends he'd lost. And she ached for his pain and despair.

It took all of her control not to give in to the urge to step close, wrap her arms around him, offer what comfort she could.

Yet with an instinct she didn't question, she knew that if he were to have any chance of healing, he had to confront the guilt that had clearly festered inside him for far too long. She took a deep breath. "And all of this is your fault…how?"

His mouth twisted. "We never should have been there in the first place. I knew—something felt off right from the beginning. Unlike CentCom, we were there, on the scene. If there'd been hostiles passing through the area, there would've been whispers in the villages, something passed along from one of our contacts."

Although she suspected she knew the answer, she asked the question anyway. "So why didn't you say something?"

"I did. But I should have recognized that it was a setup, raised hell, even refused to go—"

"And disobey orders?" she said in disbelief. "You couldn't do that. Any more than you could have lived with yourself if you'd hung back while your unit was about to walk into a situation you thought was dangerous."

"Listen, for God's sake. Maybe you're right about that, but what happened on that pass— It was just all…wrong. Teams get used to a certain pattern, into a kind of rhythm, on patrol. I should've been in front, the way I usually was, but instead I was hanging back at the rear—"

"Why? Were you sick or injured or something?"

"No. I was keeping an eye on—what the hell does it matter? The point is I wasn't where I should've been—"

"And if you had been up front, what would that have accomplished?" she demanded. "Were you so much better than the man taking your place that you could have prevented an ambush?"

"No, but—I—" He stopped, regrouped. "That's not—" He stopped again, and just stared at her.

"You're not psychic, John. If you were, you wouldn't have spent the past few days chained to the bed. Obviously your instincts were right, but it was your job, your unit's job, to do exactly what you did, to take that walk into danger no matter how you felt. The responsibility for what happened rests with the men who attacked you and whoever higher up your chain of command okayed the information about the pass in the first place."

Unable to stand the physical distance between them another second, she padded close, rucked back the sleeves of his shirt and reached up to cup his face. "I'm sorrier than I can say that you suffered such a terrible loss." She thought about her grief for Jimmy and couldn't imagine what it must have been like for him. "But what happened wasn't your fault. You're not God. Or a superhero. And I'm sure as hell not sorry you're alive. I doubt any of the friends you lost that night would be, either. They'd be as glad as I am that you made it out."

Taggart gazed down into her face. He wasn't sure what he felt, what he thought; so many things were suddenly tumbling through his mind at once that he couldn't seem to get a grip on any particular one.

What he did know was that, while he wasn't convinced Genevieve's assessment of his actions was correct, she clearly believed what she'd said with every fiber of her being. And because she did, a part of his heart that had been so damn cold since that devastating night on Zari Pass four years ago felt warm again.

What's more, as he felt her arms come around him in a fierce embrace, he realized that for the first time since he could remember, he didn't feel completely alone.

Standing on the prow of the deck, a steaming cup of coffee cradled in his hands, Taggart raised his face and soaked in the sun.

Some time during the night, a chinook had blown in. The soft breeze ruffled his hair with warm fingers while it set the surrounding evergreens gently swaying. It was as if, he mused, the immense trees were slow dancing to the music of the melting snow as it dripped from the trees, trickled off the cabin's eaves, raced merrily along dozens of narrow, winding rivulets toward the creeks and streams murmuring in the distance.

At the rate the thaw was progressing, the roads should be passable later that day.

That made it decision time.

In the past twenty-four hours he'd revealed things to Genevieve he'd never shared with another living soul. And instead of playing it safe and pushing him away,

she'd opened her heart even wider and invited him to
come closer.

What's more, in the wake of yesterday's painful dis-
closure, she'd somehow understood that he'd reached
the limit of what he could emotionally process and she
hadn't pressed him any further.

She'd led him back to bed instead, where they'd
stayed, except for a brief raid on the kitchen long after
the sky had darkened, making love with nothing held
back. They'd gone slow, been wild. They'd shared tenderness, urgency, heated whispers, raw cries of passion.
They'd kissed, clung, explored, feasted, turned each
other inside out and held each other together.

He might not be in love with her, not exactly, but he
felt more connected to her than he had to anyone since
his mother died.

So how the hell could he betray her?

For the first time since he'd told her that he'd let her
go in order to secure his own freedom, he admitted to
himself that in the back of his mind he'd been reserv-
ing the right to renege on their deal. Every reason he'd
cited at the time to justify why she'd be better off in custody still stood, with the added kicker that he felt even
more protective now than he had before.

And yet… He couldn't stand the thought of destroy-
ing her trust. Despite the fact that he had an obligation
to his brothers and the client who'd paid for their services, and that he truly felt it would be in Genevieve's
best interest to turn herself in.

Hearing the door open and the sound of her footsteps
approaching, he turned to watch her walk toward him.
Dressed in dark jeans and a pale-pink sweater, her hair

gleaming like burnished silk in the sun, she was beautiful. He wondered how he could ever have considered her merely pretty.

"You look far too serious for such a gorgeous day," she said lightly, joining him at the rail. Like a flower, she raised her face to the sun.

He shook his head. "It's the weather. It's hard to believe it can go from minus zero to fifty plus in less than forty-eight hours."

"Nature's just full of surprises," she agreed, shifting her gaze to him. "So are you."

Just for a second he thought he saw something in her eyes— But no. No way could she know what he'd been thinking, know about the internal battle he was waging over what was right and what was best. "You think so?"

"Uh-huh. Breakfast was wonderful. If I'd known you could cook like that—" her mouth turned up "—I'd have chained you to the stove instead of the bed."

"Huh. I'm not sure that's a compliment."

"No, really, it is. Although, now that I think about it, I take it back." She leaned bonelessly against him, gave a little sigh of contentment as his arm came around her. "Bed is definitely the best showcase for your talents."

He narrowed his eyes. "You do realize you're skating on really thin ice, right?"

She laughed, that soft, delighted chuckle that never failed to light him up inside. As the sound of it faded away, they simply stood on the deck together, wrapped in a companionable silence as they admired the day.

Then Genevieve gave a faint sigh. "The snow's melting off pretty fast."

"Yeah. But it's only temporary. Winter's definitely here. You can feel it in the air. Another few days and the cold and the snow will most likely be back."

"I don't suppose we could hang around for that?" she asked a trifle wistfully.

"No. I don't think we can." Steeling himself, he turned her in his arms, telling himself that the least he owed her was to look her in the eyes when he admitted he wasn't sure he could just let her walk away. "Listen—"

"I've—" she said at the same time.

They both stopped. He inclined his head. "Go."

"All right." She swallowed, then visibly steadied herself. "I've decided to release you from your promise."

For a second he was sure he hadn't heard right. "What?"

"If we start packing up right now, we should be ready to leave by this afternoon."

Stunned, he took a moment to wrap his tongue around the questions crowding his mind. "Are you sure?"

"Yes."

"But…why? What changed your mind?"

"I've been thinking about some of the things you said. About how I've done all I can, and how I'm making things even harder on Seth. And that if I go back now, with you, I won't be totally alone. That is—" she looked up at him and, for one of the few times he could remember, he could see both fear and uncertainty in her eyes "—if your offer still stands."

"Yeah, sure, but—Jesus, Genevieve." He shook his head with the vague thought that maybe that would help clear it. "I just don't get it. Yesterday, you were so adamant…."

Her expression changed, some of the tension draining away to be replaced by unmistakable tenderness. Reaching up, she laid her hand against his cheek. "You're not quite as inscrutable as you think," she said quietly. "And the longer I've had to think about it, the more I've come to realize that I've put you in an untenable situation.

"Besides—" she lightly drew her thumb over the seam of his lips, her throat visibly working as she struggled to hold on to her air of calm "—you trusted me enough to tell me what happened to you. How can I not trust you back?"

It was too much. At the same time that he felt a huge weight had been lifted from his shoulders, a part of him worried uneasily that she was making a serious mistake, that he wasn't worthy of such faith.

"Genevieve—"

"It'll be all right," she said firmly, once more seeming to read his mind.

"Damn straight." He'd see to it, or die trying, he vowed to himself. "I swear I'll do everything I can to expedite this whole thing, try my best to convince the judge to go easy on you—"

"I know you will. I trust you, remember?" She gave his arm a reassuring squeeze, then dropped her hand to her side and took a step away. "Now, I'm going to start packing things up, before I chicken out and change my mind."

And briskly turning away, she left him alone with nothing but the sunshine and his own unsettled thoughts for company.

Thirteen

"**M**y rig is *where?*" Taggart demanded, jiggling the keys to Genevieve's truck in his hand. After a very short discussion, they'd agreed his was the vehicle of choice in which to make the drive back to Colorado.

"In a barn about a mile and a half down the road from where you left it," she repeated patiently. Pausing in the task of emptying the contents of the fridge into a garbage bag, she picked a piece of paper up off the counter and proffered it to him. "Here. I've written down the directions and drawn you a map."

Taking the sheet from her, he studied it a moment, folded it and slid it into his pocket, then looked back up at her and shook his head. "You walked through the snow, in the dark, just to hide it?"

She widened her eyes, doing her best to look innocent. "I was keeping it safe for you."

"Yeah, right."

"Hey, a girl's got to do what a girl's—"

He expediently cut her flow of words by the simple act of tugging her into his arms. "Spare me the pitch," he murmured, lowering his head to rest his forehead against hers. "Bottom line, Bowen, you're a menace. How the hell you managed to make it this far—" shifting, he found her mouth and interspersed his next words with a series of erotic, unhurried kisses "—without serious injury—" his hands slowly stroked down her back as he caught her bottom lip between his teeth and bit down lightly "—is beyond me."

Genevieve felt her body start to hum. His simplest touch made her feel warm and malleable, like Silly Putty left out in the sun. "John?" she murmured, her eyelids drifting shut as his mouth slid over the curve of her jaw to explore her throat.

"Hmm?"

"If you don't go now, you won't be going at all."

"No?" Nothing happened for a moment, then his hands slowly relaxed their grip on her butt. Sighing, he met her heavy-lidded gaze with a rueful one of his own. "I suppose you're right."

She eased back, forcing herself to step away from his seductive warmth. "Yes. I am."

"All right. If you're sure you don't want—"

"*Go,*" she ordered with a breathless laugh. She watched as he strode across the room and out the door. Feeling mixed relief and regret, she started to turn back to the fridge when she abruptly remembered the distributor cap. "Wait!" she called, dashing after him onto the porch.

Already down the stairs, he stopped and turned. "What?"

"Just hang on a minute." Due to the amount of chopping he'd done the past two days, the wood pile was seriously diminished, which was good since it made her task easier. Leaning over the low stack of logs that were left, she reached down and cast about until her fingers closed over the bulbous piece of metal. Straightening, she twisted back around. "You'll need this." With a smooth, underhand toss, she lobbed it to him.

He snatched the shiny metal cap out of the air, spent a long second considering it, then once more looked up at her.

"If I'm ever in serious trouble, I want you guarding my back," he informed her dryly.

Genevieve smiled. As compliments went, it was first class and she didn't doubt it showed in her smile. "I love you, John Taggart Steele," she said softly, unable to stop herself. "Now go, so you can get back."

"Count on it." He headed for the truck.

It was done.

Standing with her back to the window, Genevieve took a slow look around the cabin's interior.

All of her things, plus John's modest bag, were packed and stacked neatly to one side of the door. The fridge was clean and unplugged, the few perishable foodstuffs that had been left bagged for disposal. She'd made sure the fire was out and closed the flue, flipped the breaker switch to the water heater and turned off the water valve under the sink. Since the power had come back on shortly after dawn and John had already dealt with the generator, she'd had only to make sure all the lamps and appliances were either turned off or unplugged.

In a gesture symbolic of her hopes for the future, she'd put clean sheets on the bed, and, in a reminder of the most life-altering week of her life, left the chain neatly coiled atop the smooth expanse of the comforter. She hoped that, when the next few days or weeks or—surely it wouldn't be more than months?—were over, she'd be able to convince John to return for a long getting-reacquainted weekend.

That is, if he still felt the way he did now when she got out of jail.

She wondered if she'd be allowed to see Seth, then realized it was unlikely. Suddenly unable to ignore the fear that had been plucking at her with icy fingers ever since she'd made the decision to turn herself in, she swallowed hard and admitted she didn't know what to expect. She'd never had so much as a traffic ticket, and, while she'd read countless books where people went to jail, the reality of actually being locked away, completely at the mercy of strangers, felt altogether different.

She just had to keep reminding herself that she wouldn't be alone. She hadn't lied when she'd told John she trusted him. And though she didn't share his optimism regarding what was about to happen—she'd known since she'd decided to run that the consequences would be grave—she'd get through it. She was young, strong, resilient, accustomed to looking out for herself.

And it wasn't as if she had a choice.

Still, it would certainly help if John would get the lead out and get back before she went from a mild case of cold feet to feeling frozen from the eyebrows down.

She glanced at the clock. He should have returned by now, she thought with a frown. Since the room felt as if it was starting to close in on her, she decided she might as well take her current book and wait outside in the sun. Just having a plan, however inconsequential, made her feel better, so she snatched up her paperback and the coat she'd laid on the couch.

She was halfway to the door when the knob started to turn.

Even as she felt a rush of relief that John was finally back, she faltered in midstep, a small alarm going off in her head as she realized that she hadn't heard him drive in.

In the next instant, the door crashed open and a tall, dark-haired stranger burst into the room.

Her heart seemed to stop as she found herself staring down the barrel of an enormous, dull-black gun. "On the floor! Now!" the intruder shouted at her. "Keep your hands where I can see them!"

She was so terrified she couldn't speak, much less move so much as an eyelash. Yet in the midst of her paralysis, time seemed to slow dramatically to the point where she registered every minuscule detail going on around her, from the pounding of more feet and the harsh cries of other male voices screaming at her to get down, to the striking features of the man now gripping her shoulder.

In the same instant that he spun her around and

forced her to the ground, she realized he bore an uncanny resemblance to John. Same inky hair, same height, same strong, straight nose and startling green eyes. His were a darker shade, however, and his features were more refined. Dressed as he was, all in black, including a long leather coat that hung to midcalf, he exuded a dangerous, fallen-angel sort of elegance.

Or would, she thought numbly, as he yanked her arms back and slapped a pair of handcuffs on her wrists, if he weren't scaring the wits out of her. Her state of mind didn't improve as she heard a swift double click of sliding metal a second before an unchambered bullet dropped with a ping on the floor inches from her face. She squeezed her eyes shut and the next thing she knew, he was patting her down, his hands skimming efficiently and impersonally over her.

Apparently satisfied she was unarmed, he rocked back onto his heels, dragged her to her knees and yanked her around to face him. "Where is he?" he demanded. Holding her upright with one powerful hand, he caught her chin in the other. "Talk to me, *Genevieve*. What the hell have you done to my brother?"

"John?"

His brows rose just for an instant. "That's right."

She tried to dredge up enough saliva so she could actually form an entire sentence. "He—" She had to stop, swallow, start over again. "He went to get his SUV." She forced herself to meet those intense emerald eyes without flinching. "He's fine. I swear. He should be back any minute."

The stare he sent her was lethal. "For your sake, you better be telling the truth."

"I am." For the first time, she started to get just the slightest bit angry. "If you'll just be patient, hold on a minute, you'll see for yourself—"

"Oh, you can count on that, sweetheart," he said grimly, effortlessly hauling her with him as he stood.

For the first time, she took note of the two other men in the room and her heart sank even lower. Unlike John's impeccably dressed brother, they were wearing uniforms that identified them as local sheriff's deputies.

Then to her horror, he gave her a slight shove toward the waiting officers. "Get her out of here," he instructed them. "Like I told your boss, somebody with the proper papers to take her back to Colorado should be at the airport by now. You can tell them I'll check in with them later."

"What about your brother?" the younger of her two guards asked. "You sure you don't want us to stay?"

"No. If he doesn't turn up in the next hour, you can bet you'll hear about it," he said, voice clipped.

Sending her one more frigid look that warned he'd meant what he'd said about her paying a steep price if John didn't turn up soon and in one piece, he turned his back and dismissed her with a single flick of one graceful, long-fingered hand.

Taggart tossed the tire jack next to the flat currently occupying the cargo hold of his rig. Closing the lift gate, he impatiently snapped the empty tire mount back into place and walked around and climbed behind the wheel.

He supposed he ought to be glad the damn tire had blown now, on a deserted mountain road where he'd been forced to keep his speed down, rather than later on the freeway when he'd have been going considerably faster.

But right at the moment, it didn't feel like much of a blessing, he reflected, as he restarted the SUV's engine, cranked the wheel and pulled back onto the road.

This entire excursion had already taken a ridiculous amount of time. While Genevieve's map had been fairly detailed, he'd still managed initially to miss the narrow track cut through a grove of sagging aspens that had eventually led him to the ramshackle barn where his SUV had been stashed.

There was just something about Genevieve, he mused. Even from a distance, she seemed able to scramble his circuits and knock him off balance. He wondered if he was doomed to spend the rest of his life a dime short and a step behind.

I love you. They were just three little words, but they'd been playing in a continuous loop in the back of his mind—and screwing with his concentration—ever since she'd said them back on the porch. It had given him more than enough time to reflect on just how desperately he wanted to hear them again.

Given the effort he'd made to get her to rescind them just a day before, there was a certain irony in that.

Yet merely this brief interlude away had made him realize how totally he'd come to need her in order to feel complete. Her quick mind, her quirky humor, her soft heart and melting touch—she was now as necessary to him as breathing. He might not have a label for his feelings, but he couldn't imagine his life without her, either, at least for the immediate future. She was the best thing to have happened to him in a very long time and he didn't intend to give her up.

Instead of jail, he'd decided to take her back to his place, enlist his brothers' help and see what sort of deal they could strike with the Silver County authorities. If that meant giving the retainer back to the client, so be it. He'd made a considerable amount of money the past few years and, since his needs were few, he had the resources to cover that as well as anything else that cropped up.

His hands tightened on the wheel a fraction as he imagined Genevieve's relief when he told her. An unfamiliar emotion swept through him and, though it took him a moment, eventually he recognized it for what it was. Anticipation. Something else he hadn't experienced in a very long while.

It vanished in a heartbeat, however, when he spotted the mud-splattered silver SUV parked on the far side of the turnoff to the cabin. Frowning, he slowed, prickles of uneasiness radiating down his spine as he took in the rental sticker on the back bumper.

Just what, he wondered, were the chances of somebody from out of town picking that spot to park out of countless miles of empty road?

And just like that he knew, even before he turned off the road onto the driveway and spotted the churned-up tracks in the snow and mud made by tires newer and wider than the ones on the old pickup he'd driven out.

Jaw set, he hit the accelerator, hands rock-steady as he took the slippery, twisting track at a speed that wasn't even remotely safe. Topping the final hill, he pushed the vehicle even harder, ignoring the thump as he fishtailed around the final curve and the loose tire in the back crashed against the wheel well.

He swore, his gut clenching, as he saw that the clearing beside the cabin was empty of vehicles, and he realized he was too late. Slamming on the brakes, he jammed the gearshift into Park and flung himself out the door while the big SUV was still rocking on its tires. Taking the steps in one powerful bound, he stormed across the porch and threw open the door.

Just as he'd expected, his older brother was the sole occupant of the room. "Goddamn it, Gabe, what the hell have you done?" he demanded, advancing menacingly on the other man as if the gun that had made an appearance at his explosive arrival didn't exist. "Where is she?"

Gabriel gave him a careful once-over, the tension edging his face ebbing away as he apparently saw for himself that Taggart was fine. "Good to see you, too, bro," he said mildly. His movements calm and deliberate, he removed the clip from the gun and uncocked the slide, then slid the weapon back into the holster hidden by his coat's custom fit.

"Where the hell is Genevieve?" Taggart repeated.

"Right this minute?" Gabe shot his cuff to glance at the deceptively simple stainless-steel watch gracing his wrist. "Most likely winging away from the Kalispell airport in the plane with the armed escort that the Silver County prosecutor sent for her."

Taggart decked him. Without stopping to think, for the first time since he'd been thirteen and Gabe fourteen, and they'd had their last major disagreement over the wisdom of his plan to steal cars for a living, he socked his big brother in the mouth with enough force to knock him to the floor.

Wisely, Gabriel stayed put. Gingerly sitting up, he flexed his jaw, then slowly wiped away the blood welling from his bottom lip with the back of his hand. He looked consideringly at Taggart, comprehension lighting his jewel-toned eyes. "It's like that, huh?" he said quietly, his expression a mixture of sympathy and dawning regret.

"Yeah. Maybe. Hell—" Taggart raked a hand through his hair impatiently "—I don't know. But yeah," he said finally. "I think so."

The realization struck him like a well-aimed boot to the head. For a second he felt dizzy and weak in the knees, and it didn't get any better as the magnitude of what he might have lost began to dawn on him.

He'd never said a word to her about what he *did* feel, hadn't put himself out enough even to tell her that he cared. And now, unintentionally or not, he'd broken his promise that she wouldn't have to face jail alone. Hell, for all he knew, she might very well think he'd driven off and callously arranged for Gabe to come so he wouldn't have to face her and own up to what she was sure to see as a betrayal.

"Damn, Taggart, I'm sorry."

His brother's voice was a welcome interruption in his tempestuous thoughts. Telling himself that it was more important than ever to focus on the here and now, to concentrate on doing what he could to make this better for Genevieve and deal with his own fear and fury and worry later, he took a deep breath and turned his attention back to Gabe. "What did you say?"

"That I'm sorry. If I'd had a clue—" he stopped, uttered a single, profane word that left no doubt as to the depth of his regret "—it never would've happened."

Taggart knew damn well Gabe was sincere; it wasn't in his brother's nature to be anything but straight with him. Even so, he was in no mood to let him off the hook just yet.

"You *should* be sorry." Reaching down, he offered his hand to the man who'd been the only true constant in his life before Genevieve and yanked him to his feet. "What the hell are you doing here, anyway?"

Gabriel gave an offhand shrug. "It's been nearly a week. After a while, when you didn't check in, Lilah started to get worried—"

"Lilah?" At the mention of their brother Dominic's bride, his eyebrows climbed and his hard-won calm deserted him. "When the hell did *Lilah* get the green light to call the shots and interfere in my life?"

Gabe sighed. "Since Dom found out she's pregnant. Trust me, the next six months are going to be long for all of us."

"Is she all right?" he asked sharply.

"She's fine. Dom's the one who's a wild-eyed maniac."

"Yeah, well I'll deal with him later. Right now, I want to hear what went down with Genevieve."

"You're not going to like it."

"Yeah. I figured." That sick feeling twisted through his gut again and he shook it off. "But for now I'm going to give you a pass." Walking toward the door, he picked up Genevieve's duffel bag and heaved it at Gabe before leaning down and grabbing a box in either arm.

"And why, exactly, is that?" the other man inquired, following him out to the back of the SUV.

"Because." He gave the loose tire a savage shove, stowed the books and turned to face his brother. "You're about to help me do whatever it takes to get Genevieve out of jail."

Again, Gabriel searched his face, then gave the faintest of sighs. "I suppose that means we're going to have to clear the brother?"

"Didn't I just say whatever it takes?" he countered, pushing past Gabe to head back to the cabin for the rest of their stuff.

Yet as he stepped inside, he felt that old, familiar bleakness settle over his heart. Because while exonerating Seth Bowen might be enough to secure Genevieve's freedom, he wasn't at all sure it would be enough to make her give him another chance.

That is, if he deserved one at all.

Fourteen

Clutching her coat, Genevieve stepped out onto the wide front steps of the Silver County Jail. After nine days spent inside, locked up in a ten-by-ten cell that had sported a single narrow, mesh-covered window, the afternoon sunlight was as welcome as it was dazzling.

She drank in several long draughts of pristine air, took a moment to enjoy the briskness of the day, then squeezed her eyes shut and said a silent prayer of thanks for her freedom.

Despite the assurances of her attorney, who had informed her he'd been engaged on her behalf by Steele Security, Genevieve still found it hard to believe that the nightmare that had consumed more than eight months of her life was finally over.

Yet the reality was driven home as she heard footsteps coming up the stairs and opened her eyes to find a familiar male face smiling crookedly down at her.

"Seth!" For one incredulous moment she could only stare at her baby brother. And then joy picked her up and sent her flying into his arms. "Oh, God, you're out! You're really free!"

Laughing and crying at once, she clung to him, patting, stroking, touching—his hands, his arms, his precious, precious face—needing that solid contact to assure herself he was really there, really all right. "I can't believe it. When? How?"

"This morning," he said, burying his face in her hair and holding on to her with the same kind of fierceness he'd displayed when he'd needed comfort as a little boy. "It was Laura's brother, Gen. He was the one. He killed Jimmy."

Her hands went still. "What?" she said in disbelief, leaning back to stare in shock at his face. "It was Martin? But why?"

"Turns out that's not his name. And he really isn't Laura's brother at all, but her lover," Seth said, more than a trace of hardness glinting in his eyes. With a little jolt, Genevieve realized that in the months since she'd seen him the last trace of boyish softness had left his face and that he was finally, fully, a man.

"They planned it from the start," he went on. "Apparently they were looking for somebody like Jimmy even before they met him. Then later, I guess Jimmy told Laura what he told me—that he'd changed beneficiaries—so they went ahead. It was supposed to look like he'd walked in on a burglary, just like I thought, only I showed up and drove Martin off before he could stage it."

"But…" Genevieve tried to take it in, to wrap her mind around it. "He was with Jimmy's folks…wasn't he?"

"Laura was. Turns out Martin was a little late, claimed he'd gotten lost finding the house. Which nobody thought to mention, since I got tagged right away."

"But the will, the insurance—"

"You know Jimmy. He was always putting things off, talking about stuff like it was a done deal before he even got the ball rolling." He shook his head. "Damn, but I miss him."

The reminder of everything he'd been through had her winding her arms around his middle and giving him another fervent hug. "I know. I know. I'm just so glad the rest of this is over."

"Yeah. Me, too." He allowed himself one more moment of comfort, then got a grip on himself. Straightening, he gently set her away, smoothed her hair back behind her ears.

There was a space of silence while they both simply stood and smiled at each other. "So?" he said finally, lifting an eyebrow. "You going to ask me who's responsible for us standing here like this or not?"

"I'm pretty sure I already know," she said, swallowing hard and telling herself she was not going to let anything spoil this moment.

That Seth was here, free, meant she owed John a debt she could never repay. The fact that she hadn't seen or heard from him since she'd been hauled away from the cabin didn't matter.

Or it shouldn't. No. It didn't. She refused to let it. She'd known there were no guarantees right from the start, known even as she was falling in love with him that their time in Montana might be all they ever had.

Just as she knew, with a certainty that didn't require reassurance or proof, that he'd had nothing to do with that last, terrifying scene at the cabin. Whatever had gone wrong, it hadn't been his fault.

"I like him," Seth volunteered.

"You've met?"

"Sure. We've talked a bunch of times, while I was in jail, then again earlier today, after I got out."

"He's a good person, a good man," she said firmly.

"Yeah. Except—" he made a soft sound that was a uniquely male mix of amusement and sympathy with just a hint of good-natured derision "—I think he's scared."

"John?" She didn't believe it for a minute. After what he'd been through in Afghanistan, she doubted anything could faze him. But she also knew her brother well enough to see he was dying for her to ask the question anyway and she was too glad to see him to deny him anything. "Of what?"

He paused just a moment, clearly enjoying himself. "You."

"Me?" she exclaimed. "That's ridiculous."

"Hey, don't kill the messenger." He raised his hands in surrender. "It's just my opinion. The guy didn't say five words on the drive over, but I could tell it was killing him to hang back at the car. One of his brothers, Dominic, I think, claims he's walking proof that the bigger they are, the harder they fall."

"John's here?"

"Yeah. Didn't I just say that?"

But Genevieve wasn't listening.

Stepping around Seth, she lifted her hand to shield her eyes from the sun as she surveyed the busy street. It only took a second for her gaze to fix on the tall man with the warrior's face staring back at her as he stood stiffly beside the shiny black SUV parked at the far curb.

Her coat fell forgotten to the ground as her heart trumped her common sense and sent her leaping down the remaining steps. She checked her motion for an instant on the sidewalk, took a quick look at the traffic and then dashed into the street.

Ignoring the bark of a horn and the screech of brakes, she dodged around a pair of cars and flung herself into his arms.

"Oh, God, I wasn't going to do this," she said, burying her face in his neck as she nearly knocked him off his feet. "And you don't have to say anything, I understand you don't feel the way I do, and I don't expect anything, really, but I've just missed you. I've missed you so much."

"Genevieve." Taggart could barely get her name out past the lump jamming his throat. He'd thought he was prepared for anything. Anger. Disdain. Demands to know where the hell he'd been. Even a sincere but distant declaration of thanks before she brushed him off and walked out of his life.

The only thing he hadn't expected was this. That she'd come straight at him with her arms wide open, her heart on her sleeve, and wrap him in the priceless gift of her love, no questions, no demands for an explanation, no words of reproach.

Squeezing his eyes shut, he locked his arms around her and lifted her effortlessly up, some of the terrible tension that had made it hard for him to get a deep breath the past ten days finally easing. Not one to hang back, she promptly wrapped her legs around his waist and twined her arms around his neck and held on like she'd never let him go.

His heart. His miracle. His love.

The woman who'd gotten the drop on him, whisked away the cloud of darkness surrounding him and taught him how to laugh again.

Until this moment he'd told himself that if it was what she wanted, he'd let her go. Yet with her safely in his arms, he could finally admit to himself that that was a lie.

She was his now. Just like he was hers.

And the least that he owed her was to tell the truth, do his best to explain why, when she'd needed him most, he hadn't been there for her.

"Genevieve," he said again, his voice stronger this time.

"Hmm?"

"You need to look at me. You have a right—" he stopped and swallowed, a hard man reduced to jelly by a woman with a Pollyanna complex "—to see my face when I tell you this."

Loosening the stranglehold she had on him, she leaned back. "Whatever it is—"

"Shh," he ordered. He'd meant to work his way up to this, but when he saw the worry suddenly darkening her eyes, he knew that he had to just say it, straight out. "Just listen. When I came back and found out what

Gabe had done—I was more afraid than I've ever been. Somehow, you'd made me take another look at what happened that night on Zari Pass, made me at least consider that I might not be the only one responsible, made me start to think that maybe, maybe, I could have a…real life. With you.

"But it was all so new, the last thing I ever expected. And then, when it was too late, when I came back and found you were gone, I just got all tangled up inside. Rather than come and see you and take the chance that you'd tell me to get the hell out and leave you alone, I thought—if I could just make things right for you and Seth—maybe then you'd believe that I hadn't just gone off and double-crossed you.

"And then, the longer it took, when the judge proved difficult and the whole thing dragged on and I was still a no-show… Well, you've got every reason to tell me to go, except—"

"It's all right," Genevieve interrupted, unwilling to allow him another second of self-doubt, wanting him to know she'd believed in him all along.

"No, it's not. Damn it, Genevieve, what I'm trying to say is—" his voice hitched just for an instant, then turned steady and strong "—I love you. I love you and I want us to be together. Forever. Say you'll be my wife."

"Oh, John." Genevieve's heart hitched as she stared into the warm green flame of his eyes. There were no longer any shadows lurking there, she realized, just a steady, blazing light. "I love you, too. Always."

"Is that a yes?"

She smiled. "How could I possibly turn down such a romantic proposal? Absolutely it's a yes."

To her amazement, he closed his eyes, obviously overcome, just for a second.

And then he was looking straight at her, his mouth slowly curving up in a smile with nothing held back.

To her shock, she saw that there was a tantalizing crease bracketing one side of his mouth that looked suspiciously like a dimple.

Then she forgot everything else as he said, "Thank God. That'll save me the job of having to chase you down again and chain *you* to a bed." Dipping his head, he kissed her, hot and sweet and tender.

And Genevieve kissed him back, knowing it was a preview and a promise of their future.

Epilogue

Genevieve sipped a glass of champagne as she stood in Gabriel Steele's handsomely furnished living room.

As much as she was enjoying her wedding reception, it was nice to have a moment to just catch her breath, reflect a little, take a look around.

People—a lot of whom were tall, striking, dark-haired men—were either scattered around the room or standing out on the terrace that wrapped the lighted swimming pool. Two of the latter happened to be John and Seth, who were listening intently to something being said by a third man she thought was either Deke or Cooper. Or was that Jake?

Candles scented the air with masculine fragrances of spice and sandalwood. Music played, a soft backdrop for the steady hum of conversation punctuated by occasional bursts of laughter.

At the other end of the room, her best friend Kate caught her eye, made a show of panning the room and its phalanx of good-looking, eligible men, mimed the word *wow* and then fanned herself, making Genevieve smile.

It was hard to believe she'd been a married woman for eight entire hours now.

Just before noon that day, she and John, accompanied by Seth, Kate, Dominic's stunning wife Lilah, and all of the Steele brothers except for the three deployed overseas, had walked out to the small, perfect meadow nestled like a jewel on the edge of the wilderness that stretched behind her house.

There, beside the little pond sparkling like glass under the pale fall sun, in the place where she'd made a home for herself, wearing the loveliest cream and ivory antique lace dress she'd ever seen, surrounded by the people she loved most and a profusion of extravagantly colored chrysanthemums, she and John had stood before a minister and exchanged their vows.

It had been beyond perfect, she reflected, glancing down at the simple emerald and diamond band that now graced her left hand.

Just the blindingly beautiful fall day, with the wind whispering through the grass and the sun kissing her cheeks. And John. Tall and straight and solemn, pledging her his love for the rest of their lives.

It had been everything she'd ever hoped for. Far more than she'd ever expected to have. And it was only the beginning.

"Genevieve? Can I get you anything? Some more champagne?"

She glanced up to find Gabriel standing before her. Handsome and charismatic, with beautiful manners—as long as he didn't think you might have harmed someone he loved—John's elegant, slightly enigmatic brother continued to knock himself out trying to make up for his rough treatment of her.

He'd not only been instrumental in securing her freedom, enlisting the governor as well as one of the state's senators to go to bat for her, but she'd had only to mention to him how she envisioned her wedding and he'd promptly taken care of all of the details, then insisted on throwing them this party.

"I'm fine, Gabriel," she said with a smile. "Or I will be, once you agree to forget about what happened between us at the cabin." She touched her hand to his sleeve. "Believe me, I know what it feels like to do whatever seems necessary to safeguard a brother you love."

"Yes." He considered her, and something in his face seemed to lighten even before he smiled. "I suppose you do." Then to her astonishment, he leaned over and kissed her gently on the cheek. "John's lucky to have you," he murmured, before he straightened, smiled again and strolled away.

Bemused, she was trying to decide what she thought she'd heard in his voice—a touch of wistfulness, a hint of loneliness?—when a pair of strong arms settled around her waist.

Everything else ceased to matter as she felt John's solid warmth at her back. "You okay?" he said softly, pressing a kiss to the sensitive patch of skin behind her ear.

"Perfect, now that you're here." Turning in the circle of his arms, she looked at him.

In sharp contrast to Gabe, who'd been the picture of sartorial splendor, John had already shed his tie and jacket. The neck of his pristine white shirt was open, exposing his strong, bronzed throat, while his sleeves were rolled to just below his elbows.

He looked big and tough and so gorgeously male that she couldn't contain a sigh of pure pleasure. "How about you?" She reached up, ostensibly to smooth his hair while actually just wanting to touch him.

"I'm doing all right. He caught her hand, cradled it against the curve of his face. "But I'd be even better if I could talk you into getting out of here with me." He slid her palm to his mouth and pressed a kiss to it that made her flush.

"I'm tired of sharing," he said softly. "I want you all to myself."

"Then I'm your girl. You may not have heard—" she leaned in, went up on tiptoe and nibbled at his bottom lip "—but I'm extremely good at disappearing."

John felt his lips quirk up as he angled his head and claimed her mouth for a brief but heated kiss. With Genevieve, life was always going to be interesting, filled with light no matter what the weather.

Tracking her down had been the best thing ever to happen to him. And if it took him the rest of his life, he meant to make sure she felt the same way.

Starting right now, he vowed, as they both straightened, joined hands and made their escape.

* * * * *

SILHOUETTE®
Desire™ 2 in 1

ENGAGEMENT BETWEEN ENEMIES
by Kathie DeNosky
(The Illegitimate Heirs)

After a scandalous rumour erupted, honourable tycoon Caleb Walker made employee Alyssa Merrick an offer she couldn't refuse…

TYCOON TAKES REVENGE by Anna DePalo

Infamous playboy Noah Whittaker gives gossip columnist Kayla Jones a taste of her own medicine, but finds that love is far sweeter than revenge.

THE MAN MEANS BUSINESS by Annette Broadrick

Business was millionaire Dean Logan's only thought until his loyal assistant, Jodie Cameron, accompanied him on a passionate Hawaiian vacation and put marriage on the agenda!

DEVLIN AND THE DEEP BLUE SEA
by Merline Lovelace
(Code Name: Danger)

Helicopter pilot Elizabeth Moore thought sexy stranger Joe Devlin was a mystery to solve—and if she hadn't just been jilted, she might have made an effort to uncover *all* his secrets!

BABY, I'M YOURS by Catherine Mann

Three months after their whirlwind affair, Claire McDermott discovered she was carrying Vic Jansen's child and that she wanted more than just an honourable offer of marriage…

HER HIGH-STAKES AFFAIR by Katherine Garbera

An affair between them was strictly forbidden, but when passion struck Raine Montgomery and rich, sexy Scott Rivers under the bright lights of Las Vegas, it was on the cards!

On sale from 19th January 2007

Visit our website at www.silhouette.co.uk

SILHOUETTE®

Desire™

Dynasties:
THE ELLIOTTS
Mixing business with pleasure

January 2007
BILLIONAIRE PROPOSITION *Leanne Banks*
TAKING CARE OF BUSINESS *Brenda Jackson*

March 2007
CAUSE FOR SCANDAL *Anna DePalo*
THE FORBIDDEN TWIN *Susan Crosby*

May 2007
MR AND MISTRESS *Heidi Betts*
HEIRESS BEWARE *Charlene Sands*

July 2007
UNDER DEEPEST COVER *Kara Lennox*
MARRIAGE TERMS *Barbara Dunlop*

September 2007
THE INTERN AFFAIR *Roxanne St Claire*
FORBIDDEN MERGER *Emilie Rose*

November 2007
THE EXPECTANT EXECUTIVE *Kathie DeNosky*
BEYOND THE BOARDROOM *Maureen Child*

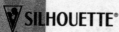

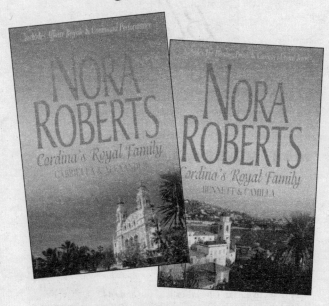

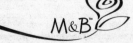

2 FREE

BOOKS AND A SURPRISE GIFT!

We would like to take this opportunity to thank you for reading this Silhouette® book by offering you the chance to take TWO more specially selected titles from the Desire™ series absolutely FREE! We're also making this offer to introduce you to the benefits of the Mills & Boon® Reader Service™—

- ★ FREE home delivery
- ★ FREE gifts and competitions
- ★ FREE monthly Newsletter
- ★ Exclusive Reader Service offers
- ★ Books available before they're in the shops

Accepting these FREE books and gift places you under no obligation to buy, you may cancel at any time, even after receiving your free shipment. Simply complete your details below and return the entire page to the address below. You don't even need a stamp!

YES! Please send me 2 free Desire volumes and a surprise gift. I understand that unless you hear from me, I will receive 3 superb new titles every month for just £4.99 each, postage and packing free. I am under no obligation to purchase any books and may cancel my subscription at any time. The free books and gift will be mine to keep in any case.

D7ZED

Ms/Mrs/Miss/Mr ....Initials ....

Surname ....
BLOCK CAPITALS PLEASE

Address ....

....

....Postcode................

Send this whole page to:
UK: FREEPOST CN8I, Croydon, CR9 3WZ